W9-BMR-850

Praise for *New York Times* Bestselling Author Virginia Henley

"Virginia Henley writes the kind of book you simply can't stop reading." —Bertrice Small

"A master storyteller. . . . With each new novel, Virginia Henley tests her powers as a writer, and as readers, we reap the splendid rewards."
—*Romantic Times*

"A brilliant author whom we come to rely on for the best in romantic fiction." —*Rendezvous*

"Colorful, sensual, masterful . . . Virginia Henley takes a classic story line, gives it a fresh twist, and gives her legions of fans exactly what they want—a nonstop, memorable read. Ms. Henley delivers."
—*Romantic Times* (Top Pick)

"Henley deftly intertwines political machinations and passion in this lusty historical romance." —*Booklist*

"In a titillating combination of historical detail and breathtaking passion, perennial favorite Henley wields her magic yet again." —Amazon.com

"Masterful." —Romance Reviews Today

Virginia Henley

SIGNET
Published by New American Library, a division of
Penguin Putnam Inc., 375 Hudson Street,
New York, New York 10014, U.S.A.
Penguin Books Ltd, 80 Strand,
London WC2R 0RL, England
Penguin Books Australia Ltd, Ringwood,
Victoria, Australia
Penguin Books Canada Ltd, 10 Alcorn Avenue,
Toronto, Ontario, Canada M4V 3B2
Penguin Books (N.Z.) Ltd, 182–190 Wairau Road,
Auckland 10, New Zealand

Penguin Books Ltd, Registered Offices:
Harmondsworth, Middlesex, England

First published by Signet, an imprint of New American Library,
a division of Penguin Putnam Inc.

First Printing, November 2002
10 9 8 7 6 5 4 3 2 1

Copyright © Virginia Henley, 2002
Excerpt copyright © Virginia Henley, 2002
All rights reserved

REGISTERED TRADEMARK—MARCA REGISTRADA

Printed in the United States of America

Without limiting the rights under copyright reserved above, no part of this publication may be reproduced, stored in or introduced into a retrieval system, or transmitted, in any form, or by any means (electronic, mechanical, photocopying, recording, or otherwise), without the prior written permission of both the copyright owner and the above publisher of this book.

PUBLISHER'S NOTE
This is a work of fiction. Names, characters, places, and incidents either are the product of the author's imagination or are used fictitiously, and any resemblance to actual persons, living or dead, business establishments, events, or locales is entirely coincidental.

BOOKS ARE AVAILABLE AT QUANTITY DISCOUNTS WHEN USED TO PROMOTE PRODUCTS OR SERVICES. FOR INFORMATION PLEASE WRITE TO PREMIUM MARKETING DIVISION, PENGUIN PUTNAM INC., 375 HUDSON STREET, NEW YORK, NEW YORK 10014.

If you purchased this book without a cover you should be aware that this book is stolen property. It was reported as "unsold and destroyed" to the publisher and neither the author nor the publisher has received any payment for this "stripped book."

For Leslie, my son Adam's wife.
She is the reason I write about
beautiful redheads.

Prologue

Hatton Hall, July 22, 1792

"Lord Hatton's heir shall not make his way into the world arse-first, if I have any say in the matter!" The red-faced midwife pushed hard on the baby's buttocks in an effort to turn it about, then brushed her hair back from her sweating forehead.

On the big bed, the young Irish girl's beauty had been replaced by a pale, haggard look brought on by the ordeal of childbirth. Lady Kathleen Hatton had gone into labor at dawn and it was now almost midnight.

Meg Riley, Lady Hatton's serving-woman, who had been Kathleen Flynn's nurse when she was a child, wrung her hands in dismay. "She's in agony, woman. Deliver the child as quick as ye can!"

The midwife, who had detected two heads when she arrived, pressed stubborn lips together. She was offended at having her authority challenged before the two young maids who hovered anxiously by the door. "The Irish think they know everything! Unless you have experience delivering twins, I suggest you keep your advice to yourself. Twin births are dangerous; naught but harm and hazard!" In spite of her air of authority, the midwife secretly felt panic. She took a firm hold of the tiny shoulder that now presented itself and pulled with relentless resolve.

Lord Hatton's heir made his appearance into the world two minutes before midnight; mercifully, the mother lost consciousness. The midwife handed the child to Meg Riley. "Wash him and I shall present him to his father immediately. The poor man has waited long enough."

The "poor man" has removed himself to his library where he'll hear no screams and where the fine brandy will ease his wait, Meg thought with outrage. As she bathed the male child, Meg examined him carefully. He was the most beautiful baby she had ever seen, with tufts of dark hair curling upon his head and black eyelashes fringing his gray eyes. She wrapped him in a swaddling blanket and approached the bed. When the midwife reached for the small bundle, Meg said, "Ye cannot leave Lady Hatton; ye have to deliver the other child!"

"Her labor has stopped, and it could be hours before it starts again." The midwife took the heir she had successfully delivered and made her way to the library.

Mr. Burke, Hatton Hall's majordomo, opened the library door for the midwife, greatly relieved that, at last, all seemed well.

"Is it a boy?" Henry Hatton demanded, arising from his leather wing chair amid a blue haze of cigar smoke.

"Yes, indeed, my lord. Congratulations on a fine son." The midwife beamed and unwrapped the blanket to display her trophy.

Lord Hatton's eyes kindled with male pride. "He's absolutely perfect, if I do say so myself. This calls for a celebration! Burke, summon the steward and the footmen and we'll drink a toast." Henry suddenly bethought himself. "How is Lady Hatton? Pleased with herself, no doubt?"

"Her work isn't finished yet, but I don't want to force things."

"Get it delivered. I don't want Kathleen to suffer discomfort."

"Twin births can be hazardous, my lord. We don't want to injure the child."

"Don't worry unduly. I have my son, my heir; that's the important thing. Just make sure no harm comes to *this* one. I've decided on the name Christopher . . . Christopher Flynn Hatton!"

* * *

By the following night, the entire household was in a panic. The second twin was still unborn, despite everything the midwife had done to induce the birth. Even the cook had been summoned for gruel and molasses and Mr. Burke, filled with alarm, had rushed upstairs a dozen times with hot bricks to warm her feet.

Kathleen Hatton lay in a torpid state with glazed eyes while Meg Riley bathed her tenderly, praying fervently as tears rolled down her anguished face. Just before midnight, Lord Hatton stormed into the chamber for the third time in as many hours.

"It must be dead, my lord," the midwife pronounced desperately in the face of his anger.

"That Spawn of Satan had better be dead!" He strode impatiently up and down the chamber, issuing threats to everyone and taking perverse satisfaction in his ability to make them cower.

As the last stroke of midnight died away, the second twin finally made his appearance into the world. Meg Riley looked down in wonder at the child whom the midwife handed her to cleanse. It was another boy, identical to the first in every detail. The same perfect limbs, the same tufts of dark hair, the same black eyelashes fringing his gray eyes, the same tiny cleft in the center of his chin. " 'Tis another boy, my lord." Meg held out the beautiful baby.

"Keep him away from me!" Lord Hatton roared. "He's a hazard to us all! Keep him away from my son, Christopher!" He picked up his first-born protectively and strode from the chamber.

While the midwife looked helplessly at her dying patient and Meg cradled the rejected child, the cook shook her head ominously. "Twins born more than twenty-four hours apart, born under two different signs of the zodiac . . . 'tis unnatural!"

The young maids nodded their agreement. A bad omen indeed.

Having at last done her job, Lady Kathleen Hatton slipped away with a gentle sigh of relief.

"Twin births are naught but harm and hazard," the midwife lamented.

"My beautiful boy," Meg Riley crooned as her tears ran freely. "Since they think ye're Old Nick's spawn, we might as well call ye Nicholas, and yer middle name shall be Flynn, after yer sweet, gentle mother, who's now with the angels, God rest her soul."

Though Henry Hatton blamed his second-born for his wife's death, as time went by he learned to grit his teeth and tolerate him, since it was impossible to keep the twins separated. From the moment they learned to walk, the boys spent every waking hour together. But from the beginning it was Nicholas, the second-born, who was the natural leader and Christopher the follower.

The servants all agreed this was because Nicholas had been born under the sign of the lion, while Christopher's birth sign was the crab. In appearance the boys were identical with not a hairsbreadth of difference between them. Their personalities, however, contrasted vividly. Though both were attractive, mischievous little rogues, Nicholas was a complete extrovert, doing everything with such passion he outshone his brother in every way.

This infuriated Lord Hatton and added to the hostility he felt toward Nicholas. Henry Hatton expected Christopher, his heir, to excel at everything, and as a result young Kit was insecure. His stronger-willed twin, Nick, became exceedingly protective of him, even doing Kit's lessons in the schoolroom so that their tutor would not make unfavorable reports to their father. Nick took the blame for Kit's sins of commission as well as omission, when he did not fulfill his responsibilities or his father's expectations.

By the time they were ten, the Hatton twins had learned to change places with each other whenever it suited their purpose, and by the time they were fifteen, it amused Nick to ensure Kit got all their father's praise, while he took all the punishment their sire meted out. The Hatton twins had truly earned the nicknames that the servants had given them at birth: Harm and Hazard!

Chapter 1

London, July 1813

Champagne Charlie's face lit up with delight as she recognized the pair of dark, dashing clients who strolled into her establishment in Pall Mall. She welcomed the handsome devils with a kiss, while the two young libertines each greeted her by placing a practiced hand upon the cheeks of her shapely derriere.

Naughty Nell, the newest nymph at King's Place Vaulting Academy, stared at the twin visions garbed in impeccable black evening attire, then turned to Moll Tempest with a breathless question. "Who are they?"

"We're in for fun tonight." Moll winked. "It's Harm and Hazard!"

When Nell gave her a blank look, Moll explained. "The Double-Dick Brothers! Champagne all around, and let the games begin!"

Suddenly, it seemed every female employed at Charlotte King's brothel had crowded into the large reception room, decorated with gilt-framed mirrors and frescoes of naked-breasted women in enticing poses. Champagne bubbled forth, as did the effervescent laughter, while the painted ladies scribbled their names on bits of paper and tossed them into the gentlemen's tall silk evening hats.

As Nell's gaze traveled from one tall, dark rogue to the other, measuring their wide shoulders, assessing their muscled thighs, and sighing over their black curly heads and devilish gray eyes, she murmured, "How do you tell them apart?"

"We don't—it's a guessing game the entire night, but in truth who cares? Just look at them! None of Charlie's other customers measure up to these two."

"In length or circumference?" Nell quipped naughtily.

"In endurance, luv! They're accomplished rakes—their father, Lord Hatton, saw to that. Brought 'em here for their fifteenth birthday to initiate them, but they were no virgins! Like turning two young stallions loose in a stable filled with mares in season."

Nell's interest intensified when she learned their father was a nobleman. "Ooo! Are they titled?"

Moll gave the new girl a pitying glance. "The elder twin is heir to his father's baronial title, but when a man is naked, the measuring stick that counts is not his nobility!"

"They seem to be on most intimate terms with Madam. Don't tell me she services them?" Nell asked aghast.

"It's the Double-Dick Twins who do the servicing. Charlie breaks her own rules for them. She's the only one who can tell them apart, but even she admits they've diddled her on occasion!" Moll whooped with amusement at her own pun.

Squeals of laughter punctuated the air as Harm drew the names of Lolly and Bubbles. "Well, lay me down and tickle me wiv' a feather," one of the curvaceous blondes giggled, taking the six-foot Adonis by the arm. The charming scoundrel bent to whisper in her ear and received a playful slap for his wicked suggestion.

When Hazard drew the name of a sloe-eyed Asian girl and then one called Desire, with the dusky skin of a houri, Charlie lifted a questioning eyebrow at him to see if he was pleased.

"Delicious appetizers, my sweet, but I'd like you for the maincourse, as always," he murmured for her ears alone. His voice was so deep, it never failed to send a thrill along her spine.

"It will give me a chance to show you my gratitude," Charlie whispered back. "As you advised, I opened a gaming room last week, and already it's doubled my business!"

* * *

Six miles from London, at Longford Manor, Alexandra Sheffield locked the bedchamber door, then quickly stripped off her clothes. She looked deeply into the bold eyes that were assessing her naked body and smiled mischievously. "Alone at last! I've been wanting to do this for weeks. Every time I looked at you, I was tempted. People gossip about me being a hellion; this'll prove them right!"

She watched the hand lift her red-gold tresses, then shuddered as she felt the bright, silky curls spill down over her naked breasts and settle about her slim waist.

"Are you sure about this? There's still time to stop."

As the question floated in the air, Alexandra ran the tip of her tongue over her lips in hesitation. It was the first time, and once it was gone, she knew there would be no putting it back. The corners of her mouth lifted at her own daring. "I'm sure! Let's kiss it good-bye and be done with it!"

Alexandra looked again at her reflection in the mirror, picked up the scissors, and sheared off her long tresses. "Oh, my Lord, I look positively outrageous!" she declared with glee. Drab, boring respectability was anathema to Alexandra, who longed to live in London and experience first-hand the follies of the *beau monde*.

She had collected all Fanny Burney's scandalous novels and had ambitions to become a writer. Last month she had read in the lively *Town and Country Magazine* that most female novelists had to cut off their hair and effect male attire before they were taken seriously, and even then they had to publish anonymously in the male-dominated profession. It was even rumored that Charles Lamb, essayist and humorist, was in reality Mary Lamb.

As Alexandra bathed and washed her newly shorn hair, she decided that when she went to London to pursue her calling she would use the male version of her name. *Alex Sheffield* had a definite ring to it! When her hair dried, she felt dismay at the myriad curls and tendrils that formed a red-gold halo about her face and feared she still looked far too feminine. As she descended the curving staircase on her way to the salon for afternoon tea, the voice of her brother, Rupert, stayed her.

"Good God, Alex, what the devil have you done to yourself? The *ton* will say you've gone as dotty as our grandmother! No one will offer for you now that you've turned yourself into a damn freak."

Alexandra spun about and lifted her stubborn chin. "That, Rude Rupert, is the whole point of the exercise! I'm only seventeen; I don't want anyone to offer for me."

"Well, they will, even though you've turned a silk purse into a sow's ear. You're an heiress, Alex; there's no help for it."

As they reached the ground floor, they were in time to see their grandmother, Lady Dorothy Longford, bid good-bye to a rather flashily dressed man.

"Nice doing business with you, Viscountess."

"A simple *my lady* will do." Dottie prodded him with her ebony walking stick. "Now remember, they must come after dark or they won't be admitted. I'll have my gamekeeper set the dogs on 'em." Dowager Viscountess Dorothy Longford was a martinet who dominated all who came into her presence.

Both Rupert and Alexandra were used to Dottie's eccentricities and odd acquaintances. Since Longford Manor had neither gamekeeper nor dogs, they dismissed the visitor from their thoughts.

Lady Longford straightened her bright red wig, yanked on the bellpull for tea, then lifted her lorgnette to examine her granddaughter at length. When she was done, she said, "Mmmm."

Alexandra waited for her grandmother's rebuke.

"I believe you've turned yourself into an *original*. A hellion with the halo of an angel . . . how unique! Those tumbled, short curls make you look taller. Your long legs make you appear quite coltish . . . difficult for a man to resist. You'll be all the rage, darling, just as I was."

It was an appalling understatement; in her day, Dorothy had been more of an outrage. Yet her scandalous, unconventional behavior had not prevented her from marrying Viscount Russell Longford, the wealthiest nobleman in Bucks County. Marriage had not tamed her, however, for it was rumored that she'd had as many lovers as Queen Charlotte had children: an astonishing fifteen!

"I don't want to be all the rage," Alexandra protested.

"Piss and piffle! You will catch a Lord of the Realm, just as I did. You will become a 'lady' just as I did, and just as your mother did *not,* to my undying shame."

Alexandra did not want Dottie to start on the subject of her mother, for there was no end to the pain it brought. Margaret had made a disastrous marriage with a commoner, Johnny Sheffield, thoroughly disgracing her parents. Then she had added injury to insult by running off with another untitled lout, and deserting her children in the bargain. Alexandra's grandmother had taken her and Rupert into her home and her heart, not only providing material comfort but lavishing them with love. Dottie had assuaged the unbearable pain of rejection, and Alexandra knew she must never hurt her grandmother the way her mother had. She vowed to postpone marriage as long as possible to avoid choosing the wrong man. Sheffield had married her mother for her money, and Alexandra was determined to avoid this pitfall like the plague.

Dottie continued, "It's all right for Rupert; he inherited his grandfather's title of *Viscount*. But you, my darling, must marry to gain the title of *Lady*."

"Marriage didn't make you a lady," Alexandra said with a wink.

"*Touché,* darling! You have inherited my wicked wit. I shall enjoy watching you set London on its ear before you settle down."

"I always hoped you'd marry my best friend, Kit Hatton, but you don't even try to attract him," Rupert complained.

"And so she *shall* marry Christopher Hatton. It is no secret that Lord Hatton and I have had an understanding for years."

Alexandra had heard those words all her life. She and Rupert had grown up with the Hatton twins, whose vast acres connected with the Longford property. The devilishly handsome brothers had fascinated her since she was a child, when she and Rupert had shared in the twins' daring escapades.

Alexandra vividly recalled an incident from the summer that the boys turned twelve. Kit Hatton had overheard the servants talking about a highwayman who had been gibbeted on Hounslow Heath at the Great West Road. He had dared his brother to ride to Hounslow and touch the grisly corpse. "Come and watch me!" Nick challenged. All four of them had thought it a great adventure in the beginning. The dangerous heath was out of bounds to them, though it was only two miles away, and none of them had ever seen a dead man, let alone a hanged felon.

Alexandra remembered the fascinated horror she had felt when the gibbet came into view. Without hesitation Nicholas rode up and boldly touched the thing, making it swing on the end of its rope, but Christopher shrank back and wouldn't even approach it. Rupert, a few months older than the twins, also lost his nerve and looked like he might be sick. Alexandra remembered her feeling of admiration for Nick's courage. He was born under the sign of the lion and would never bow his proud head. Never! No matter what!

With great contempt for Kit and Rupert, Alexandra declared that she too would touch the highwayman. She would never forget the look of admiration on Nick Hatton's face. It was that look that gave her enough courage, that and the fact that he held her hand while she did it. She could remember the goosebumps even now.

When they returned, Lord Hatton was awaiting them in a rage. Kit told his father that Nick had dared and taunted them into it and had even forced Alexandra to touch the gruesome thing. Though Nicholas knew he was in for a thrashing, he did not make a liar of his brother. Instead, he sent Alexandra a reassuring smile that told her he would bear the punishment with stoic dignity.

Alexandra's memories were interrupted when the tea arrived. She looked at her grandmother and sighed. Dottie expected her to marry Christopher Hatton because of his title, and Alexandra knew that the only way to avoid a fortune hunter was to marry someone with wealth and title. But she was torn between the twins. Though she and Christopher shared a love of painting, and he and her brother were inseparable friends, Alexandra was not certain it was the heir she preferred. She and Nicholas were true friends. She had confided in him since they were children. However, they were children no longer, Alexandra acknowledged. The Hatton twins were men grown, sophisticated and experienced beyond their years. They had taken their place in society and were the envy of their peers. She regretted that these days Nick treated her as a sister, for lately she had begun to long for him to think of her as a woman. She glanced at Dottie and was suddenly covered with guilt over her attraction to Nicholas. All her life it had been drilled into her that she must not follow her heart, must not fall in love, for that path inevitably led to disaster.

"By the by, you will give Annabelle Harding my regrets at her entertainment tonight. Tell her I am decomposed." Dorothy Longford, slim as a reed and straight as a ramrod, was a commanding figure, and though her face was now like fine parchment, it still retained traces of the vivid beauty she had once possessed.

Alex's lips twitched with amusement. "The word is *indisposed*, as well you know, but if you're not going, neither am I."

"Pish tosh! You must go. She has designs on your betrothed for that dreadful daughter of hers. And she's not the only one. Every mother in the county with eligible daughters will be there in hope of leg-shackling one of the Hatton twins. You know all the gels pursue them shamelessly."

"Christopher is not my betrothed," Alexandra protested.

"Claptrap! As the future Lady Hatton, it is your duty to keep those greedy hussies at bay. Men aren't discerning, darling; they'll lift any skirt that's offered."

At thirteen Alexandra had become aware of the way females looked at the Hatton twins. Older women as well as debutantes were avid for the company of the charming, virile devils. She hadn't understood the attraction was sexual until she turned sixteen. "We don't even know if the Hattons will attend."

"Piss and piffle! Henry Hatton will be there. Annabelle lures the men with gambling, and those decadent Chinese lanterns she strings about the gardens positively invite intrigue!"

"I'll escort you, Alex . . . wouldn't miss it on a bet. I

can lend you one of my tie-wigs to cover your hideous hair, if you like," Rupert teased mercilessly.

Suddenly, thinking of Nicholas, Alexandra wished she'd waited one more day before cutting off her crowning glory.

"What the hellfire are you doing?" Nicholas Hatton demanded as he rounded the east wing with a shaggy black wolfhound at his heel.

His twin took aim and fired, nicking the curved beak of a stone griffin that stood sentinel at the corner of Hatton Hall's roof. At the sound of the shot, the dog lunged forward and began to bark furiously. Christopher aimed his pistol at the wolfhound. "Call him off, if you don't want a ball in his brain."

Nicholas knew his brother's bravado was an act. "Heel, Leo," Nick commanded, then without hesitation strode forward and plucked the pistol from his brother's hand.

Kit grinned and pointed proudly to the griffin. "Match that!"

"Have you no more sense than to deface Hatton statuary for target practice? You value nothing!"

"I'm sure we can afford to replace a few ornaments, if they get damaged," Kit drawled.

"It isn't about money. Hatton Hall has sat here for almost two centuries. Those griffins are antique artifacts. You should cherish our ancestral home." Nicholas had a deep and abiding love for Hatton Hall and the lush acres upon which it sat. Somehow, it was the only connection he would ever have to a mother he only knew through the servants' affectionate stories and fond memories.

"Perhaps you cherish it too much, or is *covet* a better word? Since Hatton Hall will be mine some day, it is none of your damn business. You know, Nick, you have a habit of telling people exactly how they should manage their lives, and moreover, you do it in a superior, condescending manner. I suggest you save your orders for Hatton Grange."

It was understood that Christopher would inherit the title, Hatton Hall, and Hatton Great Park, while Nicholas would inherit Hatton Grange horse farm. Gray eyes stared into identical gray eyes until one pair lowered. Christopher knew in his heart that his twin coveted nothing that was his. Kit laughed and lifted his lashes. "Your lion's roar is worse than your bite; you've never mauled me yet. From now on I'll use the doves for target practice." At his twin's look of contempt, he said quickly, "I'm jesting; the only doves I'm interested in are soiled ones. I intend to pluck myself a pigeon tonight."

"So do I, but I'll be at the gaming table," Nick said wryly.

Kit winked. "That's why they call me Harm and you Hazard."

Nicholas handed back the gun. He knew his brother wanted to impress their father with his shooting at the hunt next week. To celebrate their twenty-first birthdays, invitations had gone out for a gala weekend house party, with a masquerade ball on Saturday and a hunt on Sunday. "If you like, we'll set up some targets tomorrow for a practice session. You can give me some pointers," Nick said with self-deprecation. "You're a far better shot than I am."

When they arrived at the Hardings that evening, Alexandra sought out Lady Annabelle to give her Dottie's regrets, while Rupert headed straight to the card room. The Hatton twins were there before him, and as usual, he had no notion which was which. Their taste in clothes sometimes helped—Kit liked to wear fawn and burgundy while Nick preferred blues and grays—but in their formal black evening attire they looked identical. Their dark, cropped hair curled crisply against starched, high-pointed collars. Their cravats were tied intricately, and their shirts were immaculate beneath black, superfine jackets that fit their broad shoulders to perfection. Their long fingers held their cards negligently, while they bantered good-naturedly with the other players.

Suddenly, Rupert's brow cleared as the puzzle was solved. Kit seldom won at the gaming table; Nick never lost. Rupert greeted his friend Kit, who threw in his hand, drained his glass, arose from the table, and said, "I have more luck betting on the fair sex." Before he left the card room, Kit lifted two glasses from a footman's silver tray and proceeded to drink both. "I have a keen appetite tonight, Rupert. A guinea says I can lure Olivia Harding into the rhododendron bushes."

"Didn't you know that Nick has been favoring Olivia with his attentions lately?"

Kit dug his friend in the ribs. "Don't be such a gull, Rupert. Of course I know. That's what makes it such rare sport. It's a point of honor with me to charm away every female who falls for Nick. It's so devilishly easy!"

"But you have the advantage of the title," Rupert said bluntly.

"Precisely." Kit laughed. "I'm only following in Father's footsteps. Before he leaves tonight, he'll bed Annabelle and get drunk on Lord Harding's brandy, not necessarily in that order."

In the ballroom, Alexandra turned down invitations to dance from three eligible bachelors, one of whom was heir to an earldom, before she escaped to the card room. She immediately saw one of the Hatton twins and held her breath, hoping it was Nicholas. Her heart beat wildly as she watched his gray eyes take in every detail of her cropped curls with tolerant amusement.

"Hello, Hellion. At it again, I see."

His deep voice coupled with the affectionate nickname sent a frisson of pleasure down her spine. "Hello, Nick. I hoped it would deter the fortune hunters, but I hoped in vain. I have decided to take refuge in here with you and gamble the night away."

The amusement left his eyes. "You will not, Alexandra."

He looked and spoke like a mature man addressing a child, and it never failed to infuriate her. "Why not?" she flared. "I can beat the players in this room. You should know that; you taught me."

Nicholas signaled the dealer that he would not be playing the next hand, then he smiled charmingly at the elderly ladies across the table and nodded to the other men and his host, Lord Harding. "Please excuse us." With a firm hand on Alexandra's elbow, he led her from the card room. "You cannot sit with the men and gamble all night. It would damage your reputation irreparably."

"There were other females present!" Her voice rose indignantly.

"Alexandra, they are dowagers, addicted to gambling and long past the age when they need worry about their reputations."

"Sitting with the dowagers would not have damaged my reputation," she insisted.

"Not until you began to cheat, you little hellcat. Then there would have been the devil to pay."

"Did you at least get me that copy of Laclos's *Les liaisons dangereuses*?"

"I did not." His voice was so deep it sounded like a growl, a warning growl.

Alex ignored the warning. "Why not?" she demanded imperiously.

"It's unsuitable; it's about immensely salacious seduction."

"I have to learn about sex if I am to write novels."

"Are you on that kick again? What a tiresome child you are."

She looked up into his eyes. They were like fathomless, gray pools, so deep she fancied she could drown in them. She blinked rapidly, hurt by his disapproval and dreading his rejection. "What the devil is the matter with you, Nick? We used to share such daring escapades and high adventures."

"That was when I was a schoolboy, sent down from Harrow. Since then I matured; obviously something you haven't done yet, Hellion."

She made a rude, derisive noise. "From the ancient, lofty height of twenty-one, how can you condescend to even talk with me?"

She was without doubt the most exasperating female on earth, but as he looked down at her bright head, a wave of protectiveness swept over him. He realized that if she had done something as drastic as cut off her beautiful hair, she must need to talk. "If you promise to restrain your impulse toward mischief for the next hour, I'll meet you around ten in the summerhouse and we'll talk."

Nick spotted Rupert in intimate conversation with a pretty blond creature and beckoned him with a commanding gesture. "Rupert, escort your sister in to supper. And keep an eye on her; she needs a bloody keeper." He returned to the card room, apologized sincerely for the interruption, and resumed play. During the next hour many more men joined the game, and by ten o'clock Nick Hatton was richer by a hundred guineas, which he would add to the money he'd been saving for a Thoroughbred filly for the Grange.

As he passed the supper room, he saw that it was empty, so he purloined a bottle of champagne and two glasses and headed into the lantern-lit gardens. Young people clustered about the terraces, laughing and flirting, while the more adventurous strolled across the lawns and down the pebbled paths, shadowed by yews and weeping willows. Nicholas caught the heavy scent of rhododendrons just as a young woman emerged from the bushes. His cynical gaze swept over Olivia Harding, taking in her dishevelled gown and ruined coiffure.

"Christopher," she gasped, quickly drawing up the shoulder of her gown to cover her half-exposed breast.

"It's Nicholas, I'm afraid. Christopher is behind you."

Olivia spun about with dismay and stammered, "But . . . he pretended to be you—" She delivered a stinging slap to Kit's face, confirming the act they'd committed, then fled into the shadows.

"She's lying," Kit drawled as he tucked his shirt into his pants. "Couldn't wait to compare us to see if I measured up to your . . . worthy attributes. Fortunately, I did."

"If you did, it's because your brains are in your cock," Nick said coldly. Sharing whores was one thing, even taking turns gracing the beds of the dissatisfied wives of the *ton* was a pleasure they could share, but inexperienced debutantes were another matter entirely. Nick wanted to smash Kit in the face, but he knew his twin had been drinking and would be no match for the fury he would unleash. With an effort Nick reined in his anger, telling himself that his heart wasn't involved with Olivia Harding, or with any of the other females Kit had deliberately lured away from him. Thank God he had more sense than to hazard his heart.

Chapter 2

By the time Nicholas arrived at the summerhouse, he had his emotions under control, at least for the present.

"Where the devil have you been?" Alexandra demanded. "I've been waiting for hours!"

"Must you exaggerate, Hellion?" Nick chided.

"Of course; I'm a writer! Everything must be larger than life!"

"If we are to talk, you have to be serious, Alexandra."

"Stop treating me like a child!" she flared.

Nick acknowledged to himself that he did think of Alexandra as a child; it was a defensive mechanism against her irresistible charms. "If I thought you were a child, would I have brought you champagne?" he countered, smoothing her ruffled feathers.

"Oh, how lovely! Thank you, Nick."

"I'll pour . . . you talk."

"Dottie insists on my having a fall Season when Parliament opens. But when we go to London next month, I want to become a writer, not waste my time fending off fortune hunters. I'm only seventeen; far too young to marry. I want to taste life, experience great adventures, know what it's like to be independent and have freedom, before I'm buried in the country with a husband and children."

As he looked down into her lovely face, his heart skipped a beat, before his emotions were back under his iron control. "Your grandmother wants only what's best for you, Alexandra. The Longford wealth is legendary;

you'll never have to worry over money or earn your living, so why can't you simply marry and write as a hobby?"

"Don't patronize me! I thought *you* of all people would understand. Writing is my passion, just as your great passion is horses. Your family too is wealthy, but that doesn't stop you from wanting to breed horses."

"But I am a man," Nick pointed out patiently.

"And spoken like a bloody man! Is it wrong for a woman to be ambitious?" she cried. "Times are changing, Nicholas. The Georgian way of life is old-fashioned—there is now a Regency! Powdered wigs and *chaperons* will soon be *passé*. Our generation demands less stricture and more freedom, for women as well as men. What could possibly be wrong with that?"

Lord God, she is innocent. If she thought this generation had less stricture and more freedom than the Georgians, she was woefully mistaken. None were more profligate than Georgian men, and the women were only marginally more moral, with duchesses producing as many by-blows as dukes. Even her own grandmother had led a notorious life. "Alexandra, as much as you insist upon it, you are not yet a woman, and it is wrong for a seventeen-year-old to have the freedom of London," he said flatly. "It isn't all Mayfair town houses and Almack's. Beyond the glitter of St. James's Street, there are some extremely seedy areas that aren't safe for innocent girls. And beyond those, there are vast expanses so crime-ridden that life is held very cheaply. There are miles of filthy streets where poverty and disease are the natural order of things. London has an underbelly I never want you exposed to. And it's not just the poorer sections, Alexandra. Wickedness and evil sometimes run rampant among the *beau monde*."

Her eyes sparkled with eagerness. "*That's* what I intend to write about! Every gentleman of fashion has a mistress and every beautiful woman has a lover. You are a part of that world; why do you object to me becoming a part of it?"

"I do *not* have a mistress," he denied repressively.

Alexandra whooped with laughter and held out her empty glass.

"What's so bloody funny?" he asked, pouring her only half a glass this time.

"Let me drink to your high morals! You don't need to go to the expense of a mistress because women fling themselves at you and almost fight one another to share your bed for free."

As he looked down at her, he felt aeons older and wiser. "Alexandra, you shouldn't even know about these things, let alone discuss them with the opposite sex. You are incorrigible; I aught to take you across my knee."

"Do any of your ladybirds like to be spanked?"

"Alexandra!"

"And how do you know so much about the lurid side of London?"

"I am a man," he repeated. He had no intention of telling her more. His words hadn't acted as a deterrent; they had only made London, with all its debauchery, seem more fascinating. He eyed her warily. "Promise me you won't do anything foolish like running away and—"

"And taking a lover?" she teased.

"Alexandra!"

"Would you explain why the thought of an unmarried female taking a lover is shocking, while society turns a blind eye and considers it perfectly acceptable for a married woman to do so?"

Nick, realizing she had only an eccentric grandmother to guide her, told her the unvarnished truth. "A lady must be virgin when she marries, so that a man's first-born and heir is legally legitimate. After that, paternity isn't quite as important."

It was Alexandra's turn to be shocked. "I should have known it was connected to wealth and inheritance. To me, that's obscene. In my eyes, it is more acceptable for an *unmarried* woman to have a lover, for she is not committing adultery, nor hurting her husband by breaking her sacred marriage vows. In fact, it's nobody's business but her own. Someday, it will be an accepted practice, you'll see," she declared loftily.

"Not in my lifetime," Nicholas said flatly.

Alexandra decided to take pity on him. "Of course I won't run away, at least not until after your birthday. I wouldn't dream of missing the weekend house party at Hatton Hall. I intend to write about the guests' foibles and peccadilloes. Please keep your fingers crossed for something scandalous."

"Hellion." He reached out to ruffle her hair, suspecting that she was teasing him unmercifully, and he hoped that beneath those bright curls, Alex had a sensible head on her shoulders. "Have another glass of champagne and we'll go and find Rupert."

As Nick held open the door of the summerhouse for her, he felt it suddenly wrenched from his hand. His father stood before him in a towering temper. Nicholas smelled the brandy fumes and saw the ugly look of accusation on his face. Swiftly, he ordered Alexandra to leave, and was immensely thankful that for once she obeyed him.

"You filthy lecher! You lured her down here to seduce her! Stay away from Alexandra Sheffield—you know damn well I intend her for Christopher. That's the big attraction isn't it, you young swine? You covet everything that is his!"

Suddenly Nicholas was in a blind rage. The injustice of his father's accusations smote his integrity. He had never allowed his heart to become involved in his feelings for Alexandra, never dared to consider her, let alone covet her. Nick's jaw clenched and he balled up his fist, fighting the violence that rose up inside him.

Henry Hatton looked pointedly at the empty champagne bottle. "You were trying to get her drunk so you could take her virginity—or am I too late?" he demanded, his eyes narrowing with suspicion.

It was too much for Nick. He swung the bottle, hitting his father with a glancing blow to the temple. Lord Hatton dropped like a stone and lay sprawled on the grass, motionless.

A sudden hush fell over the horrified onlookers who had gathered. Finally someone asked, "Is he dead?"

"Dead drunk," Nick muttered with contempt, then he walked swiftly away from the distasteful scene.

The following morning, when Nick Hatton called at Longford Manor to reassure Alexandra that all was well,

Dottie Longford raised her lorgnette to examine the handsome devil before her. "Are you the heir or the spare?"

"It's Nicholas, my lady," he replied with amused tolerance for her blunt enquiry.

"Mmm, I might have known it wasn't the heir paying his addresses." She straightened her black wig. "I'd offer you breakfast, but I dismissed the cook this morning. Servants—can't abide 'em!" she confided. As Alexandra arrived in the morning room, Dottie prepared to leave. "I'll be in the kitchen, cooking myself a kipper. Who needs riffraffy servants anyway?"

Alexandra rolled her eyes. "Eccentric as a bandicoot."

"I prefer a bandicoot to a mad bull. I'm sorry about last night, Alexandra."

"Why was he so angry with you?"

"I never did find out," Nicholas lied with a reassuring smile, "and Father doesn't remember a thing about it this morning. A faulty memory is the sole advantage of drinking too much. I just wanted to make sure you weren't upset by the incident."

"I've seldom seen Lord Hatton when he wasn't angry with you. How do you tolerate him, Nick?"

"He's always worse around our birthdays—it's the pain of losing our mother," Nick explained, to excuse his father's behavior.

"He'll be sorry when he recognizes himself in my *roman à clef*!"

Nick laughed. "Come early on Saturday, and pack some old riding clothes. You'll find me in the stables."

"Where else?" she asked, her fond gaze lingering on the open collar of the linen shirt that displayed so temptingly his strong neck. "I'll bring my sketchbook too," she declared, knowing exactly what she wanted to draw.

When Nicholas departed, Dottie came out of the kitchen carrying a frying pan that held a burned kipper. "I adore that boy—ah, if only I were ten years younger, I'd give the gels a run for their money with that Adonis."

Alexandra almost choked. If Dottie were ten years younger, she'd still be past fifty! Still, she had to admit, Nicholas Hatton certainly made a female long for a lover, no matter her age. She was becoming excited about the upcoming weekend. "I must think of a costume for the masquerade ball." She had almost decided to disguise herself as a young man, since the guests would be less guarded with what they said in front of a male. "What about you?"

"Oh, I shall go as a nun, of course. It will fool people into thinking I'm celibate."

This time Alexandra did choke, then had to pretend it was the smell of the burned kipper that made her gasp for air.

"The young people today have no imagination. They are a wishy-washy, namby-pamby lot! Don't ye know that fancy-dress balls were devised as a delicious excuse to wear inadequate, indecent garments? When I was younger, I wore the most scandalous costumes; one so daring it earned me the nickname Godiva." A faraway look came into her eyes. "I wonder where that long, silvery-blond wig got to? Probably in a trunk in the attic. You could rummage about up there for a costume, Alexandra."

"I think I just might . . . after I've cooked you another kipper."

"Thank you, darling. You are an angel."

Later that morning, Alexandra carried an array of costumes to her bedchamber, while Dottie clutched an old ear-trumpet as if it were a priceless, lost treasure. "Pox take it, I shall have one of the most entertaining weekends of my life with this contraption!"

Alexandra eyed Dottie warily. "As a poking device?"

"No darling, as a *provoking* device! I shall pretend that I've suddenly been struck deaf. The party won't be boring, after all!"

On Friday, July 21, the day before his birthday, Christopher Hatton was pleased when a large wooden box was delivered, marked JOSEPH HEYLIN, CORNHILL, LONDON. Heylin was the maker of the finest holster pistols in England and Christopher guessed his birthday gift had arrived. Kit had a fine gun collection and was eager to add to it. He had dropped numerous hints to his father about the pair of sterling silver–mounted officer's holster pistols he'd seen in Heylin's workshop in Cornhill, and apparently the seeds he'd planted had borne fruit.

It wasn't until after dinner that Lord Hatton stood up from the table and announced, "Well, Christopher, if you'd like your birthday present, you'd better come out to the stables."

For a moment Kit wondered why the stables, then it dawned on him that he was most likely getting a new pair of leather saddle holsters to go with the pistols. Kit winked at his twin as they followed their father out to the stables. "I love surprises."

And surprise was what Christopher got when his father presented him with the savage black Thoroughbred stallion. An unpleasant surprise. A bolt of fear akin to lightning shot through him as he stood rooted to the spot, reliving his tenth birthday. Until then, the twins had been mounted on ponies they'd had since they were three and which represented no threat. Then Hatton decided that at ten years old, his heir was ready for a spirited black hunter.

The animal had terrified Kit, and he wished with all his heart that the docile gray filly presented to Nicholas could be his instead. He remembered how he had avoided going close to the hunter for two days, until his father had demanded to see him ride. He had crept up upon the great beast with a saddle over one arm and a riding whip clutched in his sweating palm.

The hunter didn't make his move until Kit was well into the stall, then suddenly he bared vicious teeth and lunged for him. Kit lashed out wildly with the whip, but this only put the black in a frenzy. He reared up with flailing hooves, ready to trample the boy who was lashing out at him.

That was the day his twin, Nicholas, saved his life.

"Don't whip him!" Nick cried, snatching up a pitchfork and gently backing the animal into a corner of the stall. "Quick, run!" Nick cried, but Kit was paralyzed with fear. As the hunter again reared and screamed, Nick dropped the pitchfork, darted in, grabbed his brother, and rolled with him from beneath the flailing iron-clad hooves. That was the day Christopher Hatton decided his twin loved him far more than his father did.

But saving him was only half the story. Nick had donned Kit's clothes and ridden the black hunter under their father's critical eye. Later, Nick explained that the horse too had been driven by fear, and only kindness and a firm hand could win him over. It had taken a whole year before Christopher could ride the hunter without being drenched in perspiration, and another year before he could ride him with the nonchalant, hell-for-leather horsemanship that came naturally to Nicholas.

Kit again felt the familiar trickle of sweat between his shoulder blades, and the miasma of horse-lant, straw, and leather rose up to nauseate him, but he had learned never to show weakness before his father. "He has magnificent lines; how does the name Renegade strike you?" Kit drawled.

Henry Hatton smiled with satisfaction and turned to Nicholas. "There's a fine pair of guns up at the house for you, my boy. If you apply yourself and practice, you may someday achieve Christopher's skill at marksmanship."

The minute their father was out of earshot, Kit cursed, "Christ Almighty, why is he so fucking obtuse?"

Nicholas put his arm across his brother's shoulders. "He isn't obtuse, Kit. He is well aware that I have a passion for horses, and you have a passion for guns."

Kit clenched his fists impotently and swore between his teeth. "I hate the son of a bitch, don't you?"

Nick's gray eyes darkened as they stared after their father. He shook his head slowly. "No, Kit, I don't hate him. I pity him."

Because Lady Longford, Alexandra, and Rupert arrived on Saturday before the rest of the weekend guests and were old family friends, they were given their choice of bedchambers. Alexandra had a special request for Mr. Burke, the majordomo, and asked for the room that was directly above Nicholas Hatton's. She remembered once, when they were children, she had caught Rupert and Christopher spying on Nick through a peephole in the floor. Alexandra hoped the hole was still there, because she had plans to put it to good use.

As she opened the tall window that overlooked the ornamental lake, the sight of the wooden punt floating at the lake's edge evoked happy childhood memories. She spotted Christopher Hatton on the far side and remembered that today was his birthday, while Nick's was still two days away. She knew it was Kit because, even from this distance, she could see the easel and canvas. She decided to join him and picked up her sketchbook.

"Happy birthday, Kit. You've come out here to avoid your guests, so naturally I couldn't resist disturbing your peace and tranquility."

"Hello, Imp. How did you know I was avoiding them?"

"Your birth sign, of course. I know everything about you—your fluctuating moods, how you hide from things like a crab withdrawing into its shell. You are a well of secrecy, with a sensitive soul."

He was painting a still life of a pair of pheasants that he had shot earlier. The game lay on the ground beside a hunting rifle he had propped against the bole of a tree. Though his subject of dead birds was rather morbid, the variegated colors of the feathers in the painting were exact.

Alexandra would have preferred that he paint live pheasants, but she could not deny his talent. "You are a true artist, Kit. I wonder if you really do hide a sensitive nature beneath your brash exterior?"

"No, my brash exterior hides a brash interior." He lifted amused gray eyes to watch her laugh. "Why the devil did you chop off your hair?"

"I'm amazed you noticed; you're usually far too self-absorbed," she teased, drawing closer to admire his work. "Perhaps you should give the painting to Dottie. I noticed two Thomas Lawrence works of art missing from the walls of the formal dining room this morning. When I asked her where they were, she said she put them in the attic because she couldn't stomach the simpering females Lawrence portrays."

"If she prefers me to Lawrence, she's more than eccentric," he said with unusual humility.

Alexandra kicked off her slippers, which were damp with dew, curled her long legs beneath her, and took up her sketchbook. "Open your shirt at the neck, Kit. I want to draw you."

"Is this to be one of your cruel caricatures?"

"Of course not! You are one of the handsomest men I've ever laid eyes on. You endlessly fascinate me."

Kit Hatton was accustomed to women reacting with fascination when they looked at him, but he didn't welcome it in Alexandra. Though he found her beauty dazzling, he never allowed it to show. She was the only female safe from his lechery in three counties, and the reason for this was simple: If he had even looked askance at her, his father would have had them betrothed, and the trap of marriage was the last thing Kit Hatton desired at twenty-one. "I only fascinate you because I'm a twin."

"Most probably," she admitted. "At least, that's part of it." Alexandra had decided to sketch both Nicholas and Christopher, then study their discernible differences. Nick usually brushed his dark hair straight back, while Kit had a curl that fell forward on his forehead. It puzzled her that though the two magnificent males were physically identical, only one made her weak with longing.

Within a quarter of an hour, Rupert arrived on the scene. "So this is where you two are hiding yourselves. Come on, Kit. We have to lay out a racecourse. Hart Cavendish has arrived and he insists we race our horses this afternoon."

"You don't mean Lord Hartington, the Duke of Devonshire? How the devil do you know him?" Alexandra demanded. William Spencer Cavendish was the son of the late infamous Georgiana, Duchess of Devonshire, and he had come into his father's dukedom last year.

Rupert said casually, "We were all at Harrow together when we were ratty schoolboys."

"Oh, I want to have a good look at him," Alexandra declared. "He's the one who had a fit of hysterics when his cousin Caroline Ponsonby wed William Lamb, because he thought of her as his *wife*!"

"I'll bet he was bloody glad Caro was William Lamb's wife when she caused the scandal with Byron, who by the way was another school chum!"

"Oh, Kit, why did you never tell me?" Alex was wildly curious about Caro Lamb, who was reputed to be unstable and had sent George Gordon, Lord Byron, a lock of her pubic hair. "Do you know the ins and outs of that affair?" Alexandra asked with avid interest.

Kit rolled on the grass with laughter. "*Ins and outs!* Christ, Alexandra, you have a sly way with an innuendo."

Alexandra blushed and pretended her witty remark had been quite intentional. She gathered up her sketchbook and charcoal and hurried back to Hatton Hall. Young Lord Hartington—here indeed was material for one of her cruel caricatures!

Chapter 3

By lunchtime, more than half the guests had arrived, and though Alexandra knew the people who were neighbors, there were many unfamiliar faces present. Her grandmother introduced her to her friend Lady Spencer, and it was only when a tall, attractive young man with fair hair and deep blue eyes took her fingers to his lips that she realized who they were. Hart Spencer Cavendish was the grandson of Lady Spencer, her grandmother's friend.

"I cannot believe my eyes, Dottie. Alexandra is the image of my daughter, Georgiana. At seventeen she was just such a tall, slender beauty, with the same brilliant red-gold curls."

"Then it is no wonder my father fell in love with her," Hart Cavendish said gallantly. He openly gazed at Alexandra, unable to hide the fact that the long-legged redhead had bedazzled him and caught his fancy. "Would you allow me to join you?"

"With the greatest pleasure, Your Grace."

"Please, you must call me Hart. I had no notion Rupert had such a ravishing sister."

Alexandra wanted to ply him with a million questions. Here was a young man who must have had an erratic childhood, growing up at infamous Devonshire House with that rag-tag assortment of children simultaneously sired by his father upon Georgiana and his mistress, Elizabeth Foster. The scandalous *ménage à trois* utterly fascinated Alexandra. She gazed at Hart Cavendish hungrily, not seeing him as a man but as a rich lode of unmined scandal and gossip; more than enough to fill a book. The things he must know about his mother and His Royal Highness, the Prince of Wales!

"Will you come and watch us race this afternoon?" Hart invited.

Alexandra had had every intention of joining the race herself and wearing breeches to boot, but now she realized she didn't wish to appear to be an incorrigible hellion to Hart Cavendish, at least not quite yet. He had been surrounded by such females all his life. He obviously admired her and wanted to be friends, and Alexandra realized the wisdom of nurturing the friendship of a duke of the realm. Here was her *entrée* to the *beau monde.*

"I would love to watch you race," Alexandra enthused and rushed upstairs, not to don breeches but rather her prettiest day dress of sprigged muslin with the green ribbons fluttering at the high waist to draw attention to her pert breasts.

In the stables a short time later, Christopher Hatton offered his new Thoroughbred, Renegade, to Hart Cavendish for the race.

"I say, Kit, that's damn sporting of you."

"Not really," Kit drawled. "He's an unknown quantity. I'll stick with my hunter—better the devil you know, I always say."

Nicholas, busy saddling his own horse, Slate, realized his twin had found a way to save face, and was glad. The horse to beat was definitely Renegade; now he could try to win without holding back.

The course they had set ran through Hatton Great Park, around the lake to the banks of the River Crane, through the meadows of Hatton Grange, then through the Longford woods, and ended at the stables where it started. The lawn and the stable courtyard overflowed with laughing guests, making wagers.

Alexandra could overhear a conversation Henry Hatton was having with a group of older men. She recognized John Eaton, a cousin of Lord Hatton's who was a financial advisor, and she also knew retired Colonel Stevenson who had served in India under Major-General Arthur Wellesley, now known as Lord Wellington and so much in the news these days. Their talk was all of war, because Wellington had just won the Battle of Vitoria in Spain, which put him closer than he had ever been to France.

"No need to worry," the colonel declared. "Wellington has put an end to the power of Napoleon in the Peninsula. He'll beat the French hollow—no finer general ever lived!"

Suddenly, Alexandra saw her grandmother in their midst. "Bloody warmongers, the lot of you! The poor hooked-nosed bugger will have a devil of a hard time beating the French if the Horse Guards keep sending him idiots like General Lighthume and Colonel Fletcher! He needs more men with iron testicles like Sir Rowland Hill!"

"Ah, I always thought you were a Whig, Lady Longford," one of the men declared. Dottie's blue language was perfectly acceptable because of her age and great wealth.

"Whigs and Tories—they all piss in the same pot! Just so long as they are making money, they're happy to let England go to hell in a handbasket."

Henry Hatton grinned. "I'm not above making a profit from war. Eaton here will be glad to advise you about investing in some lucrative government contracts."

Dottie made a raspberry. "What a load of caca! I wouldn't dream of disturbing my investments. They've returned me a thousandfold over the years."

Alexandra saw the look of speculation on Lord Hatton's face. "Will you take tea with me, and a spot of brandy, this afternoon, Dottie? There's a certain matter I'd like to discuss."

Alexandra's curiosity was whetted, but at that moment she felt the ground rumble with approaching hoofbeats. She elbowed her way to the front of the crowd to watch the climax of the race. Two horses were neck and neck, far ahead of the others. One was black, the other gray. Nick Hatton's horses had always been gray, as far back as she could remember. The one he was riding he had bred himself. If Alexandra had had a million pounds, she would have unhesitatingly bet it on the gray, yet it had little to do with the horse. It was the man riding the gray on whom she would put her money.

The horses were full-out now. They were well matched, and their satiny sinews strained forward with brutal strength. The animals were even, head to head, and it looked as if the race would end in a draw, but Alexandra knew better. She raised her eyes to the man riding the gray and saw his teeth flash in a smile that told how much Hazard Hatton was enjoying himself. She shivered as she saw his male power dominate and harness the power of the animal beneath him. Then, triumphantly, his mount surged over the finish line ahead of the black Thoroughbred Hart Cavendish rode.

Alexandra was mesmerized just looking at Nick. Her blood pounded exactly as his did. Simply watching Nick thrilled and excited her; he had a deep and abiding lust for life, and he was more man than any male she had ever encountered. His linen shirt clung to his chest and the cords of his neck pulsed with the glory of being alive. She knew that it was not so much that he liked to win; rather, she knew he could not bear to lose. Twin he might be, but to Alexandra, there was no man on earth like him.

She watched Hart Cavendish shake his head in disbelief, then laugh aloud as he congratulated Nick Hatton. Alexandra liked the fair-haired young man immediately because he was so good-natured. At least half a dozen young women crowded past Alexandra to congratulate the winner and to flirt with all the young men who had raced. As the horses were returned to the stables, the talk was all of wagers and who would collect and who would pay. Jeremy Eaton, a second cousin to the twins, had appointed himself to handle the money, and none objected since his father was a financial advisor.

"If I'd been riding Renegade, I would have beaten you," Kit informed his brother.

"That's quite possible," Nick acknowledged generously.

Overhearing the twins, Alexandra wondered if Nick would have held back and allowed Kit to win. The Hatton twins had a close bond that was sometimes hard to fathom.

As Kit and Rupert turned their horses over to Hatton grooms, they suggested a swim in the lake to cool off.

All the young men agreed, and the young women began to giggle and whisper, making plans to follow and watch.

Alexandra did not join the other young people but entered the stables, knowing Nicholas would tend his own horse rather than turn it over to a groom. She watched him cool down the Thoroughbred as well as his gray, curious about his special touch with horses. When she posed a question about it, Nick grinned at her.

"Mr. Burke says I inherited it through my mother's Irish blood. Her family bred horses and practiced the ancient secret rituals known as horse whispering."

"I've never heard of horse whispering," Alexandra said raptly.

"You learn the animals' natural behavior and train them with kindness rather than mastering them with brute force."

"It seems to work like magic."

Nick's grin widened. "There is a lot of myth surrounding horse whispering, but I doubt there's any magic involved. I suspect that kindness works best with humans and all living creatures."

She watched his muscles flex and ripple as he gave Slate a rubdown. He had beautiful hands, and for a moment she imagined what it would feel like to have him touch her in a similar fashion. She went weak at the thought. Alexandra longed to sketch him, to capture his male beauty on paper, so that she could keep it and look at it whenever the desire came upon her. And Alexandra frankly admitted that the desire came upon her quite often lately.

"If you'd worn your old riding clothes, you could have helped me. Why the pretty gown?"

"I have decided to behave like a young lady this weekend, rather than a hellion."

His gray eyes filled with amusement. "I wondered why you didn't insist on joining the race. It makes for a nice change"—he eyed her dresss appreciatively—"but how long can you keep it up?"

"Until I get bored, I suppose. You will notice that I did not rush off to the lake to ogle the males who removed their shirts and plunged about in the water for the edification of their female audience." Alexandra hoped her words would allay any suspicion he harbored about her plans, most of which involved him.

"I wonder if maturity is sneaking up on you?" His glance roamed over her, paused on her breasts, hesitated on her mouth, then lifted to her saucy curls.

Alexandra thought the look he gave her held a tinge of regret, as if he didn't really want her to grow up.

The first thing Alexandra did when she went up to her room was move the Chippendale bench at the foot of the graceful bed. Then, filled with excited anticipation, she rolled back the green Chinese rug. *Yes! The hole is still there.* It had been cut into the ceiling below to accommodate a chandelier but had been put in the wrong place, about a foot off center of the room. When the magnificent chandelier had been installed correctly, the hole was not noticeable from below.

Alexandra knelt down and put her eye to it. She had a splendid view of the chamber below because of the eighteen-foot ceiling height. She brought her sketchpad and charcoal and tossed down a pillow from the bed to make herself comfortable while she awaited her model. She didn't have to wait long. Because of the race and the subsequent attention Nicholas had given the two horses, he was in much need of a bath. She put her eye to the hole and watched him drag a copper bath from behind a screen. In a few minutes two houseservants brought buckets of steaming water to fill the tub.

Alexandra lay flat on the floor, holding her breath, her eye to the hole, as Nick began to remove his clothes. She watched, mesmerized, as one garment after another came off. Her sketchbook lay forgotten as she became engrossed in the riveting scene below. Alexandra had never seen a naked male before, and she sighed with great satisfaction that her first viewing was of Nicholas Hatton.

His proud head, wide shoulders, and broad back looked sculpted from bronze. From behind, his hips were narrow, his buttocks small and firm, and his legs strong and muscular. When he turned to step into the water, she saw that his belly was hard and flat, but her eyes traveled lower with an insatiable curiosity that would not be denied. Between his legs was a nest of dark curls that partially hid his male sex. The glimpse she got from above, before he became submerged in water, was brief, but it told her his size was formidable. Even though the fashion of tight breeches left little to the imagination, a male's private parts were larger than she had expected. She wondered if that was true in general, or in particular where Nicholas was concerned.

To an artist, his body is absolute perfection, she rhapsodized. Then her innate honesty asserted itself. *Who the devil am I kidding? To a woman, his body is absolute perfection!* With her pulses racing, she watched him scrub his torso and lather his hair, then duck beneath the water to rinse before he stepped out to vigorously rub his body with a towel. Alexandra suddenly remembered her sketchbook. She sat up and, with rapid strokes, drew the lithe, classical figure of the male she had been studying so intently. She gazed down at the paper and saw that the naked man was indeed a superb specimen.

She looked through the spy hole again and saw him pad over to his wardrobe. She felt a pang of regret. If only he would remain naked and still for her. She wished he would lie down on the bed so she could capture every detail of his magnificent body. It was only a tiny leap for her imagination to place herself on the bed with him. She rolled onto her back with a low moan as full-blown desire filled her mind. She raised her hand to her tingling breast and touched her own fingertip to her nipple as it hardened. Amazed at her body's reaction, her fingers traced her rib cage, which rose and fell with her agitated breath. Her palm came to rest low on her belly, and she pressed down hard to ease the ache that filled her with longing. Then, unable to control her vivid imagination, Alexandra surrendered to a wicked fantasy.

As evening approached, Alexandra carefully laid out her costumes for the masquerade ball. She had brought two with her so that she could carry out her ingenious, yet simple plan. She donned a white shirt that belonged to her brother, Rupert, and pulled on fawn-colored trousers whose straps went beneath her instep to assure a taut fit, then she pulled on soft leather top boots. It was a good thing her legs were as long as Rupert's or his clothes would not have been such a good fit.

When she buttoned the gold brocade waistcoat, it flattened her breasts, and she knew the claret-colored jacket with its padded shoulders would camouflage the rest of her feminine curves. Her fingers had no trouble arranging an intricate neckcloth, then she tucked her short curls beneath one of her brother's brown tie-wigs. The transformation was amazing. Even without an eye mask, none would have guessed she was anything but a young buck of fashion.

Though Alexandra didn't know how Nick would be dressed, she did know that Kit and Rupert had chosen identical black and white harlequin costumes so people would mistake them for the Hatton twins. She smiled and shook her head, wondering how her brother expected people to believe he was Nick Hatton when his shoulders were so abysmally narrow.

She went downstairs and knew she had passed the test when her own grandmother didn't recognize her. Dottie was easy to spot in her nun's habit, brandishing the ear-trumpet, especially since she was with her oldest friend and lover, Neville, Lord Staines, who was costumed as Friar Tuck. The ballroom was filled with females anxious to dance. Alexandra thought she recognized Olivia Harding, but the proliferation of medieval headdresses and Elizabethan ruffs transformed most of the uninteresting young women into intriguing strangers. There were one or two females in powdered wigs with red ribbons about their throats who affected delicious French accents, and another disguised as a Japanese lady in a gorgeously embroidered kimono and carrying an ivory fan.

Hatton Hall's library had been set up as a card room, and Alexandra walked in and casually rubbed shoulders with the men who filled every table. Her gaze wandered from knights to pirates to men in military uniforms as she tried to decide if Nicholas was the Horse Guard or the Hussar. The latter turned out to be Hart Cavendish, who didn't recognize her, and the former was Olivia

Harding's brother, Harry, who told her pointedly that *he* was supposed to be in costume.

Dottie entered the card room and joined a circle of titled guests, which included Lady Hortense Mitford, Countess Lavinia Bingham, and the Duchess of Rutland, all leading Society matrons. George Bingham immediately arose and offered Lady Longford his chair. "Dorothy, m'dear, won't you sit?"

Dottie lifted the ear-trumpet. "Shit? Did you say *shit,* George? I quite agree that horse shit works wonders on the kitchen garden. It doesn't offend me, of course, but I don't think shit is a good choice of subjects in mixed company, m'boy!"

Lady Hortense and Countess Lavinia both gasped audibly, while Lord Staines tried valiantly to hide his amusement. The Duchess of Rutland stepped into the breach immediately, changing the subject. "Did you see Annabelle Harding's headdress at the theater last evening? She actually had a nest complete with a blackbird adorning her coiffure!"

Up went the ear-trumpet. "A black turd adorning her coiffure? I warrant it was an improvement over the battleship she wore to Prince William's naval tattoo."

At the graphic picture Dottie's words painted, the Duchess of Rutland's eyebrows raised until they touched her hairline. She welcomed the arrival of her friends Lord and Lady Brougham into the circle, hoping they would steer the conversation back to respectability. The duchess, however, was doomed to disappointment when Lady Brougham announced, "I hear the Prince of Wales is honoring Princess Charlotte with a gigantic ball."

Lady Longford slyly tapped Lady Brougham with her ear-trumpet. "I know to whom you refer," she said confidentially. "The Duke of Cumberland is reputed to have gigantic balls! Wasn't it your sister who told us that they were the size of swan's eggs?"

The gentlemen were all vastly amused; the ladies were not. George Bingham nudged his old friend. "I envy you, Neville; there's a few games I wouldn't mind playing with a deaf nun!"

Alexandra closed her eyes, prayed for patience, and heaved a great sigh of relief when her grandmother left the gaming room in search of other Society matrons whom she could torture for her own depraved amusement.

A black-caped figure entered the room. The black leather mask and slouch hat were so sinister that Alexandra would never have recognized the highwayman as Nicholas if she hadn't overheard him tell Hart Cavendish who he was. The two friends sat down at the faro table, one of Nick's favorite games of chance. Alexandra slipped into an empty chair beside him and casually picked up the cards that the dealer dealt her.

They were playing for money, of course, and Alexandra wagered everything she had won on the horse race. As she watched Nick's long fingers caress his cards, a shudder went through her at the memory of her afternoon's imaginary dalliance with the attractive devil. The felon's black attire only made matters worse, adding an air of danger to his dark, dominant presence. His closeness made it impossible for her to concentrate on her cards, and she lost her money. Before she knew it, her pockets were to let.

Affecting a curt, husky voice, she glanced at Nick and said, "A word, sir?" She scraped back her chair, stood up, and stalked from the room.

Nick Hatton murmured an excuse and followed the young man. When he lifted his black leather mask, Alexandra saw his gray eyes assess the coat by Weston and the Hoby boots and conclude that his card partner should be flush enough to pay his gambling debts.

"I can't pay," Alexandra said flatly.

"I'll take your marker," Nick said smoothly.

Alex shook her head. "It will have to be pistols at dawn!"

Nick looked at her closely, knowing someone was pulling his leg, but damned if he knew the fellow's identity.

Alex raised her hands, lifted off the brown tie-wig and shook out her red-gold curls.

"Good God, Hellion! You had me gulled!"

Alexandra laughed with him as she put back the wig and carefully tucked her own short hair beneath it. With eyes brimful of devilment she confided, "I'm going to the ballroom now to dance with all the debutantes and set their hearts aflutter. I'll wager you double or nothing I can get my face slapped!"

Nick shook his head as he watched her depart. She really was the most high-spirited and amusing female he had ever encountered. Once she grew to womanhood, she would be a devastating creature. His eyes lingered on her shapely bottom and long legs encased in men's britches, and his mouth went dry at the erotic thoughts they produced. Why on earth had their father chosen this particular female for Christopher, effectively rendering her taboo where he was concerned? His father's words from the night at the Hardings' summerhouse came back to him. *"That's the big attraction, isn't it, you young swine? You covet everything that is his!"* Nicholas knew he coveted nothing that belonged to his twin. *Nothing except Alexandra Sheffield!* his inner voice mocked. *Daydreams are for children,* he told himself bluntly and went back to the card room.

Alexandra had no intention of going to the ballroom. Instead, she went back to her chamber to change into her "real" costume. There was no hurry; she knew it would be at least an hour before Nick tired of faro. She removed her brother's clothes, observing herself in the cheval glass, and pulled on black silk tights. They emphasized the length of her slim legs, and Alexandra knew when she put on the black, high-heeled slippers the effect would be scandalously provocative.

Next, she slipped on a black velvet doublet that fitted the contour of her breasts so snugly there was no room for anything beneath it. She smoothed her hair back with a brush and drew the black silk hood over her head so that not a wisp of red showed, and she laughed with delight at the pair of pointed ears that stood up so saucily.

She painted her lips red and, with a piece of charcoal, darkened the tip of her nose and drew delicate cat whiskers beside both corners of her mouth. Next she slipped on a green sequined eye mask, through which her own green eyes gazed catlike at her reflection. Finally, Alexandra fastened the long, black tail to her derriere, looped it over her arm, and pulled on black gloves.

The effect was absolutely stunning. She posed before the mirror, arching her back, then practiced a slinky, feline walk. She was delighted with her reflection, but rather breathless at the amount of daring it would take to leave the privacy of the bedchamber and mingle with the crowd below. She reminded herself that this costume had once been worn by her grandmother, Lady Longford. *She must have been a little hellcat in her day,* Alexandra mused, and she decided on the spot that she possessed just as much courage as Dottie ever dreamed of having.

Chapter 4

When Alexandra joined the crowded party, she soon realized by the murmurs and whispers that she was attracting the attention of every Tom, Dick, and Harry. She was dismayed, for there was only one man she hoped to attract. She wanted the floor to open up and swallow her when she saw Lord Hatton walking a direct path to her. He did not even try to conceal the lust he was feeling.

"Pussycat, Pussycat, where have you been?"

"Rat catching," she hissed, then deftly lifted a drink from a footman's silver tray and placed it in his hand. "Try quenching your insatiable thirst with this, Henry." Alexandra disappeared into the garden for her own safety, knowing she would be almost invisible in the shadows.

Presently she saw a man wearing a black-and-white harlequin costume and a mermaid with their arms entwined. Alexandra could clearly hear their conversation and realized the mermaid sounded exactly like Olivia Harding.

"I propose a moonlight dip," the male suggested persuasively.

"But how can I go back to the party dripping wet?" The mermaid sounded disappointed.

The harlequin laughed. "Darling, you remove your costume, of course." The pair moved toward the lake without even noticing her.

Alexandra strolled around the house and looked in at the library window. She watched the highwayman rake in his winnings and arise from the table. She could see that inside the air was filled with blue smoke and guessed that Nick would seek fresh air. She returned to the stone terrace that opened from the ballroom and stationed herself in the shadows beside a French door, watching carefully through its glass. More than anything she wanted Nick to pursue and woo her. She would not make it easy for him, for the sheer pleasure of having him bend her to his will and refuse to take no for an answer. When she saw the tall, dark figure approach, she tossed her long, black tail into his path.

Nicholas touched it with the tip of his boot, then he bent and picked it up with curiosity. When he pulled on its tail, the cat emerged with a plaintive *meow.* His eyes widened with appreciation at the feline contours of the female in the alluring costume. "It could prove dangerous prowling about in the dark," he murmured.

"I have nine lives," she purred, "while you, my insolent night rider, are on the reckless road to Tyburn." Alexandra deliberately retreated one step.

"There is something irresistible about danger, don't you think?" Nicholas advanced one step.

Alexandra could tell that her identity eluded him and that his curiosity was piqued by her provocative disguise.

"Do I know you, Puss?" he asked suggestively, as his avid eyes roamed over her.

"You should; I'm one of your stable cats."

He laughed. "Then what the devil are you doing up at the house? I think I should take you back to the stable." His voice was teasing and filled with suggestive innuendo.

Alexandra caught her breath, and her pulse raced wildly as she rubbed her cheek against her own shoulder in a seductive feline gesture. Then she bared her teeth and hissed, "Touch me and try to take me anywhere at your peril, sir!"

He tickled her chin with the end of her tail. "Black cats are symbols of witchcraft, and you certainly have me spellbound."

"I thought all cats were gray in the dark," she purred.

"Whoever said that knew little about felines and even less about females." He took possession of her hand and, with his other hand at the small of her back just above her tail, urged her in the direction of the stable.

Alexandra's knees turned to water at his touch. It was the first time he had ever done anything as intimate as hold her hand, and she felt the warmth from his body seep up her arm, making it tingle. He was so overtly masculine, so tall and powerful as he took command, she wanted to follow wherever he led. It also was the first time she had experienced the legendary charm and she was prepared to play out the game to its conclusion. For a year now she had dreamed of such a wooing, and the anticipation didn't come close to the excitement of the reality. His undivided attention threatened to overwhelm her.

Inside the darkness of the stable very little could be seen, but that heightened Alexandra's other senses. The rustling sounds of the animals were familiar and soothing, yet the smell of the hay and leather had the complete opposite effect, arousing slumbering emotions and titillating her excitement.

Nicholas drew her into the privacy of an empty box stall. "Do you like to be stroked, Puss?"

In the shadowed darkness she gazed up at the tall, dominant male who towered above her. He was as tempting as sin, and she knew she could not resist him. "That depends upon the hand doing the stroking," she replied huskily from lack of breath.

He cupped her shoulders with strong, possessive hands, making sure she did not turn capricious and attempt to leave. "My strokes can be short and fast, or long and slow like this." One hand rubbed firmly down the length of her back all the way to her rounded bottom cheek, then he repeated the sensual motion. "Which do you prefer?" he whispered.

"Long and slow," she purred, arching her bottom into his hand. Alexandra felt quite safe from discovery. An unmarried girl would never paint her lips bright red, nor wear a costume that was so bold it tempted a male's very manhood.

"Have we ever exchanged kisses?" he murmured intimately, still trying to discern her identity.

An uncontrollable shiver ran up her spine where his

hand had stroked her. "You tell me." She lifted her mouth in invitation, hardly daring to breathe as the long-anticipated kiss was about to become a reality.

Tentatively at first, his lips brushed hers, then his mouth took possession and he deepened the kiss. Alexandra was lost. Her arms lifted about his neck as he pressed her close. Desire snaked through her, turning her longing to craving.

Nick pulled her into his hard body, cupped her buttocks firmly, and pressed her woman's center against his marble-hard arousal. Then he lifted her in a circular motion so that her softness moved around his erection, making sure that she could feel it pulsate as his heat seeped into her.

Her hands slipped down from his neck and splayed against his taut chest muscles, knowing she should push him away. But her thighs strained against his, as if she wanted to imprint forever the feel of his body against hers. His mouth, by turns inviting and demanding, easily persuaded hers that it wanted to be ravaged. Her arms crept back about his neck, and she pressed her body so close that their heartbeats mingled.

His sensual mouth urged her lips to soften and cling to his. The way she responded excited him, making him want more. She tasted different than any female of his acquaintance, arousing both his desire and his curiosity, tempting him to explore further. He took off his cloak, wrapped it about her, then pulled her back to his body, his hands roaming over her secret places now hidden beneath the soft black cape. One hand came to rest on the swell of her breast, the other hand tipped up her chin so he could recapture her lips. Against his persistent pressure, her lips parted to allow the tip of his tongue to slide inside the sweet warmth of her mouth. "You taste like wild honey—I don't believe I've ever tasted you before, Puss."

"Are kisses so different?" she asked in breathless wonder.

Slowly, he unbuttoned her doublet, and his possessive hand stole inside to cup the silky globe of her breast. "I sincerely hope so. Are mine not different from other men's?"

Alex knew that she should not allow him to touch her

in this intimate way, and a tiny spark of fear ignited. She willfully ignored it because his touch felt so deliciously wicked. She caught back the words *I have no idea,* realizing it would be a confession of her inexperience and would probably cause him to stop. She felt his fingers brush across the tip of her breast until her nipple turned diamond hard and experienced a feeling of shock that a male would do such a thing to a female.

She gasped as a shaft of desire shot from her breast, spiraled through her belly, and came to rest between her legs. She tried to focus, so she could answer his question. "Perhaps another kiss will give me the answer." Surely she had not meant her words to be so blatantly inviting?

He laughed, deep in his throat. She too wanted more, and he was ready to satisfy all her feline desires. He plucked his cape from her shoulders and spread it upon the hay, then he drew her down beside him. Unerringly, his hand slipped back inside the doublet, and as his warm palm cupped her breast, he felt it harden with arousal. With the fingers of his other hand, he traced a tantalizing path up the inside of her thigh. "Do you like cream, my little Puss?"

Alexandra shivered. When had she lost complete control of the situation? How on earth had he managed to lure her to lie with him? She had always known that Nick Hatton was devilishly dark and dominant; now she knew that he was also dangerous. Unbelievably, it added to his attraction.

He covered her high mons with his hand and was mildly surprised at her reaction. He felt her stiffen and close her legs, trapping his hand between. He squeezed softly, knowingly, and her thighs opened slightly to his questing fingers. Through the soft material, he stroked her cleft and circled the tiny bud with his thumb, eliciting a moan that was music to his ears. He covered her mouth with his and thrust his tongue inside, imitating what he longed to do with his cock. Imitating what he fully intended to do with his cock. He found the waistband of her tights and began to draw them down.

She murmured, breathless with desire, "I had no earthly notion a man could arouse a woman to madness."

The movement of his hands paused. *Is this female telling me she is not a cat; that she is still a kitten?* He gazed into her eyes through the green eye mask, and in the dimness wondered if his imagination was playing tricks on him. Then she spoke again.

"Nicholas, are you really going to make love to me?"

His heart slammed against his chest wall, and it was all he could do to prevent himself from jumping back in alarm. *Goddamn it, it is Alexandra, playing the little hellcat!* After seeing her and touching her this way, it was no longer possible to think of her as a child. She was a sensual female on the brink of womanhood and ripe for the plucking. Nicholas knew a moment of panic, then his common sense took over and his resolve hardened. He knew he must teach her a lesson that she would not soon forget. If he could put fear into her heart, then so much the better. Thank God she had chosen him for this seductive encounter; any other man of his acquaintance would have plucked her by now!

His voice took on a mocking tone. "You are enjoying my kisses, and my touching your body, but I know exactly what you are up to. You have allowed my twin to make love to you, and like every other female, you want to compare us!"

"No, I've never dreamed of making love to anyone but you, Nick!"

He cupped her breast, caressed it knowingly, and laughed nastily. "You have no way of knowing if I am Nicholas or Christopher. We share our costumes as we share our conquests. It is obvious you like playing guessing games as much as we do, Puss."

His confession horrified her; for a moment she was convinced that she had mistaken Christopher for Nicholas.

Nick felt Alexandra stiffen and draw back from his possessive hand, and his other arm swept about her waist, holding her against his hardened body. "The smell of the hay is most inviting . . . a stable cat like you must enjoy rolling about in it quite often."

"I have never rolled in the hay! Let me go!"

Nick, ignoring the indignation in her voice, straddled her and imprisoned her between his hard thighs. His demanding mouth, no longer gentle, covered hers, effectively smothering her protest as he pressed her down onto the fragrant dried clover. "Why don't I remove everything except your mask and see if I can identify you by your delicious body? Your breasts feel most familiar, but I need to taste them before I can be absolutely positive."

Alexandra gasped as she realized the man lying on top of her in the hay was about to lift her breast to his lips and suck her nipple into his wicked mouth, as if it were a cherry ripe for the plucking. She felt his hot mouth murmur suggestively against her throat, "Open your legs and let me stroke you, Pussy. I will soon fill you with the cream you crave."

Full-blown fear now mingled with flaring anger as Alexandra extricated herself from the lecherous male who was intent upon ravishing her. "I cannot believe this is how you amuse and enjoy yourself!"

Nicholas heard a sob escape from Alexandra as she tried to flee from the stall. *Oh, my honey love, I enjoyed it far, far too much.* He grabbed her and pulled her back to stand before him. He could feel her body trembling and hated himself for what he had done to her. He lifted off her green mask. "Alexandra, you have no idea of the danger you were in. I almost ruined you. When I last saw you, you were dressed as a male. . . . Obviously this was a deliberate plan. Thank God it was me you chose for your experiment! Alexandra, most men wouldn't have stopped." With firm hands he wrapped his cloak about her. "You will go upstairs and take off this scandalous costume immediately."

Now that she knew it really was Nicholas, and that he had only behaved in a salacious way to teach her a lesson, she sagged with relief. Her fear of him now mingled with defiance. "How can you behave like a moralistic father, when a moment ago you were ready to seduce me?"

"That's enough sauce, you little hellcat. Go now. We mustn't be seen together. My father has already accused me of poaching on Christopher's territory, and I would never, ever do that."

Because his rejection hurt her and covered her with

shame, Alexandra's temper flared higher. Why in the name of hellfire did everyone assume she belonged to Kit? She wanted to protest at length, but the lump in her throat almost choked her. She pulled the cloak more closely about her and began to run. "I hate you, Nick Hatton!" she shouted over her shoulder.

The following morning, when Christopher was summoned to his father's chamber, he assumed the discussion would be about allowing Hart Cavendish to ride Renegade. He had decided to ride the Thoroughbred himself in the hunt today to avoid a browbeating from his father. He'd practiced his shooting all week and fully expected to bring down a stag, perhaps more than one. *I'll show the old swine,* he vowed as he tapped on the door and was given permission to enter.

The two men who faced each other were dressed alike in fawn riding breeches and tan leather riding boots. Both wore "pink" hunting jackets, which in actuality were red. Christopher's father offered him ale, which he accepted though he didn't want any. He preferred whiskey. He had acquired a taste for hard liquor, knowing that Henry Hatton admired a man who could handle drink at any hour of the day or night.

"I spoke with Dottie Longford yesterday, and we reached an understanding about a betrothal between you and Alexandra."

"A betrothal?" Kit asked sharply.

"Yes, I think we should announce it tonight at the hunt dinner. You may present her with your mother's diamond and sapphire ring."

Christopher Hatton seldom challenged his father—he usually left that job to his twin—but today he did not hesitate. "Absolutely not! It's out of the question."

"What the devil do you mean?" Lord Hatton roared.

"I'm too young to be leg-shackled."

"Girls like Alexandra Sheffield are few and far between, you stupid young fool."

"I have no objection to Alexandra, or marriage either for that matter, but goddamn it, Father, not yet. . . . Perhaps when I'm twenty-five."

"Are you insane? She'll be snapped up like a trout

fly if she goes to London. Haven't you noticed young Hartington sniffing around her? The Longford heiress won't sit about twiddling her thumbs until you decide you have enough guts to take the bloody plunge."

"What about my Grand Tour? I want to travel Europe before I'm dragged to the altar."

"We're fighting a bloody war in Europe, or has that slipped your mind, you imbecile?"

"Then I'll go east . . . to Turkey perhaps. I want to study art."

"Turkey, my arse! Only fops and weaklings are interested in art! You forget, young sir, I am the paymaster here. I control the purse strings!"

"I'll pay my own traveling expenses. My allowance doubles now that I am twenty-one."

"Don't dare to defy me, Christopher! I shall cut off your allowance today unless you promise you'll do your duty and beget a Hatton heir."

There was a low tap on the door, then it swung open to admit Nicholas.

"What the hellfire do you want? You are forever sticking your bloody nose in where it isn't wanted," his father spat.

"Well, *I* want his opinion, if you don't!" Kit shouted.

"Are you aware our houseguests can hear you both?" Nick asked quietly.

"He actually wants to announce my betrothal at the hunt dinner tonight! What the hell would you do, if he insisted that you marry Alexandra Sheffield?"

Nick masked the surprise he felt and quickly controlled his emotions. He saw the look of pure panic on his twin's face at the thought of marriage. "I'd take her in a heartbeat," Nick said quietly.

"I'm not ready for marriage!" Kit cried.

"You gutless young swine! You haven't the balls for anything save gambling, drinking, and whoring!"

"He had a good teacher," Nicholas defended his brother.

Kit's gray eyes narrowed with hatred. "I've far more guts than you realize, Father."

"Good! Then you'll act like a man when I announce the betrothal at the dinner tonight." He glanced at the ormolu clock on the mantel. "Ten o'clock; the whip will have the staghounds ready." He lifted a hunting rifle from the gun case. "Are you coming, or are you as squeamish about hunting as you are about marriage?" he asked contemptuously.

Alexandra, along with the other guests, could hear Lord Hatton and his son having a terrible row. Though no one could make out the words exchanged, the timber and tone of the voices told everyone they were having a fierce argument. Since the Hatton twins' voices were identical, none knew which son had invoked Henry Hatton's fury, but all knew he frequently vented his vile temper on Nicholas. Alexandra too assumed it was Nicholas, since he was the usual recipient of his father's wrath, and relief washed over her when the shouting abruptly ceased.

She tapped on the door of the adjoining bedchamber. When she opened it she was surprised to find Dottie wearing a silk morning gown rather than a riding habit.

"I'm not joining the hunt, Alexandra. Lord Staines isn't up to it, and it will give Neville and I a chance to be alone."

"Did you hear all the shouting?"

"Fiddle-faddle, darling; it doesn't signify. In a household of men, shouting and brawling is the order of the day. The morning after men have imbibed, their tempers have hair triggers. Best to avoid them at breakfast. By the by, what are you planning to wear tonight to the hunt dinner?"

"My jade green silk, I think."

"No, no, darling, wear that blush pink thing; it's more maidenly. Take that rebellious look off your face, Alexandra. I'll come along to help you dress and we can argue about it then. No point in ruining the day with an argument that can be postponed until the evening, is there?"

Alexandra laughed. "I suppose there is logic in that." It was only when she got to the ground floor of Hatton Hall that it struck her as being odd that her grandmother planned to help her dress.

* * *

The hunters gathered in the courtyard made a colorful tapestry in their bright coats and fashionable riding habits. Today they were not after fox, but deer. The staghounds were straining on their leashes and baying loud enough to frighten off any game within a five-mile radius. The men's mounts were equipped with saddle holsters and guns; the ladies, however, were not armed. They joined the sport today as mere spectators.

Alexandra tightened the girth on her hunter and thanked Rupert for saddling her mare. She spied the twins across the courtyard, guessing that Kit wore red, and Nick wore green. A furious blush rose to her cheeks as the intimate details of the encounter with Nicholas came flooding back to her. The humiliation of Nick's rejection still stung her pride. Moreover, both twins seemed to be avoiding her, so she deliberately snubbed them and trotted over to join the ladies. She eyed Annabelle Harding's full figure, pictured her without her stays, and wondered if it were true that Lord Hatton was bedding her. The corners of her mouth went up. What a wickedly amusing lampoon it would make, with Annabelle clutching the bedpost as Henry struggled with her laces, trying in vain to stuff her abundant flesh back into her corsets!

The Hatton twins held their hunters on short reins as they conversed. Nicholas had given his new pistols to his brother in an effort to cheer him up, but Kit's dark brows were drawn together as he tried to solve his dilemma. "If I tell the old man I'll start paying court to Alexandra, do you think it will get him off my back? I could hint that I'll agree to some sort of understanding; anything so long as he doesn't announce my betrothal tonight!"

"Alexandra is very young. She isn't ready for marriage either, Kit. I think it's a good idea to postpone things." Why did the thought of Alexandra and Christopher seem so appalling to him when their families had had an understanding since they were children that they would marry some day? He loved his brother deeply and wanted him to be happy. The trouble was he loved Alexandra too, *like a sister* he assured himself, and he couldn't bear the thought of her unhappiness. *That's the biggest bloody lie you've ever told yourself. You don't love her like a sister at all!* But Nicholas knew it was a lie he would have to desperately cling to and live with for the rest of his life.

A hunting horn sounded and the dogs were unleashed. "I'll go and talk with him. Hunting usually puts him in a good mood," Kit told his brother and determinedly spurred Renegade and took off after their father.

An hour into the hunt, Nick spotted a doe with a fawn that must have been born late in the season. He did not raise his horn to his lips to summon the other hunters but watched the pair disappear into the woods that led to a dense forest. He could hear the staghounds baying in the distance and was glad they were not close enough to pick up the doe's scent.

Alexandra, riding with the ladies, had long since ceased to listen to their incessant chatter about what they planned to wear to the hunt dinner. Her mind wandered back to the strange conversation she had had with Dottie that morning, predicting that an argument was in the offing. She had a feeling that it was going to be about more than her choice of gown. Her brows drew together as she remembered Dottie and Henry Hatton going off for their private talk yesterday. Then, like a revelation, it dawned on her that their plans concerned a betrothal between herself and Christopher. She had nothing against Kit Hatton, of course—nothing except that she was secretly in love with his twin! Alexandra immediately drew rein and turned her hunter about. She'd be damned if she'd allow them to arrange her future for her. The Hellion would mount a rebellion!

Nicholas, who had become separated from the hunt, raised his head to pick up the sound of the horns or the baying of the staghounds. Suddenly, he heard a shot that sounded quite close and urged his horse in that direction. He drew one of his hunting pistols from the saddle holster just in case a stag bolted through the trees from the direction of the shot. He came to a clearing and recognized his brother. It took him only a moment to spot another red-jacketed figure crumpled on the ground.

Kit's head jerked up with alarm as his brother approached. "There's been an accident!" he cried.

Nick holstered his gun and was out of the saddle in a split second, running to the man lying on the ground. "Good God, it's Father!" Nick saw the ugly chest wound, smelled the metallic scent of blood, and heard his own heartbeat hammering in his ears. He felt for a pulse in vain. He looked up at Kit, who was still clutching his pistol. "He's dead!" Nicholas said with disbelief.

"It was an accident, I swear! Oh Christ, what am I to do?" Kit dismounted, took one step closer, threw down the pistol and clutched his head with his hands. "It was an accident!"

"Of course it was an accident," Nick assured him.

"But they'll never believe me . . . they'll say I murdered him. . . . Everyone heard the terrible row we had this morning. . . . Dear God, Nick, help me!"

Nicholas looked down hopelessly at the body he held; his father was already going cold. "Of course I'll help you. We'll explain it was an accident."

"No one will believe me! I killed him, and I had a motive. . . . They'll arrest me!"

"They won't arrest you if it was an accident, Kit. Try to get hold of yourself and tell me what happened."

"A stag . . . we both saw it . . . I had a clear view. . . . He rode directly into my path as I fired."

Nicholas eased his father's body back down to the ground, then got up from his knees and bent to retrieve the silver-mounted Heylin pistol from the grass where Kit had thrown it.

"It's *your* gun, Nick. Say *you* did it . . . please help me!"

Nicholas stared at his twin's chalky pallor and saw he was trembling like an aspen leaf. He felt his brother's plight as sharply as if it were his own. Nick wished he *had* been to blame; how in the name of God would Kit carry the burden of guilt? He walked over to his brother. "Pull yourself together, Christopher." Nick didn't put his arms about him, because one hand held the gun and the other was covered with his father's blood.

A look of crazed panic came into Kit's eyes as they heard the hounds approaching. "I'll shoot myself! It's the only way out."

Nicholas prevented him from snatching the gun, even though it was no longer loaded.

Three hunters rode into the clearing. "What the devil has happened?"

"Keep the dogs off!" Nicholas ordered. "I accidentally shot my father."

Chapter 5

The three mounted men stared in disbelief at the horrific scene before them. As more members of the hunting party rode into the clearing, Nicholas realized with a sinking heart that some of them had been spectators that night at the Hardings' summerhouse when their father had lain stretched out upon the grass. He experienced an eerie feeling of *déjà vu* when someone asked, "Is he dead?"

As it happened, the two legal authorities required to attend an accidental death were among the weekend guests. Colonel Stevenson was a Justice of the Peace; Lord Staines was the County Coroner.

Lord Harding was the first out of the saddle. He glanced at Christopher and said with his usual air of authority, "Help me get your father up to the house."

Kit stepped back in horror, but at that moment Colonel Stevenson quickly intervened. "No, no, Harding. The scene must not be disturbed until we establish exactly what happened here. The body must not be touched until the Coroner has pronounced him dead."

Nicholas saw his twin's deathly pallor and the terrified look in his eyes. He feared that Kit would either begin to confess his hatred for their father or pass out from shock, and he knew he had to get him away from the body. "Christopher and I will be up at the house, Colonel. The accident has unnerved us. I shall inform Lord Staines that you need him immediately, then I will answer any questions the two of you may have." Nick turned to Hart and Rupert, who had just arrived and stood gaping helplessly. "Will you see to the horses?" he asked quietly, then moved to his brother's side and touched his arm as a signal that they should leave.

Mr. Burke took one look at the twins' faces as they entered the hall and knew something terrible had happened. "Whatever is amiss?"

"There's been a hunting accident," Nick said quickly.

Kit ran his hand distractedly through his hair, over and over again, trying to brush back the curl that fell over his forehead. "Father's dead!"

Mr. Burke stared and shook his head in disbelief.

"Burke, would you be good enough to inform Lord Staines that he is needed at the accident scene? Rupert will show him." With a steadying hand on his brother's elbow, Nick guided him up to his bedchamber. Kit, shaking from head to foot, stumbled on the stairs as his legs threatened to give out under him.

The moment they were inside the chamber, Nick locked the door and shoved his brother into a leather chair.

"Whiskey," Kit muttered.

Nicholas poured water from the jug and washed his father's blood from his hands. Then he went to a cabinet and sniffed at the contents of two decanters. "Brandy will do you better at the moment . . . it's a restorative." He splashed the golden liquor into a goblet and brought it to his brother.

Kit tossed the fiery liquid down his throat and gasped as it took his breath away. He shook his head as if to clear it. "I cannot believe he's dead! Any minute I expect him to come crashing through the door, raving and shouting his orders, browbeating me into a bloody betrothal."

"Kit, we haven't much time. They'll be here with their questions very shortly."

"They won't question *me*! It was *your* gun! *You* admitted doing it. . . . They won't question me, will they?" he asked desperately.

"They might, Christopher. They may ask if you witnessed the accident." In a calm voice Nick explained, "They are within their rights to ask anything they wish. They are investigating the death of Lord Hatton, a Baron of the Realm."

"*I* am Lord Hatton!"

Nicholas stared at his twin, thinking it a strange thing for him to say. "So you are," he said slowly. Nick suddenly had second thoughts. He never should have given in to his brother's pleading to take the blame upon himself. It was time that Christopher took responsibility for his own actions. He was a man grown; it was high time he started acting like one.

"You won't change your story?" Kit demanded fearfully. "You've always been there for me. . . . We're in this together, Nick, always together, right?"

Nicholas let out a long, slow breath, knowing he would capitulate. "I won't change my story. It would draw suspicion to both of us—they might begin to think we conspired to kill him."

"It was an *accident*, Nick. You *do* believe me?"

Nicholas knew his twin had left him no choice in the matter. "Yes, I believe you."

As Alexandra rode into the courtyard, she saw a small group of hunters who were accompanied by two grooms transporting something heavy from the woods. For a moment she thought they carried a stag, but then she saw the red hunting jacket and realized it was a man. She spotted Rupert leading Renegade into the stables and spurred her mount to catch up with him.

"There's been an accident." Her hand covered her thudding heart as she searched Rupert's ashen face. "Kit's been injured—the black threw him!"

"No, no, Alex. It's Lord Hatton. He's been shot."

"Oh, no! Is he badly injured?"

"He's dead, Alex," Rupert said through stiff, bloodless lips.

Alexandra sat stunned as she watched the grooms carry the body into Hatton Hall. Her very first thought was of the shouting match she had overheard this morning between Lord Hatton and his son. *Nicholas, no!* Her heart contracted. *Nick would be blamed—Nick was always blamed.* She rejected the thought instantly, then her own words about the house party came back to her.

She had said to Nick, *"Keep your fingers crossed for something scandalous."* Alexandra closed her eyes as guilty remorse washed over her.

Nicholas opened his brother's bedchamber door and admitted the two men who knocked. The questions by Colonel Stevenson, Justice of the Peace, were perfunctory. He completely ignored Christopher Hatton and addressed Nicholas. "Tell me what happened."

Nick looked the colonel directly in the eye. "There was a stag. I thought I had a clear view. Father rode directly into my path as I fired."

The colonel held out a gun. "Is this Heylin pistol yours?"

Nick did not hesitate. "Yes, sir."

The colonel nodded to Lord Staines, who had brought a death certificate with him. Neville wrote *accident* against the cause of death, then signed it in his capacity as County Coroner. Colonel Stevenson added his signature as witness, and that put an end to the legalities. In a trice the matter was set right and tight as a drum; all clean, and legal, and above board. The gentlemen offered the twins their condolences and departed.

The members of the upper class were adept at cleaning up their own messes; they happened on a regular basis. Appearances were what mattered most to Society, and took precedence over any other consideration. Once the legalities were airtight, however, the gossip and conjecture of the *beau monde* would run rampant. The upper class was addicted to blood sport.

When Stevenson and Staines departed, Kit asked eagerly, "Is that it? Is it over?"

"Perhaps the legalities are over, but there is a plethora of things to do, arrangements to make, plans for the burial—"

Kit recoiled. "I can't face any of that!" He strode to the cabinet and filled his glass with whiskey.

"Things have to be faced," Nick insisted. "We have to go down and see what they've done with Father's body. And we can't just ignore a houseful of guests."

Kit took three gulps of his whiskey. "Let the servants look after the bloody guests."

"The people who serve us will be overwhelmed. They'll be looking to us for direction."

Kit lifted his gaze from his glass and looked into his brother's eyes. "I'm still shaking. Since you're so cool and calm, you give them direction."

Nick threw his twin a look of contempt as he watched him lift his glass to his lips. Kit despised their father, yet he had many of Henry Hatton's weaknesses. He got dog-bitten-drunk far too often. Nick rubbed the tension from the back of his neck. Perhaps he was expecting too much of his brother. He'd just gone through the horrendous ordeal of causing a fatal accident, and the guilt of it must be eating him alive. Kit would need time to come to terms with it all. "I'll go down and cope with things."

Lord Staines tapped on Lady Longford's chamber door and entered discreetly. "It is as we feared, my dearest. The accident was fatal. Henry was shot through the heart. I've just signed the death certificate."

"Well, it's a wonder he wasn't shot years ago. Who shot him? Was it Annabelle's husband?" she asked bluntly.

"Dottie, my dearest, I shall never get used to the outrageous things you say." He took her hand as if to soften the news. "Hatton was accidentally killed by his own son."

Her hand went to her throat. "Not Christopher?"

"No, it wasn't his heir; it was Nicholas. It is best that I go to the courthouse and file this death certificate immediately. I want everything tidy, with no loose ends; it's the least I can do for the Hattons. Rupert is coming to take you home; I do apologize for not escorting you, my dearest."

"*Tush,* Neville, it is only the next estate after all. I am perfectly capable of managing."

When he had gone, Dottie sat down heavily in a padded boudoir chair and stared into space. *I am perfectly capable of managing . . . capable of managing . . . managing . . .* She had been managing for as long as she could remember. She had laid her plans so carefully, so cunningly. At long last she had secured her beloved Alexandra's future by manipulating Henry Hatton into agreeing to the betrothal between his heir and her granddaughter. Now, only hours before it became a *fait accompli*, it had all been swept away. Fate was a hideous bitch!

It was all a *charade* . . . the great wealth, the investments, her insistence that Alexandra have a Season. Even her eccentricity was an invention to explain away the oddities and disparities of appearing to be rich as Croesus, when not a groat remained in her bank account at Barclays. So long as she was able to keep up the facade, Society would fawn upon her, but Dottie knew time was running out, and she was almost at her wit's end.

Oh, it had all been true once upon a time. She had married the wealthiest lord in Bucks County, Viscount Longford. Her husband had then proceeded to squander his fortune on the gaming tables and notorious women. Fortunately, Russell had drunk himself to death before all the money ran out, leaving Dottie with magnificent Longford Manor.

She clenched her fists with outrage at the thought of Johnny Sheffield, her untitled lout of a son-in-law who had gone through her daughter's dowry like a dose of salts. No wonder Margaret had left him, but she had also left two penniless children behind in the wake of her shipwrecked marriage. *It was my fault. I should have taken a firmer hand with Margaret and insisted she marry a man of wealth and title!* She vowed again that she would not let the same fate overtake Alexandra.

Her sharp mind rapidly went over her alternatives. One thing was certain: There would be no betrothal announced tonight. Still, she clung to her hopes doggedly, refusing to allow them to be snuffed out like a guttering candle. Perhaps, after a short period of mourning, a quiet wedding could be arranged. She straightened her wig with an impatient tug, and resolved to discuss the matter with Christopher before she left. As she packed she looked on the bright side—perhaps the Thomas Lawrence paintings had sold.

Alexandra opened Dottie's chamber door, breathless from rushing up three flights of stairs. "Have you heard about the terrible accident?" She did not wait for her grandmother's answer, but rushed on, "I cannot find Nicholas . . . I've looked everywhere. I must go to him! He'll need to talk with someone."

"Alexandra, come and sit down for a moment. Lord Staines has gone to the courthouse to file the death certificate. He certified it as an accidental death, so there will be no legal complications for Nicholas. Go and pack your things, darling. Rupert is taking us home."

Alexandra decided that it was best not to argue with her grandmother, but her resolve hardened. She had no intention of leaving until she had spoken with Nicholas.

"Mr. Burke, I shall be forever grateful to you for stepping in and directing the servants in our family's hour of misfortune." Nicholas knew the words sounded stilted, but he meant them with all his heart. He thanked Meg Riley for her ministrations to his father's body. Cleaning up the wound, and bathing the corpse, must have been no easy task for the aging nursemaid. The valet too had played his part, selecting the clothes in which Lord Hatton was now laid out and disposing of his hunting attire.

Nicholas said decisively, "We'll leave him lie here in his bedchamber until the coffin I've ordered arrives, then we will move him to the library for the customary viewing. I've sent word to the church; let me know when Reverend Doyle arrives, so we can make the burial arrangements."

Mr. Burke nodded his understanding and departed with the valet. Meg Riley placed her hand on Nicholas's sleeve to comfort him, but her eyes welled up with tears over the disaster that had befallen the young man she loved most in all the world, and she could find no words. Nicholas covered her worn hand with his and squeezed firmly, infusing her with his strength. "It will be all right, Meg. Go and get some rest."

As Nick stood looking down at his father, he expected to feel only numbness, but to his own amazement he realized that he was in mourning. He mourned the lifetime of rejection his father had shown him. He mourned the love and acceptance for which he had strived so hard but never achieved. And he mourned the fact that matters could never be set right between them, for their time had all run out.

As Nicholas descended the great curving staircase that led down to the vaulted foyer, he saw that it was crowded with guests who were awaiting their carriages. They were leaving *en masse,* and apparently couldn't get away fast enough. The Duchess of Rutland's voice carried clearly up to him. "Devilish queer! It staggers the senses to think that he not only caused his mother's death but twenty-one years to the very day, he has killed his father!"

A cynical smile tugged at the corner of Nick's mouth. Surely he had not expected compassion from these people? He squared his shoulders and descended into the vipers' nest, bracing himself for their artificial condolences. Yet it was suddenly brought home to him that he still deeply mourned the mother he had never known, who had died giving him life.

After the guests departed, Nick ran upstairs to check on his brother before the minister arrived. What he found did not completely surprise him. The room was in disarray, with clothes strewn everywhere. The whiskey decanter as well as the one that had held the brandy lay empty upon the carpet. Kit lay sprawled across his bed in a drunken stupor. Nick decided there was no earthly point in trying to revive him. It was probably best to let him sleep it off.

As he quietly closed the chamber door, he looked up and saw Dottie Longford coming down the hall.

"Christopher, my dearest boy, please know that my heart is with you on this sad day. If there is anything we can do for you and Nicholas, please don't hesitate to ask."

Nick realized that she had mistaken him for Kit, but surprised himself by not correcting her. He took her arm and gently led her away from Kit's door. "That is extremely kind of you, Lady Longford. My brother and I appreciate your friendship."

"I am devastated that the circumstances make it necessary to postpone the betrothal, but I want to assure you that nothing has changed. After your mourning period . . ."

Nicholas realized that here was his chance to give

Alex the year of freedom she longed for. "My heart aches that a whole year of mourning must be observed before I may betroth Alexandra."

Dottie's shoulders sagged. "A year is a devilish long period, Christopher. Well, now is not the time to speak of it. . . . Another day soon, my dearest boy."

Alexandra went to her bedchamber and changed from her riding habit into a soft day dress. Once more she rolled back the rug and looked down into the chamber below. It seemed to be empty; she saw no movement and no sign that Nick had even been there. She got up from her knees and went over to the window. When she drew back the lace curtain, she saw him walking with the minister in the direction of the church, which was on Hatton land. She was sure it was Nick because he was still wearing his green riding jacket.

She dropped the curtain quickly as a sharp tap came on the door and she heard Rupert call her name. "Alex, we're ready to leave." She held her breath and remained perfectly still. Rupert's voice came again. "Alex, are you in there?" A moment of silence passed, then she heard the sound of his retreating footsteps. Alexandra let out a relieved sigh. Until she had spoken to Nicholas, she knew there was no way on earth she could bring herself to leave Hatton Hall.

Nicholas made all the arrangements for the funeral and then went into the churchyard with Doyle to approve the burial site. He knelt at his mother's Celtic cross and spoke to her silently, as he always did. With reverence he traced his fingertips over the name carved upon the cross: KATHLEEN FLYNN HATTON. Then he got to his feet, nodded to the grave digger who had been standing patiently waiting with his shovel, and quickly departed.

With his hands in his pockets, Nick walked over the Hatton land that he loved so deeply. As twilight descended he headed for Hatton Grange. The sight of the mares with their foals in the grass paddock filled him with a sense of well-being. He had bred most of them himself and was proud that, due to his hard work and long hours, Hatton Grange horse farm had become a successful venture. It now brought in high profits from the contract he had negotiated to supply mounts for the Royal Horse Guards.

Nicholas knocked on the grange-house door and went inside to give the horseman and his wife the news about the fatal accident. Tom and Bridget Calhoun were aghast at the dreadful tidings. Nick knew they were familiar with Lord Hatton's famous temper and were glad that these days they worked for him rather than for his arrogant father, who was notoriously difficult and demanding. Nick assured them that there would be no changes at Hatton Grange, and he saw the relief on their faces as the Irish couple offered him words of comfort for his troubles.

When he left the Grange, he made his way into Hatton Great Park, pausing as he looked across the lake toward the hall. Its beauty and permanence had made him feel secure since his earliest memories, and tonight it seemed to emanate strength. It had stood there for almost two centuries, sheltering the people who dwelled within its massive stone walls. He knew it would remain a bastion against the storms of life for future generations, and he hoped that a hundred years from now his great-great-grandchildren would love it with the same deep and abiding passion that he felt.

The beauty of the rising moon reflected in the lake took his breath away, and he threw back his head to gaze up at the stars.

He easily found the constellation of Leo the Lion; its star Regulus was one of the brightest in the sky. Tomorrow was his birthday. Twenty-one years ago on just such a night as this he had been born. The vastness of the universe helped him to view the day's troubles somewhat in perspective, and he felt a small measure of calm descend. He had learned not to dwell on the past, and in that moment Nick made a conscious decision not to look back. Instead he vowed to look forward, to embrace the future.

The warm, comforting silence of the house wrapped itself around him as he climbed the stairs to his chamber. The feel of the oak banister, so sturdy beneath his hand, seemed to lend him strength, and the familiar touch of his wolfhound as it brushed against his thigh in the darkness brought a smile to his lips. He lit only one candle, then he undressed and threw the casement wide. He braced his arms upon the windowsill, filled his lungs with air, and took one last look at the stars. As he sat down on the bed, Leo jumped up beside him, and a female scream rent the air.

Chapter 6

Alexandra's eyes flew open to observe a naked man and a gigantic black animal looming above her. The scream escaped her throat before she could stop it.

"Alex, what the hellfire are you doing in my bed?" His words, shot at her like steel arrows, reverberated with anger and outrage.

She was suddenly filled with a dismay that was tinged with fear. Before dark it had seemed perfectly acceptable to await him in his chamber. Now she realized how compromising it was to awaken in his bed. "I—I must have fallen asleep while I was waiting for you."

"Waiting for me for what? This is a whore's trick! You have no more goddamn sense than a five-year-old!" Vivid memories of last night's encounter in the stables filled his head. It had been hard enough to resist her in the hay; here in his bed it was almost impossible. Anger was his only possible defense against Alexandra's potent allure.

A whore's trick? Alex was stricken. Would he teach her another lesson? She was breathless at the thought. Her intentions had been completely innocent. She had longed to comfort him, share his trouble, and show her compassion for his anguish. How could she have forgotten how dangerously male he was at close quarters? To cover her fear she allowed her temper to flare. "Well, you are the expert on whores! In my extreme ignorance I thought I was being a friend."

"A lady does not come to a man's chamber, nor does

she wait for him in his bed, Alex. She guards her reputation."

His words told her she was in for a lecture, not a lesson, and she experienced a moment of disappointment rather than relief. "If you are so worried about my reputation, why are you standing before me completely nude?" she challenged.

Nick uttered a foul oath, strode to his wardrobe, and pulled on a bedrobe. He lit another candle and set it down on the bedside table so that he could see her face. "Alex, you must know that your betrothal to Kit was to be announced at the dinner tonight."

"I know no such thing!" She denied it, but she knew that was exactly what her grandmother and Henry Hatton had planned.

He held his patience. "You cannot deny that Dottie and my father have always had an understanding that you would marry Christopher and become Lady Hatton."

"My grandmother's wishes are common knowledge; how can I deny them? But you know I long for a year of freedom in London, before I bury myself in the country with a husband."

"The terrible accident today guarantees you a year of freedom. Kit cannot marry until a year of mourning has been observed. But you don't seem to realize that your reckless behavior tonight could ruin your future. Christopher is now Lord Hatton. Do you think for one moment that if my twin discovered you in my chamber, in my bed, he would ever make you Lady Hatton?" Nick pulled on the riding breeches he had discarded. "I am taking you home, Alex."

"I can find my own way home!" she flared. "I don't need a father, or a keeper; I am not a child!"

"Then for Christ's sake stop acting like one." He threw off the bedrobe, donned his shirt and jacket, then pulled on his boots. "Keep your voice down," he cautioned, as he picked up her bag and moved toward the door.

"Any more orders?" she asked tartly.

"Not another bloody word, Alex!" His forbidding tone told her clearly he was at the end of his patience.

"Stay, Leo," he commanded, then swept her through the doorway.

Though she could feel the ironlike grip of his fingers bruising her arm, she obeyed his order to remain silent as he pulled her along the hallway and down the dark staircase. Outside, she suffered in silence as he half dragged her across Hatton Park in the direction of Longford Manor. When they reached a copse of trees that separated their properties, Alex finally rebelled and dug her heels into the soft earth. "I refuse to take another blasted step until we talk, Nicholas."

He towered above her, determined to get her safely home without anyone knowing they had been together until close on midnight. "Then you leave me no choice." He picked her up, slung her unceremoniously over his shoulder, and strode forward.

Alexandra's eyes flooded with tears of frustration. It wasn't supposed to be like this, she told herself fiercely. All she had wanted to do was comfort him in his hour of need and offer him a woman's warmth and tenderness. All he wanted was to be rid of her as quickly as possible. His words and actions made it plain that she was just a nuisance. His outright rejection made her heart ache. It was obvious by the way he carried her that he did not even think of her as a woman. It was also apparent that Nick Hatton didn't need anyone, least of all her.

As his long strides covered the distance between their homes, Nicholas knew his feelings for Alexandra were totally inappropriate. This fierce need to protect her at all costs came from the deep affection he had always felt toward her. Lately, his fondness had turned to desire, deny it how he may. He knew that shouldering the blame for the shooting accident that killed his father would not only protect Christopher but would keep it from touching Alex in any way. Nick was under no illusions. The Society matrons who had wooed him for their daughters yesterday, would now fall on him like ravening beasts. He suspected that he would be vilified, crucified, and then ostracized. He would be *persona non grata*. He knew that Society lived for scandal, thrived upon it in fact. He knew he would be fodder for the gossip mills for the next year at least. As his arm tightened on Alex possessively, he assured himself that he had done the right thing.

Nick deposited Alex on her own doorstep without arousing anyone at Longford Manor. When she was safely inside, he sprinted back through the trees that separated their properties. When he passed by the library, where his father now lay in his oak coffin, Nicholas said a silent prayer, then slowly, quietly ascended the stairs that took him to the sanctuary of his own chamber.

Leo greeted him with great affection and a thumping tail, and Nick rubbed his head fondly, grateful for the animal's devotion, no matter what the rest of the world thought of him. Once more he undressed and climbed into bed; the great wolfhound contentedly stretched out on the rug beside him. As Nick lay with his arms folded behind his head, the day's bizarre events replayed themselves. Though he doubted he would be able to sleep, gradually his body relaxed and he slipped into a dream.

Nick undressed and threw the casement wide. He braced his arms upon the windowsill, filled his lungs with air, and took one last look at the stars. As he sat down naked on the bed, he became aware that he was not alone. "Alex," he murmured huskily, "I knew you would come." His hands cupped her shoulders tenderly as she came up from the bed.

"I—I must have fallen asleep while I was waiting for you."

"You know you shouldn't be here, sweetheart. You should be thinking of your reputation, not of me."

"Nick, you are more important to me than anything in my life."

He felt her touch his cheek and covered her hand with his to keep it there, hungry for the physical contact between them.

"Nick, I know you didn't do it. You took the blame, as you take the blame for everything at Hatton Hall. In my heart I know that you didn't shoot your father."

"Hush, Alex, no one must know." He opened her hand and dropped a kiss into her palm. "It will be so much better this way. I have no crushing burden of guilt to

bear. Christopher will get through this if there is no one to point the finger at him or whisper behind his back."

"No matter how strong you are, I couldn't bear for you to be alone tonight. Let me stay, Nick; let me comfort you."

He gathered her in his arms, so that her cheek pressed against his heart. He could not deny how much he needed her warmth, how much he wanted her love. His possessive hand stroked her silken curls, and the scent of her hair filled his head, almost stealing his senses. He knew that Alexandra was still sexually innocent, and a wave of protectiveness swept over him. He removed his arms and reached for his bedrobe to cover his nakedness. When she came back into his arms, he imagined the black velvet that covered his bare flesh would be barrier enough to keep her safe from his rampant desire, but Nicholas had not reckoned with Alexandra's irresistible allure. She lifted her lips in sweet invitation, and his mouth touched hers softly, gently at first. The sensations she aroused were so heady a temptation that he deepened the kiss. When her lips parted, he entered the hot cave of her mouth and lingered there, reveling in the taste of her and the warm, sensual scent of her skin.

"Nicholas, please let me love you."

Her whispered plea was too hard to resist. He pulled her down beside him, opened the velvet robe, and drew her inside. They touched, and caressed, and whispered for hours. At last he undressed her slowly, exploring, savoring, stroking, and tasting her until she cried out in her need. Finally, in desperation, he knew he must bring her release the only way he could without taking her virginity. He opened her slender thighs and trailed his lips across her warm, satin flesh.

Nick awoke with a start. His erection throbbed painfully and his body was covered with a fine sheen of sweat. The dream was still with him in vivid detail, even her jasmine scent lingered on his sheets. Christ, he had actually been making love to Alexandra with his mouth! He threw back the covers and quit the bed, as disgust for his lust engulfed him. What the hell was the matter with him? His father lay dead, yet all he could think of was making love to the woman who would become his brother's bride. He went to the window and filled his lungs with the cold, fresh air of the night. When his blood cooled and a semblance of sanity returned, a rueful smile lifted the corner of his mouth. "Thank God it was only a dream, you randy swine," he whispered mockingly.

The week that followed confirmed all of Nick Hatton's suspicions. Condolences poured in for Christopher, the new Lord Hatton, while Nicholas received nary a card. Nick was relieved that the solicitous attention Kit received buoyed his brother's spirits and helped him pull himself together to play the role of bereaved but dutiful son. Though Nick knew his brother cringed inwardly, Kit agreed to act as pallbearer, along with his twin, his father's cousin, John Eaton, and Eaton's son, Jeremy.

The funeral, which was well attended by the wealthy families of the surrounding counties, gave polite society the opportunity to pay their respects to Henry Hatton and to curry favor with the new baron. At the same time, it allowed them to slake their curiosity about the younger twin, who, on the day before his twenty-first birthday, had shot his father to death. Accidentally, of course.

July turned into August before the late Lord Hatton's solicitor made the journey from London to Hatton Hall for the reading of the will. Mr. Burke showed Tobias Jacobs into the library, where shortly he was joined by the Hatton twins.

The solicitor introduced himself, trying to hide his amazement that the two men were physically identical. As he wondered which twin was the heir, he indicated his heavy leather portfolio and asked, "May I take the liberty of using your father's desk?"

"My desk," Christopher corrected. He waved a negligent hand toward the mahogany desk. "Please, feel free."

Jacobs cleared his throat. "Thank you, Lord Hatton."

The twins seated themselves and waited politely as the silence in the room stretched out until it became awkward. They watched Jacobs shuffle his papers and heard him clear his throat two or three times before he found his voice.

"Lord Hatton's will differs from the norm in many respects. Please bear with me while I explain. It is usual under the circumstances for a man of wealth and position to acknowledge those who have given lifelong service and make provision for them. When I brought the oversight to his attention, your father informed me that it was not an oversight. He insisted that the servants received adequate wages for their services, and I could not persuade him to bequeath them even a token stipend." Jacobs cleared his throat again and glanced over his wire-rimmed glasses at Christopher Hatton. "You may rectify this, of course."

The solicitor picked up another piece of parchment and read:

"To my beloved son and heir, Christopher Flynn Hatton, I hand down my baronial title. To Christopher I also bequeath Hatton Hall and Hatton Great Park, with all its property and acres." Jacobs drew in a deep breath before he continued, "To Christopher I also bequeath all monies deposited in Barclays Bank and all investments held in my name by John Eaton, my financial advisor and sole trustee of this my last will and testament."

Jacobs cleared his throat once more as he selected another sheet of parchment. His hand shook slightly, making the paper rustle.

"To Christopher I also bequeath Hatton Grange horse farm, its stock, and all the attached property and acres."

"You mistake, Jacobs," Christopher pointed out. "I believe my father left Hatton Grange to my brother."

Nick sat like stone as a cold finger of premonition touched his heart. Before Jacobs spoke, he knew what the solicitor would say.

"No, Lord Hatton, there is no mistake. Your father bequeathed Hatton Grange to you, his heir." Tobias Jacobs dropped the parchment and spread his hands apologetically. "It is usual that when the elder son inherits the entire estate from his father, the younger son inherits any maternal property brought to the marriage by the mother. I am speaking, of course, of the Curzon Street town house in London, which was part and parcel of Kathleen Flynn's dowry. Once again, the late Lord Hatton has deviated from the conventional path. He has bequeathed the Curzon Street town house to his heir, Christopher."

Again, Jacobs looked over the rim of his glasses, then his glance dropped to the will. "These are your father's own words: 'I give, devise, and bequeath my entire estate, both real and personal, to my first-born son, Christopher Flynn Hatton.' " He stood up from the desk and looked from one twin to the other. "I will give you some privacy. When I return there are certain legal papers, documents, and deeds that will require your signature, Lord Hatton."

When the twins were alone, Christopher burst out laughing. "Well, I'll be damned. The old swine didn't hate me after all!"

"No, Kit, he loved you." *In his own twisted way.*

"Christ, the old pisspot sure as hell held a grudge against you, though. Right up to the end he blamed you for killing our mother. I can't get over it . . . he left me everything, and you nothing!"

"My name appears nowhere in the will. He avoided it as if I didn't exist." Nick was stunned, though he suddenly realized that he should not have been surprised in the least that their father was reaching back from the grave with his all-controlling hand to wreak havoc. What he had done was deliberately designed to destroy the bond between his twin sons. He had never been able to affect their closeness while he lived, so his will was his last desperate attempt to cause a breach between them. Nick clenched his jaw and vowed that his father's devious methods would never succeed in alienating them.

"If Hatton Hall, Hatton Grange, and the Curzon Street town house now belong to me, where the devil will you live?" Kit asked.

"Champagne Charlie's, perhaps," Nick replied lightly.

Kit laughed uproariously. "I'm jesting! Hatton Hall may be in my name, but it will always be your home too, Nick."

"Thank you, I accept your generous offer."

"And I shall give you an allowance too, of course."

Nicholas, a master at masking his emotions, inwardly recoiled at his brother's words. *Give me an allowance?*

Surely, you are not serious, Christopher? The insult was horrendous! The lion raised his proud head and stared at his brother with disdain. "I am a grown man, Kit. Don't cast me in the role of beggar, while you play magnanimous lord of the manor, offering me your charity."

"Damn you, Nick! Can't you even pretend to feed my vanity? I simply thought you might need me for once, instead of it always being the other way about."

I have too much pride, and you, too little. God help us both, Nick thought grimly. He was no saint. Indeed, he felt a great deal of resentment that though he had worked like a demon to make Hatton Grange horse farm a financial success, he would reap none of the benefits. It was most ironic that last month he had sold a dozen sleek geldings to the Horse Guards, helping to fill Hatton's coffers. It was even more ironic that though Kit had never lifted a finger to help with the work of the Grange, he would now receive every penny of the profits. The only animals left at the Grange were the breeding mares and the colts they had foaled in the spring. Nick had bred them all himself, so he knew the proprietary feelings that rose up within him were only natural. He realized that he had always thought of the Hatton Grange land as his. It was where he had planned to build his own house when he married. A mocking smile curved his mouth at the thought of matrimony. Who the hell would wed a penniless second son?

Nicholas realized he was dangerously close to self-pity, and he was saved by a low knock upon the library door. Tobias Jacobs entered and cleared his throat. "Am I intruding, Lord Hatton?"

"Of course not," Christopher replied, moving toward the desk. "Let's get the legalities out of the way." He read the papers that Jacobs spread before him and signed the documents.

"I shall file copies of the title deeds so that they may be registered in your name, and herewith present to you the original property deeds for safekeeping." The deeds he handed Kit bore official red seals. "As soon as it is convenient, you should present yourself at Barclays Bank, my lord. They too will require your signature. It would also be prudent to see John Eaton, your late father's financier, who will advise you about Hatton investments. As sole trustee of the will, he'll no doubt be anticipating your visit."

"You know, Jacobs, I take offense that I wasn't named as a trustee along with John Eaton," Kit complained petulantly.

"I am sure that your father meant no offense to you, my lord. When the late Lord Hatton made his will, you were not yet twenty-one, and he trusted Eaton's advice implicitly regarding the family's finances."

Nick frowned. "As trustee, I presume that John Eaton is already in possession of a copy of our father's last will and testament?"

"You presume correctly, sir," Jacobs replied.

Nicholas wondered fleetingly who else knew that he had been cut out of his father's will without a penny. His reputation as black sheep would assuredly be complete once word got around.

When their business was finished, Christopher took up the whiskey decanter and offered Jacobs a drink for the road. The solicitor declined quickly. "I never indulge in strong liquor, Lord Hatton. I am sure you will appreciate that men in my position need be in control of their wits at all times."

Amused, Kit raised an eyebrow, along with his glass. "I certainly appreciate that men in my position need *not.*"

Jacobs was not amused. He gathered up his papers, secured the straps on his leather portfolio, and walked directly to the library door. "I bid you good evening, Lord Hatton." He exited with a slight bow.

"Humorless old stick! His mind's as dry as a bloody desert."

Rather like your throat these days. But Nick knew if he voiced his disapproval, Kit would imbibe twice as much.

Kit winked at his twin and hoisted his glass in an irreverent toast: "Here's to being first!"

Nick's mouth curved in a sardonic smile. He appreciated the irony, if not the humor. He said on a more sober note, "It was shameless of Father not to mention Mr. Burke or Meg Riley in the will. You must rectify that immediately."

"Must I?" Christopher drained his glass and grinned. "Thirsty work, coming into an inheritance. Since my presence is required at Barclays Bank, let's go up to London tomorrow and celebrate. I'll invite Rupert to join us. I definitely feel the need to shake off the gloom of Hatton Hall."

"Not tomorrow. You should call on John Eaton before you go."

"What the devil for?" Kit brushed back the hair from his brow.

"You have business matters to discuss." Nick schooled himself to patience. "You need to know how he has invested Hatton money. You need to know how much there is and what return he is getting on your money. I don't believe Father ever discussed these matters with you. . . . You are completely in the dark, Kit."

"I don't give a fiddler's fart about business. If you're so interested, you go and talk with him, for Christ's sake!"

"Don't be so obtuse. It would be highly unethical for Eaton to discuss your investments with me. I've been cut off without a farthing. What the hellfire would it look like if I went to him with questions about your inheritance?"

"You are the one who is being obtuse, old man. Simply visit Eaton and present yourself as the very charming and wealthy Lord Hatton. You take care of business and I'll take care of pleasure!"

Nicholas kept a tight rein on his thoughts and emotions until he retired to the privacy of his own chamber. There, however, he gave vent to his anger and to his sense of loss. It felt as if a great, gaping hole filled his insides and was rapidly expanding toward his heart. Once more he was in mourning. This time it was over the loss of his dreams—and his future. A scratching at the door distracted him, and he moved across the room to admit Leo.

He walked slowly to the mirror and looked at the face reflected there. The gray eyes that stared back at him were filled with self-righteous indignation, and suddenly he began to laugh at himself. He was still Nicholas Hatton, unchanged in any way by the events of the last fortnight. Just as he was still the younger twin, he was also still the stronger one. He had thumbed his nose at fate all his life; he sure as hell wasn't about to stop now. He was a man who was comfortable in his own skin. Neither his father's death, nor the will, could affect who he was at his core. He, and he alone, was in control of his life; no one could take his future from him, least of all a dead man.

Nicholas poured water into the bowl and stripped off his shirt. He eyed his naked torso and acknowledged with male pride that his shoulders were certainly broad enough to withstand the slings and arrows of outrageous fortune. He took up his razor, knowing it was male pride that made him shave twice a day. Born under the sign of the lion, he had an abundance of regal pride, and he had always ruled his own domain. He looked down at the wolfhound and spoke aloud. "Remember, there are no timid Leos. They are courageous, fierce, and wild, and they can bear anything with stoic dignity. The lion holds center stage and never lowers his proud head."

Leo gave a sharp bark of agreement that made Nick throw back his head in laughter. When he finally lay in bed with his arms folded behind his head, Nicholas felt as if a great burden had been lifted from him. He vowed to put boyhood dreams aside and plan for the future. Suddenly, a vision of Alexandra came to him full-blown, and he examined his feelings honestly. For the first time he admitted that he wanted her and acknowledged that he had been toying with the notion that if his brother truly didn't desire her for his wife, perhaps he could woo and win her for himself. With a bittersweet pang of regret, Nick realized this was the first dream that must be set aside. Alex could never be his now. More than anything in the world she feared becoming the wife of a penniless fortune hunter. Her future lay with Kit. She was destined to become Baroness Hatton. So be it.

Chapter 7

Alexandra Sheffield sat engrossed, reading a novel by none other than Georgiana, Duchess of Devonshire, which Dottie had provided when Alex had plied her with questions about Hart Cavendish's notorious mother.

"Read this if you wish to satisfy your curiosity about the infamous Georgiana. *The Sylph* is a thinly disguised autobiography in which she pours out her heart on the unspeakable twaddle that obsessed her, namely husband, marriage, friends, and herself. It was written as revenge when she learned her husband had a mistress," her grandmother informed her.

The book was written in a series of letters by her sweet, young heroine, Julia, an innocent from the country who came to London to marry a wealthy man of fashion.

All my hopes are that I may acquit myself so as to gain the approbation of my husband. Husband! What a sound has that when pronounced by a girl barely seventeen . . . and one whose knowledge of the world is purely speculative.

It was obvious to Alex that Georgiana/Julia longed for her husband's adoration when she described attending a ball: *I saw his eyes were on me the whole time; but I cannot flatter myself so far as to say that they were the looks of love; they seemed to be rather the eyes of scrutiny, which were on the watch, yet afraid they should see something unpleasing.* Alexandra knew exactly how Georgiana had felt. Nicholas Hatton looked at her this way!

Before long, Georgiana/Julia was describing her husband's extravagant gambling, a vice in which she too indulged because her husband soon became bored with her. As Alex turned the pages she realized that Georgiana's chief complaint against her husband was the lack of romantic love.

My person still invites his caresses . . . but for the softer sentiments of the soul . . . that ineffable tenderness which depends not on the tincture of the skin . . . of that, alas, he has no idea. A voluptuary in love, he professes not that delicacy which refines its joys. He is all passion; sentiment is left out of the catalogue.

Alex again thought of Nicholas Hatton and was taken by a delicious shudder. She couldn't understand why the woman was complaining when she admitted that her husband was *all passion* and a *voluptuary in love.* Alex shook her head in disbelief as she realized that Georgiana had turned from her husband to the Prince of Wales *for the softer sentiments of the soul.* Prinny was a figure of fun, a caricature of a man. How could Georgiana have been so foolish? She finished the book and returned it to Dottie. "You were right; it is pure twaddle. I had a devil of a time trying to finish it."

"Georgiana conveniently solves her heroine's problems by having her husband kill himself. Unfortunately, in her own case, the Duke of Devonshire wasn't quite as obliging."

Alexandra's lips twitched with amusement. "Admit it, you gave me Georgiana's novel to discourage me from trying to write my own. It won't work, of course; mine will be of a much higher calibre."

"Yes, darling, and as a result it will be much more difficult to get published. Mediocre claptrap appeals to the masses. My advice would be to concentrate on lowering the quality, not elevating it."

Their conversation was interrupted by Rupert's arrival. His friend Kit Hatton had called earlier and the two had gone out riding. When the handsome Hatton twin had appeared at Longford Manor, Alexandra's heartbeat had become erratic until she realized that it was Christopher seeking out the company of Rupert.

Her brother had the sort of open, friendly countenance that could never hide his thoughts. Newly returned from his ride, Rupert threw his tall beaver hat and his riding crop onto the hall table and strode into the sitting room. His face showed clearly that he was bursting to tell them something of great import.

"The Hatton solicitor came yesterday to read the will," he blurted. "Christopher has inherited!"

"Heirs usually inherit," Dottie said dryly.

"No, no, Christopher has inherited everything! The title, Hatton Hall, Hatton Great Park, Hatton Grange horse farm, the money, the investments, and even the London town house. The old man cut Nicholas out of his will completely!"

"I don't believe you. That is impossible! Have you been drinking, Rupert?" Alex asked, suddenly suspicious.

"No . . . well, yes, Kit and I took lunch at The Cock and Bull so we could drink to his great good fortune. But I'm not making this up; Christopher has inherited everything!"

The color drained from Alexandra's face. Dottie curled her lip. "A leopard never changes his spots; Henry hated his second son before he was even born. This is his petty revenge."

"Nicholas gets nothing?" Alex whispered through bloodless lips.

"Not a sausage!" Rupert confirmed, eager to expound on what he had learned. "Kit has invited me to London. He has immediate business at Barclays Bank, of course, then we shall paint the town! Kit's fortune is Nick's misfortune—get it? Missed-fortune."

Rupert's attempt at humor horrified Alexandra.

"When men have imbibed, darling, they think everything amusing."

"Please don't try to excuse him; he's loathsome!" Alex snapped.

"Men have an inexhaustible supply of loathsomeness, I'm afraid."

Rupert gave his grandmother a speculative look. Emboldened by the liquor he had consumed, he decided to broach the subject of his allowance and thought it amusing to refer to himself in the third person. "By the by, if Viscount Longford is to accompany Lord Hatton to London, he will need to be considerably more plump in the pocket. The viscount has been wondering why his allowance wasn't increased when he turned twenty-one, four months ago."

"Tell the viscount that I shall be happy to discuss the matter with him when he is sober," Dottie replied.

Rupert bowed solemnly. "Very good, ma'am. I must find my valet and have him pack my things for London."

That should prove a sobering exercise, since you no longer have a valet. Dottie sighed. The time had come when she must apprise Rupert of the financial facts.

"My God, how could Lord Hatton do this to his sons? It will set them at each other's throats!" Alexandra began to pace up and down. "He was nothing but a devious, loathsome, worthless swine!"

"Not worthless, darling. He has left his heir a fortune."

"But it is so unfair! Nicholas must be devastated! What the devil has he ever done to deserve such cruel, vengeful treatment?"

"Shot his father, perhaps?" Dottie reminded her.

"That is a vile thing to say!"

"Men are loathsome, women vile . . . it is our natures."

"I'm going to Hatton Hall," Alexandra said with resolve.

"Wise decision," Dottie agreed. "Lay your claim on your future husband now, for once the wealthy Lord Hatton arrives in London, every Society matron with a whey-faced daughter will set a matrimonial trap for him."

Alex rolled her eyes in exasperation. Her grandmother deliberately tried her patience. Surely it was obvious she was going to see Nicholas. She ran upstairs to change into a riding habit, wondering wildly what she could say to make him feel better. Nothing came to mind as she saddled her palfrey Zephyr and rode to Hatton Hall. It was only after Mr. Burke told her that Nicholas had gone to Slough to visit John Eaton that an ingenious plan came to her. She laughed out loud as she thought about it—it was the perfect solution!

* * *

Nicholas Hatton, astride his brother's hunter Renegade, took the Bath Road to Slough and shortly thereafter rode into the courtyard of Eaton Place. When Kit had suggested that he visit the Hatton financial advisor and pass himself off as his twin, Nick hadn't taken him seriously. This morning when Kit still refused to deal with John Eaton, Nick decided that he would ride up and speak with their father's cousin himself.

He had no intention of passing himself off as Christopher until he encountered his second cousin in the stables. When Jeremy looked down his long nose with contempt and said, "Hello, Kit. It didn't take you long to sniff out the money trail, I see."

Nicholas was furious. He had always disliked the youth. He was an absolute snot and obviously resented the fact that Kit had come into a title. Nick decided to rub salt into his wound. "I prefer to be addressed as Lord Hatton," he said in his most arrogant drawl. "Be a good lad, Jeremy, and tell your father I'm here on business."

Jeremy's eyes narrowed. "The name *Harm* suits you far better than *Lord* Hatton." His glance slid over Renegade. "Nice mount . . . the one you rode in the fatal hunt, I believe."

Nick was instantly aware that the young snot was on a fishing expedition and decided to nip it in the bud immediately. "Are you accusing me of something?" When he received no reply, Nicholas deliberately turned his back upon his cousin and handed Renegade to an Eaton groom. When he turned around, Jeremy was gone.

Nick was greeted at the front door by a majordomo wearing livery so fancy he had a difficult time hiding his amusement. As he looked around the entrance hall, he was surprised at the luxury of the furnishings. Though Eaton Place lay only a few miles west in the next county, he had not had occasion to visit in years, and he was amazed at the show of wealth. Directing the finances of others must assuredly be a most profitable profession, Nick concluded.

John Eaton greeted him warmly. "Come along to the

library, my boy. You are looking much improved since the funeral, Christopher. I am glad you are bearing up, under such difficult circumstances."

"Thank you, John. I only just learned that Father named you sole trustee to his will. His . . . my solicitor, Tobias Jacobs, advised me to consult with you immediately."

"Ah, no hurry my boy. I shall take care of business for you, just as I did for Henry. No need to worry about it at all."

Nick was immediately aware that Eaton's cold, agate eyes belied his words. They were far more paternal than their father's had ever been and rang false in his ears. "I'm sure I need not worry. I am simply here to go over the investments I have inherited."

John Eaton smiled and wagged his finger. "Ah, Christopher, I detect a note of censure in your voice. You feel slighted that your father did not make you a trustee, but under the circumstances it is far better that he did not."

Nick raised a dark brow. "Under the circumstances?"

"You inherited everything, your twin nothing whatsoever. Under the circumstances it was best that you not be named a trustee. You may be safely confident that I have your best interests at heart. Your father took my advice in naming you sole beneficiary."

Nick wanted to smash his fist into Eaton's long arrogant nose. "So I have you to thank?"

"In no small measure, you do indeed, my boy. You are well aware of the animosity between your father and Nicholas; he made no secret of it. I knew he begrudged handing over Hatton Grange horse farm and its profits to his second born, so I advised him to make you his sole heir."

"A conspiracy." Nick's mouth curved in a half smile that did not reach his eyes. *Father's motive was hatred, but yours could only have been greed. I warrant your advice was expensive.*

"As I said before, I have only your best interests at heart. Do you see now, Christopher, why you can place complete trust in me regarding your investments?"

"Yes, I see things clearly now." Nicholas lusted to

reveal his true identity to the son of a bitch. It would be almost worth it to see the look on his face. He clenched his jaw until it ached to keep from flinging his name in the bastard's face. Instead, he said, "I would like a list of my investments and what interest they are earning. I would like a full accounting."

He saw that Eaton was momentarily taken aback. Likely he had never thought his cousin's heir particularly shrewd. He did know however that he was spoiled and used to getting his own way, just as his own son, Jeremy, was spoiled rotten.

"Of course I shall give you a full accounting. These things take time, you understand, Christopher. It shall be delivered to you the moment the tally is finished."

Nick suspected that he was stalling, but there was little he could do, other than make it clear he expected the accounting. "Thank you, John. I won't take up any more of your time. I'll expect to hear from you in two days. You may send it to the Curzon Street house—another bequest I no doubt owe to you."

The reception he had received from both Jeremy Eaton and his father gave Nicholas much food for thought on his ride home.

At Longford Manor, Dottie walked into her grandson's chamber and noted its disarray. Shirts and neckcloths were strewn across his bed, while mismatched riding boots and Hessians lay upon the carpet. Rupert stood jangling the bellpull.

"Why the devil doesn't Wilson answer my summons?"

"I don't imagine he can hear it."

"Why the devil not?"

"London's too far away."

"What the devil is he doing in London?"

"Looking for a new position, since he no longer works for you."

"Damn it, Dottie, you've insulted the fellow!" he accused.

"I warrant you did that when you didn't pay him."

Rupert had the decency to look guilty for a moment. "But I've been so short lately. It was an oversight I fully intended to rectify once my allowance was increased."

"Sit down, my boy. It is the allowance I have come to discuss." She lifted a neckcloth with her ebony cane and flipped it out of the way, then sat down on the bed. "Life is filled with ups and downs. . . . Everything on earth has its advantages and its disadvantages. . . . We must take the good with the bad. . . . Oh, plague take it, enough platitudes! I'll cut the palaver and be specific. You inherited your grandfather's title, Viscount Longford—"

"And I have tried to live up to it," Rupert assured her.

"Indeed you have, my boy. Russell would be proud. You've managed to go through a great deal of money in an amazingly short time, following in his hallowed footsteps."

Rupert rolled his eyes. "Don't tell me I must go on a budget and cut corners, just when I've been expecting an increase! Are you telling me that I shall have to divide the interest into even smaller amounts so that it will last longer?"

"You've spent the interest, Rupert."

"Good God! Don't tell me I've been dipping into my principle?"

"Plunging would be a better description."

"How much is left?"

"Nothing."

"Nothing?" He jumped to his feet, a note of panic in his voice.

"Nothing," Dottie confirmed.

He paced across the chamber, considering for a moment, then concluded, "Well, in that case it is quite obvious that the amount my grandfather set aside for me was inadequate. I throw myself upon your generosity and beg that you make arrangements more befitting to my station as Viscount Longford."

"When I married Russell Longford he was a wealthy man. He pissed away half his fortune on drink and women. The gaming tables got the other half."

The look of hope was wiped from Rupert's face.

"Blessedly, there was a large amount of money set aside for your mother's dowry."

Rupert's look of hope began to return.

"Your father, Johnny Sheffield, pissed that away."

Rupert's face fell, his expectations once more dashed. He sighed with deep resignation. "It is most fortunate that you are a wealthy woman in your own right. I throw myself upon your mercy, Grandmother. My fate is in your hands."

"No, Rupert, your fate is in your own hands. My money is a mirage, a myth, I am afraid."

"It cannot be true! After all these years of thinking I'd inherit a fortune and be able to spend like a nabob? I'll be a bloody laughing stock! I won't be able to face my friends—I'd rather put a bullet in my brain!"

"I wouldn't try, Rupert. Too small a target," Dottie advised.

"What am I to do?" he asked blankly.

Dottie gave a sharp bark of laughter. "Typical male response! Not *What is my grandmother to do?* or *What is my dear sister Alex to do?* The remedy, rather like you, Rupert, is simple: Marry an heiress. The county seems to be chockablock with such gels."

A glimmer of renewed hope dawned on Rupert's face. "The sacrifice might not prove too overwhelming, since I would wed an heiress regardless. It will simply have to be sooner rather than later," he said decidedly, demonstrating amazing practicality. "Our money troubles must be kept secret, Dottie. My friend Kit would drop me like a hot chestnut if even a whisper of this got out."

"You cod's head! I shall be as silent as the tomb, my dearest boy. Especially where young Hatton is concerned. Alexandra would have no chance of becoming Lady Hatton if she were a pauper. Now, Rupert, I am trusting you to keep your lip buttoned around your sister. Under no circumstances is Alexandra to know that we are no longer wealthy. If she thinks like an heiress and acts like an heiress, then everyone will assume she *is* an heiress."

The "heiress" in question left Hatton Hall and headed in the direction of the Bath Road, hoping to meet up with Nicholas on his return ride from Slough. As she cantered along the banks of the River Crane, she wondered why he had gone to see John Eaton, his father's financial advisor. Perhaps he was clutching at straws, hoping Eaton would find some sort of a loophole, she reasoned, or perhaps he was trying to borrow money. Whatever his mission, her heart ached for his plight.

The river ran through Hatton Grange, and Alexandra's sense of fairness became outraged at the thought that the thriving horse farm had been snatched away from Nicholas and bestowed upon Christopher. She reined in Zephyr to a slow trot as she passed through the lush fields of the Grange, but when she saw the foals with their dams, the temptation to stop was too great to resist. She dismounted, climbed the wooden rail that surrounded the meadow, and held her hand out to a dappled gray mare that was cropping the grass. The horse ambled over and Alex laughed when the colt followed its mother and attempted to suckle.

Presently, the mare pricked its ears, and Alex lifted her head and shaded her eyes with her hand as she scanned the distance. When she spotted the rider mounted on the powerful black Thoroughbred, her heart lifted with joy as she recognized Nicholas. Nobody rode as well as he did. She waved to him, and the anticipation of their meeting made her breath catch in her throat. Excitement bubbled up inside her, causing her heart to flutter and her pulse to race madly. She couldn't wait to lay her ingenious plan before him; it would solve every difficulty and change their lives forever.

Chapter 8

Nick, deep in thought over Jeremy Eaton's taunt about the name *Harm* suiting his brother better than *Lord*, didn't notice Alexandra perched upon the meadow rail until she began to wave madly. His dark brows drew together, and he hoped nothing was amiss as he galloped toward her. A feeling of relief washed over him when he was close enough to see that her face was lit by a radiant smile. He dismounted and tethered Renegade. As he drew close he saw the smile fade and tears flood her eyes. "What's wrong, Alex?"

She slipped down from the rail and dashed the tears from her eyes with an impatient hand. "Nick, I simply cannot bear what your father did to you!"

His steps slowed to a halt. "So, Rupert couldn't wait to tell you." Nicholas was angry that Alexandra had been told of his misfortune, yet he knew it was inevitable. The news would spread faster than wildfire, for gossip was far more difficult to contain. Suddenly, Alex smiled through her tears, and he was reminded of the sun coming out from behind a dark cloud.

"It's all right, Nick. I have the solution to all your money troubles. You don't need his rotten money—you can have mine!"

"Yours?" The cool note in his voice held a warning.

"I'm an heiress. If you marry me, you'll be rich!"

Nicholas Hatton stepped back from her as the slight anger he was feeling exploded into fury. She was actually crying tears of pity for him. The profound insult was like a blow to his solar plexus. The idea that a woman, any woman, could feel sorry for him mauled his pride. The thought that this particular woman who was so dear to his heart felt sorry for him was unendurable. "Alex, I shall pretend I did not hear that," he said stiffly.

"Piss and piffle! It is the solution to all your problems."

His jaw clenched like a lump of iron, and he tried to suppress the rage he felt. If a man had uttered such a thing to him, he would have struck him. With rigid control he demanded, "What on earth gives you the notion that you must solve my problems?"

"Because I care about you, Nicholas!" she cried passionately.

His wrath turned to chagrin. He had no right to be enraged at Alexandra. She was so sweetly innocent and touchingly naive, to say nothing of overwhelmingly generous, it brought a lump to his throat. It did not diminish his humiliation, however. Without knowing it, she had struck at his very manhood. She saw him as a victim, a pathetic victim who needed her charity. "How can you cast me in the role of a fortune hunter who would marry you for your money, when you have feared such a fate all your life?" His voice was so deep, it sounded like a growl.

She closed the small distance between them. "Nicholas, I care about you more than I care about money!" She gripped his arms with her small hands to emphasize her words and looked up at him in supplication.

"What sort of a man would I be, if I allowed you to sacrifice yourself through some sense of misguided sympathy?" His eyes were the gray of storm clouds.

She thought of his rigid honor, his unwavering integrity that made him dismiss all her pleading arguments. She shivered; he was so wickedly handsome, yet so stern and powerful. "For God's sake, Nick, I don't feel sympathy; you must know that what I feel is lo—"

"Alexandra!" He used her name as an invocation to stop her words, to prevent her from uttering such blasphemy. He was well aware that Alex thought she loved him, but knew he must disabuse her of such a notion immediately. His mind darted about like quicksilver, searching for a way to make her understand once and for all that he could never take advantage of a love-struck girl without coming to loathe himself. On top of everything else, Alex was taboo to him because it was known by all that she was his brother's future bride. Nicholas did not want to hurt her, but he realized it was the only way. He had no choice.

He took hold of her hand gently and held her gaze with his. "I thank you from the bottom of my heart for your generosity, Alexandra, but marriage between us is out of the question. I have always thought of you as my little sister, Alex. It would be impossible for me to think of you in any other way."

She looked up at him in dismay. His words made him seem far older than he was and emphasized the difference in their ages. Like a mature man addressing a child, he gently pointed out that the gulf between them could never be narrowed, that their feelings for each other were totally disparate.

He released her hand and patted her head, ruffling the bright curls. "This infatuation you feel will vanish like a puff of smoke once you go to London and are swept up in the social whirl."

Alexandra wished that the earth would open up and swallow her. She had never felt more gauche in her entire life. Her cheeks were stained with the humiliation of his rejection, and inside her chest, her heart actually hurt as if cruel, ruthless fingers had just crushed it. She dropped her lashes so that he would not see the pain reflected in her eyes and brushed imaginary dust from the skirt of her riding habit. "I promised to help Dottie with dinner. . . . We are between cooks at the moment," she said awkwardly.

Nick fought the impulse to gather her in his arms and hold her until she stopped hurting. He knew he must be cruel to be kind. He forced himself to remain still as she untied Zephyr's reins and mounted. Her back was ramrod straight and her chin high as she galloped off in the direction of Longford Manor. Only when she was out of sight did he mount Renegade and ride home.

Kit Hatton was directing Mr. Burke and the valet he shared with his twin as they packed for London. Nick decided to wait until dinner to tell his brother of the disquieting reception he had received at Eaton Place. He went to his chamber and did his own packing, knowing that Kit would monopolize the servants.

Kit arrived in the dining room preoccupied with tomorrow's journey to London. "Oh, I forgot you visited Eaton today. Did you have any trouble convincing them you were Lord Hatton?"

"When I rode in on Renegade, they assumed that I was you."

"Did you learn anything, or was it a complete waste of time?"

"I learned that John Eaton lives in splendor. I learned that Jeremy envies you your title."

Kit picked up his fork and laughed. "Who wouldn't? Here I sit, Lord of the Manor at just twenty-one, dining on my own trout from my own river."

Nick watched his brother covertly to gauge his reaction. "Jeremy hinted that he knew something about the hunting accident."

Kit put down his fork. The trout seemed to have lost its appeal. "What did the snotty swine say?"

"He said the name *Harm* was more suitable to you than *Lord* Hatton."

"You're jumping to conclusions," Kit said defensively.

"I challenged him immediately, demanding if he was accusing me of something."

"What did he say?" Christopher asked, holding his breath.

"Nothing whatsoever."

Kit laughed. "There you are then. He's simply green with envy that I have a title and he never will!" Because Mr. Burke was otherwise employed, a young serving-maid brought in the second course and removed the fish. "What's your name?" Kit asked, immediately distracted from the conversation by the female servant.

She bobbed a curtsy. "Ellen, my lord."

Kit's glance swept over her from nose to knees. "Very pretty," he drawled. When her cheeks flushed scarlet he laughed. "Better stay out of *Harm's* way," he teased.

"John Eaton reassured me again and again that he had your best interests at heart and would take great care of your investments." As soon as Nicholas spoke, the maid spied her chance to escape.

"Nothing to worry about then."

"I didn't believe him," Nick said flatly.

"Father wouldn't have used him as his financial agent if he hadn't made money, cousin or no cousin."

"That's true. Father had a nose for money, and Eaton wouldn't have dared cheat him. I tried to convey the impression that the present Lord Hatton also has a nose for money. I asked him for a complete accounting, and when he tried to put me off by telling me these things took time, I told him I would expect it in two days."

"But we'll be in London in two days."

Nick schooled himself to patience. "I told him to send it to Curzon Street."

"You know, old man, you have an extremely suspicious nature."

"No, if I had a suspicious nature, I'd think you had dishonorable designs on young Ellen."

Kit almost choked with laughter, then threw down his napkin. "You are a shrewd bastard, Hazard Hatton. I warrant John Eaton would have one hell of a time cheating you."

You're wrong, Kit. He has already cheated me. "It is you I wish to keep Eaton from cheating."

"Now that Father is gone, don't think to set yourself up as my guardian, Nick. It is most insulting to imply that I am not as shrewd as you are, either regarding money matters or human nature. I believe I am quite capable of handling my own affairs. Since everything is now mine—*including the servants*—I'll thank you not to meddle. Perhaps you should concentrate on your own problem. If I were in your shoes, I would solve my dilemma immediately by marrying money." Kit held up his hand when he saw Nick open his mouth to reply. "Pardon my presumption in advising someone with your great wisdom; I warrant the predatory lion has already marked his prey."

Nick's pride had taken too many blows today. He knew he must remove himself from his twin's presence to prevent violence from erupting. "A truce? I shan't meddle in your affairs if you don't meddle in mine."

Later, as he lay in bed, Nick realized that he had done to his brother what Alexandra had done to him. Presuming to solve someone's problem implied that he was not capable of doing it himself. He had not intended to offend Kit; nevertheless, his twin had taken offense, and Nick decided that this was a good sign. If he was ready to take on the responsibilities of the vast Hatton estate, it would free Nick to get on with his own life.

He pushed away thoughts and suspicions about Jeremy and John Eaton. He had warned Kit, and decided that was enough; he would keep his word and meddle no further. Though he tried to banish thoughts of Alex, she pervaded his senses. She had offered herself up to him, and her compassion and generosity filled him with awe. Here in the solitude of his own chamber, he admitted how tempted he had been. He searched his motives honestly and knew the temptation had nothing to do with her money. She was adventurous and hungry for life. Courage and laughter were second nature to her. She had wit, intelligence, and a radiant beauty that came from within. Nick let out a slow breath of appreciation; her glorious red-gold curls and long slim legs weren't bad either! She was a prize beyond compare, and Nick couldn't deny that he coveted her.

He closed his eyes and imagined that her fragrance of jasmine stole to him in the darkness. As he drifted into sleep, her presence permeated his dreams.

Nicholas found himself entering the doors of the ancient Hatton church and realized with joy that it was his wedding day. It was, however, a pagan ceremony, and as he approached his bride, he saw that a sleeping Alexandra was lying naked upon the altar, amid glowing candles and flowers of jasmine. His mind denied that she was a sacrificial offering, as his possessive glance roamed freely over her alabaster flesh and the red-gold curls that covered her high mons. He bent his dark head and placed his lips upon her heart in a reverent kiss that sealed their union. He removed his dark cape and draped it over her exquisite body, cloaking her innocence. Then he lifted her and with infinite tenderness carried her to his bed. He laid her down upon linen sheets, whiter than driven snow, and worshipped her with his eyes. The moment he threaded his fingers into her silken curls and claimed her lips, she lifted her lashes, slipped her arms about his neck, and arched her body to fit his. The mating that followed was a wild, pagan affair, erotic, exotic, and sensual in the extreme. They lay panting, entwined in each other's arms, when a knock came upon the chamber door. He heard his twin's voice clearly. "I have come to claim my bride." Wildly, Nick looked down at the lovely female in his arms and saw the vivid spots of crimson blood upon the pristine sheet. "Judas! What have I done?"

Nick awoke with a start. His body was glistening with perspiration. Christ, it had happened again. He swung his legs out of bed and paced the chamber like a lion in his cage. With relief he remembered that tomorrow he was leaving for London. The sooner he put a safe distance between himself and Alexandra, the better it would be for all of them. And never again must he imagine making love to her; not even in his dreams!

The moment she got home, Alex wanted to retreat to her own chamber to lick her wounds. Three obstacles—dinner, Dottie, and Rupert—stood squarely in her way. She surveyed the larder with dismay; its contents were diminishing in alarming fashion. She picked up a cold ham, along with some vegetables from the garden, and entered the kitchen with resolution, prepared to tackle the evening meal.

"I shall help you, darling," Dottie declared brightly.

"Cooking is not your *forte,*" Alex said decisively, taking a carving knife from Dottie's hand before she did herself an injury.

Rupert came into the kitchen with a look of desperation on his face. "Alex, I'm at my wit's end. You must help me pack for London. My valet has deserted me and I am flummoxed!"

"It will have to wait until after dinner."

"Why?" he demanded.

"Because, Rude Rupert, I have been appointed head cook and bottle-wash. Unless you would care to take over?"

He threw up his hands in horror. "This is a madhouse; I shall be glad to see the back of it."

"When you are gone, there will be one less lunatic," Dottie pointed out. *And one less mouth to feed.*

Alex met the challenge of dinner, but later, when she stood on the threshold of Rupert's chamber, her courage almost failed her. The entire contents of his wardrobe engulfed both bed and carpet in a storm-swept sea of clothing.

In an effort to help, Rupert gathered together a dozen clean neckcloths and held them out. "These need starch."

Alex swallowed a curse and deftly dodged the chore. "It would be far more practical to starch them when they are unpacked." She eyed his valises that stood gaping, ready to be filled, and sent him off to the attic. "As well as these, you will need a large trunk, perhaps two. You have morning, evening, and riding clothes. You have greatcoats, boots, hats, and wigs, to say nothing of shirts and waistcoats."

"I need a valet," he said plaintively.

"You need a kick up the arse!"

"There's no need to be offensive, Alex."

"Then stop offending me. You are about as much use as a chocolate teapot!"

"Perhaps Dottie is right; I need a wife. She suggested that marriage would solve my problems."

Alexandra saw how easily he accepted such a solution, and suddenly the contrast between him and Nicholas Hatton was brought home to her. Rupert was an immature youth, while Nicholas was a man, and Alex realized that that was Nick's great attraction; she wouldn't want him any other way.

It was late when she retired, and she fought the impulse to fling herself upon her bed and cry herself to sleep. Though her emotions had been deeply wounded, she knew that sooner or later she was going to have to come to terms with reality. Nick Hatton did not return her affection. She told herself that it was her own fault that she felt such despair. Dottie had warned her since she was a child that she must follow her head rather than her heart. Under no circumstances must she ever fall in love, for love was disastrous. She told herself that she would get over him, but deep down inside Alexandra knew it was a lie.

The pain in her heart slowly melted away and was replaced by a feeling of excitement. She felt the wind in her face, felt it whipping her long hair into a wild tangle, heard herself laughing with sheer joy as she bent low over Zephyr's sleek black neck and urged her to gallop faster. She was in a race with Christopher and Nicholas Hatton and she was the prize! She turned her head to watch Kit astride Renegade and knew he could outrun her mare. He was so handsome mounted upon the black stallion that she longed to sketch him and capture this moment forever. She smiled a secret smile when he pulled ahead of her. She turned her head to the other side to watch Nick astride Slate and felt jubilant. She had bet her entire fortune upon the gray, but it had little to do with the horse. It was the man riding the gray on whom she had put her money. Her secret smile widened as she watched him pull ahead. The two horses in front of her were full-out now. They were well matched, and their satiny sinews strained forward with brutal strength. The animals were even, head to head, and it looked as if the race would end in a draw, but Alexandra knew better. She raised her eyes to the man riding the gray and saw his teeth flash in a smile that told her how much Hazard Hatton was enjoying himself. She shivered as she saw his male power dominate and harness the power of the animal beneath him. Then, triumphantly, his horse surged over the finish line ahead of the black Thoroughbred.

Alexandra was mesmerized just looking at him. Her blood pounded exactly as his did. Simply watching him thrilled and excited her. His linen shirt clung to his chest and the cords of his neck pulsed with the glory of being alive as he reached up and lifted her down from the saddle. As she went down into his arms, she knew that it was not so much that he liked to win; she knew he could not bear to lose. Twin he might be, but to Alexandra there was no man on earth like him.

Handclasped, they ran laughing into the stables. When he pulled her down into the hay, she went willingly. His possessive hand slipped inside her doublet, and as his warm palm cupped her breast, she felt it harden with desire. The fingers of his other hand traced a tantalizing path up the inside of her thigh. As his dark head dipped to take possession of her mouth, she whispered breathlessly, "Nicholas, are you really going to make love to me?"

Suddenly, Alexandra's eyes flew open. Her hand went to her hair, which was now cropped short, and she felt a pang of regret over its loss. When she realized that it had only been a dream, she experienced a far greater loss and could hold back the tears no longer. She sat up in bed and hugged her knees. If she was ever to get over her longing for Nick Hatton, she knew she must put distance between them. In the morning, she would talk Dottie into their going to London with Rupert.

Chapter 9

Alexandra's feet touched the floor long before sunrise, and by seven she was packed for London. When Rupert opened his door to her polite tap, he was standing amidst his trunks and valises. "After you've taken your luggage down, will you come back up for mine?"

"Do I look like a porter?" Rupert asked. "Ring for a servant."

"I cannot believe how unobservant you are. Dottie went on a servant rampage about a week ago, and Longford Manor's staff now consists of Mrs. Dinwiddie, our ancient housekeeper, and Old Ned, who takes care of the horses. Never mind, I'll carry my own bags."

"But who'll carry my— Where the devil are you going, Alex?"

"To London, of course. The Berkeley Square house has a full staff of servants, all idle at the moment. I cannot bear the thought of them catering to your every whim, so I am joining you. Since our carriage is away for repairs, I assume you will be using the Hatton coach?"

"To transport our luggage only. We intend to ride."

"Then there should be plenty of room for Dottie and me."

"Dottie?" Rupert looked alarmed. "What if she starts sacking the London servants as soon as she arrives?"

"That should make little difference to you. When in London you sleep all day and prowl all night. Besides, you can always go and stay in Curzon Street with your very dear friend Lord Hatton."

"You seem to have an answer for everything," he said testily.

"Well, I do know who is going to carry your bags downstairs, Viscount Longford," she informed him sweetly.

At ten o'clock Rupert rode off to Hatton Hall, but it was two more hours before the huge black berline coach with the Hatton baronial crest emblazoned on its doors pulled up in the courtyard of Longford Manor. The coachman obligingly stowed all the luggage aboard and was about to help Lady Longford climb the carriage step when she threatened to strike him with her walking stick. "Stand back, sirrah! I'm not ready for the knacker's yard yet!"

"Beg pardon, ma'am."

Dottie watched Alexandra mount Zephyr before she climbed into the well-padded carriage and lowered the window. "You'll be much more comfortable inside with me. The long ride to London will fag you out, darling. Won't you change your mind?"

Alex laughed. "It's six miles, not sixty! Hardly far enough to give the horses a good gallop."

Dottie put up the window and settled herself against the leather squabs. How could she argue with Alexandra when she had come up with the clever idea of going to London? Closing up Longford Manor for the next several months would cut the upkeep expenses to the bone. Mrs. Dinwiddie and Old Ned were adequate caretakers who would cost nothing.

They made great time along the Great West Road, passing the lovely flower gardens of Osterley Park, whose perfume drenched the warm summer air. They galloped past Syon House, a huge square mansion that was ugly on the outside but had magnificent Adam interiors. They had to slow down when they reached the outskirts of the city, but London held such fascination for Alexandra that she welcomed the slackened pace. The coachman turned onto the Cromwell Road, which took them to Knightsbridge, then along bustling Piccadilly to Mayfair. He pulled up outside the tall, stone house in Berkeley Square, jumped down from the box, and went to the leader's head and secured its rein to the cast iron carriage post. He then began to unload trunks and valises, making sure the Hatton luggage stayed onboard for the short journey to Curzon Street.

"Where the devil is the man?" Lady Longford complained loudly. When the wary driver approached the viscountess, keeping a weather eye on her ebony stick, she read him the riot act. "A coachman's first duty is to his passengers, not his portmanteaus! Death and damnation, you wouldn't have dared treat Henry Hatton in such a cavalier fashion. Give me your arm, man, your arm!"

Alexandra, who had trotted Zephyr to the stables behind the town house, hadn't witnessed her grandmother's about-face, so it amused her when she came around the corner of the building to see Dottie leaning heavily on the coachman's arm. He turned her over to the butler who awaited Lady Longford at the solid mahogany doors, picked out in gold.

"Welcome to London, my lady. The staff and I are delighted to see you and are most honored to be serving you again."

"Lud, I'll soon change that, Hopkins," Dottie declared dryly.

The butler, familiar with her eccentricities, merely bowed.

Alex slipped inside behind her grandmother. "Hello, Hopkins."

"Good afternoon, Mistress Alexandra. Viscount Longford has been impatiently awaiting your arrival."

She grinned at the butler. "Addressing him as Viscount Longford bestows far too much respect upon Rude Rupert. How do you do it with a straight face, Hopkins? And I assure you it's his trunks that he awaits impatiently."

As Rupert came rushing downstairs, Alex's wicked juices began to bubble. "You're just in time to carry up the luggage!"

"No time for hilarity. I need evening clothes. We ran into Hart Cavendish at Barclays Bank and he invited us to dine at Devonshire House tonight."

"I take it you secured invitations for Alexandra and me?" Dottie's tone brooked no refusal. Though she had no intention of going, the invitation was important to her.

"Er, well, since Old Lady Spencer will be there, I warrant you are more than welcome."

"You will refer to her as Countess Spencer in my presence, you young lout! Here, you may carry this up first." Dottie handed him a huge hatbox that held all her wigs. "Your bosom friend, Hatton, is in mourning when it comes to his betrothed, but not apparently when it comes to Devonshire House entertainments. Come, Alexandra, we must choose a gown that will make you irresistible to the males of the species."

By six o'clock, Alexandra was adorned in a cream silk faille gown whose *décolletage* showed her firm young breasts to perfection. Peacock velvet ribbon adorned the gown's empire waist, and Sara, their competent ladies' maid, was busy threading the same shade of peacock ribbon through Alex's red-gold curls to make a brilliant contrast.

"You look lovely, darling, but you need something to give you flair, drama!" Dottie cocked her head to one side, then the other. "I've got it! You need one of my fans."

Alex looked alarmed. Dottie had a collection of feather fans in every shade imaginable, which added to her wardrobe's vivid theatrical look. Her grandmother disappeared into her own chamber and returned holding one of her treasures. When Alex picked up the huge turquoise ostrich-feather fan and wafted it slowly, she loved her reflection in the mirror. It didn't make her look the least bit eccentric; it made her look ravishing!

"Damn and blast, the carriage will be here at six and I cannot manage this neckcloth." Rupert stood helplessly on the threshold.

Alex ignored him. "Dottie, it's almost six; you must dress!"

"Lud, child, why would I dine at Devonshire House? We have an incomparable chef right here in Berkeley Square, who has promised me *coq au vin,* followed by sherry trifle. Rupert will escort you, but remember to treat Lord Hatton with disdain and save your smiles for Hartington. It will drive him mad!"

The butler came to announce that the carriage had arrived.

"Alex, tell them I shall be there in a jiff," Rupert directed. "Hopkins, help me with this blasted neckcloth. I was trying for an Oriental, but I suppose the waterfall will have to do."

Alex picked up her wrap, kissed her grandmother good night, and ran lightly downstairs. The coachman bowed and opened the door, but for a moment she stood rooted to the pavement as she realized that the carriage was occupied by both of the Hatton twins.

A pair of dark brows lifted in surprise. "Alex, you look—"

"Ravishing? Well, don't panic. I give you my assurance that neither one of you is in danger."

The twins exchanged a sardonic look of appreciation for both her dazzling appearance and her sharp set-down. Privately, Nick was just as dismayed as Alex; he'd had no idea she was coming to London. He cursed silently. His nights were already flooded with dreams of her, and he had hoped putting distance between them would banish her tantalizing presence. But their close proximity tonight guaranteed his erotic dreams would increase.

Alexandra swept up into the carriage with the outward confidence of a woman who knew she looked glorious. On the inside, however, she was a quivering mass of indecision. The men's black evening clothes, combined with the dim interior of the carriage, made it impossible for her to tell them apart. She sat down beside one of them, which placed her across from the other, and pointedly ignored both. *Dear God, I came to London to escape from him, and now I find myself sitting beside him, brushing thighs!* She abruptly changed seats, murmuring that she did not like to ride backward.

Rupert arrived and took the seat she had just vacated. As the coach lurched forward, her brother smiled happily. "Ah, this is like the old days . . . the four of us together!"

"Except you're now a viscount and I'm a lord," Kit jested as he jabbed his elbow into his friend's ribs.

Alexandra was mortified. She had just quite deliberately

moved to sit beside Nicholas Hatton, the man she was running away from. She stared out the window, pretending a great interest in the passing scene, but in reality she saw nothing, as Nick's close physical presence silently overwhelmed her. When the carriage turned into Piccadilly and her body swayed against his, she blushed furiously. She could swear that she could feel his heat seeping through her gown, threatening to melt her icy reserve.

Nicholas clenched his fist to keep his hand from covering hers. When Alexandra was this close, the temptation to touch her was difficult to resist. His nostrils flared as her scent stole to him, and he told himself firmly that her attraction was fatally irresistible only because she was forbidden to him.

"We're going on to White's later," Kit told Rupert. "Our memberships should be confirmed by now." Hart Cavendish had sponsored his three friends to become members of the oldest gentlemen's club in London, renowned for its gambling.

"What are the annual dues?" Rupert asked. "I've forgotten."

"I'll take care of it, old man," Kit offered negligently.

Alexandra blushed. How clumsy of Rude Rupert to bring up the subject of money when Nicholas had nothing. How generous of Christopher to cover her brother's insensitive *faux pas*.

The carriage turned in at the gates of Devonshire House, the largest mansion in Piccadilly. Rupert remembered his manners and jumped out first so he could escort his sister. Kit was about to dismiss the carriage since they intended to stay out all night, but Nick instructed the driver to wait and take Alex home safely.

Alex felt a mutinous resentment that they were free to carouse in London all night, while she was to be packed off home to bed like a child. *Goddamnit, life is unfair for females!* She glanced at Nicholas, saw the forbidding look on his dark face, and knew he was expecting her to protest vigorously and make a scene. Vowing to disappoint the dominant devil, she lifted her chin, wafted her ostrich-feather fan, and swept up the steps of Devonshire House. Outside it resembled a barracks, but inside it was magnificent!

It was Alexandra's first visit, and her eyes widened with appreciation as she ascended the marble stairs and witnessed the glittering throng gathered beneath the great crystal chandeliers. A liveried footman took her cloak and she gazed about, wondering how on earth this many people would sit down to dine at one time.

Hart Cavendish, the young Duke of Devonshire, spotted her immediately, flanked by the darkly handsome Hatton twins, and came forward to claim her. "Alexandra, welcome to Devonshire House. You look absolutely dazzling." He lifted her hand to his lips. "Rupert, you old reprobate, why didn't you tell me your sister was in town? I would have sent flowers. Come, let me introduce you." He plucked her from amidst her three escorts and carried her off on his arm like a trophy.

Alexandra said the first thing that came into her head. "I'd no idea so many people would be in London at this time of year."

"Oh, there'll be lots of entertainments throughout the fall and winter. Tonight's dinner is in honor of the Earl of Liverpool."

Alex couldn't hide her amazement. "You mean Robert Banks Jenkinson, the new Prime Minister of England?"

Hart gave her a quizzical smile. "I doubted anyone as young and lovely as you would have the least interest in politics."

"You are wrong. I have a great interest in politicians . . . both in what they do and what they leave undone. Please point Jenkinson out to me. I'd like a good look at the man who served under Spencer Perceval as War Minister only last year and was so ruthlessly ambitious he shoved old Perceval out on his . . . ear!"

Hart laughed. "I believe it was another part of his anatomy."

London's *élite* fascinated Alexandra. She was both observant and perceptive as she watched the bi-play that went on between Society's sexes. She watched the matrons maneuver their daughters of marriageable age among the most eligible bachelors and saw that Kit Hatton and her brother were soon surrounded by this year's crop of debutantes, who'd been in London since the Season opened in May.

Her glance roamed the glittering crowd, looking for Nicholas. He had made it plain that she was not his type, and she was most curious to see who was. When she saw him, she was surprised to see him in conversation with a male friend, with no young women whatever vying for his attention. She watched him surreptitiously from behind her fan and saw that the women who approached him were older, sophisticated creatures who bestowed smiles upon him that were far too familiar. Alex was immediately green with jealousy, though she told herself she didn't give a damn about his conquests. When he made his way to the Prime Minister and engaged him in what appeared to be serious conversation, she felt inexplicable relief.

Alex returned her attention to her escort and saw they were surrounded by young men awaiting introductions. She could not help but be flattered as Hart presented her to Lords Fitzmaurice, Tavistock, and Burlington. There were so many titles that soon she could not sort out the earls from the viscounts.

Hart's sister Harriet, Lady Granville, affectionately known as Hary-O, greeted her warmly. "How lovely to see you. I hope Lady Longford came up to town. Since our grandmothers are such dear friends, I expect we'll be seeing a lot of each other. Do you mind if I steal my brother? I need him in the dining room if we are ever to get this crowd seated."

Hart steered Alexandra toward a group of young ladies with whom she was acquainted. Deborah Mitford, Elizabeth Cecil, and Lucy Lyttelson, all debutantes who had been presented this Season, were there with their mothers. When Hart begged her leave, their looks were envious. Dukes of the Realm were few and far between, and Hart Cavendish was second only to royalty in wealth and position.

Finally, the double doors to the dining room swung open and were flanked by footmen resplendent in Devonshire livery. This appeared to be a signal for the start of a race, as the young women about her eagerly rushed forward in an attempt to find themselves seats next to eligible dinner partners, as their mothers had obviously coached them to do.

Alexandra decided upon a more aloof approach. She languidly wafted her fan and watched the other guests elbow their way into the dining room. When she reached the double doors, she was duly impressed by the size of the opulent chamber and the length of the tables. There were two of them, each about forty feet long, set with magnificent damask linen, Georgian silver, and Venetian crystal glasses. One footman stood behind every second chair, ready to lavish attention upon the two people assigned him.

She saw that her brother, Rupert, and Christopher Hatton both sat with young heiresses of the *ton.* Neither had apparently given her a thought. Then she saw that the chair beside Nicholas Hatton was conspicuously vacant, and she wondered wildly if he had saved her a seat. Like a revelation, it dawned upon her that he was *persona non grata* with the matrons who had eligible daughters in tow. He was being deliberately snubbed because of the hunting accident and the ensuing scandal.

Her heart turned over in her breast. How could they be such hypocrites, such utter snobs? She lifted a defiant chin and walked a direct path to Nick Hatton's side. He stood immediately and held her chair with an outward show of gallantry. She slipped into the seat and rewarded him with a radiant smile, fully expecting him to be furious with her.

Instead, he was wryly amused. "You are far too tenderhearted, Alex," he murmured for her ears alone. "It is not necessary to take pity on me."

"I cannot believe they are treating you this way," she whispered angrily. "They know it was an accident."

Nick began to chuckle. "As well as tenderhearted, you are endearingly naive. The worthy matrons of the *ton* are not snubbing me because I shot my father; I am being ostracized because I now have no part of the Hatton wealth."

She sat stunned as his words sank in, and she realized that he spoke the gospel truth. "It is the mothers and daughters who are savage bitches! The men seem civil enough. I saw Robert Banks Jenkinson speaking with you."

"The Earl of Liverpool was War Minister before he became Prime Minister." Nick, about to add something, changed his mind.

"Apparently the earl lets nothing stand in the way of ambition."

"Ambition in a man is an admirable trait, Alex."

She arched a brow. "And what would you consider an admirable trait for a woman?"

"Loyalty . . . something you have in abundance. Courage . . . something else you display when you deliberately choose to sit with me."

"Utter rot! I simply have a defiant nature and enjoy spitting in the *ton*'s evil eye."

His mouth curved. "Hellion."

Oh God, Nick, don't look at me that way. Why the hellfire can't you set your stupid scruples aside and marry me? Alex curbed her thoughts and lowered her lashes, before he could guess how lovesick she was. When the gentleman sitting to her right spoke, she had no idea what he said. She gave him a polite smile and feigned interest, while her emotions ran riot throughout the entire meal.

When she turned her attention from him, Nick was thankful. Her closeness played havoc with his senses, and her lush breasts exquisitely displayed in the empire gown had so physically aroused him that his breeches were stretched to the bursting point. By the end of the meal, the dull ache in his groin had spread up to his heart.

Lady Harriet Granville ascended the dais and asked that everyone repair to the music room, where cake and cordials would be served. There was to be no dancing tonight, though the Devonshire musicians would play in the background while most of the guests socialized by conversing, currying favor, or cutting up their acquaintances.

"There you are." Hart Cavendish had obviously been searching for her. "I wanted you to sit with the family for dinner, Alexandra. Hary-O and I were so looking forward to your company."

"Nicholas and I were perfectly happy back here in the cheap seats," she teased, wafting her fan.

"Forgive me, I thought you were Christopher," Hart apologized, relieved that she was not with her rumored betrothed.

"Thank you for rescuing me; the Hattons are naught but Harm and Hazard." She took his arm. "Shall we repair to the music room?"

Hart bit his lip and looked torn; the rest of the evening at Devonshire House would be one long yawn from start to finish.

Nick laughed. "The little hellion is teasing you unmercifully, Hart. She knows damn well we are on our way to White's. If you'll round up Kit and Rupert, I shall escort the lady to her carriage."

Alexandra went to get her wrap and returned to find Nick awaiting her at the top of the marble steps. With his firm hand at her elbow they descended to the courtyard and walked to the black berline coach in silence. He signaled to Todd to keep his seat on the box and opened the carriage door himself. She broke the silence. "You're not being the least gallant. You just want to make certain I'm packed off home to bed."

"Yes." He stood gazing down at her, imagining her in bed. His bed. She made no move to get into the carriage, and the silence stretched between them. They swayed slightly toward each other, then away. The noise of the street beyond faded, and the darkness enfolded them for a moment in their own private world. Swiftly, he gathered her in his arms, dipped his head, and covered her mouth in a demanding kiss. She opened her lips and melted against him.

"Good-bye, Alex."

He was gone before her thoughts became coherent. In a daze she climbed into the carriage and was halfway home before she realized he had said "good-bye" rather than "good night."

Chapter 10

The quartet of gamblers left Devonshire House and hired a hackney to take them the short distance to St. James's Street. White's Club, number 37 on the east side of the street, was opposite Brooks's and distinguished by its big bay window. Hart Cavendish forked over twenty guineas, the entrance fee for all four of them, and the porter took their top hats and canes to the cloakroom. Since they had already dined, they went straight into one of the card rooms, which was crowded with men in formal attire. The air was redolent with blue cigar smoke and the chink of drinking glasses as the four friends waited for chairs to become vacant.

Nick sat down at the baccarat table to the left of Lord Sefton, who was the dealer, which ensured that he would be next in line to take over the "shoe," the dealing box. Rupert quickly offered to be the croupier, to assist the players in making their bets, so that he would not have to participate in the gambling. The object of baccarat was to reach a count of nine with either two or three cards. On the first deal Nick drew a four and a five, giving him a "natural." He showed his hand immediately, and the dealer paid his bet. On the second deal Nick drew a three and a six, giving him another natural, and with a sniff, Lord Sefton again paid his bet. Nick decided to stand on his next two hands, while most of the other players drew.

"Devil's own luck, Hatton," Lord Sefton muttered, though he had no notion which Hatton twin he was addressing, and voluntarily gave up the dealing box to Nicholas.

Nick shuffled and cut the cards, dropped them back into the shoe, placed the fifty guineas he had won in the bank, and dealt the cards. Lord Worcester immediately called out, "banco," accepting Nick's entire bank as his wager. Using only his index finger, Nick dealt Worcester one card facedown, then one to himself, and repeated the procedure. When both men turned over their cards, the dealer had eight, Worcester only seven, giving Nick the win again. Nick spotted a vacant chair at the faro table, raked in his counters, which now totaled more than a hundred guineas, and turned over the bank to a grinning Hart Cavendish seated on his left.

Nick sat down at the faro table next to his brother, and Rupert came up behind them to watch the play. He secretly admired the risks Nick Hatton took, wishing he could emulate them. He was in the same penniless boat, though no one knew it, but didn't dare wager money he didn't have, or he'd end up in dun territory. "The list of new members should be posted. I'll go and take a look." Hart Cavendish had submitted his friends' names when they were about to turn twenty-one, and a list of those who had been accepted was posted every three months.

When Rupert returned to the table with a paper in his hand, his cheeks were flushed. On the list of new members he had found his own name beneath that of his dearest friend, Lord Hatton, but glaringly conspicuous by its absence was the name of Nicholas Hatton.

Kit drained his glass of whiskey, glanced up at Rupert's face, and jested, "What's the matter, old man? Didn't you make the cut?"

"No, I'm right here, but, er, perhaps the list is incomplete."

Kit, who had lost three hands in a row while his twin had consistently won, grabbed the paper from Rupert and scanned it. "Well, I'll be a dirty dog's dinner!"

Nick looked from one to the other, then plucked the list from his brother's fingers. His glance quickly went down the names; there was no need for him to read it twice. He handed the paper back to his twin and slowly gathered his winnings. "I'm sure you gentlemen will excuse me," he said with utmost civility.

"For Christ's sake, sit down, Nick. You can stay as my *guest;* there's no need for you to leave," Kit assured him.

"There is every need," Nick said quietly.

He cashed in his counters, which came to almost two hundred pounds, then he retrieved his hat and cane and gave White's porter a generous tip. Outside, a fine drizzle had begun to fall, but Nicholas barely noticed as he put on his top hat, pushed it rakishly forward over one eye, and sauntered down St. James's Street. He ran his stick along the iron railings to produce a satisfying racket and whistled carelessly through his teeth.

He turned into Pall Mall and headed for Champagne Charlie's. A sudden cloudburst turned the drizzle into a downpour, but Nick didn't quicken his pace. By the time he strolled into the establishment, he was soaked to the skin. The nymph who came forward to greet him had an amazing pair of breasts, and as he tipped his head to gaze down at them, a trickle of rain water from the brim of his top hat splashed down upon her glorious globes.

"Ooo, that's cold! Come in to get warm, did you, luv? I know a game that'll make you hot as fire!"

Nick grinned down at her. "I didn't come for that sort of game. I'm here for a game of chance."

As he headed toward the gaming parlor, Charlotte King spotted him. "You're drenched to the bone! Get upstairs, for God's sake, before you ruin my Axminster carpets."

"You are guessing that I am Nick."

"I don't need to *hazard* a bloody guess. I've been expecting you." She took his cane from him and pointed it upstairs. "You're the talk of the sodding town!"

The moment they entered her private bedchamber, she stripped off his evening coat and hung it over the tall brass fender in front of the fire. Nick unfastened his soggy muslin neckcloth, while Charlie removed the studs from his evening shirt. She decided to let him undress himself, for already the glimpse of black curls on his muscular chest was making her greedy, and she knew she must put his needs before her own tonight. "I'll get you a towel."

When Charlie returned, she found him standing naked with his back to the fire. "Ah, that feels good." He held out his arms to her and she went into them, cupping his buttocks with her palms and massaging them. "That feels even better." He took the elaborate feathered ornaments and pins from her hair and set them on the mantel. Her champagne-colored curls fell to her shoulders, and he threaded his fingers into them to bring her closer.

She gazed up into his gray eyes, expecting to see them stormy, but all she saw was calm, as if he had come to a decision and was at peace with it. "So, what will you do? Will you marry?"

He cocked a dark, amused brow. "Is that a proposal?"

Her easy laugh was full-throated. "I'll make you another sort of proposal. We could be partners in a gambling venture."

His sharp bark of laughter rent the air. "Ha, as if my name isn't blackened enough!"

His hands were busy disrobing her, and she knew better than to argue with Hazard Hatton. He was a man who knew what he wanted, and no power on earth would keep him from his goal. Charlie doubted he'd ever marry for money, for that would give a woman the upper hand over him. The lion would never bow his proud head. He was cloaked in a devil-may-care attitude even when he was naked. Especially when he was naked.

"So, what are you going to do?"

"Fuck you, of course." He lifted her onto his cock and carried her to the big curtained bed.

Much later, when Charlie came out of her dressing room wearing a chamber robe, she found Nick with the towel about his hips, reclining on her bed, smoking a cigar. Now he was ready to talk.

He blew a smoke ring. "I've decided to join the army."

"My God, you can't!" She came to the bed and knelt before him. "There's a war on with the French. . . . They'll send you to Spain!"

"Charlie, that's the whole idea. You know I like risk, adventure, challenge. Actually, I can't wait."

"Will you at least buy yourself a commission?"

"I shall try."

"The Duke of York's mistress sold commissions, but after the Parliamentary scandal, Frederick had to resign as Commander-in-Chief."

"The Regent has restored his brother as Commander-in-Chief. Frederick has an office at the Horse Guards. I've been advised to speak with his private secretary, Sir Herbert Taylor."

"Oh, Nick, is there any way I can make you change your mind?"

He winked and held his arms wide, "You're welcome to try, luv."

When the coach drew up outside the house in Berkeley Square, the well-trained butler hurried out with an umbrella. "Oh, thank you, Hopkins. You are so very considerate." Alex wanted to tell him that she liked rain, but it would have diminished his thoughtfulness.

Upstairs, the maid awaited her in her chamber to help her get ready for bed. "This is absolutely unnecessary, Sara. I am perfectly capable of undressing myself. Promise you won't wait up for me again?"

Sara bobbed a grateful curtsy. "Your grandmother asked if you'd pop in and tell her about your visit to Devonshire House."

Alex put on the nightgown and robe Sara had laid out for her. She found Dottie reading in bed, propped up by half a dozen lacy pillows and drinking Madeira.

"Ah, there you are, darling. I hear it's pissing down outside." She held up her glass. "I did the wise thing tonight; Berkeley House has a very good cellar."

Alexandra's eye was caught by a painting over the fireplace. As she drew closer, she saw that her suspicions were correct; it was an erotic painting of a nude female lying seductively upon a black leopard skin. Alex blinked; the red-gold curls framing the familiar face and upon the female's high mons gave her pause. "Death and damnation, she looks exactly like me!"

"Naturally, darling. It was one of your ancestors who posed for the painting."

"Who?" Alex asked, wide-eyed.

"Well, actually, it was me," Dottie admitted.

Alex was stunned. "But it's so . . . racy."

"Raciness is quite acceptable. A little sin in the soul makes a woman irresistible. I have done a dreadful job of bringing you up, if you think nudity is shocking. The artist left out the tattoos on my bum cheeks that say BOTTOMS UP!"

Alex spun around to look at her grandmother, but when she saw the arch look of amusement on her face, she knew she was embroidering the facts. "I had no idea I got my coloring from you."

"Ah, yes, once I was as dazzling as you are, darling. I've worn wigs so long, you don't remember. Speaking of dazzling, how did you enjoy Devonshire House?"

"It was opulent beyond my wildest dreams. The Kent-designed reception rooms are particularly sumptuous. There were more than a hundred and fifty people seated. It was like a royal dinner."

"Royalty can't hold a candle to the Devonshires . . . the Germans are a tatty lot! I hope you didn't sit with young Hatton, and instead reserved all your smiles for Hart Cavendish."

"I didn't sit with Christopher."

"Serves the young bounder right. Competition from Hartington will bring him up to snuff, mark my words."

Alex refrained from saying she didn't want to bring him up to snuff and changed the subject. "What are you reading?"

"Rousseau's *Confessions,* the bible of Romanticism. I'll let you have it when I'm done, but in the meantime you'll have to content yourself with something less prurient from my bookcase."

Alexandra ran her finger along the titles, avoiding the romances, and finally selected a book about astrological signs. She had kept all thought of Nicholas safely caged until she gained her own chamber, but once she was alone it was impossible. She relived the delicious, demanding kiss, then wondered why he had bid her good-bye, rather than good night. She did not want to examine it too closely and pushed the thought away, where it crouched like a lion, waiting to pounce.

She climbed into bed and opened the book at her astrological sign of Sagittarius. *You are an unforgettable and charming character with a blithe and friendly spirit, who attracts attention and affection.* "Ha, I wish I could attract his affection," she muttered aloud. *You always have a sparkle in your eyes, an easy laugh, and magically light up a room. Your gregarious nature and sense of humor are powerful forces in any social situation. However, you often rebel and live according to your own laws which require personal freedom.* "Well, I cannot deny that part," she admitted. *You are far more romantic than most people think. Your ideal mate will be someone strong enough to hold you, yet flexible enough to let you spread your wings.*

Alexandra's fingers rapidly turned back the pages until she found the sign of Leo the lion. *This is the ruler of all the signs. The big cat has an arrogant pride and sunny playfulness. There are no introverted or timid Leos. They are strong, determined, and dignified as they await their royal moment in the sun. He walks straight and proud with feline grace. The lion always has a commanding air and stately bearing. He holds center stage with dramatic action, and his commands are effective because he is a master of straightforward speech. The lion has a knack for telling you with a superior, condescending manner exactly how you should manage your life.* "This is what Kit has always accused Nick of doing," she murmured, "and he does it to me too."

The lion never leans on others; he prefers others lean on him. He is fierce, wild, passionate, and courageous, and can bear anything with stoic dignity. He is a spectacular gambler, who will bid higher than anybody, anytime on anything. He is a loyal friend, but a powerful enemy. Leo has a forceful temper, and often gets away with murder. Alex closed the book, slid down beneath the covers, and thought about Nick. Was it possible that he had murdered his father? No, no, murder was a coward's act, and Nicholas was the most courageous boy and then man she had ever known. She began to daydream about the kiss he had given her tonight; it had been both tender and savage. A good-bye kiss!

When Alex slept, Nicholas once again dominated her

dreams, and it seemed that indeed she *was* able to attract his affection. He kissed her for hours, in all the ways she had dreamed of being kissed. Sometimes his lips were tender and teasing, persuasive and playful, sensual and sinful. Then his mouth became rough and ravenous, hot and hungry, passionate and possessive. But finally he withdrew and stood apart from her, and she heard herself begging, "Please, Nick, please don't leave me." He would not heed her, and as he walked away, she saw that he carried a gun and wore a scarlet jacket. A feeling of dread began to overwhelm her.

A few hours before dawn, Nicholas had returned to the Hatton town house in Curzon Street with plenty of time to change from his damp, wrinkled evening clothes, bathe, shave, breakfast, and present himself to Prince Frederick's secretary, Sir Herbert Taylor, in the War Office at the Horse Guards in Whitehall.

After he introduced himself, mentioned the Prime Minister's name, and informed Taylor that he had been supplying the Guards with horses for the past year, Nick Hatton had no difficulty in purchasing himself a lieutenancy with the Royal Horse Artillery for the sum of two hundred pounds.

"The war effort is strapped for cash, my boy, as well as fighting men. In Wellington's last dispatch to Lord Bathurst, the new Minister of War, he revealed that his Spanish soldiers had been robbing, murdering, and burning so viciously he had to send them packing in disgrace."

Nick learned that he would be serving under General Rowland Hill, who was presently fighting in Spain, close to the French border. Reinforcements were sailing every week from Portsmouth to Bilboa and San Sebastian, so he could embark immediately. He went directly from the War Office to be outfitted for his uniform and equipment.

When he arrived back at Curzon Street, he found that Christopher had only just arisen. His twin was dressed for riding and intended to meet his friend Rupert in Hyde Park's Rotten Row, which was conveniently close by at the end of the street.

Kit eyed Nick's morning coat, which told him that his twin was not just crawling home from a night's debauch. "Where did you get to last night?"

"I visited a friend."

"I'm surprised you still have any, now that you are *persona non grata,*" Kit jested. "I don't remember a thing past midnight. Rupert must have brought me home and poured me into bed. The post just arrived, by the way, and it appears John Eaton sent the accounting as promised. I asked Hart Cavendish about him last night. Seems Eaton has so many wealthy clients he has opened an office here in London. He's nicknamed the Corkscrew since he can prise money out of anything. So you can stop worrying and making noises like an old woman."

"Well, I'm relieved you can get along without my advice, Kit," Nick said good-naturedly, "since I'll be leaving in a day or two."

"Leaving for where?"

"Portsmouth."

"I warrant Brighton has much to recommend it, but what the devil is in a *démodé* place like Portsmouth?"

"A ship that will take me to Bilboa. I've joined the army."

"The devil you say!" When Kit saw Nick was not jesting, he slashed his riding boot with his crop. "Well, that was a selfish, vainglorious thing to do. How the hell do you expect me to run Hatton on my own? Being a land baron carries a great deal of responsibility."

"Kit, let's be honest. You reject my advice and abhor my interference." *Learning responsibility will do you a world of good.* "We have an agreement not to meddle in each other's affairs."

"Actually, this move is absolutely brilliant on your part. A military man embodies the masculine ideal of the *ton.* In uniform you will represent all the essential male traits of honor, fearlessness, and aggression. Martial readiness paints a rugged picture of masculinity and brute strength. The *beau monde* will forgive a military man anything." Kit sounded resentful. "What's your regiment?"

"I am a lieutenant in the Royal Horse Artillery."

"You fool! You'll be on the front lines . . . in the

thick of all the gunfire." He shuddered. "Well, better you than me. What's the uniform? Blues like the Royal Horse Guard?"

"Dark blue, yes, riding breeches and short tunic jacket with gold buttons, collar, and epaulets."

"I suppose it has those tall, black riding boots that come halfway up the thigh?"

"Yes, they cover the knee to protect it."

"And a polished breastplate and helmet with black and red plumes? Christ, the women will grovel at your feet." Kit couldn't hide his envy. "What's the dress uniform?"

"I don't know. I can't afford one. And there will be no time for the women to grovel; I'm leaving tomorrow or the next day."

Alexandra hurried along Charles Street, then crossed over into Curzon Street. When she had awakened this morning, only fragments of her dreams remained with her. The strong image of Nick's red jacket and his guns floated in and out of her mind, though she tried to banish it. She remembered kissing. Had she dreamed it, or had it actually happened? Then she remembered what she preferred to forget: He had kissed her good-bye! Her dream insinuated once again and she saw Nick clearly. She suddenly realized that he was not wearing a hunting jacket, he was wearing a uniform! *Dear God, is that what he meant by good-bye?* She knew she must stop him.

As she neared the tall, stone mansion, the front door opened and Nicholas, she assumed, dressed in his favorite gray riding clothes, descended the steps. He saw her and stopped to wait. "Oh, thank heaven I have found you before you do anything rash!"

"Alex, you look particularly lovely today." His gray eyes looked her over with appreciation.

"Don't change the subject! Tell me truthfully: Do you intend to join the army?" As she gazed up at him, his dark beauty was so compelling her breath caught in her throat.

"On my sacred honor, Alexandra, I have no such intent. Where did you hear such a rumor?"

"Oh, thank God, Nick. It wasn't a rumor; it was just a silly dream I had about you."

Kit's white teeth flashed in a smile. He knew she had mistaken him for his twin, but he wasn't about to enlighten her. "You know, Alex, you shouldn't be walking the streets without an escort, or at least your maid."

"Please stop treating me like a child."

"I'm treating you like a lady, Alex. It's very sweet of you to be concerned, but I assure you I will never, ever join the army."

"Then why did you bid me *good-bye* rather than *good night*?"

"Did I do that? It was just a figure of speech, I warrant. I'm not going anywhere, and I shall probably see you at Burlington House on Friday."

Alex went weak with relief, and she felt more than a little foolish to have come running to Curzon Street like a lovesick girl. "You're going riding; I won't keep you."

"Why don't you get Rupert to take you riding in the park one morning, and I'll join you?" he asked.

Alex couldn't believe her ears. Was Nick actually inviting her to ride? Her heart skipped several beats as she thanked him and bade him a breathless good-bye.

Chapter 11

Dottie, desperate for money, decided to pay a visit to Coutts Bank. In her younger years Thomas Coutts had been an admirer, and if she remembered correctly, had once offered her *carte blanche.* Since Barclays Bank knew she did not have two coppers to rub together, Coutts it would have to be, she concluded. All the banks were in distant Lombard Street, so she decided to pay a visit to Spinks and Co. to see if the disreputable devil Spinks had sold her Lawrence paintings. If not, she'd demand an advance from the old reprobate, then take a hackney to Lombard Street.

"Oh, are you going out, Dottie? I'd love to come too; I am simply dying to have a ramble about London," Alex said eagerly.

"You don't want to be shackled to a dowager, darling. You may explore on your own, providing you take Sara with you, of course."

Alex was privately delighted at her grandmother's suggestion, for a maid would undoubtedly go wherever she led without voicing grave disapproval. She found the young maid belowstairs, ironing petticoats and some of Rupert's starched neckcloths. "I have something much more *pressing* for you to do, Sara, pun intended. I want you to accompany me about London."

Sara bobbed a curtsy. "Do you wish to go shopping, mistress?"

"No. Actually, I wish to go prowling. I need you more as a guide and fellow conspirator, than a *chaperon*. Are you game?"

Sara's eyes sparkled. "I know how to keep my mouth shut, if that's what you mean."

"That is exactly what I mean! How perceptive of you, Sara. Let me get my sketchpad and put on my comfortable half boots, and we shall be on our way. You don't mind walking, do you?"

"I'm a servant, mistress; shank's mare is my usual mode of transportation."

"When we are out together, and I warn you now that it will be often, I want you to call me Alex." She decided a little discretion might serve her at this early stage and did not tell Sara that she planned to sometimes dress as a male.

When they were safely outside the Berkeley Square house, Alex said, "Now, first I want you to show me all the exclusive men's clubs where they gamble, dine, and whatnot."

Sara raised her hand to her mouth to cover a giggle. "The closest is Alfred's." She led the way from the square along Berkeley Street to Albermarle and pointed to number 23. " 'Tis rumored to be the dullest place in existence."

Alex watched two octogenarian gentlemen enter. "I can see why!"

Sara laughed and led the way across Piccadilly. "Down there on the corner of Bolton Street is Watier's. He used to be the Prince of Wales's chef, and the food is reputed to be the best in London, not that females will ever get the chance to eat it."

Don't be too sure of that, Sara. These exclusive male haunts may have a few surprises in store!

They entered St. James's Street. "Boodle's is number twenty-eight, and Brooks's is number sixty, both on the west side, and directly facing is White's, the oldest club in London."

"Oh, I'm particularly interested in White's; it's where my brother and his friends went last night." Half a dozen fashionably dressed dandies gave Alex and Sara appraising, speculative looks before they strolled inside, but Alex ignored them, pulled out her pad, and began to draw the famous bow window.

"There's a gentleman in the window waving at you."

"Good God, as if I'd be interested in the sort of wastrel who idles away his daylight hours in a gaming house."

"You shouldn't really be here, staring, mistress. Respectable young ladies don't even drive down St. James's. This is strictly male territory, except for—"

"Except for?"

"Well, you know, dollymops—"

"Dollymops? The girls who sell mops?" Alex asked, puzzled.

"St . . . streetwalkers," Sara whispered.

"You mean prostitutes? Oh, how vastly amusing! The fellow has mistaken me for a strumpet." Alex laughed. "The cheeky sod!"

Sara hurriedly led the way into King Street. "This is Almack's. Finally, a place where ladies are allowed, but of course you must have a subscription from one of the patronesses."

"Ah, yes, my grandmother will be sure to get me a subscription. The supper balls are held on Wednesday nights, I believe, and if you don't manage a subscription you are socially dead. Is that correct?"

"I'm afraid so. It is the primary London marriage market for debutantes. There are gambling rooms to attract the gentlemen."

"Marriage market? I warrant it's more like a meat market where flesh is sold! Moreover, intelligent females are shunned, since everyone knows young women enjoy being inferior to men, and marriage is a lady's natural condition."

"Don't you wish to attend?" Sara asked in disbelief.

"Oh, I can't wait! It will supply me with endless material for drawing clever, but devastatingly cruel caricatures."

They strolled along to Pall Mall. Alex spied a pie-man and bought them a couple of pasties. Sara didn't mind eating in the street, but it was the first time she had ever seen a lady do so.

"I should like to see the theaters. How do we get to Covent Garden and Drury Lane?"

Sara was torn. She knew that Alexandra should not walk in such a seedy area but had to admit that the prospect was exciting. Stage actresses and the various classes of people they attracted to their performances were fascinating. Sara decided to compromise. "I shouldn't really take you there, but if we leave before it starts to get dark, I don't think we'll come to any harm."

Death and damnation, if she has reservations about taking me to the theater district, what will she think when I want to visit the prisons and Bedlam?

As they made their way up Charing Cross Road, Alex noticed there were far more pedestrians about, and not many in the throng were fashionably dressed. Hawkers with barrows were shouting the praises of their wares and doing a brisk business. She looked up and saw some church spires, but she also saw many taverns and smoke shops dotted among the playhouses. Their doors were ajar and the racket from inside was raucous; the smell of cheap ale, gin, and tobacco permeated the air, along with curses, screeches, and laughter. Though it was only afternoon, some patrons staggered in and out of the public houses in a drunk and disorderly fashion, spitting on the pavement and spewing in the gutter.

Sara and Alex exchanged glances, held their skirts close, and hurried past. In Drury Lane, the theaters had just finished their matinee performances, and the crowds of people leaving littered the street with orange peel, chestnut shells, bread crusts, and various other remnants of the refreshments they'd enjoyed while watching the play. Mangy dogs and pecking pigeons vied for the scraps, while the miasma of sweating humanity made Alex pinch her nostrils.

"I should never have brought you here," Sara declared.

"No, no, I absolutely love it! London isn't all Mayfair town houses and Almack's, and I am determined to see it all for myself." Alex stared at an extremely good-looking young male who was with three gaudily dressed women, none of whom were clean, young, or pretty. She wondered fleetingly whatever he saw in them, then it suddenly dawned upon her that they were whores, and he their whoremaster! She knew an overwhelming desire to sketch the tableaux but had more sense than to pull out her pad. She knew she'd have to wait until she got home, but they made such a vivid impression, she'd have no trouble remembering them.

The smoke from London's chimneys made the afternoon light fade earlier than it did in the countryside, and with great reluctance Alex decided they had better head back to Mayfair. "Well, Sara, we didn't get far, but we saw a lot. We had a late start; next time we'll go out for the whole day. This must surely be the most fascinating place in the world. I want to go into the bowels of the old walled city. I want to see London's beauty and her underbelly, but most of all I want to see her people," Alex said passionately. "Let's go back a different way."

As they walked down Long Acre, Alex was just about to buy them a drink of asses milk from a milkmaid when she saw a beggar woman with a child clutching her ragged skirts and another little mite clinging to her back. With an apologetic look at Sara, Alex gave the woman the only money she had left, then they made their way along Shaftsbury, up Regent to Conduit Street, and thus home.

Dottie arrived by hackney just as they reached Berkeley Square. "Ah, Alex, you are so like me; neither of us could resist racketing about town the entire afternoon."

Hopkins gave Sara a look of disapproval, but she returned it with one of angelic innocence. He turned his attention to Alexandra. "Flowers have arrived for you, Mistress Alexandra. I took the liberty of putting them in water."

"Oh, how lovely!" As Alex bent her head to breathe in the fragrance of the roses and freesias on the hall table, her heart raced. She read the card quickly and felt immediate disappointment. "The flowers are from Hart Cavendish," she told Dottie. "He is inviting me to attend a play tonight."

"And shall you go?"

"Oh, yes. I've been longing to visit the theater district!"

Less than three hours later, Alex sat at her dressing table while Sara fastened the small buttons that ran up the back of her jade silk evening gown. She had spent two hours sketching people and scenes she had encountered earlier, wolfed down late-afternoon tea and scones, and taken her bath.

"You know, darling, you must be fitted for a couple of new gowns. I have neglected you shamefully; your clothes are definitely not up to crack. Those puff sleeves will be *hors de mode* this winter, mark my words." Dottie was feeling most expansive, since Spinks had managed to sell the Lawrence paintings, and she had bamboozled Thomas Coutts into loaning her five thousand pounds. Of course she'd had to put up Longford Manor as collateral, but that was a mere technicality, she assured herself. She laid a ten-pound note on the dressing table. "This is mad money, darling. You can't go about London with your pockets to let." Her glance met Alexandra's in the mirror. "You won't be alone with Hart this evening, will you?"

"We are to meet Hary-O and Lord Granville at the theater, and Hart's other sister, what's-her-name, Countess of Carlisle."

"She was christened Georgiana for her mother. When she was a child they called her Little G, but now she uses her middle name, Dorothy. Named after *moi*, actually. She married George Howard, Earl of Carlisle. He's a bit of a corkbrain, but infinitely more interesting than Leveson-Gower Granville, who's a dead bore. Hary-O and Dorothy are up for any old gig—not as flighty as their mother by a long shot, but a pair of prime goers."

"I think I hear the carriage." Alex stood up from the dressing table and picked up her cloak.

"Let him cool his heels. It wouldn't do to seem to eager. I think my jade and turquoise earbobs will look splendid with that gown." Dottie's diamonds and emeralds had been pawned more than two years ago, but she clung to her semiprecious jewels for sentimental reasons.

Hart awaited Alexandra downstairs. She thanked him for the flowers and the invitation to the play. The black carriage, which had the Devonshire ducal emblem emblazoned on its door, had polished brass oil lamps fore and aft, a coachman, and a tiger in livery who sprang down from his rear platform to open the door for her. Inside, Hart sat facing her so that he would not crush her skirts, and Alex sat with lashes lowered as a refined young lady was expected to do.

That didn't last long, of course. Inside, Alex's wicked juices were bubbling as she lifted her eyes and gave him a conspiratorial smile. "I have a great desire to see Goldsmith's play *She Stoops to Conquer,* rather than the Sheridan play. Do you think your sisters would mind if we didn't join them tonight?"

Hart covered his surprise quickly and winked at her. "Do we care?"

"Not a whit," she said, laughing. "I've read Oliver Goldsmith's comedy of manners and would love to see it performed onstage. It pokes such delicious fun at the *haut monde*." She produced an eye-mask. "I shall wear this to be on the safe side; being alone with a man flaunts every convention."

Darkness covered up a multitude of sins in the theater district and lent it an air of glamour. Fashionably dressed people were alighting from carriages, oblivious to the prostitutes who were arriving in droves and the child beggars huddled in doorways. Young girls stood on every corner selling flowers or matches to gentlemen in evening attire; boys hawked playbills and lampoons.

When Alex showed an avid interest in the cartoonists' lampoons, Hart grinned down at her and paid the grimy urchin a crown for a couple of them—more than the lad usually earned in a month. In the theater foyer, it seemed that every member of the *ton* went out of his way to greet the Duke of Devonshire and cast his eye over the lucky lady with the red-gold curls who accompanied him.

They sat upstairs in a private box; when Alex enjoyed a farcical moment in the play, she laughed out loud, making Hart appreciate a companion with such a unique and natural personality who did not pay lip service to convention. He decided immediately that he would invite her once more to see Sheridan's play *The Rivals*. Since his sisters were seeing it tonight, they wouldn't be there to cramp his style.

After the play as they exited the theater, Alex took her courage in her hands. "Are some of these fashionably dressed women mistresses?"

"It's not a subject I should be discussing with you, Alex."

"Oh, I know that, but since I need educating, I didn't think you'd mind giving me lessons."

What man could resist? "Yes, the beautiful companions are mistresses, the plainer ones are generally wives. You could easily be mistaken for my mistress tonight, Alexandra," he warned gravely.

That's a step up from the strumpet I was taken for in St. James's Street today! With a straight face she inquired, "What does a mistress cost?"

"Gowns, jewels, carriage and horses, plus a house in Chelsea."

"Why are the streets filled with . . . ladies of the night?"

"Ah, the 'Duchesses of Drury Lane.' After the first act is over, the theaters lower the admission price. The doxies flock inside to ply their trade. Why does this lurid subject interest you?"

"Because it's lurid, of course," she said, laughing.

"This whole area, from the Strand to Holborn, is *quite* lurid—not at all suitable for unwed ladies, though." He tried to change the subject. "Would you like some late supper?"

"If you take me somewhere close by that's interesting."

"Well, I cannot guarantee that the company will be *élite*."

"If you could, I wouldn't want to go."

They passed a man on the corner playing a barrel organ. His tiny, red-capped monkey held out his tin cup to them, and when Hart dropped in a half crown, the fey little creature doffed his cap. Laughing, they turned down Russell Street, where Hart took her into an interesting establishment that served food and drink. It had a bar with a brass foot-rail where the patrons could stand, or they could sit at small round tables and rub elbows with the *habitués*.

Hart ordered for her, as was the custom. It was a custom Alex abhorred; though she did not object to the potted lobster *hors d'oeuvre* when it arrived, she drew the line at the ladies' drink of sherry. "How about a wager? I'll order a typical male supper of raw oysters and cognac, followed by one of your cheroots. If I get through it without casting up my accounts, you must agree to take me wherever I wish to go one night next week. If I don't pass muster, you may choose the place."

Hart Cavendish was fascinated. Alexandra Sheffield wanted to be treated as an equal, rather than being placed on a pedestal like most debutantes. "The place you want to visit must be strictly off-limits, for you to make such a drastic wager."

"Perhaps, but I shan't tell you where until the very night."

"You make the mystery so intriguing! I accept your wager." He promptly ordered them each a dozen oysters and a cognac.

Alex made short work of the oysters on the half shell; however, she knew the cognac would be a challenge. But when Hart opened his gold cigar case and offered her a cheroot, she took it without much anxiety; the Hatton twins had taught her to smoke when she was fourteen.

When he lit her cheroot with an amused look of skepticism on his face, Alex knew she had to pull it off. She sipped and puffed very, very slowly, and her eyes narrowed against the smoke. She looked about the room in a leisurely fashion until she heard sudden applause. "Isn't that the famous singer from Ranelagh Gardens?"

Hart turned his head. "Sophia Baddeley, yes. She's Melbourne's current mistress, but he and I won't acknowledge each other tonight, because I have a lady with me."

"But I'm smoking like a chimney; how will he know I'm a lady?"

"Because I will give him the *cut,* and he'll know immediately."

"Oh, Hart, how ridiculous the rules of Society are. We didn't need to attend a play that was a comedy of manners; we are *living* a comedy of manners!"

"Being with you is more entertaining than any play, Alex. You win the wager; I shall take you wherever you wish to go." He grinned at her. "Even if you had lost, I would have taken you."

"I know." She grinned back. "I just wanted to show off!"

Hart threw back his head and laughed out loud. Alex joined him and realized that the cognac had gone straight to her head. The fresh air helped sober her a little as they strolled back to where the Devonshire carriage awaited them.

Inside, she deliberately spread her cloak, her reticule, and the lampoons he had bought her along the seat, so that Hart was forced to sit opposite her again. She was sending him a message that she wanted a safe distance between them, with no attempts at kissing.

When the coach stopped in Berkeley Square, Hart inquired, "Will I see you Friday night at Burlington House?"

"Yes, we received our invitation. I shall finally get to meet your sister, Lady Dorothy Howard, Countess of Carlisle. I wouldn't miss it for the world," she assured him, her mind immediately filled with the image of Nick Hatton.

Hart escorted her to her doorstep and placed a chaste kiss on her forehead. "Thank you for a most memorable evening, Alex." When he returned to the carriage he was in a quandary. Because of his parents' disastrous marital *ménageries,* he had no desire for a wife; he had in fact sworn off marriage for life. He was the wealthiest nobleman in England and could afford any mistress he desired. But now he had a dilemma. He was badly smitten by Alex and longed to become her lover, but she was an heiress, and offering *carte blanche* to a lady with her wealth would be no inducement whatsoever.

Chapter 12

Christopher Hatton watched as Nicholas packed his trunk. He envied his twin the Royal Horse Artillery uniform, especially the firearms he had been issued. The silver-mounted flintlock pistols, made by Godsall, had twelve-inch barrels and ornate handles. Their lockplates bore the emblem of the Crown with the initials GR for *Georgius Rex*.

"You are taking your own mount, Slate?" Kit asked.

"Yes, I know his value; I bred him myself. I'll ride him to Portsmouth, and I've arranged to hire a packhorse for my baggage."

"Do you have to leave today?" Kit's tone was grudging.

"What would be the point in delaying my departure?" Gray eyes stared into identical gray for a long, drawn-out moment.

Finally, Kit broke their gaze. He felt a great deal of resentment toward his twin brother for what he had done. He truly did not mind him being an army officer, but why the hell hadn't he joined the Horse Guards, so he could be stationed in London? It was the looming separation that angered Kit. He had refused to think about it for the last two days, but now that it was Thursday, and Nick's departure was imminent, he could think of nothing else.

Kit feared that, without Nick, he would lose his identity. They were twins, for Christ's sake, a pair, always together. Twins supported each other, leaned on each other, championed each other. Now Nick was deserting him, leaving him in the lurch, and moreover, he seemed happy about doing it! A feeling of panic rose up within him, and it took a steely effort to keep it from overwhelming him. Kit asked himself what the hellfire he had done to deserve such unjust treatment from his brother.

Nicholas was quite aware that Christopher resented his going, but he honestly believed that Kit would ultimately benefit from their separation. He had long overshadowed his twin, and this would allow Kit to stand on his own two feet and become his own man.

When it was time for him to leave, Nick decided a gesture was necessary to show his brother that he needed his help. "I'm flat broke, Kit. Could you cough up a tenner for my journey?"

"You bloody fool! Why didn't you say something?" Kit emptied his pockets of all the money he was carrying, then went to his room and brought him another twenty pounds, which was everything he had in the house.

"Thanks, old man. I owe you." Nick embraced his brother, bade him take care of himself, then hoisted his trunk to his shoulder. "Don't come down with me; I have to do this on my own."

Kit stared at the door long after he had gone. *You bastard, Nick! You* prefer *doing things on your own!*

By nightfall, Christopher Hatton was dead drunk. When Rupert came to call in Curzon Street, Fenton, the butler, told him that Lord Hatton was not receiving visitors. Rupert stood there a moment or two with a furrowed brow. What the hell was his friend playing at? Then his brow cleared. "Must have a bit of muslin upstairs," he muttered to himself. "Oh, well. I suppose I shall see him at Burlington House tomorrow night."

Christopher Hatton's first order of business the next morning was Barclays. He withdrew a substantial amount of funds, reasoning that spending lavishly would banish his blue devils. Before he left the bank, however, he came face-to-face with Jeremy Eaton.

"H'lo, Harm. I was hoping I'd bump into you."

Kit bristled when his second cousin did not use his

title, but he masked his irritation because he sensed that young Eaton was there for a purpose. Since he was showing no deference, Kit was on his guard immediately. "How do you know I'm not Nicholas?"

Jeremy chuckled. "What business could Nick possibly have at Barclays when you got all the money? Unless, of course, you paid him off for taking the blame."

"I don't know what the devil you're talking about!"

"Oh, I think you do, *Harm*. Remember, I was there the day of the fatal *accident*."

The blood drained from Kit's face, and he thought he might faint. "What the hellfire are you insinuating?" he bluffed.

"I am insinuating nothing, *Harm,* though I certainly could. I know how to keep my mouth shut. I would never divulge to a soul that I was close enough to the scene of the *accident* to hear you arguing with your father in the woods that day."

Panic rose up in Kit Hatton; blood returned to his brain and his head began to pound. Nick had warned him about this slimy piece of offal, but he had ignored his twin. Kit's panic suddenly doubled; Nick was gone and would not be able to take care of this trouble. Kit silently cursed his brother for deserting him and leaving him to cope with this nightmare on his own.

Jeremy smiled. "Blood is thicker than water, cousin; you may trust me implicitly. On another subject entirely, I wonder if you would stand me a loan? I have the inside track on a good investment but find myself five hundred pounds short."

Kit knew it was blackmail, but if five hundred would keep the scurvy swine from revealing that it was he and not Nick who had fired the fatal shot, it was worth it. "I think that could be arranged," Kit said stiffly.

"Thank you, *Lord Hatton;* I hoped I could count on you."

"Don't mention it," Kit murmured politely.

"Absolutely not," Jeremy promised.

That same morning, Dottie Longford accompanied Alexandra to Madame Martine's, a very chic Paris dress shop in Bond Street. "The only time Madame Martine ever saw France was on a clear day from the cliffs of Dover, but her clothes are *haut monde.*"

The establishment was only a five-minute walk from Berkeley Square along Bruton Street, so Alex got to see none but fashionable shoppers like herself. The moment they crossed the shop's threshold, they were fawned upon, and she knew Madame Martine had recognized the wealthy dowager.

"M'granddaughter needs a gown for the Burlington House reception tonight. Something in a shade that will contrast the glorious color of her hair."

"Tonight, Lady Longford, *mais—*" Martine sounded aghast at such short notice.

"But nothing. If you cannot accommodate us, we shall go elsewhere."

"*Non, non,* it weel be my great pleazzure," Madame assured her.

"Indeed it will," Dottie agreed.

Alex hid a smile and sat down in a fragile gilt chair to wait. A shop assistant brought out two white gowns, both of which were infinitely suitable for a young debutante.

"We don't want white." Dottie waved a dismissive hand.

"But Lady Longford, white ees in such good taste."

"I deplore good taste; it's so lacking in courage."

The assistant took away the white and brought out a pink gown and another in a subtle shade of lavender. Alex tried on the latter and stood before the mirror to see if the gown liked her as much as she liked it. Tiny knife-pleats of chiffon fell from its high waist, and when she walked the effect of light and shadow made the material change color. Her eyes lit up and she was just about to say that this was the gown she wanted, when she saw Dottie place a cautionary finger to her lips.

"Mmm, it might do," Dottie said doubtfully, "but it obviously lacks something. I suppose we'll take it," she pointed her ebony stick, "if you throw in that violet wrap you have on display."

Madame Martine, seeing her profit fly out the window, protested, "But, Lady Longford, that ees the finest cashmere!"

"I should think so . . . none of your rubbishy stuff for

us. A couple of pairs of long kid gloves wouldn't be amiss. Don't lollygag about; wrap 'em up! We can't dilly-dally all day. We'll be back for a fitting for a full wardrobe when we have more time."

When they got outside the shop, Alex said, "Thank you for the gown and the lovely cashmere wrap. You are a shrewd shopper."

"I love to haggle. Had an ancestor who was a famous rug thief at a bazaar, or was it an ancestor who was famous for being *bizarre*? I forget which."

Just as they arrived back at Berkeley Square, Rupert was about to go riding in Hyde Park to see if Kit Hatton was there, since he hadn't seen hide nor hair of him for two days. When he saw Alexandra's dress box, however, his eyebrows rose to his hairline. "Madame Martine's, begod! The most expensive shop in Bond Street!"

"Do keep a civil tongue in your head when you address the ladies of the family and where they shop." Dottie looked him up and down and stared pointedly at his expensive riding breeches, weskit, and jacket. "Bond Street is no more pricey than Savile Row, I warrant." She pointed her stick in the direction of the breakfast room. "I'd like a word, Rupert."

Dutifully, he sought the breakfast room, for Dottie was too formidable for him to disobey. When she used that tone, she could render a man to cooking oil.

Dottie closed the door and spoke frankly. "How are you coming along in the heiress department? Do you have your eye on anyone?"

"Well, not yet. . . . I've been here less than a week!"

"According to the Bible, God created the earth in less than a week," she said dryly. "Rupert, to keep the wolf from our door, I was able to arrange a bank loan, and I have earmarked a thousand pounds for your business venture."

"Business venture?" he questioned uncertainly.

"The business of securing a rich wife, you young cork-brain! I shall give you five hundred now for your expenses, ring and such frippery and fallals, and five hundred when you are betrothed."

"A thousand to secure a rich wife is stretching it a bit thin."

"Think of it as a challenge, Rupert. You are titled, you have youth, passable looks, and are sound of wind and limb. What more could a gel want?"

He thought of his empty pockets. "Could I have it today?"

"I shall give you the five hundred today, if you give me your solemn word that you will not run yourself into debt. I don't want a bum-bailiff plucking you off the street and throwing you in Fleet Prison, which is what happened to your disreputable father, for I shall have neither the means, nor the inclination, to bail you out. Now, not a word of this to Alexandra. I shall set aside a thousand for her dowry, but we cannot count on her becoming Lady Hatton for at least a year, until Christopher is out of mourning." Dottie pointed to the door. "Off you go. Size up the birds you see in the park . . . and Burlington House will be fertile hunting grounds tonight; make the most of the opportunity."

Alexandra found herself intensely excited as the hired carriage drove along Piccadilly to Burlington House. She hadn't seen Nicholas since she'd rushed to Curzon Street after dreaming of him in a military uniform. Nick had made a point of telling her that he would see her tonight, and she could think of nothing else.

Rupert, his grandmother on one arm and his sister on the other, escorted them up the marble steps of the great mansion, which the Earl and Countess of Carlisle leased from the countess's brother, Hart Cavendish, Duke of Devonshire. Dottie, resplendent in orange wig and black beaded gown, played counterpoint to Alexandra's lavender chiffon.

They were greeted by Hart's grandmother, Lady Spencer, who hadn't seen her friend since Henry Hatton's funeral. "Dottie, we meet under happier circumstances. I missed you at Devonshire House last week."

Rupert spied his chance to escape, but Alex stayed beside her grandmother quietly, though inside she felt a riot of bubbling excitement. When the host and hostess stepped forward to welcome them, Alex hoped Hart's sister Dorothy would not enquire why she hadn't joined them at the theater, and she breathed a sigh of relief when her attention was taken by Alex's cashmere wrap.

Hart joined the gathering and soon spirited Alex away on the pretext of showing off Burlington House. Her glance swept the crowd for a glimpse of Nick. In the ballroom she was surprised to see Annabelle Harding and her daughter, Olivia. "Good evening, Lady Harding. Hello, Olivia."

"So, Lady Longford has brought you up to London early; how nice." Annabelle's look of vexation denied her words.

Alex noticed that Olivia Harding, usually blooming with robust health, looked decidedly peaked.

"Lord Harding and m'son, Harry, have disappeared into thin air. Have you seen them, Your Grace?"

"They're most likely in the card room, Lady Harding." Hart bowed politely and extracted Alex and himself from their company. "I always feel slightly uncomfortable when addressed as Your Grace; I much prefer being called Hart or Hartington."

Alex looked up at him with an impish look on her face. "Really, *Your Grace*? I cannot imagine why, *Your Grace*."

"You are a terrible tease, Alex. Since we're in the ballroom, I imagine you would like to dance, *mam'selle*?"

"And I imagine you are only asking because you think it your duty. I much prefer we finish the tour of the house, *Your Grace*."

They were about to ascend the sweeping staircase to the gallery, when Hart's sister Dorothy rushed up and clutched his arm. "The Regent's carriage just pulled up at the curb," the Countess of Carlisle said, all aflutter. "I had no idea he would attend tonight; please help me greet him, Hart."

Alex released him. "Go quickly; I see Dottie over there." But instead of joining her grandmother, Alex headed to the gaming room, seeking the one person with whom she longed to spend time. Her heart began to hammer as she saw the familiar tall, dark figure ahead of her in the hallway. "Nick," she called, hurrying her steps to catch up with him.

He turned with a welcoming smile that reached all the way to his gray eyes. "Alex, it's Kit. But you won't be mistaking us again anytime soon. Nick left yesterday."

"Left?" Alex caught her breath.

"Left England to join his regiment. Surely he told you, Alex?"

He gave me his word. "On my sacred honor, Alexandra, I have no such intent," he said when I asked if he had joined the army. You bastard, Nick Hatton, you deliberately lied to me! "No, actually he didn't say a word. He told me he would see me here at Burlington House tonight." Her head began to pound painfully.

"He deliberately lied to you? What a scurvy thing to do! Nick was in such a hurry; it was almost as if he was running away from something. Couldn't talk him out of it, though I tried my utmost."

He was running away from me! Dear God, I am going to faint.

"You look exceptionally lovely tonight, Alex. I'd like to paint you in that gown. . . . Its subtle color changes with the light and shadow whenever you move."

He was being gallant and paying her compliments, yet she could hardly respond; all she could think of was Nicholas. *What he told me when I suggested we marry was true. He said, "I have always thought of you as my little sister, Alex. It would be impossible for me to think of you in any other way." I didn't believe him until this minute. What a blind, stupid little fool I've been. God, how I hate you, Nick Hatton!*

Rupert joined them. "There you are, Kit. His Royal Highness, the Prince of Wales, has arrived. Oh, Alex, have you heard the astonishing news? Nick has joined the Royal Horse Artillery! How I envy him his courage."

"Some men cannot live without vainglory!" she said dismissively. "I must get a look at the Prince Regent, I hear that he is heavy as a hippopotamus these days. Do show me where he is, Rupert."

"I'll see you in the card room, Rupert, and perhaps I'll have the pleasure of seeing you later in the supper room, Alex." As Kit watched her leave, the smile on his face was most satisfied.

* * *

When Christopher passed the library on his way to the card room, he saw Olivia Harding, hovering just inside the doorway, beckon to him. "Hello, Olivia. Your family came up to London early, I see."

"Would you step inside, Kit? I have something I must tell you."

He was warned immediately by the hushed, pleading quality he heard in her voice, a marked contrast from her usual assured tone.

Her blue eyes were wide with anxiety as he took a tentative step across the library threshold. "Kit, I'm in trouble," she blurted.

He stiffened immediately. "What sort of trouble?"

"You know . . . oh, please, don't make me say it." She touched her belly. "We . . . I think I'm going to have a—"

"What the devil does that have to do with me, Olivia? Oh, I see: Nick has gone to fight the French, and this no doubt explains the reason why he ran off in such a bloody hurry!"

Olivia was aghast. "It wasn't Nick . . . it was you, Kit!"

"You are quite mistaken, Olivia," he said coldly. "We are often mistaken for each other."

"I did not mistake you, though obviously I did make a terrible mistake." The anguish in her voice was palpable. "If you won't offer for me, Kit, whatever am I going to do?"

"Olivia," he said stiffly, "you must know that when I take a wife it will be Alexandra Sheffield. It was Father's last wish before his tragic accident. It is common knowledge that it was arranged when we were children."

Olivia's face was no longer pale but flushed with the humiliation of Christopher Hatton's cold rejection. Her shoulders slumped, but she managed to lift her chin as she walked past him.

As Kit watched her depart, the satisfied smile on his face had been wiped away. All he felt was panic as he nervously brushed the hair back from his forehead. *Christ Almighty, Nick. You've only been gone a day and already the vultures are attacking their prey. First that bastard Eaton, and now Olivia-fucking-Harding! You have left me vulnerable to every scheming swine who sees easy pickings!*

Alexandra's flaming anger at Nick Hatton made her head pound and her mouth go bone dry. She lifted a glass of champagne from the silver tray offered her by a liveried footman and drained it. She put her hand to her head and knew the champagne had only made it feel worse. She decided what she needed was fresh air and went out onto the ballroom's balcony. She saw a lone female figure standing in the darkness.

"Oh, Olivia, you startled me. I have such a pounding head, I had to seek a refuge."

"I too have a terrible headache, Alexandra." She could not keep the sound of tears from her voice. "I feel quite ill."

"Oh, I'm so sorry. Are you going to be sick?" Alex asked, her hot anger suddenly replaced with sympathy.

"Of course not!" Olivia snapped. "Why would you think such a thing?"

Alex could hear the fear in her voice and guessed that what Olivia feared was gossip. She was hurt that Olivia thought her capable of starting rumors. "It was just a figure of speech. I feel like going home, but with the Regent here, it might be thought rude."

"None would ever think badly of *you,* Alexandra Sheffield!"

Alex could clearly hear the resentment in her voice, and she wondered what the devil she had done to Olivia to deserve it. "Perhaps if I have something to eat, I'll feel better. Excuse me." Food was the last thing Alex wanted, so she left the balcony and returned to the ballroom. It wasn't long before Hart came searching for her. She pasted a bright smile on her face and wondered how much longer she could endure the dreadful evening.

An hour later when Hart took her to the supper room, they found his two sisters and their husbands flanking His Royal Highness, Prince George. The food and drink with which they had plied him had obviously put him in a sentimental state of mind, for the moment he saw Alexandra's red-gold curls, he became weepy over memories of his beloved Georgiana.

"He may drown in bathos," Hart murmured to Alex.

"No such luck," she murmured back tartly. "If he sheds any more crocodile tears, it is we who may drown."

Christopher strolled into the supper room and approached Alex and Hart. "I had hoped you would favor *me* with your company for supper, Alexandra." His tone was proprietary.

Alex frowned as the pain in her head increased. What the devil had suddenly made Kit so possessive? Her glance went from him to Hart, and she thought they resembled two dogs with raised hackles.

"I refuse to be a bloody bone," she muttered, *or a bitch,* she added silently, and went to find her grandmother.

She wrapped the violet cashmere about her shoulders and turned to see Hart. He smiled at her and spoke to Dottie. "I would like your permission to give Alexandra a ride home, Lady Longford."

"By all means, my boy. And may I say how very gallant you are to offer a ride home to a young lady with her grandmother in tow."

In spite of the pain in her temples, Alex couldn't help the bubble of laughter that rose to her lips. When the carriage with the ducal Devonshire crest arrived in Berkeley Square, Hart dutifully escorted both ladies to the door and bade them a warm but circumspect good night.

Dottie and Alex ascended the stairs together. "Men are all alike, darling; they just have different faces so we can tell them apart," Dottie said, laughing.

Alex reflected miserably that that wasn't quite true. The Hatton twins were not at all alike yet had the same face, and it was almost impossible to tell them apart!

Chapter 13

Nicholas Hatton watched the Port of Plymouth and then the coastline of England disappear from the horizon. Though he deeply regretted the things he was leaving behind that would never be his—Hatton Grange and Alexandra Sheffield—he was determined to face facts and let them go. With deliberate steps, he moved forward to the bow of the frigate, symbolically turning his back upon the past and welcoming the future, no matter what it held.

The ship was crowded with infantry soldiers who were going to various regiments to augment the troops fighting the French. He had safely stowed Slate belowdecks with the other horses that were replacements for those killed in battle. While waiting for supplies to be loaded, Nick had made the acquaintance of at least a dozen soldiers who had been posted to his regiment, the Royal Horse Artillery, as well as a sergeant, Tim O'Neil, who had served in India. O'Neil, originally from Cork, still spoke with an Irish brogue.

It took only three days to reach Bilboa because the Bay of Biscay, always unpredictable, was unusually calm. Nick took Slate from the hold, and when O'Neil helped him load his baggage on the packhorse, he realized that everything he owned in the world stood there before him on the dock. Though it was a sobering thought, he was given no more time for reflection. The recruits were gathered together and a Field Captain informed them that Wellington's army was fighting and winning the battles of the Pyrenees against overwhelming odds. "In the last fortnight we have inflicted thirteen thousand casualties on Marshal Soult's army and taken seventeen hundred prisoners." A great cheer went up from the men standing on the dock. "However, when we took San Sebastian, we suffered two thousand casualties."

The raw recruits suddenly sobered. "The troops behaved badly; drunkenness gave way to pillage, arson, and rape when the town fell. Several officers, who tried in vain to restore order, were murdered by their own men. Inevitably there is anti-British sentiment here, and the Spanish are blaming the generals, even Lord Wellington himself. Be warned now that such behavior will no longer be tolerated." A blanket of silence descended.

"The Commander-in-Chief's headquarters are in Lesaca; soldiers in the Life Guards will proceed there immediately. The recruits in General Thomas Graham's divisions will proceed to San Sebastian, on the coast fifty miles east of here. Those men in General Rowland Hill's artillery division have orders to proceed south of Lesaca to Pamplona. Hill has had the town under siege for the whole of August. Wellington refuses to sacrifice men in a direct assault on Pamplona because the fortress there is impregnable. But fighting is going on in the surrounding towns."

Lieutenant Nicholas Hatton was given a map, as were the handful of other new officers, then each man who had disembarked was left to his own devices.

Nick Hatton, with the help of Sergeant O'Neil, immediately rounded up the new recruits assigned to the Royal Horse Artillery. He then organized the two dozen men into a troop, secured wagons and supplies, and set out for Pamplona, which Nick estimated would be a journey of eighty miles over hilly terrain.

Lieutenant Hatton decided to make camp early the first night. He assigned jobs to the men, and those not involved in making campfires, cooking food, or tending the horses were given a lesson in the use of their firearms and bayonets. Some of the younger men had never fired a gun in their lives, and Nick decided that they would hunt for food rather than wasting ammunition on fixed targets. Before dark descended they had bagged a small number of rabbits and game birds. By the time they were ready to move on at dawn, Lieutenant Hatton knew every man's name and the basics of his background.

At dusk, two days later, near Ostiz, a handful of French Dragoons lay in wait for them. Lieutenant Hatton gave his first rapid-fire order. "Take cover!" He decided the enemy stragglers were looking for supplies, and when he saw that his men were reasonably safe behind the wagons, he crept along the line and asked for volunteers. Only three spoke up, but Nick was willing to bet that others would follow if he and O'Neil charged the dragoons without hesitation. They killed only four but the others fled, and it was a complete rout—with only one of Nick's soldiers, young Jake Smith, catching a ball in his left arm.

They made camp immediately, and Nick had the pleasant duty of removing the ball with his knife. He washed and dressed the wound, then tore up one of his linen shirts to make the youth a sling. He took the first watch, till midnight, then bade O'Neil awaken him at four so he could also take the last watch before dawn. Already the men trusted and respected him as a leader who put their welfare before his own.

By afternoon the following day, they arrived at Pamplona. Nick reported to General Rowland Hill, who immediately gave him permanent command over the recruits he had brought with him and gave him another half dozen who had experience. He was able to keep Sergeant O'Neil as his *aide-de-camp,* and he met his immediate superior, Captain Troy Stanhope. Nick now had thirty men under his command; Captain Stanhope had four times that number.

While his men settled into camp, Nick rode the perimeters of seiged Pamplona and surveyed the ramparts of the impregnable fortress, bristling with guns. Captain Stanhope then assigned him two artillerymen to explain the siege guns, the six-pounder light guns, the various size cannon, and the caissons of artillery ammunition. Nick asked many pertinent questions so that tomorrow he could teach his men exactly what they needed to know.

It had been a long day, and Nick was grateful for the hot food O'Neil brought him, along with a bottle of Spanish wine. He washed and shaved before he retired, and as he lay abed in his bivouac tent he felt a sense of accomplishment. He rehearsed what he would say to his men tomorrow. Before their lesson on guns, he would lay down the law about drunkenness. Experience of his father's drinking had taught him it was often responsible for the vilest excesses of brutality. Nick was thankful his days had been so busy that he had had no time to waste in wishful thinking about Alex.

In London, Alexandra was doing some wishful thinking of her own. She had visited some publishing houses with a proposal for a satirical book about the *beau monde.* All had rejected the idea. They were only interested in a real-life confession and *exposé* by a leading hostess of Society, providing that it was salacious enough. So, for the moment, she realized that writing fiction was out, and picked up her sketchpad.

An hour later she had completed a satirical lampoon of His Royal Highness, the Prince of Wales, at the Burlington House reception. It was George's head on the body of a bloated hippopotamus, in a pond filled with food and drink, all floating toward his open mouth. She drew bottles of champagne, as well as peacocks, swans, and pheasants sporting alarmed looks as they neared his gaping maw. Then she sketched eels, lobsters, and oysters, trying to swim away as they awaited their turn to be devoured. She thought for a moment, then underneath the picture she printed: HIS ROYAL HIPPO ATTENDS BURLY HOUSE RECEPTION.

Alex waited until Dottie went out with Lady Spencer in her carriage, then with the help of Sara she went to Rupert's chamber and gathered some articles of clothing from his wardrobe.

"You don't really intend to go out dressed in your brother's clothes, mistress?" Sara sounded shocked.

"Don't call me mistress; it is *mister,* if you please!" said Alex, pulling on trousers with a strap that went under her instep. She fastened the shirt buttons and pleaded, "Help me with this infernal neckcloth. See, I'm growing more like Rupert every minute," she said with a grin. "God, how does the male sex put up with starched shirt points that cover their ears?"

Sara giggled. "Gives them an excuse not to hear anything a female has to say!"

When Alex tucked her red-gold curls beneath the brown tie-wig, Sara stood shaking her head in disbelief. "I'd never know you were a girl."

"I'm not a girl; I'm a woman, a devious woman," Alex asserted. "Now, if my grandmother returns while I'm out, pull the lace curtain back on the upstairs front window as a signal."

Alex walked to the office of William Cobett, who turned out a weekly newspaper advocating reform called the *Political Register*. She asked to speak with the editor, and her spirits lifted as the man looked at the lampoon she had drawn and gave a great guffaw.

"I'll take it," he said decisively. "Four bob."

Alex blinked. "Four shillings?" Her spirits sank. "Surely, it's worth a guinea?"

" 'Oo the bleedin' 'ell do ye think ye are, Cruickshank?"

Alex knew well that George Cruickshank was London's leading caricaturist, whom Society feared with a vengeance. She began to bargain and finally lowered her price to five shillings.

"Four bob, take it or leave it! Maybe next time I'll raise it to five, or 'ow about an article on reform? Climbin' boys, or reducin' child-labor hours? Somethin' to pull the 'eartstrings, and sell papers."

Alex thought it over and agreed to the four shillings. As she walked back to Berkeley Square, she turned the money over in her pocket. *What a pittance! It's a bloody good thing I don't have to earn my own living.*

Tonight was the night that Hart Cavendish was to pay his lost wager and take Alexandra wherever she wanted to go. Once again she called on Sara to conspire with her. She needed to borrow evening clothes from Rupert, but had to wait until he finished dressing and left for the night. Alex poked her head around his chamber door and whistled with appreciation. "Death and damnation, Rupert, who the devil are you trying to impress?" He was wearing new black satin knee breeches and a new blue brocade evening coat.

"That's for me to know, and you to find out, Miss Inquisitive."

"*Cherchez la femme,* unless I miss my guess!" Alex chortled.

Rupert colored. He had learned from Harry Harding that his sister, Olivia, was definitely in the marriage market and her family would welcome a viscount with open arms. Harry had told him confidentially that the entire family would be at Almack's tonight, and Rupert was determined to put his best foot forward. The only thing that bothered Rupert was the fact that Kit had shown a marked interest in Olivia, and he knew he could make no definite plans regarding the heiress if Kit was still interested.

"Good night, and good hunting!" Alex called after her brother as she watched him descend the stairs and pick up his hat and cane. Then she slipped into his chamber and took his black formal clothes from his wardrobe. For good measure she also took his black evening cape.

Sara helped her into her brother's starched white shirt and assisted her in arranging the neckcloth. Alex was almost ready when they heard the carriage. "Sara please go down and tell Hart Cavendish not to come in, but to await me in the carriage."

Sara blinked. "I will go down and *ask* the duke if he would be so kind as to await you in the carriage."

Alex laughed. "Don't worry, Sara. He *will* be so kind." She draped the cape over her male attire, hid Rupert's best wig beneath it, and grabbed a hand mirror. She passed Sara on the front steps as she was coming back into the house. "I left Dottie a note, filled with evasions of course. Thank heaven she is late."

Hart opened the carriage door from the inside and helped her up. "Where am I taking you?" he asked with a grin.

"Hold this," she said, thrusting the hand mirror at him. "I'll tell you in a moment." She positioned the mirror he was holding, whipped out the tie-wig, pulled it over her hair, and tucked in the straying curls and wisps. Then she threw the cape from her shoulders to reveal her formal male attire and answered his question. "You are taking me to White's."

Hart's mouth fell open. "Alexandra, you cannot be serious!"

"I have never been more serious in my life."

"I cannot take you to White's; it is a club for males only."

"Hence the male attire. Oh, Hart, don't turn all prudish; please go along with this mad lark."

His glance traveled over her from head to toe, then back up again. "If I wasn't honoring a wager, I would refuse you, Alex."

She began to laugh. She was well aware he would have refused if she'd asked him to take her. That's why she'd made the wager. Making good on a bet was a point of honor for gentlemen of the *ton*.

Hart Cavendish held his head high as he and his companion strolled into White's, but he could not prevent the two spots of color on his cheekbones. He took Alex into the dining room, not because he was ravenously hungry but because it would delay the hour when he must take her into one of the gaming rooms.

Alexandra immediately noticed that the deference rendered to a Duke of the Realm was above and beyond that which ordinary mortals received. Everyone from doormen to porters and waiters bowed and scraped the moment they departed the carriage with the Devonshire ducal crest on its door. Even the other members who were at White's tonight went out of their way to greet Hart, revealing that they were both eager and flattered to be acknowledged by a duke.

Alex perused the menu, trying to decide what to eat for dinner. The waiter gave all his attention to Hart, who ordered rump of beef with shallots and mushrooms and was about to order for her when he caught the warning look in her eye. "I shall have roast duck stuffed with oysters and walnuts." The waiter took her order without even looking at her. When Hart ordered a bottle of Burgundy, Alex added, "I'll have rum shrub." This was a popular drink she had never tasted, made with rum, lemon, sugar, and almond.

When Hart saw that none paid particular attention to

Alexandra, he began to relax and enjoy their conspiracy, though he was still nervous about taking her into the gaming rooms. They both declined dessert; Hart was about to reach for his cigar case and order a brandy when he thought better of it, knowing that Alex likely believed what was good for the gander was also good for the goose.

Alex leaned closer across the table. "I want to read the infamous betting book."

Hart rolled his eyes and moaned in mock resignation. "Is there no depth of male folly to which you will not sink?"

"I'm not sure; I'm not yet familiar with all your follies."

Hart led the way toward the front bow window, where the betting book was kept on a nearby high desk. Alex ran her fingertips over the great leather-bound volume, wondering if she was the first female to ever open and read it. She saw that many of the entries were mundane bets on horse races at Epsom or Newmarket, cricket games or boxing matches, but every so often there was an entry that seemed utterly preposterous. On a rainy April day, Lord Alington had bet a friend a thousand pounds on which of two drops of rain would first get to the bottom of the glass in the bow window!

There were pages of bets regarding various battles in the Peninsular War, and Alex closed her eyes and offered up a silent prayer to keep Nick Hatton safe. When she opened her eyes she saw a bet that His Royal Highness, the Prince of Wales, had made. "Good God, even Prinny records his wagers in this book!"

Hart laughed. "The most outrageous bet he ever made was with the late Charles James Fox. They wagered on which side of Bond Street the most cats would be found. The wily Fox, knowing how felines liked sunshine, took the sunny side and won thirteen to naught!"

Alex imagined the ridiculous picture the pair must have made, searching for cats up and down Bond Street. "You will be relieved to know that I do not wish to place a wager in the book; there is a limit to my folly. However, I am avid to go into a gaming room."

When Hart adamantly refused to allow Alex to buy her own counters, she did not argue, for all she had was the ten pounds pin money that Dottie had given her. They walked around the room, and when Hart saw that Alex was paid no particular attention, he relaxed his vigil and sat down to play baccarat, while Alex stood to watch. In a short time she wandered off, curious about the other games of chance in the smoke-filled room.

Alex stopped to watch a game of *vingt-et-un*, or twenty-one. Just as she decided to sit down to try her luck, she felt someone pinch her bottom! She turned around quickly to find two gentlemen behind her but could not decipher which one was guilty. One was Lord Brougham, and Alex blushed furiously, thinking he may have recognized her. She turned back to the game and waited apprehensively for Lord Brougham to say something. She heard nothing, but all at once she certainly *felt* something. It was Brougham's hand caressing her buttock. She mastered the urge to slap his face and slipped away, back to the safety of the duke.

Hart was raking in his winnings. When he stood up from the table, Alex confessed in an urgent whisper, "I'm afraid I have been recognized. Lord Brougham pinched my bottom!"

Hart Cavendish looked angry. "I don't think he recognized you, Alex, but for pity's sake stay away from the old rue."

"But he must know I'm a female, Hart, or why would he touch me there?"

Her companion stared down at her with a perplexed look on his face. "How the devil am I to explain such behavior to you?" He ran his hand through his blond hair a couple of times, then said carefully, "There are some men who are attracted to boys, Alex."

She thought that over for a moment, then for clarification asked, "You don't mean *sexually* attracted?"

"I'm afraid I do, shocking as that must seem to you."

Alex found it more puzzling than shocking, but the thing that filled her with chagrin was that young males in society were well-informed about the facts of life, while females were kept in virtual ignorance. "Lord Brougham has a wife," she said tentatively. "Do you suppose she knows?"

"Good God, no. Such a vice is not bandied about, Alex," he said repressively. "It would cause a horrendous scandal."

Alex tucked the information away, delighted that she was becoming privy to the salacious peccadilloes of the *beau monde*. She had enjoyed herself excessively, and as they drove back to Berkeley Square, she told Hart and thanked him for being such a good sport. She covered her male attire with the long evening cape and removed her brother's tie-wig. "My grandmother may still be up." She ran her fingers through her hair to ruffle the flattened-down curls.

"Let me do that," Hart said huskily.

Before she knew it, he was beside her with his long fingers threaded through her hair. "You have a natural audacity that calls out to me." He held her captive for his kiss.

Alex took a deep breath and knew she must tell him how she felt. It was unfair to let him think she wanted him to romance her. "Hart, you are going too quickly. I just want us to be friends; I have no interest in marriage."

He looked into her eyes and smiled. "I have no interest in marriage either, my sweet."

Alex was startled. "Oh" was all she could think of to say, then his lips claimed hers in a lingering good night kiss. On the spot she decided it was lovely. It was not, however, as cataclysmic or heart-stopping as Nick Hatton's. "Good night, Hart." She slipped from the carriage and ran into the house before he had a chance to do anything more.

At Almack's, Rupert danced with Olivia Harding three times; not in succession, of course, but it was enough to alert her mother, Annabelle, that the solution to their family's delicate and pressing problem could be at hand. She made her way to the gaming room and made a furtive sign, beckoning her husband and son.

"Lady Longford's grandson is showing a marked interest in Olivia," Annabelle said with great urgency.

"I was the one who dropped a hint to Rupert that Olivia was on the marriage block," Harry Harding murmured, "and assured him our family would be here tonight."

His mother bestowed a look of approval upon him and said to Lord Harding, "Rupert inherited his grandfather's title years ago, and I believe he turned twenty-one a few months back. Do you think we might consider a viscount for Olivia?"

"If we don't act with alacrity, we will be lucky to get a commoner to offer for the little wanton!"

"Hush, for pity's sake, my lord. It is only *innocent* girls who can be seduced and brought to the brink of ruin." Her voice held a note of accusation that plainly said she spoke from experience.

"Hhmmph," Harding replied, remembering well just how fecund a debutante Annabelle had been. "Better get back down to the ballroom and seize upon any opportunity that presents itself. Viscount Longford would be a gift from the gods."

Annabelle Harding found Olivia in the supper room, with an attentive Rupert fetching her ratafia.

Rupert bowed gallantly. "May I bring you some refreshment, Lady Harding? A glass of ratafia, perhaps?"

"My lord," Annabelle addressed him formally, "it does my heart good to see a young man with such fine manners. Might I be so bold as to ask for a small sherry and a slice of seed cake?" When he left to do her bidding, she turned to Olivia. "Do you think you can bring him up to scratch?"

Olivia blushed. "I'm trying, Mamma."

"Hint that you often take a carriage ride in the park in the afternoons." Her mother plucked the lace fichu from Olivia's *décolletage* to display her daughter's ample cleavage. "If he takes the bait and meets you, you must have him escort you home and invite him in for tea. Just get him into the parlor and your father and I will do the rest."

Chapter 14

In Pamplona, Spain, summer weather spilled over into September, keeping conditions hot, dry, and dusty. Military food supplies were scarce, and Wellington had made it plain that soldiers would have to forage and live off the land. Lieutenant Nicholas Hatton taught every man under his command to hunt for food, then turned a blind eye as Sergeant O'Neil taught them to filch poultry, eggs, and vegetables, as well as fodder for their animals, from the farms in the vicinity. At the same time Hatton and O'Neil taught the men to be ever vigilant for ambush as they scouted the countryside and to be on guard every moment when they patrolled around the walls of the seiged town.

Hatton set his own rules for his own men. Drunkenness was forbidden, and he commanded that they form bonded pairs and foursomes so that they never hunted or patrolled alone. After one of his men caught a bullet in the shoulder from the ramparts of the seiged fortress, he taught them to be one another's eyes and ears. "You must watch one another's backs. We all have strengths and weaknesses. The stronger must watch out for the weaker; for all to survive, you must be your brothers' keepers." It was a concept Nick had practiced all his life. The men learned the wisdom of this when one of Captain Stanhope's lieutenants was killed by an enemy bullet from those same ramparts. Stanhope immediately put the dead lieutenant's men under Hatton's command, doubling the size of Nick's troop less than a fortnight after he arrived at Pamplona.

* * *

In London, Christopher felt the weight of his responsibilities as Lord Hatton. Invariably, he found that a double whiskey in the morning lightened his spirit. Kit was feeling no pain when John Eaton, the Corkscrew, paid him a visit in Curzon Street.

"I trust when you received the accounting I sent last month, Lord Hatton, that you found it to your complete satisfaction?"

Kit, who had not exactly scrutinized the lists of stocks and investments he had inherited, waved a negligent hand and urged, "Please call me Christopher, just as you used to call my father Henry. You were cousins, after all, John."

"Not only cousins but good friends too, Christopher. He relied upon me to keep him advised about fail-safe investments when they presented themselves, and I shall do the same for you, my boy. That is the reason I am here today. This war is a golden opportunity for those who seek to make a killing. If you will study the market and choose the right investments, they will return your money a hundredfold. You must make your money work for you."

"John, my responsibilities as Lord Hatton will make it almost impossible for me to spend my days studying the market. My twin has deserted me for the glory of fighting in the war, which doubles my burden. You are in a far better position to know where to invest my money. I shall trust your judgment implicitly."

"Rather than take ready cash from the bank, I suggest you take out a loan against Hatton property and sink it into new investments."

"Who do I see about securing a loan? And what would be a fair amount of interest the bank should charge?" Kit asked vaguely.

"No need to bother with the bank, my boy. I shall be more than pleased to lend you the money—at a lower interest rate than the bank would charge—and put it straight into solid investments. There is the bonus here too of doing your part for the war effort. Winning a war takes more than playing soldier, you know."

"So I imagine, John. Actually, I've had some large expenses lately. My bank account seems rather depleted."

"No need to worry about money. I shall deposit funds into your account as you need them." Eaton pulled a paper from his leather case. "Just sign this authorization, giving me power to act on your behalf in all your financial business affairs, and I shall take care of everything, just as I did for your father."

"I appreciate this very much."

Eaton held up his hand. "I am merely doing my job. My London office is on Jermyn if you need me for anything, Christopher."

Before matters became serious between himself and Olivia Harding, Rupert called round to see Kit at Curzon Street. "I've seen precious little of you the last couple of days. What have you been doing with yourself?"

"Actually, I've been scouting the galleries and art shops for paintings that appeal to me. Father never had much use for art—thought my hobby unmanly—and it occurred to me that I am now free to indulge my tastes. Spending his money on paintings gives me perverse delight, Rupert. What have you been up to?"

"Don't laugh, but I've decided to enter the marriage market."

Kit looked horrified. "Has a maggot eaten your brain?"

Rupert could not bring himself to confess to his best friend that he was penniless and must marry for money, especially not now that Kit was Lord Hatton and had just come into his fortune. Therefore, he lied, "I inherited my grandfather's title, Viscount Longford, but the bulk of his money doesn't come to me until I am twenty-five. Actually, Kit, I've been on a pretty short string lately, and I am sick and tired of being in queer street."

"Why the devil didn't you tell me you were temporarily short of funds? You know I have plenty! No need to commit suicide and marry. You haven't pledged yourself yet, have you?"

"Well, no, that's the thing, you see. I wanted to be sure you had no proprietary feelings for Olivia Harding before I committed."

Kit Hatton paused before he replied. *Here is a perfect solution to a problem that is not rightfully mine.*

Damn, now I will have to do an about-face. "Rupert, I had no idea you had Olivia in mind. That puts a different complexion on things! I have no proprietary feelings for her, but Nicholas certainly had. Their relationship was becoming so serious, I thought they'd make a match of it. Heiresses as attractive as Olivia don't cross our path every day, you know. If I were you, old man, I'd snap her up while my twin is off playing soldier."

"Do you think Olivia was in love with Nick?"

"More than likely she was, Rupert. Tall, dark, dangerously virile men play havoc with women's hearts, but look on the bright side: If she's on the rebound, she will fall into your arms."

"Well, truth to tell, Olivia seems to be quite receptive, but I don't look forward to presenting myself to Harding. You know what an officious air of authority he has."

"Rupert, you are Viscount Longford; your grandmother is rich as Croesus. You are one of the most eligible bachelors in *England,* let alone *London.* Harding should grovel at your feet! I would advise you not to appear too eager. I warrant Harding will double her dowry, especially if you are reluctant to wed immediately."

"But I'm *not* reluctant to wed immediately; that's what I need."

"Christ, Rupert, don't be the carpenter of your own cross! Harding doesn't know that. Drag your feet, and Olivia's old man will throw money at you."

"Thanks, Kit. You do wonders for my self-esteem. Don't know what I'd do without you."

"That's what friends are for, Rupert." *You scratch my back, I'll scratch yours.*

Alex helped Sara to brush and sponge Rupert's black formal attire and hang it back in his wardrobe. Then she helped herself to a pair of fawn trousers, a russet jacket, and an ecru waistcoat. "I'm going out this afternoon, Sara. Would you come with me?"

Sara eyed the male attire. "Are you wearing those, *sir*?"

Alex laughed. "You have a quick mind; that's why I like you."

"Where do you plan to go?"

"I intend to explore farther afield, in a poorer section of the city. I want to write an article about a worthy cause, and I need to sketch something that tugs at the heartstrings."

"That shouldn't be hard to find; there's heartbreak 'round every corner in London. We're so lucky to live in Mayfair."

Alex pulled on the trousers and tucked in Rupert's shirt. "Yes, Sara, I know. Where were you born?"

Sara hesitated, then answered vaguely, "North, up past Soho."

"Shall we go there today?"

"No, miss," Sara said quickly. "Let's go along the river. We could visit Whitefriars and perhaps go as far as Blackfriars Bridge. If our time runs short, we can take a boat back."

"Good idea. We'll save even more time if we take a hackney cab to Charing Cross and walk from there."

There was nothing remarkable about the couple who climbed from the cab at the Golden Cross Hotel except that the young man carried a sketchpad under his arm. Alex gazed up at the huge lion atop Northumberland House and fleetingly thought of Nicholas. *Devil take you, Nick Hatton.* They strolled through Hungerford Market, where Alex made a quick sketch of a fish stall that sold everything from cockles and winkles to cods' heads and black eels, a few of which were still writhing. Finally, the fishy stink drove them out the back entrance by the river and they stood on the Hungerford water-stairs near Warren's Blacking Factory to catch their breath. The stench from the river, however, propelled them to hurry east toward the Temple.

On Thames Street the odor improved as the air became redolent with malt from a brewery. The people on these streets were raggedy and dirty, especially the children, who ran about barefoot. When a pathetically thin little girl with matted hair begged, "Spare a penny, mister?" Alex put aside her sketchpad to find some coins for the child, but suddenly her attention was diverted by something that really caught at her heart.

A chimney sweep and his assistant were making their

way toward the brewery. Both were covered with black soot from head to foot, and Alex was outraged that the apprentice was a little boy who she thought could not possibly be older than five. "How old is that child?" Alex blurted.

"I'd say eight, if it were any of yer bleedin' business!"

"He's too small to be eight."

" 'Ee's small so 'ee can squeeze up chimbleys, mate." The sweep twirled his long-handled brush, which rested on his shoulder, deliberately sending a cloud of black smut toward Alex.

"You don't mean to tell me you actually send that child clambering up chimneys?"

"No, 'ee sits in the parlor eatin' bread an' 'oney, while I do the dirty," the sweep replied with typical cockney sarcasm.

"I want to draw you both."

"Sod off, mister!"

"I'll pay you a shilling."

"*Two* bob . . . chimbley sweeps is lucky."

Alex agreed but had more sense than to give him the money before the drawing was complete. When she looked closer at the little boy, a lump came into her throat; she could see that his knees and elbows were covered with burn scars beneath the soot and that his hair was badly singed. But it was the child's look of hopelessness that made her eyes flood with unshed tears.

After Alex paid him the money, she could not bear to watch the sweep take the child into the brewery. "My God, Sara, house chimneys are bad enough, but the thought of the tall factory chimneys is unendurable!"

"Sweeps are wicked, cruel masters. They starve the boys, so they'll stay undersized, and I've heard tell they light fires under them to make the poor little mites climb faster."

"Let's go home, Sara; I've seen enough." Sadly, Alex turned toward the river to find a ferry.

When the two young women entered the house, the first person they encountered was Dottie. She swept them with an arch glance and said to the maid, "Though you make an attractive couple, don't allow the young bounder to talk you into eloping."

"Oh, Dottie, please don't cavil at my wearing Rupert's clothes. They make it so much easier for me to go about London, and I did have Sara with me, as you advised."

"If you think I've never impersonated a male, think again. I advise a little discretion though. Don't allow Christopher Hatton to see you in trousers, if you expect to become Lady Hatton."

"I encountered the most heartrending situation today. I saw a chimney sweep who had a little helper no older than five or six."

"London is chockablock with social injustice, darling. Child workers, particularly climbing boys, should be against the law. I read in the paper there's a hearing tomorrow in the House of Commons on that very subject."

"Then I shall attend!"

"Ah, then they'll have an audience of one. Unfortunately, there isn't an iota of interest in reform, which can be blamed directly upon His Royal Haughtiness. *Ninny* would be a more apt sobriquet than *Prinny,* I warrant."

"I made a sketch of the sweep and his climbing boy, but I want to do a few more while they are still so vivid in my mind."

"And I had better get the soot specks off the viscount's marino wool jacket if we don't want him to have apoplexy," Sara murmured.

At that moment, the least of the viscount's worries was his jacket. He had been riding in the park for an hour, hoping to encounter Olivia Harding, but feared he had missed her. He was about to ride over the Serpentine bridge toward Rotten Row, when he saw her riding in an open phaeton beneath a parasol. Rupert removed his hat and gave her a warm greeting, and he was both surprised and pleased that Olivia ordered her driver to stop.

"Rupert, how very romantic of you to remember I would be in the park in the afternoons." She closed her parasol and handed it to the maid who sat across from her. "Can I persuade you to come and ride with me?" She patted the seat beside her, fanned her lashes to her cheeks, then raised them to gaze at him with large brown doelike eyes, by far her prettiest feature.

"It would be my pleasure, Mistress Harding." Rupert dismounted. "May I tie my horse behind the carriage?" He climbed in, sat down beside her, nodded to the maid, and placed his hat on the seat.

"Rupert, you have my permission to call me Olivia. Longtime friends permit liberties." She smiled coyly, then shared her carriage rug with him by placing it across his lap.

He was about to protest that he didn't need its protection on such a warm day when he felt Olivia's hand upon his thigh. He flushed slightly and glanced at the maid but saw that her attention was riveted upon Hyde Park's trees. He quickly covered Olivia's ungloved hand with his, then was at a complete loss whether to move it or not.

Olivia, however, was not at a loss. She quickly turned her hand into his so that their palms met, then she gave his hand a meaningful squeeze.

Her actions aroused him instantly, and much to his embarrassment he hardened and lengthened to within an inch of their clasped hands. Trying to be discreet, he slowly slid their hands away from his groin but in doing so found that their clasped hands now rested in Olivia's lap. "Forgive me," he begged.

Olivia gripped his fingers tightly to prevent their escape. "I love it when you are impetuous," she whispered intimately and dragged his hand across her thigh to rest upon her plump mons.

Rupert's cock began to pulse wildly, and he was thankful for the lap robe. He had enjoyed a fair number of sexual encounters with various *women*, but this was the first time he had ever crossed the forbidden boundaries with a debutante of good family. It slowly began to dawn upon him that perhaps sensuality was something a good girl could possess. The thought excited him beyond measure and gave him the courage to explore this new idea. Almost imperceptibly, Rupert stroked his thumb across Olivia's pubic bone, and he watched with delight as her pupils began to dilate. As he felt the heat of her feminine core radiate upward into his hand, he pressed down and applied a circular motion. He was rewarded when Olivia began to squirm with his toying and teasing and drew in a long, quivering breath. Her obvious arousal made his cock buck uncontrollably, and he knew that part of his excitement was due to the forbidden factor of what he was doing, especially while sitting directly across from her maid.

Olivia opened her legs to give him greater access. She looked up into his eyes and said breathlessly, "Rupert, I want you to come inside."

His mouth went dry at the blatant invitation.

"I want you to come inside . . . for afternoon tea."

Rupert blinked and realized that they were drawing up before the Harding town house on Clarges Street. After a moment of panic, he grabbed his beaver hat to cover himself, scrambled from the carriage, and helped her down from the phaeton.

Olivia turned to her maid. "Have a groom take care of his lordship's horse, Emily." Then she took possession of Rupert's arm and held him captive until he was in the Harding parlor. When she saw that the room was empty, she moved against him and lifted her chin in invitation.

Rupert dipped his head and sought her lips. Her mouth clung to his and her lips opened softly, sweetly, luring him inside. He almost came out of his skin when he heard a woman clear her throat.

"You are just in time for afternoon tea, Lord Longford. May I take the liberty of calling you Rupert?" Annabelle asked archly, extending her hand.

Since he had taken some liberties of his own, Rupert could hardly refuse. He bowed low over her hand and relinquished his beaver, which he no longer needed now that his cock had shriveled.

While they waited for tea to be served, Olivia chatted incessantly about how thrilling her ride in the park had been, and Rupert felt a measure of relief when the tea cart was rolled into the parlor. He found himself at a disadvantage, however, holding a cup and saucer in one hand and balancing a plate of watercress sandwiches on his knee when Lord Harding happened upon the scene.

"Don't get up," Harding ordered him. "Paying your addresses to m'daughter, are you m'boy?"

"Yes, sir; that is, with your permission I hope to pay my addresses, Lord Harding."

"You're not *toying* with Olivia, are you Sheffield?" Harding bent an agate eye upon him, and Rupert wanted to slide under the chair, hearing the verb her father had chosen.

"I assure you, my lord, my intentions are completely"—his tongue stuck to the roof of his mouth—"honorable."

"Ha, 'course they are; my little jest! Let's see now, you inherited your grandfather's title, what?"

"Yes, sir; Viscount Longford," Rupert said lamely.

"Which carried a substantial inheritance, I understand?"

Before Rupert could decide whether to answer in the affirmative or the negative, Annabelle arose from the settee and swept her daughter from the room on a flimsy pretext, which meant that they would leave the men alone so that they could discuss money matters.

Rupert swallowed hard and remembered the advice his best friend, Kit Hatton, had given him. "I came into my inheritance when I was eighteen, sir." Rupert did not tell him that he had gone through it like a dose of salts, as Dottie so graphically put it.

"So, you are in the marriage market, are you, young sir?"

"The subject of a prospective bride has crossed my mind, Lord Harding; however, I wouldn't deprive Olivia of the fall and winter entertainments. I don't believe these things should be rushed."

"Since the Season started, I've already turned down two offers for my daughter's hand. A young woman with eight thousand a year will be snapped up quicker than a trout fly."

"Amazing how small a dowry will attract fortune hunters, but with a father as diligent as you are, my lord, I am sure Olivia will be safe until the end of the year."

Harding's eyes narrowed with suspicion. *Does the*

young devil know my daughter's shameful secret? Both he and his wife suspected the culprit was that rakehell Nicholas Hatton, who had just bolted across the channel to fight Napoleon. Until he had shot his father, they had anticipated a marriage between Nicholas and Olivia, but after that fateful weekend, it was out of the question. Harding sighed heavily. "To my way of thinking, the social whirl and being presented at Buckingham Palace fills a young girl with conceit. I'd prefer it if Olivia avoided the entire thing, what?"

Against his better judgment, Rupert clenched his fists until his fingernails dug into his palms, and he doggedly clung to Kit's advice. "I'm sure Olivia would be disappointed, my lord."

"Not a bit of it. She's not one of your flighty girls with her head in the clouds. I might see my way clear to increase her dower to ten thousand per annum for an early wedding. Your grandmother, Lady Longford, for all her wealth would not sneeze at that amount, what?"

Rupert slowly uncurled his fingers and let out his breath. *Kit was right! And perhaps Dottie can persuade him to raise it a bit. By Jupiter, with that much per annum I'll be able to own a racing curricle and matched pair!* "My grandmother does not discuss her wealth with me, Lord Harding. The viscountess is extremely closedmouthed when it comes to her money and investments."

"Yes, yes; rightly so, rightly so!" Harding got to his feet. "Annabelle! Ah, there you are m'dear. We must issue a dinner invitation to Lady Longford immediately. Who knows, soon we may be one happy family, what?"

Rupert felt sure that Dottie would be impressed with the progress he had made; he had even impressed himself! Moreover, once the betrothal was a *fait accompli,* she would give him the other half of the money she had promised him. *Every little bit helps!*

When he returned to Berkeley Square, he found his grandmother in the dining room sipping an aperitif before dinner. "You will be receiving a dinner invitation from Lord and Lady Harding. I am paying court to their daughter, Olivia, and naturally they want to be assured of our wealth from the horse's mouth, so to speak."

"I may be an old gray mare, but I'm not ready for the knacker's yard quite yet. May I say well done, my boy? You have outdone yourself; Harding has money to burn! What's the catch?"

"*I'm* the catch, Dottie. I shall make Olivia Harding the Viscountess Longford. Lord Harding was so eager that he promised to up Olivia's dowry for an early wedding."

Alex, who had just come into the dining room, heard her brother's news. Like mercury her mind flashed back to the night of the masquerade ball when she had seen the harlequin slip off to the lake with a female who had sounded like Olivia. "Oh, Rupert, you haven't gotten her in trouble, have you?"

"In trouble? What the devil are you talking about?" Rupert was in high dudgeon at his sister's insinuation.

"Early *weddings* are often the result of early *beddings,*" Dottie explained dryly.

Rupert suddenly recalled Kit's words: *"I have no proprietary feelings for her, but Nicholas certainly had. Their relationship was becoming so serious, I thought they'd make a match of it." Does Kit have suspicions? Is that how Kit knew Harding would throw money at me for an early wedding?* Rupert immediately closed his mind to such unsavory suspicions. Not only was Olivia considered to be an innocent young lady but he didn't want to examine circumstances too closely; beggars could not be choosers. "I know everyone thought Olivia would make a match with Nicholas Hatton, and I know that tall, dark, dangerously virile men play havoc with ladies' affections, but I assure you Olivia did not lose her heart to him."

Complete silence blanketed the dining room. Dottie tried not to look cynical. Alex tried not to look devastated.

Chapter 15

Alex, attired in Rupert's clothes, sat in the House of Commons, furiously scribbling notes about the evidence that was being given to the Parliamentary Committee on climbing boys. Then she wrote her article for the *Political Register* before she left the House.

DEATH OF A CLIMBING BOY

More than two years ago, a chimney sweep by the name of Grundy was hired to sweep a chimney at Calvert's Factory in Upper Thames Street. He was accompanied by one of his climbing boys, eight-year-old Tom Boggs. When they arrived, Grundy put out the fire, which had already been burning for six hours, and sent the boy down the chimney from the roof.

The boy became stuck in the narrow flue, and the red-hot pipe inside the chimney caused the child to burn to death in inexpressible agony. Though they knocked down part of the chimney to remove him, all attempts to restore life were ineffectual. Upon examination, it was found that the child's elbows and knees had been burned to the bone as well as the fleshy parts of the legs and most of the feet, which is evidence that the suffering child attempted to climb from the chimney as soon as the horrors of his situation became apparent.

His efforts were in vain.

The Committee that delivered this report to

Parliament recommended that the use of climbing boys be prohibited. This writer fears that their efforts, which took more than two years, will also be in vain. Attendance at this hearing was sparse. Few members of the nobility or clergy bothered to attend. Those who did attend talked or slept throughout the presentation. The chances of these recommendations being carried out are as slim as eight-year-old Tom Bogg's chances were for surviving to adulthood.

Alex turned in the article at the newspaper office, accompanied by two drawings. One was of a sweep and his soot-covered climbing boy with sad, hopeless eyes; the other was a caricature of the Members of Parliament eating, drinking, and sleeping on the benches while a speaker droned on unheeded. She received the grand sum of seven shillings for her efforts. *If only one person reads my article and feels outrage, it will be worth the pittance,* she thought to herself as she made her way home.

Rupert called around to Curzon Street so he could tell Kit his good news. "I believe congratulations are in order. I took your shrewd advice, for which I am deeply grateful, and pushed old man Harding into upping the ante to ten thousand a year."

"Then congratulate you I do! I gave the advice, but you acted upon it; two heads are better than one."

"Well, I warrant a twin knows that better than any. By the way, do you miss Nick excessively?"

"I'd be lying if I said I didn't miss him. A twin isn't just a brother; he is a part of yourself. I wish he hadn't run off, but I know he had his reasons."

Rupert changed the subject. "I haven't exactly made plans for the wedding yet, but when I do, I want you to be my groomsman."

Kit Hatton had the decency to flush. *Bloody bad form, as I'm the one who impregnated the bride!* Instead of retreating into his shell, he made a crablike, sideways maneuver. "Rupert, I am extremely flattered, but I would advise you to ask Olivia's brother, Harry. Giving him the honor would put you in such good standing with your new in-laws."

"I hadn't thought of that. Sure you won't feel left out?"

I want to be left out of this one. "You should ask Harry."

"Then it's settled! Do you know where I want to go today? Tattersall's to have a look at the horses. I saw the Earl of Jersey tooling his cattle through traffic this morning and suddenly I fancied a phaeton, or even a racing curricle."

"Then let's do it. We're both men of means, so why shouldn't we indulge our fancies?"

After two hours inspecting horses, Rupert looked on with longing as Kit bought himself a pair of well-bred, matched chestnuts. They spent another two hours at the coachmakers, where Kit chose the most expensive perch-phaeton in the coachyard. "Let's celebrate. Why don't we go home and change, then meet at White's for dinner?"

"Sorry, Kit, I must dance attendance on Olivia at Almack's."

Christopher patted Rupert's back to console him. "It happens to the best of us sooner or later. Wait till I'm courting your sister, Alex. The imp will lead me on a merry chase, I have no doubt."

Later, at White's, after Kit had eaten dinner and made his way to the gaming rooms, he saw Jeremy Eaton across the room and wanted to hide. He had been successful in putting thoughts of his second cousin out of his mind, but seeing him made Kit's hackles rise. He watched with sinking emotions as Jeremy approached.

"H'lo, Harm. I was hoping I'd bump into you."

Kit experienced *déjà vu. Those were the exact same words the devious swine used last time we met!* Kit dreaded what was coming.

"I understand my father tipped you off to some fail-safe, lucrative investments, cousin?"

Kit summoned an arrogant attitude and stood his ground. "Surely your father isn't foolish enough to discuss my private business affairs with you, is he, Jeremy?"

"Ah, no. My father does not have a foolish bone in

his body, Harm. He has no idea the special interest I take in you. Only the two of us know . . . *so far,*" he added with unsubtle emphasis.

"What the devil do you want?" Kit demanded with a bravado he did not feel.

"Since my father isn't nearly as generous toward me as your father was toward you, I find that I am short of funds again. I too would like to put some money into investments. It's ironic that your father left you everything, don't you agree, Harm?"

The avaricious swine knows it was me who shot Father and not Nick. I wish the bastard would have a fatal accident himself! But why the devil am I worrying, when I have enough money to keep the bloodsucking scum quiet? "This is the last time Jeremy. How much?"

"A mere five thousand buys my undying loyalty and gratitude."

Kit's eyes narrowed. His demands had gone up tenfold since last time. "Meet me at Barclays in the morning." He turned on his heel and walked a direct path to the faro table. Within minutes Jeremy Eaton sat down at the same table and enjoyed the devil's own luck. Soon, he had all Kit's blunt and graciously accepted a marker from his second cousin. Kit ordered a double whiskey. *This is one of the times that I miss you, Nick. The two of us together would demolish this bastard, but I can't do it alone, curse you!*

Lieutenant Nicholas Hatton wondered if the Fates were cursing him. October brought such a sudden change to the weather that he and his men were caught off guard. October was as wet as September had been dry. The deluge began and would not cease; the dusty earth turned into a sea of mud, and the area outside Pamplona where they had made their camp became an ankle-deep quagmire.

Nick gave orders to strike their tents and set up on higher ground. On the second morning at the new camp, he discovered that not only was food and wine missing but supplies and weapons had been stolen. With Sergeant Tim O'Neil at his side, he ferreted out who was to blame. Apparently, the four young soldiers who were on guard had crept inside in the middle of the night to escape the torrential rain and had downed a few bottles to warm their blood.

Grim-faced and with hard, crystalline gray eyes, Nick surveyed the four culprits who stood at attention before him. His natural instinct was to protect the young devils, and his quicksilver mind darted about exploring avenues that would excuse them from the consequences of their actions. Because he had always protected his twin and covered for him by taking the blame upon his own shoulders, he was tempted to do the same with his soldiers. With a sinking heart he realized that he must mete out discipline; to do otherwise would be grossly unfair to his other men who were not derelict in their duty. He knew they must be taught responsibility.

"There will be no more wine available in my camp. You will give every bottle to the villagers, then you will replace the food that was stolen plus an extra three days' supply of game for the entire camp." His eyes darkened; his face looked hard as granite. "Your watch-time will be doubled, and I shall be there with you to see that you do not shirk one moment." He saw their shoulders slump and hardened his heart against softening their punishment. "Your pay will be forfeit until the stolen guns are paid for." *Death and damnation, how long will this siege last? My men need action. Pamplona was out of food and water and ready to capitulate but then the bloody rains came!*

The next day, Wellington himself rode into camp astride his great charger, Copenhagen, to converse with General Hill. Lieutenant Hatton, along with the other officers, were privy to their conversation. "Tomorrow I mount a surprise attack on Bidassoa. My men will be the first British soldiers on French soil. It will be a symbol, a foretaste of what is to come. General Hill, you will remain in charge of the siege of Pamplona until she surrenders, before you lead your men into France. Any French disasters in the Peninsula have been largely due to their cruelty to civilians. I am convinced that good behavior in conquered France will pay off!" The hooked-nosed Wellington spoke matter-of-factly. He was an impatient commander who did not suffer fools. "Inform your men that we are at war with the government, not with civilians."

Wellington departed as swiftly as he had arrived, riding Copenhagen into the wind and the rain. Clearly, General Hill was disappointed not to be among the first to set foot on French soil, but he ordered his officers to keep up their men's morale and above all warned that when Pamplona surrendered, they must keep their soldiers on a tight rein and maintain discipline at any cost.

During the next fortnight, Nick drummed discipline into his soldiers as they relentlessly pounded the fortress with cannon. "Pamplona is close to surrender. I am responsible for your behavior. I will not tolerate acts of vengeance upon conquered people. If I see any man commit murder, arson, or rape, I will not hesitate to shoot him on the spot. Do I make myself clear?"

Not one man present doubted he meant it. They had come to respect him for his untiring energy and his genuine concern that put their welfare before his own, never asking aught of them that he would not willingly do himself. He patched up their wounds, dosed them when they came down with dysentery, and counseled them when they became homesick—even writing letters for those who were illiterate. Hatton was a natural leader, far better in their opinion than any other of Hill's officers. Moreover, they knew that Lieutenant Hatton's word was his bond.

Occasionally, mail arrived from England, which never failed to cheer the men. Nick had written a letter to his twin but had received no reply from Kit. A dozen times since he had been in Pamplona, he had begun a letter to Alexandra, then stopped himself from posting it. He did not want to do anything that would encourage her to daydream of him. Though she constantly filled his thoughts, he dutifully pushed them aside. His dreams, however, he had no control over whatsoever, and strangely, the most vivid ones occurred whenever the day's events had been horrific. His dream sex was highly erotic, like riding wild horses on a magic carpet!

Nick thought he was too tired to dream, but he was wrong.

He felt a sense of joyful anticipation that went beyond

happiness, for he knew that soon, very soon, Alexandra would come. After what felt like an eon, he saw her running toward him, laughing, naked. He gathered her into his arms and watched her lashes flutter to her cheeks. Like the delicate flutter of a butterfly wing, he touched the corners of her mouth with the tip of his tongue. She smiled a secret smile, without opening her eyes, and slid down his bared body to her knees. He went down with her, kneeling before her, and his longing was like a hunger in the blood. Slowly, his fingertips traced her cheek, her throat, her shoulder. Then his hand brushed across her heart and he felt its rapid beat beneath his fingers.

His mouth moved closer to the tip of her breast, and he gently blew warm breath on the hard little bud and watched it ruche tighter. His hand trailed beneath the curve of her breast, along her ribs, and down her belly. He heard her indrawn breath of excitement when he drew one fingertip along her cleft. Then, very deliberately, he licked and tasted her from throat to navel as his fingers drew circles about the rosebud that nestled in the damp red curls at the tip of her cleft.

A wild thrill ran through him at the love noises she made, for they told him that she had never been sexually pleasured before. He untangled her arms from around his neck and gently pushed her down into the flower-filled grass. His hands slipped beneath her buttocks, and his fingers slid into the cleft between her cheeks as he lifted her onto his muscled thighs. Then he bent his head and dropped a kiss onto her high mons, which tempted him to madness. As her lashes lifted, he saw the look of shock in her eyes turn into a sultry look as he thrust his tongue into her hot, silken sheath. With the tip of his tongue he felt the pulse point deep within, then he felt her sheath tighten, throb, and pulsate, as it gripped and squeezed his tongue. He felt her open her legs fully so she would not impede the hot, sliding friction, and he knew what she wanted. With a heavy rhythm that matched their heartbeats, he thrust deeply for long breath-stopping minutes. When her climax came, it was hard and fast. He felt exultant as her hot shudders melted into liquid tremors.

* * *

In London, plans for the Harding-Sheffield wedding began to jell and became solid. For Rupert, time seemed to flash by like a racing whippet; for Olivia, time seemed to have slowed to the pace of a sloth, as she surreptitiously but constantly surveyed her figure in every available mirror.

The Hardings wisely decided to hold the wedding in London rather than at their stately home in Bucks County. They used the excuse that the fall Season had begun, but in reality it meant that the wedding could be a much smaller affair.

"Did Olivia tell you how long she is willing to wait for the wedding?" Dottie asked Rupert.

"Just until I kill myself."

"Oh, not long then," Dottie said dryly. "Rupert, don't whinge; it is most unmanly."

"The wedding is to be a week from Saturday. I have asked Olivia's brother to be my groomsman." Rupert sounded resigned.

"Mmm, I suppose with Christopher Hatton in mourning, you had little choice, but that means Olivia will reciprocate and ask your sister to be her maid of honor. Such short notice is indecent!" Dottie wanted to bite her tongue the minute she said the word, so she quickly added, "Well, there's nothing to be done but take Alexandra round to Madame Martine's in Bond Street." She carefully counted out Rupert's five hundred pounds and sighed at the expense of another new gown for Alex. "Here, m'boy, you've earned it by rising so precipitously to the occasion. I'm proud of you, Rupert."

Though Dottie would have preferred to dispatch Annabelle Harding to the devil, she curbed her evil impulses and allowed Lady Harding and Olivia to accompany Alexandra and herself to the Parisian dressmaker, since Madame Martine also was doing the wedding gown.

"I've always wanted my bridesmaids to wear pink." It was Olivia's favorite shade, as it flattered her dark coloring.

"You are not having bridesmaids, dearest, only a maid of honor, but I am sure Alexandra will be amenable to pink."

"Actually, I'm not," Alex replied. "I have screamy-colored hair that clashes with pink."

"Then what about puce?" Annabelle suggested.

"Puce is not only pink, it is *offensive pink*," Dottie declared. "I think *you* would look good in goose-turd green, Annabelle."

Olivia giggled. "Baby blue wouldn't clash with your hair, Alexandra," she said, wistfully abandoning all hope of pink.

Alex tried valiantly not to grimace. "Forget-me-not blue would be more striking, don't you think, and carries such an appropriate sentiment for a wedding?"

The color agreed upon, they moved on to style. "I simply love the French Empire style, don't you, Alexandra?"

"I must confess that I do," Alex said, smiling at Olivia.

"Did you know that Josephine Bonaparte made the Empire style fashionable in order to conceal the fact that she was *enceinte*?" Dottie had no patience for subtlety.

Olivia turned pale, while Annabelle flushed, confirming Dottie's suspicions. Alex said quickly, "Madame does the French style exquisitely. My last gown was Empire, and I had many compliments."

So Rupert is the scapegoat! Dottie thought. *Now that Annabelle knows that I know, I shall squeeze a consolation prize from the harpy.* "Olivia, my dear, have you given any thought to a town house of your own? Surely a viscountess won't want to live with Mamma and Pappa?" Dottie saw the speculative look that Olivia bent upon her mother.

"Actually, Mother, there is an empty town house in Clarges Street, not too far away from ours. Perhaps Daddy would give it to us for a wedding present?" Since Daddy had given her everything she ever wanted from the age of two, Olivia considered it her due.

Dottie threw Annabelle a look of triumph. Annabelle smiled resignedly; she knew she was getting a bargain by saving her daughter from disgrace.

Alex was aware of the bi-play, and worse, she understood it. *Olivia is with child and Dottie knows about it! Does Rupert know? He flatly denied the innuendo, yet he has agreed to a hurried wedding, so he must know!* Alex firmly stopped her inquisitive mind from digging deeper; she feared uncovering something worse.

When she returned from the dressmaker, Alex was careful not to allude to anything remotely connected to Rupert and Olivia's secret. Thoughts were one thing, but words, once uttered, changed everything and moreover could inflict painful wounds. She gave her brother an especially affectionate smile. "By the way, Rupert, did you write to tell Nick that you were getting married?"

Rupert stiffened. His blue eyes turned to ice. "I have no intention of writing to the coward."

"Whatever do you mean?" She held her breath, terrified of his reply.

Rupert hesitated for a long moment, then said, "The *ton* ostracized him when he accidentally shot his father, and instead of facing them down, he bolted with his tail between his legs."

Alex knew his eyes had not turned to ice over anything to do with the shooting accident. Only something devastatingly personal could do that. She turned on her heel and fled up the stairs. In her chamber she picked up a book and flung it at the wall. It didn't nearly relieve her of the emotion building inside of her. She snatched up an inkpot and hurled it after the book. The hideous mess it made of the primrose wallpaper gave her a moment of satisfaction, but it was not until she threw herself on the bed and sobbed for an hour that she began to purge herself of Nick Hatton.

Rupert allowed his curiosity to mix with a little excitement when he received Olivia's note telling him she had a surprise for him. It would not be the first surprise she had given him. When they had been left alone in the Harding's parlor and he had formally proposed to her, she had flung herself into his arms with great abandon. Olivia had a lovely rounded figure, and when she pressed her soft curves into his long, lean length, it had heated his blood with lust. His kisses were tentative, but her answering kisses had been so hungry he began to think that perhaps a wife and marriage were things to be desired rather than dreaded. If her parents had not been lurking in the house, Rupert was certain that he could have seduced Olivia and persuaded her to a giving mood.

He decided that when he called in Clarges Street, he would take her a present. Flowers was his first idea, but he quickly decided on chocolate bonbons instead. With the ribbon-wrapped box beneath his arm, he ran up the steps of the town house and lifted the brass knocker. Though it was the butler who opened the door, he immediately saw Olivia descending the stairs to the entrance hall and knew she had been waiting for him. She wore a pink morning dress but was carrying a bonnet and her reticule, which told him they were going out.

"Rupert"—she lifted her cheek for his chaste kiss—"how lovely of you to bring me chocolates! I shall take them with me. I have the most wonderful surprise for you."

He smiled down at her. "What is it, dearest?"

"Ah, I want to *show* you, not *tell* you about it, Rupert." She had decided that the advantages of showing him far outweighed those of merely telling him. She took his hand and led him from the house and along the pavement of Clarges Street with a conspiratorial air. She took him past three houses, then turned in at the fourth and pulled him up the steps.

Rupert's excitement withered as he assumed they were going visiting. Her idea of a wonderful surprise obviously differed from his. When Olivia went in without knocking, he thought that she must know these friends extremely well, and he felt reluctant to follow. He stopped in the black-and-white tiled entrance hall, glanced up at the chandelier, then let his curious gaze roam about the well-appointed home. "Whose house is this?" he murmured.

Olivia's eyes shone with suppressed excitement. "It is *ours,* Rupert! Daddy has bought it as a wedding present."

Rupert was stunned. Pleasantly so. He had dreaded the thought of living with the Hardings. "Well, that's most generous of your father, I must say, Olivia."

"Come on." She again took his hand and, clutching the box of chocolates to her breast, urged him up the stairs. She led him into a richly furnished bedchamber, set the beribboned box down on a bedside table, opened her reticule, and withdrew an iron key. "Lock the door."

It took Rupert a moment to comprehend that this was a planned rendezvous, but in the very next moment, his body responded. Vigorously. He quickly did as Olivia bade him, then returned and handed the key back to her. He removed her bonnet and opened his arms wide.

When she stepped close and lifted her lips in eager invitation, Rupert knew instantly that he would not be able to control his desires. Alone, in a locked room, with a bed inviting dalliance, his resolve to be patient until their wedding night went up in smoke. His lips sought hers, but before his mouth even began to make demands, she opened her lips for him, luring him inside. When her tongue began to duel with his, he gave an inward sigh and enjoyed to the full the provocative little thrusts she initiated.

Her soft curves brushed against his hard leanness, tempting his hand to explore them. Olivia's breasts were full, the nipples already taut as his fingers closed over one lush globe. She gasped with pleasure, and her own fingers unfastened the bodice of her morning gown, giving him full access to what swelled beneath. When his hand closed over naked skin to caress and knead, Olivia's hands began undressing him with great urgency.

For one moment he fought to stop her, but he had no willpower to deny himself, not when his body burned for her touch. Instead, he began to remove his garments, leaving her hands free to roam over his hard, heated flesh. In seconds he was naked, and rampant. His impluse was to shield her from such male sexuality, but before he could collect his thoughts, Olivia took possession of his cock, wrapping proprietary fingers about it so tightly he almost came out of his skin.

He knew if he did not remove her lovely dress, he would ruin it. With gentle, shaking hands, he raised the skirt and lifted the gown over her head. Olivia's own hands tore off her pretty undergarments quickly, and Rupert knew he had never before reduced a female to a state of nakedness this rapidly. Before her chemise joined her other garments on the carpet, she stood on tiptoe, wound her arms about his neck, and lifted herself onto his jutting arousal. Olivia was frantic for the joining.

With his hands beneath her buttocks, he managed to get them both to the bed, where they collapsed in a tangle of limbs. Olivia scrambled quickly to the dominant position, molding her breasts to his chest and her plump thighs to his groin. She rose above him, breathlessly, and sank down with a heartfelt moan.

Rupert gazed up at Olivia; she was panting and moving up and down on him voraciously. Over and over, she lifted herself high, then plunged down, greedily swallowing him whole, urging him to do his part as she rode him relentlessly. Soon, she was begging him to go faster, harder, and though he did his level best, he knew he could not satisfy her hunger unless he was on top and in control. Before he could roll her beneath him, she thrust so vigorously that she brought herself to her own rapture, and in doing so, made him spend. He melted into her as she milked him of his seed, then she collapsed onto her back beside him. He closed his eyes and was drifting in a warm sea of surfeit, when he felt her rub her body against his side and heard his name upon her lips. "Rupert?"

He lifted his head from the pillow and watched her pop a chocolate bonbon into her mouth whole. Then she took another, bit into it with sharp little teeth, and dipped her tongue into its soft pink center, licking the cream filling with relish. She swirled her tongue over her lips and cast him a sensual look that left no doubt in his mind. *Again? She wants to fuck again?* Rupert thought he had died and gone to heaven.

Chapter 16

A few days before the wedding, Alexandra volunteered to help Rupert pack his personal belongings and his clothes so they could be sent around to the house in Clarges Street. She enlisted the help of Sara, and the conspirators sorted through Rupert's wardrobe, culling garments that Alex deemed too shabby for a newlywed viscount. When they were finished, Alex ended up with a pile of male shirts, neckcloths, trousers, and jackets, numerous and varied enough to garb herself for any occasion.

Rupert gave his trunks a cursory check. "Where is my black formal attire? Perhaps you took it to be pressed?" he asked Sara.

Since Alex knew Sara had an aversion to lying, she quickly cut in, "You left it at Longford Manor, I imagine, along with copious amounts of other fashionable garments that you didn't bother bringing to London."

"A couple of wigs also seem to be missing," he said, puzzled.

"That's something I've been meaning to mention, Rupert. Wigs are going out of fashion. It is becoming *de rigueur* to wear your own hair."

"Not that I noticed at Almack's recently," he said dryly. "Are you sure you haven't pinched them, Alex?"

"Whatever would I want with a man's wig?"

"There is no end to the things my mind conjures. Oh, well, I shall have to take a run into the country. Kit has a brand-new phaeton and matched pair of chestnuts we're avid to try out."

"Ah, anxious to take the reins into your own hands, are you?"

Rupert laughed with good nature. "Tweaking me about marriage, Mistress Sly Boots. One day soon it will be your turn."

When Alex and Sara were alone, Alex began to change clothes and posed a question to the maid. "I've heard talk of places called 'flash houses' where scores of young boys are trained to be thieves. Have you heard of them?"

"Certainly I have. Girls are trained too, but the danger of being put in prison and flogged for thievery pushes girls into prostitution as soon as they are old enough."

"And when are they considered old enough?"

"Twelve or thirteen, if you want the truth, miss."

"I do want the truth, Sara, though it's heart-scalding. These flash houses are purported to be in an area called the Rookery of St. Giles. Where is that exactly?"

"It's up north of Soho somewhere, around High Street." Sara gestured vaguely with her hand.

"Isn't that where you used to live?"

Sara flushed and pressed her lips together.

Alex pounced. "You don't want me to see where you used to live, do you, Sara?"

"No, miss. My mother was so relieved to see me escape from that terrible place and the wretched life that most of the people who live there endure. When I was lucky enough to secure a position as maid in the wealthy part of town, she made me promise not to go back more than two or three times a year."

"I insist upon seeing it; we'll go there today."

"It's not a fit place for a lady."

"Then I shall wear men's clothes, and you must call me Alex."

"Better not wear anything fancy, or you'll be set upon and robbed the minute you set foot in St. Giles."

Alex, garbed in her brother's oldest clothes, and Sara, wrapped in a shabby shawl, made their way up Charing Cross Road. The farther north they walked, the more the streets deteriorated. The buildings they passed were successively more dilapidated, then decayed. The area was filled with foul alleys and tumbledown houses. Raggedy, barefoot children mingled with emaciated dogs, rummaging among the offal of the rat-infested streets for scraps. Men slept, huddled in doorways, and girls on the streets were falling-down drunk. It seemed that every woman they passed had a baby suckling a pendulous breast, while swollen-bellied with another child.

Alex slipped her hand around Sara's and squeezed. "I'm sorry, Sara. I had no idea." *No idea that such slums even existed!*

"If Hopkins, the butler, ever finds out where I came from, I shall get the sack."

"I promise that you will always have a position in Berkeley Square, Sara, and I shan't let Hopkins know anything about you; I know that servants can be bigger snobs than the *ton*."

The maid took Alex into a ramshackle building occupied by dozens of one-room hovels. The stench was putrid. Alex pinched her nostrils together and waited while Sara knocked on a battered door. It was opened by an old woman; Alex realized with a shock that this was Sara's mother, only in her forties but aged beyond her years.

"Lawks, ye shouldn't bring yer fancy man 'ere, luv!"

Sara lapsed into her mother's cockney and explained who Alex was. They spoke so rapidly, often in rhyming slang, that Alex only understood every tenth word, though she was fascinated.

Sara's mother was clean and the room was neat, a marked contrast from the other hovels in the squalid four-story building.

"Are you an only child?" Alex was clearly mystified how such a place had produced Sara.

"No, my mother had seven; I was the youngest. The boys are all grown and gone, Lord knows where; two older sisters are dead, God rest their souls."

"Who taught you how to speak? How did you acquire the airs of a lady, Sara?"

"That was Maggie, who lives across the hall. She took me in when I was a little girl and my mother had too many mouths to feed. Maggie was a gentlewoman fallen on hard times. I owe it all to her. I'll take you to meet her, but don't get too close," Sara warned. "She has the consumption."

Before they left, Alex watched Sara hug her mother and give her money. She decided on the spot that she would speak to Dottie about giving her maid a raise. Then they went across the hall. Maggie's face radiated pure joy when she saw Sara, but a lump came into Alex's throat when she saw the hollow cheeks and sunken eyes of the woman who had saved Sara from a living hell.

"Maggie, this is my friend Alex."

"How do you do, sir? It is a distinct pleasure to make the acquaintance of a gentleman who is Sara's friend."

Alex bowed. "My lady, the pleasure is all mine." Alex wondered if Maggie had ever been beautiful. If so, the only thing of beauty that remained was her voice. Alex imagined she had once been tall, slim, and elegant; now, however, she was thin and hunched, as if she protected a painful chest. Alex stepped a distance away so that the two could talk privately. *How unendurable this existence must be for a woman who was born to privilege. How does she bear it?* Alex's hand closed over the money in her pocket. She drew out the seven shillings she had earned from the newspaper, and slipped it onto the mantelpiece above the empty hearth.

As they left, Sara pointed to a four-story derelict building across the street. "That's a flash house—the top two floors."

Alexandra now understood that the children who became thieves to better their lot in life were completely justified. Since Society didn't give a tinker's damn about them, they had no choice but to look after their own interests, no matter what laws they broke.

"That's where I would have ended up if Maggie Field hadn't intervened."

"Have you any idea what her circumstances were?"

Sara shook her head once, then said, "I think I took the place of her own daughter, who she lost through tragic circumstances, perhaps of her own making."

When the young women arrived back in Berkeley

Square, unfortunately, Dottie was in the reception hall. She swept a disapproving glance over shawl-wrapped Sara and shabbily-clad Alex. "I would like a word with you upstairs, Alexandra."

Dottie entered her own chamber, and Alex had no choice but to follow her grandmother into her territory. "When I saw you before in male attire, I assumed it was a one-time lark. What in the world are you playing at, Alexandra?"

"Dottie, I'm doing what I love: learning about the world and writing articles for the newspaper. There are so many wrongs that need righting! Let me show you my article on climbing boys."

"I read it in the *Political Register.* It was most commendable, but what happened to the novel you were intent upon writing? Such an endeavor, while wearing a morning dress and sitting at a writing desk, would be far more suitable for a lady, I warrant."

"The novels I've read recently are piffle! We need reform, and the government does nothing. My articles just might fire up the public into demanding that the government make changes. My next article will be about flash houses. Disguising myself as a male makes it both easier and safer to move about London."

"And if I forbid it?" Dottie looked as militant as a warhorse, ready to breathe fire.

Alex clasped her hands together in unconscious supplication. "Oh, please don't forbid me. Doing this has given me the freedom for which I've longed and opened my eyes to what goes on beyond the narrow confines of the *ton.* It makes me feel alive, as well as worthwhile. It also is broadening my mind and giving me an education that I couldn't get from books alone."

"Fiddle-faddle! You think those arguments will sway me? You must make the most of being in London, Alexandra. You should be socializing and using it to your advantage. Men are not enthralled by ladies who devote themselves to good causes; they view them as fanatics!"

"I promise I won't become a fanatic! Please allow me this taste of life before you compel me to settle down to marriage."

"You will have to promise far more than that, Alexandra."

Alex clutched at straws, ready to bargain. "I will promise anything within reason."

"If I allow you freedom to pursue this *calling*, racketing about London with all the riffraff and ragtag, I want your faithful promise that you will marry Lord Hatton next year."

"I . . . Christopher may not choose to marry me!"

"Piss and piffle, Alexandra! That is the biggest load of claptrap I've ever heard! The man does not do the choosing; the woman does. Females are far more interesting and fascinating to males than vice versa. A clever woman such as yourself can hold any man in the palm of her hand and make him do her bidding."

"Are you willing to give me *complete* freedom?"

Dottie hesitated, thought about qualifying it to *within reason,* then decided against it. "Complete freedom in exchange for your promise to become Lady Hatton."

Fleetingly, Alex thought of Nicholas, her first love. The love that was now dead. She had mourned it, and purged herself of it, and now accepted the fact that marriage with Christopher was inevitable. She realized that it had always been inevitable. "I faithfully promise, Dottie."

"And I promise you won't regret it, darling."

Lieutenant Nicholas Hatton asked himself if he regretted joining the Royal Horse Artillery, and though it had turned out to be a supreme challenge, he knew he had acquitted himself well so far and had few regrets.

His men, however, were becoming extremely restless, because the end of October was in sight, yet still besieged Pamplona had not surrendered. Finally, Lieutenant Hatton decided to go on the offensive to help matters along. The Artillery forces had an excess of gunpowder that had not been used in the siege of the Spanish town, and Hatton came up with an idea to put it to good use. He asked for volunteers, and selected young, unmarried men who as yet had no families.

On the last day of October, they carried twenty barrels of gunpowder and spaced them out along the outside walls of the town near the fortress. He instructed his volunteers to form a line like a bucket brigade, but what they were to pass from hand to hand were barrels of gunpowder. Hatton and Sergeant O'Neil stationed themselves at the ready with fuses and lit tapers, and as the gunpowder was thrust into their hands, the two men lit the fuses and flung the barrels over the high wall. The barrel brigade kept up a steady rhythm, never missing a beat, as one explosion followed another, filling the air with acrid black smoke.

Lieutenant Hatton's arm was totally numb from wrist to shoulder before they finally saw the white flag of surrender, fluttering through the choking clouds of smoke. A great cheer went up from his men and from the other soldiers who had gathered at the first explosion. When General Rowland Hill entered the town to accept its surrender, a grinning Nicholas Hatton went down his line of courageous volunteers to shake each man's hand and murmur a brief "Well done." The two words felt like the greatest praise they had ever received.

As his troops entered Pamplona, through his vigilance and aided by Sergeant O'Neil, his men did him proud. Because they committed no vile acts upon the conquered men nor depraved lust upon the females, he turned a blind eye to their looting, happy that they set no fires. Nick was vastly relieved that Pamplona fell with no casualties to his men.

The good fortune did not last. Now that Pamplona was secure, General Hill gave his officers orders to move their men toward the French border to join with Wellington's force, which would soon be doing battle with General Soult's army. Nick bade his men break camp. Because of the unrelenting rain, which had turned the ground into a quagmire, it was a gargantuan task to move the gun carriages upon which the cannon were mounted, especially in such hilly terrain. For more than a week, Nick spent eighteen hours a day in the saddle, riding the line. The only times he dismounted were to help dig out wheels sunk into mud over their axels, tend a lame horse, or fall into his bedroll for four or five hours of sleep.

As Hill's army got close to the border, the French,

fearing retaliation for the atrocities they had committed against the Spanish, attacked with a vengeance. In the bloody skirmish, two of Hatton's men were killed and one was struck by a shot that shattered both bones in his left leg. Nick was out of the saddle in a flash; he cut makeshift splints from a nearby tree and put on a field dressing. He knew if the leg was not tended properly, the soldier would lose it. He ordered two recruits to use a blanket to carry the wounded man to the medical officers who had set up a field hospital. Only then did he turn his attention to the dead. He knew their names by heart and where they came from in England. In the cold, wet hours before dawn, he wrote to their families, offering his sympathy and describing their courage.

When Hill's forces arrived at the River Nivelle, they found the rushing, swollen waters impossible to cross. Wellington's forces, on the far side of the river, were fighting off attacks from General Soult's French army, and Hill's battalions would mean the difference between defeat or victory. Hill directed his officers to have their men search up and down the riverbank for boats, but their efforts proved fruitless. Lieutenant Hatton sought out General Hill. "Sir, Wellington's men obviously had to cross the River Nivelle before us."

"I warrant that it was less swollen than it is now."

"Undoubtedly, General. But cross it they did, and I conclude that the boats and watercraft they used must all be on the other side of the river."

"A logical supposition, Hatton. Can you suggest a solution?"

"I volunteer to swim across to get the boats, sir."

"Swim those raging waters? The risk is great, Lieutenant."

"At Hatton, we not only have a lake on our property but the River Crane, a branch of the Thames that swells every spring. I could swim it at seven, sir; both ways at eight. I won't allow a foreign river to defeat me, General."

Nick Hatton put his men in the charge of Sergeant Tim O'Neil, as well as his pistols and his mount, Slate, then he slipped into the icy water of the Nivelle and began to swim against the tide. He wasn't even halfway across before the cold seeped into his bones, and he realized that the sparse rations coupled with long days in the saddle had robbed him of his usual energy. But he knew the strenuous activity of his duties had toughened and hardened his muscles, so he cut through the roiling, brown water as cleanly and efficiently as he could.

When he was in the middle, a memory from his youth suddenly surfaced. He had been swimming the River Crane, egged on by his twin and Rupert, when suddenly Alexandra decided to try it. She jumped in and managed a few strokes before the swirling current dragged her under. In a flash he had swum to save her, but as he held her bright head above water and began to stroke toward shore, she had hit him and cried, "No, no, I want to go to the other side! Help me to get there, Nick."

He smiled inwardly as he eyed the water with grim determination. *Help me to get there, Alex.*

He feared his lungs might burst, but eventually he reached the far side of the Nivelle and dragged himself up on the muddy bank, gasping for breath. He searched up and down the river for more than an hour, finding only a skiff and a small rowboat; finally, when his legs were starting to shake with fatigue, he struck gold! He came upon four large, flat, wooden barges roped together. The find sent renewed energy surging through his body. He attached the skiff to the barges, cut their mooring rope with his knife, and began to pole slowly back across the river, thanking all the saints in heaven that on the return journey the current was with him. When he got back to camp, not only his own men cheered him; all General Hill's forces celebrated his daring feat.

That night, under cover of dark, the men, their animals, and all the cannon and artillery were transported across the river so that Hill's forces could join with Wellington's. The following day, Lieutenant Nicholas Hatton was promoted to captain. Nick didn't know whether to be flattered or dismayed; now he commanded four times as many troops.

Wellington was overjoyed. "Soult has been building

up fieldworks. Now I can pour greater force on certain points than the French can concentrate to resist me!"

For the first time, Captain Hatton and his men fought in all-out battles. Wellington's words proved prophetic. When one French position after another fell to overwhelming attacks, Soult was forced to order the abandonment of his right wing. The English defeated four divisions in a single day and captured fifty-nine guns. The weather alone prevented Wellington from following the fleeing enemy. Since every river was impassable and the ground was knee-deep with sticky mud, he ordered his soldiers to hunker down and wait. Nick found some abandoned ruins and directed his men to make camp, which afforded some shelter to his shivering troops.

Once the rain let up, they didn't have long to wait. The Battle of the Nive lasted for five days. Though one of Wellington's top generals, John Hope, was captured by the French, the British forces gained steadily. Defeat for the French came when three German battalions deserted from their army and Soult ordered that all his German troops be disarmed. Filled with a euphoria they hadn't known in months, the British soldiers celebrated the victory.

At first flush, Nick Hatton experienced the glory of victory, but it was short-lived. As he searched for wounded men on the battlefield and learned that more than four thousand of the enemy had been killed, his euphoria vanished. As he moved among the carnage of mangled bodies and looked into the faces of the dead French soldiers, he saw how young they were. All thought of celebration was wiped from his brain.

Though the wedding was small by the *ton*'s standards, everyone was eager to celebrate the nuptials of Olivia Harding and Rupert Sheffield, Viscount Longford. The bride wore traditional wreath and veils, the maid of honor looked ravishing in vivid forget-me-not blue, and the mother of the bride was resplendent in puce.

Lady Longford was gowned in tasteful gray but wore a bright orange wig, hoping to annoy Annabelle Harding. As they left the church, she swept the mother of the bride's puce gown with an amused glance and murmured to Lord Harding, "She would have been wiser to take my advice and wear goose-turd green."

Alexandra, escorted by groomsman Harry Harding, rode the short distance to the reception in the carriage with the bride and groom. *I warrant all four of us know Olivia's secret.* Alex looked at the bride and forbade herself from conjuring pictures of her and Nick Hatton. *Olivia is smiling serenely as if she hasn't a care in the world, which now, of course, she hasn't! But what a wretched position this puts me in; Olivia is now my sister-in-marriage.* Alex glanced at her brother and felt immediate guilt for her thoughts. *Rupert's plight makes my position pale into insignificance.* She wondered why on earth he had married Olivia, and came to the conclusion that he must have a deep affection for her. Her heart went out to him. When they alighted from the carriage in front of the Clarges Street house, Alex reached for her brother's hand and squeezed it. "I love you, Rupert."

The rooms of the town house were crowded with guests, some of whom hadn't attended the church ceremony. Lady Spencer came because of her friendship with Dottie. She was accompanied by her grandson Hart Cavendish, who came mainly because Alexandra would be there. His wedding gift was a magnificent set of Georgian silver engraved with the Longford crest of a *Stag Couchant.*

Rupert was thankful when his best friend, Kit, arrived to give him moral support. He was astounded at Hatton's generosity; he had bought the newlyweds their own carriage, and the card stipulated that Rupert was free to select his own matched pair of carriage horses from Tattersall's.

Christopher Hatton toasted the newlyweds. The wedding present would cut a deep swath into his Barclays account, but it would completely eliminate any need for guilt.

Olivia watched Kit from beneath her dark lashes. There was no doubt that he was one of the handsomest men she had ever set eyes upon, and his close proximity made her pulses race and played havoc with her heart.

However, Olivia had been taught a hard lesson. She was no longer ruled by her heart but by her head, and she could clearly see that Rupert was far more malleable husband material than Kit Hatton would ever be. Rupert had been bought and paid for, and he would dance to her tune on a daily—and nightly—basis.

Alexandra found herself with three escorts vying for her attention. Hart Cavendish had no trouble elbowing Harry Harding aside, but Kit Hatton was impossible to dismiss. When the hour grew late, Hart slipped a possessive arm around her. "Weddings are supposed to have a salubrious effect upon females. Are you feeling the impulse?" he murmured wickedly in her ear. "Are you coming home with me, darling?"

She laughed up into his face. "You must have mistaken me for an opera dancer, if you are offering me *carte blanche.* I fully intend to leave with Dottie tonight, but if you would again like the company of young *Master Alex* one evening this week, I shall pass along your invitation."

A short time later, Kit also asked her to leave with him. "My mourning deprived me of the pleasure of dancing with you tonight, but I would love to take you for a long carriage ride, Alexandra."

"How utterly tempting you are, Lord Hatton. However, my grandmother would never allow me to leave with you this close to the wicked hour of midnight. Perhaps another time."

The two rejected friends, having liberally imbibed, left together with the intention of consoling themselves at White's, Brooks's, then Watier's, where the play was particularly deep.

At least two hours after midnight had passed, Rupert lay abed with his bride. He reflected upon how eagerly he had carried Olivia to their own house in Clarges Street, how excited he had been to embark upon his wedding night. Olivia, however, had been much more demanding than he had anticipated. In point of fact, her appetite for the flesh had exceeded his own. Though he lay sprawled in utter exhaustion, sleep eluded him. He pictured the Longford crest engraved upon the Georgian silver. The *Stag Couchant* was so bloody apt. Not only did it have horns but it was lying down—a position no doubt he would have to assume whenever Olivia wished. An adage he had once heard from Dottie drifted through his thoughts: *With Caesar's coin comes the obligation to submit to Caesar's rules!*

Chapter 17

A week later, when Hart Cavendish picked up Alex Sheffield, she was again dressed as a young man about town. "And where does your dissolute fancy dictate this evening, old man?" he teased. "May I suggest a pub called The Noble Rot?"

"My fancy isn't dissolute tonight; it's profligate. I wish to observe prostitutes," Alex announced casually. She needed another article for the *Political Register.*

"Prostitution is not a subject that interests a *lady*."

"It should be! Every woman should make it her business to learn what other women have to suffer. Prostitution is something that should be abolished."

Hart threw back his head and laughed at her innocence. He moved across the carriage and took her hand. "Alex, my love, if a drab heard you voice such an opinion, she would likely scratch out your eyes. Doxies are doxies by choice."

"Piss and piffle! That is the biggest load of claptrap I have ever heard!" *Good God, I'm turning into my grandmother!* "Doxies become doxies because they have no *other* choice. Moreover, if you continue to address me as *Alex, my love,* people will think you are one of those men who are attracted to boys."

He raised her hand to his lips and nibbled on her fingertips. "Ah, but to this one I am. *Sexually* attracted," he teased wickedly.

"Stop that," she said impatiently.

"You said that you fancy being profligate, darling."

She eyed him with speculation, and her wicked juices began to bubble. "I feel a wager coming on."

"Well, I am a betting man."

"I dare you to address me as *darling* all evening."

"I'll do it if the prize I win is worthwhile . . . if you will allow me to kiss you, for instance."

The corners of her mouth went up, then she said wickedly, "You may kiss me as many times as you fancy . . . if you do it in public."

"I believe outrageousness excites you. I'll stick to *darling* in public; the kisses will have to be private."

"Kiss. Singular," Alex corrected.

This time it was the corners of Hart's mouth that went up. He tapped his silver-headed cane on the carriage ceiling, and when the driver slid back the panel, Hart said, "The Mollies' Club."

When they alighted from the carriage in lower Piccadilly, Hart bade the driver wait. He gave a password to gain admittance, reached for the door, and held it open. "Permit me, darling."

Alex removed her top hat, handed it to the porter, and gave Hart an adoring glance. "Thank you, darling." She was disappointed when the porter's face registered no shock but remained passive.

The club was filled with gentlemen in evening attire and ladies in costly but flashy gowns. The noise level was extremely high as the couples crowded round the gambling tables, laughing, drinking, and flirting outrageously. "By the raucous laughter, everyone seems to be enjoying themselves."

Hart's laughter rang out.

"What's so bloody funny?" she hissed.

"You are, darling. What would you like to drink, rum shrub?"

"I'll have champagne . . . darling," she added through her teeth. As she sipped from her glass and the bubbles tickled her nose, her avid glance swept about the dimly lit room. Most of the women were statuesque, the plumes in their wigs making them tower over their partners. A few were rail thin, with no curves whatever. Alex was admiring a diamond choker on the throat of a woman in black when she noticed her Adam's apple.

She leaned close to Hart and murmured, "I suspect the woman at the roulette table is a man."

"What a profligate mind you have, darling." Mirth made him almost choke on his brandy.

A couple walked past their table from the dance floor. "Evening, Hart." Alex was astounded that it was Hart's brother-in-law, the Earl of Carlisle. His companion, however, was not Hart's sister Dorothy; she was a very pretty female with a painted face and delicate hands and ankles. "His lordship is with a prostitute! She's so young it is an outrage."

"Take a closer look at all the women, Alex."

As she did as he bade her, Alex's eyes widened with shock.

"You are the only female in the entire room, Alexandra."

She was shocked to the bone. "I'm leaving! This isn't what I asked you to show me, Hart. You deliberately deceived me!"

"Half of them are prostitutes. Male prostitutes."

Alex headed for the exit as quickly as she could.

Hart followed, pleading, "Darling, don't be angry."

As they left, they drew every eye, and with flushed cheeks she hissed, "Don't call me that!"

As they walked to the carriage, she muttered with chagrin, "Hoist on my own petard. But truly, it is disgusting!"

"Why is it disgusting for males to dress as females, when you think it perfectly acceptable to go about dressed as a male?"

She stopped and turned to look up at him. "You were teaching me a lesson? Was that your point in taking me to such a place?"

His arms slipped around her and he bent his head and kissed her. "Yes, darling. And there are so many other lessons I would like to teach you."

She tasted the brandy on his lips. "Not another kiss until you fulfill your part of the bargain."

Hart sighed and opened the carriage door for her. "Waterloo Road," he instructed his driver. He sat down beside her and capitulated. "You win, Alex. I'll take you to a 'finish.' "

"What's a 'finish'?"

"It's where London's prostitutes finish up after the theaters let out. It won't just be a lesson; it will be an education."

They rode over the stone bridge at Westminster and alighted from the carriage close to where the new bridge was being built across the Thames at Waterloo Road. "Keep your wits about you," Hart warned his coachman.

Alex stared about her, for though the weather was chilly, scantily dressed drabs filled every dark doorway. All the buildings' windows were shuttered, as if their eyes were closed in slumber, but Hart, with a proprietary hand at the small of her back, led her through a small door. She was momentarily blinded by the light of a thousand gas lamps, and she realized immediately that she was inside a gin palace.

At one end of the room was a long row of tables with seats like upholstered couches. Each was separated by a wooden screen for a modicum of privacy. At the other end of the room was a raised dais where prostitutes were parading in all their tawdry finery, doing their utmost to arouse their audience of men making their selections. The strumpets both lifted and lowered their garments to expose their female charms to best advantage and accompanied their actions by lascivious banter. The air was filled with laughter, blue smoke, cheap scent, and the stink of unwashed bodies. Alex stared in fascination as one whore after another led the man who had chosen her to one of the drink-filled tables. Then she noticed that both Hart and herself were being singled out for particular attention because they were richly dressed.

A young girl, with hair dyed the color of burgundy, solicited Alex. " 'Ow would y'like me to suck yer duck till it quacks, luv?"

Alex shot Hart a look of panic.

Hart, unable to hide his amusement, shrugged. "You know what they say about redheads!"

Alex quickly recovered. "No, but I warrant it's nowhere near as outrageous as what they say about dukes!" She suspected the brandy he had consumed had clouded his judgment in bringing her here.

As the hour of midnight passed, Alex was amazed at

the number of men who had been drawn to the gin palace; most appeared to be regular customers. "The number of male members present who belong to the aristocracy is disgraceful."

Hart grinned. "Male members indeed; you have a delightful way with words, Alex."

Well, I shall certainly write about this debauchery! As the hour advanced, the gentlemen of the *ton* began to remove their coats, waistcoats, and cravats as they lounged on the couches with whores either straddling their laps or kneeling between their legs. *This is an eye-opener about the men in High Society that I shall never forget!* "Are these brutes actually entertained by plying girls with gin until they fall to the floor dead drunk?"

"Entertained and infinitely amused."

A crowd of men had formed around a few females who lay nearly unconscious in the middle of the floor. One male bent down and fed one of the whores a bright yellow concoction. "Whatever is he making her drink?" Alex asked with alarm.

"A mixture of mustard and vinegar, I believe. The result produces great hilarity among these swine, who have more money than brains."

Suddenly the young prostitute began to spasm in a convulsion, and as her half-clad body writhed and contorted, a great cheer went up. Alexandra ran from the room and once outside promptly vomited. "Please take me home," she said to a white-faced Hart.

As the carriage rumbled back to Mayfair, Nick Hatton's words came back to her. *London has an underbelly I never want you exposed to. Wickedness and evil sometimes run rampant among the beau monde.* Alex sat huddled in a corner of the carriage; she didn't much like Hart Cavendish at the moment. Nor did she like herself and her own prurient curiosity.

Alexandra stayed close to home the next couple of days. She worked laboriously over an article for the newspaper, condemning the squalid slum conditions and devastating poverty that spawned prostitution in girls as young as twelve. Then she ripped the aristocracy up one side and down the other, not for turning a blind eye but for condoning and exploiting the situation. Then she invited the public to go and see for themselves the debauchery that went on in the city's gin palaces.

Alexandra had to steel her emotions before she could sketch a scene to accompany her article, but when she was done, she was satisfied that it would tug at the heartstrings of even the most hardened politician.

Alex looked through her bedroom window; watching the first snowflakes of the year fall made her feel melancholy. She decided to take afternoon tea with Dottie since she hadn't spent much time with her grandmother lately. Actually, the place seemed too quiet since Rupert had moved to his own town house, and Alex admitted that she missed him.

Dottie stood at the hall table sorting through the mail that had just arrived. "Grieves and Hawks, Goggin Brothers, Huntsman and Sons, all Savile Row tailors, and all, thank heaven above and all the cherubim and seraphim, are bills for which Rupert is now responsible! God rot the boy; you'd think he'd call round for his mail, if nothing else."

"I've missed him too."

"Missed him? Then I advise you use a bigger shovel to hit him with next time."

Alex laughed. She felt better already. "I'd be happy to take his mail around to Clarges Street. Being a new husband keeps him busy, I suspect."

Dottie opened an invitation and threw the other letters on the hall table. "Busy spending money, by the look of things. Well, speak of the devil—or the devil's mother-in-law—here's an invitation to dine with the Hardings. I'm afraid that Annabelle is too much to stomach, even with my cast-iron gut."

"Cast-iron gut? How graphic."

"The secret of my longevity: a cast-iron gut and a callous heart."

"Dottie, you do not have a callous heart!"

"Of course not, darling. I disparage myself for the sheer pleasure of hearing others beg to differ. You needn't bother reassuring me." Dottie scrawled their regrets across the bottom of the invitation. "The dinner will be to apprise us of the news that Olivia is with child, which we will be expected to greet with wide-eyed surprise and two-faced congratulations. The men will all be smoking Harding's cigars, and you know how I loathe a man with a cigar . . . makes him look like he's sucking on a dog turd! You may take your brother's letters and drop this off at the same time."

Dottie and she were jumping to the conclusion that Olivia was with child. Perhaps it wasn't true; they should give her the benefit of the doubt. If it were true, it was conceivable that Rupert was the father and doing the honorable thing.

Alex decided to walk in the snow. She would go to Clarges Street and be back in time for dinner, so did not take Sara. She put on a warm velvet cloak and scooped up the letters from the hall table. The lamps along Curzon Street were being lit, and Alex lifted her face and laughed with delight when snowflakes fell onto her eyelashes. She knocked on Olivia and Rupert's door in Clarges Street, and it was opened by a maid she had never seen before.

"I'm sorry, ma'am. Lady Longford is not at home. She is visiting Lord and Lady Harding, but she will be back for dinner."

"Oh, actually it is Rupert I am here to see; I'm his sister."

"His lordship is engaged, ma'am. Would you care to wait?"

"Yes, thank you." Alex wiped her feet upon the mat, removed her cloak, shook the snow from it, and hung it on the hall stand. The maid bobbed a curtsy and disappeared. As Alex stood waiting with the letters in her hand, wondering with whom Rupert was engaged, she heard male voices coming from the drawing room.

"I thought we would go to Champagne Charlie's tonight. We haven't been for months; she'll think we dropped off the face of the earth."

Why, that's Christopher's voice. The Hatton twins had such deep voices they could never be mistaken, except for each other's, of course. She moved closer to the door. Then Alex heard her brother groan. "Not Charlie's. Can't we go to White's or Watier's?"

"I've dropped so much money at White's lately that I've become an easy mark. At Charlie's my luck might change; let's give it a try."

"Well, so long as we're just going to gamble, and not for the other sport—"

"Speak for yourself, old man. What the hell's the matter with you? You used to enjoy heaving dumplings and writhing rumps. Don't tell me your bride has you on a short leash?"

"Actually, Kit, no. She doesn't give a tinker's damn where I go or what I do, so long as I satisfy her before I leave—and after I return."

"And you're complaining?" Kit asked.

"Nightly command performances can be fatiguing. Why don't I meet you at Charlie's?"

"Why can't I just wait for you?"

"I never know how long it will take; she's an indefatigable bedfellow."

Kit's laughter rang out. "Christ! She who must be serviced!"

Alexandra wanted to sink through the foyer floor as the two men came out of the drawing room and nearly hit her with the door.

"Alex, how lovely to see you. How are you, Imp?" Kit asked with familiar affection.

"I . . . I'm cold. I just walked in the snow." Her burning cheeks belied her words. She avoided her brother's eyes and tried to make a joke. "I brought your mail, Rupert. You must inform the people who are dunning you that you have a new address."

No one laughed. "Well, I was just about to leave. Will I have the pleasure of seeing you at the opening night of the new opera at Covent Garden next week?" Kit enquired.

"Perhaps," she said tentatively.

Christopher took her hand and lifted her fingers to his lips. "Elusive females are irresistible. Good night, Alexandra."

When she was alone with her brother, she quickly filled the silence with a gentle jab. "We haven't seen you since the wedding."

Rupert, shuffling through his mail, said dryly, "You'll be receiving a formal invitation to dinner shortly."

"Yes"—Alex held up the envelope—"I am about to drop off our regrets at the Hardings."

Rupert ripped open a letter, then frowned. "This isn't for me, it's for Dottie."

Alex took it back, stuffed it into her reticule, then turned as Olivia arrived home.

"Oh, hello, Alexandra. Were you just leaving?"

"Yes, actually," she replied lamely.

"Sorry we can't invite you to stay and dine with us tonight, but Rupert and I are otherwise engaged." Olivia gave Rupert a hot, sideways glance.

Alex noticed that the look her brother returned was decidedly cool. "I quite understand," she murmured. *I don't really understand. I thought Rupert loved you exactly as you are. . . . Why else did he marry you?*

Before returning to Berkeley Square, Alex left her and Dottie's regrets with the Hardings' butler. As she turned the corner from Clarges Street onto Curzon, she pondered the conversation between Rupert and Kit Hatton. Apparently, they were going to a place called Charlie's to gamble. She had never heard of it, but from their conversation she gathered that there were more games than faro going on there. Despite her disgust with what she'd seen at the despicable gin house, her curiosity remained strong, and she made an immediately decision to go and see for herself. First, however, she would have to find out where Champagne Charlie's was.

As soon as she got back to Berkeley Square she sought out Sara. "Have you ever heard of a place called Champagne Charlie's?"

Sara pressed her lips together.

"I promise I won't make you go there."

"It's called King's Place Vaulting Academy; it's in Pall Mall."

"You are a mine of information, Sara; I intend to ask Dottie to raise your salary."

Sara grinned. "Her ladyship said to tell you that she is dining in bed tonight. She found a new book about Lord Nelson's notorious affair with Lady Hamilton and intends to devour it along with her sherry trifle."

* * *

The next morning Alex rewrote her article, emphasizing the deplorable moral decay of England and the reforms that were needed. After lunch she donned her male attire and delivered her story and sketches to the *Political Register* office. She received seven shillings for her efforts and knew that was top price.

"The bleedin' Regent has suppressed all lampoons about himself, primarily by payin' off caricaturists like Cruickshank. People are hungry for stuff about Prinny. A drawin' that ridiculed His Royal High-an'-Mightiness would sell papers. See what you can do."

Knowing it would be easy money, Alex promised the editor, William Cobett, a lampoon. Now that she had money in her pocket, she decided to go to Champagne Charlie's and gamble. It wasn't the gaming that drew her, of course, but what else might be going on there. Pall Mall was a fashionable district and she felt sure that she would find nothing that was lurid.

Alex tried to affect a nonchalance she was far from feeling as she walked into Champagne Charlie's in the late afternoon. The first thing that struck her was the luxury of her surroundings. The second thing was that the females she encountered did not look like the prostitutes she had seen on the streets of London or at that horrible gin house. Not only were they beautiful and well-groomed, most were laughing and looked genuinely happy.

Two females, who were conversing and apparently enjoying a jest, looked over the young man who had just arrived. By mutual consent, the younger of the pair approached Alex and gave her a radiant smile. "Hello, luv. You're not a regular patron, but I hope that will change. My name is Reggie; welcome to Charlie's."

"A boy's name," Alex blurted, disconcerted.

"Well, if Charlotte can be Charlie, Regina can be Reggie."

"Ah, yes, my name is Alex—" She just caught herself from adding *Sheffield*.

"A mutual friend recommended us, no doubt?"

"Yes, yes," Alex admitted nervously. "Kit Hatton."

Another smile wreathed Reggie's face. "You know the

twins, the Double-Dick Brothers? Well, any friend of Harm and Hazard is certainly a friend of mine!"

The Double-Dick Brothers? Alex was rendered speechless. When Reggie reached for her hand, she slipped it behind her back; Alexandra's hands were slender and feminine. Undaunted, the pretty blonde took her arm. "I came for the gaming," Alex said quickly. Realizing her double *entendre,* she added, "Cards, but perhaps I'll see you later."

"I hope so, luv, but be warned: When evening descends, Charlie's gets pretty busy, and I may not be available."

"I can only imagine," Alex murmured.

The gaming room was just as luxuriously furnished as the spacious reception room, minus the mirrors. And there were many paintings of nymphs in enticing poses to distract the players. *Gives an edge to the house, no doubt,* Alex thought cynically as she took a seat at the *vingt-et-un* table. The dealer of the permanent bank was female and attractive, but she was not young. Somehow Alex felt pleased about this; at least the establishment didn't discriminate against age.

She handed the dealer five of her hard-earned shillings, and when she received only one chip, she tried not to flush. It was fortunate that Alex enjoyed an immediate run of luck; it increased her number of chips tenfold. She played on, and whenever one of the six men at the table demanded a reshuffle, she took time to observe the rest of the room. Technically, it was still afternoon, yet already the room was more than half filled with gentlemen who seemed to have money to burn. Most played negligently and indulged in the free-flowing liquor, so by focusing on the game and keeping her wits about her, Alex's losses were minimal and her pile of chips increased steadily.

There was no clock in the room, but she had been playing for a couple of hours and gauged the time to be about six, when a female strolled in who could only be described as stunning. She was sleekly beautiful, with champagne-colored hair swept up into a sophisticated French roll. She wore a low-cut evening gown in a shade of sable, and her throat and wrists were adorned with topaz jewels. Alex guessed who she was before she exchanged pleasantries with the gentlemen who called her Charlie. Alex experienced a sharp stab of envy, mixed with jealousy, as she suspected this woman knew Nick Hatton . . . *most likely in the biblical sense!*

A young female, dressed as a maid in a frilly, short skirt, was regaled with cheers as she went to a sideboard and took out a chamber pot. Alex stared in disbelief as the girl carried it to the gaming table where she was sitting. The blonde handed it to the gentleman sitting on Alex's right, who stood up immediately to relieve himself. Alex looked down into the pot and saw a pair of eyes painted on the bottom, one eye closed in a suggestive wink. She stood up immediately, almost knocking over her chair, and the dealer cashed out her chips, pushing her winnings toward her. Alex scooped up her money and fled.

As she strode through the busy reception room, her steps slowed and she chided herself for being a coward. She had come to learn about the prostitutes who worked in this high-class brothel, and unless she struck up a conversation with one of the females employed here, she would learn nothing. Taking her courage in her hands, Alex sat down on a divan in an alcove and glanced about for Reggie. Finally, she spotted her. She was now wearing a white muslin coat dress that opened all the way down the front. Beneath it she wore a matching white corset, white stockings, and fetching black garters. When Alex beckoned to her, Reggie flashed her a radiant smile and came across the room.

"Were you lucky tonight, darlin'?"

"Extremely lucky; I won thirty pounds!"

Reggie laughed. "Ooo, that will buy you five minutes of my time, luv."

"Are you teasing me, or are you serious?" Alex asked, aghast.

Reggie sat down, crossed her legs, and stroked Alex's thigh. "Now I'm teasing you."

Alex captured her hand to hold it still. "How much do you get for . . . you know . . . pleasuring a man?"

"It varies. Usually a hundred guineas, unless you want to stay all night—then it's five hundred."

Alex's mouth gaped open, then it snapped shut. "Do you enjoy the work here?"

"Well, it certainly beats being a bloody servant for starvation wages. Actually, I *am* in service, but my working conditions are better than anyone else's in London. Shall we go to my room, luv?"

"Er . . . I'm a little short."

"Ooo, darlin', don't let that worry you; men come in all shapes an' sizes. Don't be shy."

"No, no, I mean *a little short of money,*" Alex explained lamely.

"Oh, I see!" Reggie laughed good-naturedly. "Well, luv, come back an' see me when you scrape enough blunt together."

Alex made her way back to Berkeley Square in a bemused daze. Some of her ideas about prostitutes and their plight had been turned upside down. Apparently there were whores, and then there were *whores*. They had a pecking order, and the intelligent ones at the top of their game flourished from the fruits of their labor.

Chapter 18

When Alex arrived home, the house seemed empty. She ran upstairs to her chamber and found a book and a note from her grandmother:

Gone gallivanting. Don't wait up. Enjoy Emma's exploits! Dottie.

Alex smiled; her grandmother had left her the book about Lady Hamilton and Lord Nelson. She decided that she would work on the lampoon and asked Sara to bring her dinner upstairs. As she tried to concentrate on Prinny, her mind kept wandering back to the brothel in Pall Mall. A full-blown picture of Charlotte King wearing the fabulous topaz gems came into her head. *The wages of sin are not death, after all; they are jewels!* It gave her an idea for the lampoon.

Alex sketched Prinny with wheels and pedals, as if he were a bicycle. Then she drew his mistress, Lady Hertford, riding him, adorned with all the Crown Jewels. Beneath the lampoon she wrote: ENJOYING THE FRUITS OF HER LABOR.

She took a bath and climbed into bed to enjoy the exploits of Emma Hamilton. Suddenly, she remembered the letter for Dottie that she had stuffed into her reticule the previous evening. Alex got out of bed, found her bag, and extracted the torn envelope. It was addressed to Lady Longford and came from Coutts Bank. Alex, consumed by curiosity, was tempted to read the letter.

Guilt at such a despicable act stayed her hand . . . for about thirty seconds.

Please be advised that the payments on your bank loan have never been met and are overdue. This is the third and last reminder Coutts Bank will provide regarding the account, which is now in arrears. If you continue to ignore this matter, it will be placed in the hands of our solicitors. Respectfully,

Alex couldn't quite make out the signature, but it looked suspiciously like *Thomas Coutts*. She let the letter slip from her fingers, totally confused. Why on earth, with Dottie's wealth, had she taken out a loan from Coutts Bank? In any case, wasn't Barclays her bank? And if she had taken out a loan for some eccentric, whimsical reason, why hadn't she paid the interest due? Alex ran her fingers through her curls, absently noticing that her hair was no longer short. *I must have a serious talk with her in the morning*. She picked up the book, and soon all thoughts that tried to intrude were banished as she lost herself in the story.

When Alex awoke the next morning, her first thoughts were of Champagne Charlie's Vaulting Academy. Her subsequent thoughts were of Emma, who had become Horatio Nelson's mistress. Then she remembered the dunning letter from Coutts Bank. She slipped a chamber robe over her night rail and tapped on Dottie's door. She found her grandmother in bed, enjoying her morning chocolate. "Was the gallivanting good?" she asked, tentatively.

"Relentlessly! After the usual regimental piss-up, we engaged in mindless pranks like sticking our arses out the window."

"Dottie, please be serious. I am in a serious mood."

"Ah, I cannot be serious after the hilarity Lady Spencer and I enjoyed last night. We were invited to play mah-jongg at Melbourne House. When we arrived we realized Liz Melbourne was showing off the new chinoiserie *décor*. It is in such execrable taste that it will make the Prince of Wales feel perfectly at home. My face almost cracked from trying to hide my amusement, and the mah-jongg tiles rattled merrily in my hand as I strove to keep my laughter silent. The conversation was an orgy of pejorative blather; there was enough hypocrisy in the air to choke a rhinoceros!"

"I'm so glad you enjoyed yourself." Alex handed her the letter. "This was among the mail I delivered to Rupert the other night. He opened it by mistake, then gave it back to me."

When Dottie read the letter, she did not even raise an eyebrow. "Darling, perhaps we *should* attend the Hardings' dinner. Wouldn't it be absolutely divine if we both wore puce?"

"It would be more divine if you could stay on the subject. What's all this loan nonsense about?"

"You've put your finger on it exactly, Alexandra. It is a jest. Thomas Coutts is a dear old friend of mine. Once offered me *carte blanche* . . . must be in his second childhood!"

Alexandra wanted to believe her, but some intuition told her to probe deeper. "It's not a jest, Dottie. It is a demand for money, and if the money is not forthcoming, it threatens legal action."

"Tush, darling! You mustn't fret about such things. I'll take care of the matter in a trice."

"Dottie, I know that you are older and wiser than I, but I'm no longer a child. Please talk to me, woman to woman."

Alex saw a speculative look come into Dottie's eyes, as if she were assessing her granddaughter. The look changed to one of acceptance, then complete capitulation. "You would be much happier not knowing, darling. But if you are the young woman I believe you to be, the truth will not destroy you. I only hope it won't make you feel as desperate as I do sometimes."

Alex touched Dottie's liver-spotted hand. "Tell me."

"My wealth is a myth, a mirage. It was true once upon a time, but it slowly evaporated into the mists of time. Your grandfather drank and gambled away his fortune. To his credit, he set aside a sizable dowry for your mother, but the untitled lout she married followed in her father's footsteps. When the money was gone, he left her with two children, and to solve her problem, she ran off with another untitled lout. Fortunately, she left you behind."

"Fortunately?" Alex asked softly.

"Most fortunately. She left behind the real treasure—one of purest gold. Oh, death and damnation, I've sunk to being maudlin! Russell left me Longford Manor, and when the well dried up at Barclays Bank, the furnishings, the paintings, and finally the servants slowly evaporated. Your suggestion that we come to London bought us time. I closed up the manor and left it with trustworthy caretakers. I took out the loan with Coutts to help Rupert secure a rich wife, and to set aside a small dowry of a thousand pounds for you, darling, which I will not touch on any account."

Alexandra felt as stunned as a bird flown into a stone wall. Then her thoughts winged back to the signs that should have told her Dottie's actions were more frugal than eccentric! "The solution to our money problems is staring us in the face. If you sold this town house, it would bring a very good price, certainly enough to safeguard Longford Manor. This London house is a luxury we must manage without."

Dottie's bark of laughter was sharp. "Ah, darling, if only it were that simple. Lord Staines owns this town house. He pays the servants' wages, even pays the food and wine accounts. It's a well-kept secret; Neville is generous enough to allow people to believe it belongs to me." Dottie heaved a sigh. "Well, at least Rupert's money problems are solved."

Alexandra's eyes widened. "Rupert married Olivia for her money. Of course! That answers so many puzzling questions. How naive I was to think he married her for love." She sat down on the bed as a horrendous thought struck her. *I offered to marry Nick Hatton so that he could share my fortune! Good God, how utterly humiliating if he had accepted me!* His rejection still stung. *How very fortunate that he was not attracted to me!*

"Love, Alexandra, is a bigger myth than my wealth. I've attempted to instill that since the day you came to live with me. I imagined I was in love with Russell Longford, your mother imagined she was in love with Johnny Sheffield, and look where it got us both. Men don't fall in love, darling; they marry for expedience, then take their pleasures where they find them. A woman, if she has any intelligence, will do the same. And I do credit you with intelligence, Alexandra."

"That's the reason you made me promise to marry Christopher Hatton. It's not just the title; it's the money and security."

"Exactly! Thank God you understand. But you must keep this secret as sacred as I have. In Society, money is everything. The *ton* will fall on us like a pack of hounds and rend us apart like foxes, if they discover we are not wealthy."

Nick said the same thing when I was the only one who would sit with him! She heard his words clearly: *As well as tenderhearted, you are endearingly naive. The worthy matrons of the ton are not snubbing me because I shot my father; I am being ostracized because I now have no part of the Hatton wealth.*

Alex gathered her thoughts to focus on the problem at hand. "We must pay the interest on this loan. I have thirty guineas I won at cards, and I have expectations of a little more with my latest lampoon. Did you win anything at mah-jongg?"

"A couple of pounds. I shall take it round to Coutts to shut them up. We shall manage somehow, darling."

"I suppose you pledged your precious jewels for this loan."

"Jewels, my bum! I had to sell those long ago. I pledged Longford Manor; what else did I have?"

Alexandra's heart plummeted. *Judas Iscariot, Dottie! You're not just eccentric, you're raving mad!*

Dressed again as Alex Sheffield, she delivered the lampoon to the newspaper. When she was paid only five shillings for it, her despair deepened. On the way back to Berkeley Square, it dawned on her that she would never be able to earn enough to get Dottie out of debt. The amount of money she earned from scribbling wouldn't even feed them, let alone keep a manor like Longford from being devoured by the wolves. Circumstances had left Alex homeless when she was a child, and the specter of it happening again frightened her. It suddenly occurred to her that she hadn't even asked

Dottie how much she had borrowed, nor the interest rate she was being charged.

When she got home, she ran up to Dottie's room but found that the bird had flown. She tried to control the rising panic within. She glanced up at the portrait of her grandmother and murmured, "What have you done?" The naked redhead gazed back at her with an enigmatic smile, and Dottie's words from the past floated back to her: *A little sin in the soul makes a woman irresistible.* Alex realized that this painting was displayed above the fireplace because it belonged to Neville Staines.

Back in her own chamber, Alex rifled through the pages of the book about Emma Hamilton until she found the chapters she was looking for. As she reread them, the glimmer of an idea began to form in the back of her mind. She put down the book and stripped off her clothes, then she stood in front of the mirror and assessed her naked form with critical eyes. What she planned would take more reckless daring than anything she had ever contemplated in her life. She knew it would entail bundling up her morals and firmly casting them aside.

Alexandra dressed carefully. She knew she needed to look striking and decided to wear the cream silk faille whose low *décollatage* showed off her firm young breasts to perfection. Then she called Sara and asked her to thread the turquoise velvet ribbon through her curls, knowing that the vibrant color was a vivid contrast to her red-gold hair.

When Sara displayed curiosity about why she was dressing in evening clothes in the afternoon, Alex replied, "Don't ask questions; you won't like the answers, Sara."

She put on her dark cloak and at the last moment decided she again needed Dottie's ostrich-feather fan for dramatic effect. Then, before she lost her courage, Alex took a cab to Pall Mall.

When she arrived at the building, Alexandra knew she dared not hesitate, but must act while the impulse was upon her. She closed her eyes, took a deep breath, and stepped across the threshold. Every female in the reception room stared at her knowingly. There was only one reason for a young woman to come here: She was on the game and hoped to be employed at the high-class brothel. When one of the girls approached her, she said, "I wish to speak with Charlotte King."

Alex averted her eyes from the gentlemen who were in the reception room, bantering with the girls. She was weak with relief that she had never met any of them. It seemed like a lifetime before Charlie came strolling into the room; Alex noticed that she exchanged pleasantries with the men before she sauntered over.

Alexandra looked directly into the madam's eyes. "I have a business proposition I'd like to discuss with you, Mrs. King."

Charlie raised a perfectly curved brow. "Propositions are certainly my business."

Alexandra laughed at the witty riposte. It was a nervous response she could not control.

Charlie swept her from head to foot with a glance that missed no detail. "Follow me." Charlie led the way upstairs to her own private suite. When the door closed, she watched Alexandra remove her cloak. "Why do you want to work for me?"

"For the money, of course."

Charlie laughed. "Of course. Are you good at what you do?"

"I don't know; I've never done it before."

Charlie's eyebrows rose. "You're virgin? I need girls with experience. Some of my clients have specialized sexual tastes. We don't have amateur night; our business is pleasuring men."

"Oh, the service I am offering will definitely pleasure men—but not physically."

"Is there any other way?" Charlie couldn't hide her amusement.

"There are many other ways. But I am speaking of *visually* pleasuring men. I would like to be a posing girl. It is like a little play or vignette behind a sheer curtain. Lamplight makes it more than a silhouette yet lends mystery to the exotic performance. Basically, a posing girl starts out fully clothed and ends up naked. She could remove her clothes and climb into bed, or remove her clothes and take an imaginary bath. All her poses are very tasteful and high-class yet extremely erotic. What makes it so provocative is the sheer curtain that separates her from her male audience, giving the illusion that she is untouchable, unobtainable. Which of course she must be."

"Undress for me."

Alexandra's mouth went dry, and she swallowed with difficulty. Yet some instinct told her that if she hesitated, Charlie would show her the door. Alex drew herself up to her full height, lifted her chin, and slowly, proudly began to remove her garments. As her shift drifted to the carpet, she forbade herself to be embarrassed. If she could not show off her body to one woman, how on God's green earth would she be able to posture before the opposite sex, with only a sheer curtain between herself and them?

When Charlie motioned for her to turn around, Alexandra did so slowly, gracefully, moving in a tiny circle. Then she reached for the ostrich-feather fan and wafted it before her, alternately concealing then revealing her body.

"Get dressed. You are a young enchantress, as well you know. Your figure is lovely, but that isn't the reason I'm considering you. It is your attitude. It makes you look every inch a lady—a unique quality in a brothel. What is your name?"

Without hesitation, Alexandra replied, "Caprice." She dressed much more quickly than she had disrobed.

"Well, Caprice, I'll pay you two hundred and fifty, for five nights a week, and provide free room and board."

Alex was dismayed. She had only anticipated performing once a week. "Two hundred for one night a week. More often than that would make it seem commonplace, rather than special. But, I shan't need room and board; I cannot live here."

"Two hundred guineas a performance? My best girls only command the high price of one hundred!"

"For a hundred guineas they are pleasuring only one man; I will be pleasuring many."

A long silence stretched between them. "One hundred; take it or leave it. I'll give you a trial. If you increase my business, we have a deal. You can start on Friday."

"Saturday. I shall come on Saturday, so that the gentlemen will have something pleasant to think about while they are in church, enduring the Sunday sermons."

Champagne Charlie threw back her head and laughed. "You have wit, a quality I admire."

"A quality you possess." Alex picked up her cloak. "Thank you, Mrs. King."

Alex's knees felt weak as wet linen as she walked home. She had certainly torn a page from Dottie's book. She wasn't just eccentric; she too was raving mad!

There were times when Captain Nicholas Hatton thought he would go raving mad during the long winter nights. The days were filled with desperate fighting—Napoleon had added another fourteen thousand troops to General Soult's command—and they went by in a quick blur of blood, guts, destruction, and death. He and his men had no time to do anything but advance and retreat, attack and defend. But the nights were endless, almost unendurable. The hours spent on watch brought a longing for Hatton Hall, with its verdant green pastures filled with the horses he had bred. He was desperately homesick for England, his ancestral home, his twin brother, and his dog, Leo. In his memory, the night sounds and scents of England were different, even the air seemed softer in retrospect. His need was like a craving in the blood.

Soon, it would be Christmas and then a new year would dawn. It would be a difficult time for the men he commanded, who were far from home with no idea when they would be able to return. He reflected that it would be a lonely time for Kit too; until now, the twins had spent every Christmas together. It would be the first holiday season since his brother had accidentally shot their father, and Nick felt guilty that he would not be at Hatton to comfort him. At night he was haunted by the thought that he could easily die here in France. Yet it wasn't death that he feared, it was the thought that he might never see England again.

With a rigid control, he kept his thoughts to himself, for he knew that if he felt this way, the men who fought under his command must have the same longings and fears. Nick had come to hate war with a vengeance. He had started out a fervent warrior, ready to take on the enemy with a knife between his teeth, but then he'd faced so many moral dilemmas and demons that his conscience had become shadowed. Some of the men he commanded, like Jake Smith, were no more than boys, risking their lives and killing people in the name of England. This war had made Nick lose an innocence he hadn't known he possessed. War was insanity; it made killing a virtue rather than a vice. He had killed so many that he feared that his eternal soul was damned—if there were such a thing, he reflected cynically.

He banished all thoughts of Alexandra, for that way lay true madness. But his dreams took on a life of their own, and in them he did not deny his hunger for her. They always began the same. His kisses were hot and demanding, taking not giving. His lips were ravenous, rapacious, and savage. Yet once he slaked himself with kisses, his arms clasped her tightly. The feel of her body was so comforting it gave him solace. When he was at his lowest ebb, she never failed to restore and replenish him. He always awoke at the same point in the dream, immediately after making love to her with his possessive mouth but before he made love to her with his body. Even as he cursed, he knew the reason for never consummating their union, even in his dreams, was obvious. Alexandra was forbidden to him; she belonged to Christopher.

Chapter 19

Christopher Hatton, along with his friend Rupert, became members of the prestigious sporting Four-In-Hand Club. Kit agreed because there was no actual racing involved. Whenever they met, the club members simply drove their perch-phaetons and curricles to Salt Hill, about twenty miles from London. There, they dined at The Windmill, imbibed until they were cup-shot, then returned to town.

As Kit tooled along St. George Street to Hanover Square, where the club members gathered for their outing, the street was fast becoming clogged with sporting vehicles. Thinking he saw Rupert in his new white drab driving coat, he drew up to the curb and jumped from his phaeton. When the tall, slim man turned, however, Kit saw that he had mistaken Jeremy Eaton for Rupert.

"What the devil are you doing here?" Kit could not hide his irritation. The members were mostly titled lords; this was the last place he had expected to see Eaton.

"Hello, Harm. Seems we frequent the same haunts."

You are certainly haunting me, you bastard!

"Nice cattle; I heard you'd bought yourself a perch-phaeton. Your investments must be paying off. Mine didn't pan out."

"Too bad. You should ask your father for advice."

"My father and I are forever at odds . . . rather like you and your father were," he drawled.

"What the devil do you mean? My father doted on me."

"Bloody ironic, isn't it, that your hand was the one to pull the trigger?"

"Look here, I've had about enough of your insinuations. If you want to shout it to the world that I, not my twin Nick, accidentally shot my father, be my guest. None will believe you."

"Accidentally?" Jeremy queried, blowing on his hands to warm them. "If I reveal there was nothing *accidental* about it, all would be ready to believe me, I warrant."

Kit began to shiver, and he pulled his caped coat closer about his neck. "I'd keep my mouth shut, if I were you."

Eaton laughed. "Mouths aren't for shutting unless there are flies about."

"How much?"

"Ten thousand sounds fair enough to me." He glanced up at the sky. "Could be in for trouble. There's a storm threatening; wouldn't want you to get caught in the deluge. I'll see you at White's tomorrow evening; I'm always there on Tuesday. Or better yet, I'll see you at Barclays Bank in the morning. Ten o'clock sharp."

As his second cousin left him, Kit reached into his greatcoat pocket and pulled out his flask. He raised it to his lips and noticed that his hand shook. *That fucking parasite! If I ever see him in the road, I'll run him down!* The whiskey warmed and comforted him. *What the hell's the difference? If I empty my bank account, his old man will fill it up for me.* Kit began to laugh. *Now there's irony for you!*

Alexandra had second thoughts about what she had done; then she had third and fourth thoughts, all filled with misgivings. She removed Dottie's long, silvery-blond wig and the flesh-colored net garment she had worn as Lady Godiva from the costume trunk. It was her only hope; Alex knew she could never perform stark naked. She also knew that if some other way to acquire money presented itself, she would jump at the opportunity. To take her mind off her performance tomorrow at Charlie's, which was rushing upon her with the sickening speed of a runaway carriage, she agreed to attend the Covent Garden opera with Hart Cavendish.

The moment she accepted, the Duke of Devonshire penned a note to Aberdeen, the Prince of Wales's secretary, asking if he could use Prinny's box at Covent Garden. When Aberdeen gave his consent, as he had in the past for the duke's father, Hart went shopping. He knew what he wanted and laid his plans carefully.

When Hart arrived at Berkeley Square, Alexandra came down the stairs with an indulgent smile on her face. It would make a pleasant change for him to take her out dressed as a female.

"You look so lovely you take my breath away. I love that lavender gown on you; I hoped you would wear it tonight."

Alex picked up her violet cashmere shawl and handed it to him. "How very gallant, Your Grace."

As he wrapped it about her shoulders, he bent to whisper in her ear, "What happened to *darling*?"

"That was a wager, and if you remind me of that particular evening, I shall no longer think you gallant."

"I promise to make it up to you tonight, Alexandra."

In the carriage, Alex was relieved that Hart behaved like a perfect gentleman and sat opposite her. Bemused, she wondered how long that would last. The area around Covent Garden was thick with the carriages of the *ton*. Everyone was eager to see the new opera, or more precisely, *to be seen* seeing the new opera. Few of them even liked opera, let alone understood it.

The Covent Garden piazza was crowded. She glanced about, searching for Hart's sisters, but didn't see them. Hart reached for her hand and said, "Follow me." She was surprised when he led her upstairs and they were ushered into the Prince of Wales's private box. "How on earth—? Hart, I thought we were joining your family." *I shouldn't be alone with him in the Prince of Wales's private box. Being on public display will cause gossip and set up clear expectations!*

Hart held her chair. "I wanted you to feel special tonight."

Alexandra sat down, surveyed the theater, and suddenly froze. Every eye in the gallery was upon her. Upon *them*. She saw ladies whisper behind their fans. By displaying her in the Regent's private box, the Duke of

Devonshire was declaring them a couple. Just before the lights dimmed, she saw Christopher Hatton gazing up at her with stunned disbelief.

As the curtain rose, Alex felt her cheeks turn rosy, and she quickly moved her chair farther back in the box. *Better get used to being stared at,* she admonished herself. *Tomorrow night you'll be on stage!* Though she assured herself that she wouldn't be able to see her audience because of the curtain and the lamplight, it didn't give her much comfort. Her audience would certainly be able to see her. *All* of her.

La Cambiale di matrimonio was a comic opera by Rossini, a new composer who was all the rage in Venice. Alex didn't understand Italian, but soon she was laughing at the antics of the bride and groom and the price they paid for marriage, which was a universal theme. She thought of Rupert and Olivia, and then her thoughts drifted to Hart and herself. Suddenly, she stopped laughing. *He wants tonight to be special! Good God, don't tell me Hart is going to propose!*

She quickly glanced at him and saw that his whole attention was focused upon her rather than the stage. He definitely had the rapt look of a man who was totally infatuated. And come to think of it, why else would he have agreed to go along with all her outrageous demands?

When their eyes met, he smiled. Reaching into his breast pocket, he drew out a long, slim velvet case, which he placed in her hands. "For you, Alexandra."

Her pulse quickened; the brilliant aria faded into the background as her fingers felt the plush velvet and her attention became riveted upon the jewel case. Unbidden thoughts flashed into her mind. She had promised her grandmother that she would marry Christopher Hatton, because Dottie wanted her to have a title and security. But the Duke of Devonshire had the wealth of royalty and could make her a duchess; Dottie would have no objections whatever!

The curtain descended amid applause, and the lights were lit for the interval. Most of the audience arose to make their way to the piazza for refreshments, but Alexandra and Hart remained in their cocoon, isolated and private. She took a deep breath and opened the jewel case. The white diamonds and purple amethysts of the necklace glittered against the black velvet. She stared, fascinated by the brilliance, mesmerized by the dazzling gems.

Hart bent close. "Alexandra, I want to be your lover."

She blinked and looked up at him. It *was* a proposal. An *indecent* proposal! She didn't know whether to laugh or to cry. She couldn't say that he hadn't warned her. The first time he had kissed her and she told him she wasn't interested in marriage, Hart had declared emphatically that he was not interested in marriage, either. He was asking her to be his mistress, his paramour, and he was perfectly serious.

Alexandra knew in her heart that she did not have the right to be offended. She had brought this on herself with her outrageous behavior. How could she expect him to treat her like a lady, when she had never behaved like one? She had encouraged Hart to take her to every disreputable haunt in London. Was it any wonder that he expected to become her lover? As she thought about it, she acknowledged that accepting his proposition would give her as much *cachet* as having a royal protector—more, since the Duke of Devonshire was not a caricature. She glanced down at the diamond necklace and realized she was holding the answer to all her and her grandmother's financial difficulties. The jewels were a temptation beyond belief. If she let him fasten them around her neck, she would not have to go to Charlie's. But then she looked back up at Hart, and she reluctantly admitted to herself that it would be impossible for him to be her lover, for *love* was not involved.

Alexandra closed the velvet case and handed it back to him.

"Damn it, Alex, I know you can buy your own jewels, but won't you allow me the pleasure of buying you a present?"

"Of course I will," she said lightly, "but certainly not diamonds. I'm not for sale, Hart."

"I don't want to *buy* you, I just want to—"

"Bed me?" She gave him a provocative glance from beneath her lashes. "You and a thousand others; better get in line."

Hart laughed, and the tension between them was broken. The lights in the theater were snuffed, the curtain lifted, the music rose and fell in great crescendos. When the opera was over, the performers took their curtain calls to great applause.

In the Covent Garden piazza, Alexandra stopped to admire the pretty items that were on sale. "You may have the pleasure of buying me that mask, Your Grace."

As he paid for it, he remarked, "Why would you want to cover your lovely face, Alexandra?"

"To hide my blushes from indecent proposals, of course."

She heard Hart say, "Oh, hello, Kit. Did you enjoy the opera?"

Alex looked up into Christopher's dark face and felt guilty.

"I did; Italian is one of my favorite languages. Magnificent artists, the Italians. I recently bought Canaletto's *Regatta on the Grand Canal.*" He looked at Alex. "I'd like you to see it."

Hart frowned. "I think you're mistaken about the title, old man. *Regatta on the Grand Canal* hangs on my wall at Chatsworth."

Alexandra saw Kit's reaction to Hart's words. His face had a closed, masklike expression, but his gray eyes changed dramatically. They took on the color of pewter storm clouds. Alex had drawn enough attention to herself tonight, the last thing she needed was an escalation of angry words between these two men. She said quickly, "It was lovely to see you, Kit. Good night."

Christopher Hatton was angry at the entire world. Fate was conspiring against him, and he felt impotent to do anything about it. Hart Cavendish escorting Alex all over London was the last straw! The past few days had been a nightmare in which his money was being syphoned from him in a never-ending stream. First by that bloodsucking swine, Eaton, and now by a fucking unscrupulous art dealer. *First thing in the morning, I'll return the Canaletto painting and demand my money back. Then I'll have the bastard arrested and lay criminal charges!* He would go tonight, except the shop would be closed. So Kit did the only thing he could. He walked the short distance from Covent Garden to the Hoops and Grapes and got quietly, steadily drunk. When he was offered opium, he bought some and smoked it.

By Saturday afternoon, Alex was resigned to her fate. Before she dressed, she donned the flesh-colored net garment, which clung like a second skin, then put on double petticoats and two sets of garters on the theory that the more articles of clothing she had to remove the less time she would have to spend exposed. When Dottie spied the long, blond wig and new mask lying on her bed, Alex knew she would have to tell her grandmother a white lie.

"Masquerade party tonight?" Dottie sounded puzzled.

"Yes." *It could be called a masquerade party, I warrant.*

"Who is your escort, and who's giving the party?"

"Olivia and Rupert. Some friends of the Hardings, I don't even recall their name." *That lie is doubly devious to make sure Dottie won't want to come with me.*

"Better you than me, darling. I'd prefer being buried alive."

An hour later, Alex took her courage in both hands, stiffened her backbone, and walked into Champagne Charlie's. A room with a dais at one end had been set aside for tonight's performance. Charlotte King, knowing exactly the atmosphere she wanted to create, had had transparent drapery installed, made from golden gauze. It would be backlit by the warm glow of gas lamps. On stage, Alexandra's performance would be softly illuminated, while her audience would be in darkness. Alex was thankful that the curtain separated them, making it feel as if she were alone. Though this was an illusion, at least she would not be able to see her all-male audience.

"What props will you need for tonight?" Charlie asked.

Alex had thought long and hard about this and knew it would be more effective if it were kept as simple as possible. "I'll need a bed and a chair . . . perhaps a small screen to hang my garments on as I remove them?"

Two servants brought a white iron bedstead to the stage, and another carried a feather mattress, sheets, and pillows. Alex stared. "Black satin sheets?"

"All the sheets at Charlie's are black satin. Makes female flesh look erotically decadent and tempting, don't you think?"

Alex did indeed. Once the stage was set, she watched the servants carry in chairs for the audience. Three dozen was a preposterous number; Alex hoped only half a dozen would be filled. When one of the girls showed her the invitations Charlie had sent out to her clients, Alex was rendered speechless.

Charlotte King commends herself respectfully to Lord —— and takes the liberty of advising him that Saturday evening at 8 o'clock precisely the beauteous, virginal Caprice will present her celebrated performance of poses, in the style of posture artiste, Lady Emma Hamilton.

At seven-thirty, Alex withdrew behind the curtain and stood just inside a stairwell door on one side of the dais. The long, fair wig was firmly anchored to her head and her mask was in place. She pulled her cloak more closely about her as she felt her heart race; she wanted the floor to open up and swallow her. This didn't happen, of course. She strained her ears, but all she heard over her own heartbeats was the sound of a door opening. Minutes later the gaslamps were lit, which was her cue. For one horrific moment Alex felt paralyzed, and her limbs would not move. She closed her eyes, held her breath, and launched herself into the void.

Her movements were languorous, yet studied. She entered her bedchamber through the door and slowly, gracefully closed it. She posed prettily before she removed her cloak. As her hands moved delicately to take off that first piece of clothing, she heard an audible intake of breath. She hung her cloak over the screen, then sank down in a curtsy for her next pose. When she straightened, she twirled around, sending her skirts billowing about her like the petals of a rose in full bloom and at the same time allowing a glimpse of ankle. Alex knew she was creating a magical image in the imagination of her audience. She was a young debutante, just returned from a masked ball.

Suddenly, she yawned. Then her next pose was a full stretch. It was a tantalizing hint of being tired, so that her audience would anticipate that she wanted to go to bed. Slowly, she began to remove one long kid glove an inch at a time. When her arm was finally denuded, she heard a collective sigh. Even more slowly, she unfastened the buttons of her gown, one provocative button at a time. She pushed the sleeves down from her shoulders, leaving them bare, and posed again. She stepped from her skirts, and in a swirl of petticoats, hung the gown over the screen. She sat down on the chair and went through the titillating female ritual of brushing her hair. Then she lifted one leg and posed before she removed a garter. She repeated the movement with her other leg, then stood and removed her second petticoat. She sat down again, this time to take off her slippers, her second set of garters, followed by her hose. As she inched a stocking down her leg, Alex heard a collective *aahhh.*

The appreciative murmur told her that her performance was a success so far. She stood up, clad only in her short shift, and posed, hands on hips, wondering how she would gather the courage to move on to the next revealing step. Modesty prompted her to turn her back to the curtain, while she unlaced her small busk. She set it on the chair, then slipped off her drawers. As she posed before them with the curve of her buttocks revealed, it drew spontaneous whistles, and she realized that there were more than a half dozen spectators on the other side of the curtain. Alex feared if she didn't finish this performance quickly, she would faint.

Cupping her hands over her breasts, she turned slowly, and suddenly it dawned on her that the red-gold curls on her mons, which clearly showed through the netting, did not match her silvery-blond tresses. She removed her hands from her breasts to give her audience something else to look at. She forced herself to yawn and stretch one last time, then climbed onto the bed and lay down on the black satin sheets. Mercifully, the gas lamps were snuffed.

The applause was instantaneous and thunderous. To Alex's burning ears, it sounded like a huge crowd. She became aware of male voices shouting something, and it finally occured to her that they were shouting, *"Encore, encore!"*

Someone backstage hissed, "Curtain call!" Alex jumped from the bed and grabbed her cloak from the screen. She straightened her wig and touched her mask to make sure it was in place, then covered from throat to toes with her cape, stepped through the curtain and bowed. Her mouth almost fell open; not only was every seat filled but many more men were standing. She backed through the curtain and vowed that she would never again step through the curtain that served as her barrier of protection.

Christopher Hatton, fearing that if he showed his face about town he would be laughed at, withdrew into a protective shell. The shop where he had bought the Canaletto painting was empty; the art dealer vanished into the night. Kit had spent a fortune, and he had been royally swindled. End of the year bills came flooding in, and to add insult to injury, he received a note from Barclays Bank informing him that his account was overdrawn. Whenever his balance had been low before, John Eaton had filled the coffers. Kit cursed his financial advisor and sent a note to his London office, asking him to come round to Curzon Street.

John Eaton arrived in the midst of a December sleet storm. He shook off his caped greatcoat, handed it to the butler, and was shown into Kit's presence. "Ah, Lord Hatton, how wise you are to remain before your own fire with a decanter of whiskey at your elbow on such a day."

Kit poured Eaton a drink and wasted no time with small talk. "My account is overdrawn, John. How could such a matter slip past your attention?"

"I assure you it hasn't. I am most concerned about the state of your finances, my lord."

"What is the 'state of my finances'?" Kit asked with sarcasm.

Eaton coughed. "It is obvious that your expenditures far exceed your income."

"But I inherited my father's wealth; where is it?"

"The answer lies with you, my lord."

"I beg to differ, sir! You are in charge of my investments; the answer lies with you!"

"Your father made wise investments in shipping and cargoes. Unfortunately, war with the United States has resulted in many of the vessels being seized. Henry also invested heavily in America; since then, however, we have lost possession of thirteen colonies."

"I thought we were at war with France!"

Eaton rolled his eyes. "We are, my lord, and wars drain a country of its money. Wars have led to the breakdown of the narrow personal management of Parliament by the Regent and the ministry."

It was double-talk to Kit Hatton. "You said there was money to be made from war."

"Only if one wins, my lord," Eaton said dryly. "These two wars are rapidly depleting England's wealth. They have resulted in high prices, heavy taxes, and massive unemployment."

"It is *my* depleted wealth I care about; I need money!"

"I warned you about using ready cash, did I not?"

"You did," Kit acknowledged, "but you also said you would loan me whatever money I needed, at lower interest than the bank would charge . . . two percent I seem to recall."

Eaton coughed again. "That is two percent per month."

"But that's twenty-four percent a year!"

"As opposed to bank rates of twenty-six percent, my lord."

"What about these bills?" Kit pointed to a sheaf of papers beside the whiskey decanter. "I signed an authorization for you to handle all my financial business affairs."

John Eaton picked up the bills and examined them. "These must be paid annually: taxes on Hatton Hall, land taxes, tax on this London town house, annual wages for the servants and staff." Eaton didn't even acknowledge the clothing or food and wine bills.

"Dear God, if the taxes go unpaid, I shall lose my property! You should have at least paid the taxes!"

"I am a financial advisor, not a nursemaid."

"Then advise me, Goddamn you!"

"Your investments are almost depleted; they are worthless as collateral. I'll make you another loan to cover your year-end expenses, but I shall have to hold the original title deed on Hatton until the loan is paid off."

Kit reluctantly went to his bedchamber and returned with the original deed for Hatton Hall. He handed over the document with its official red seals, warning, "I want this back, understand?"

"You can easily pay back the loan if you cut down on life's luxuries, slash your expenditures, and abjure self-indulgence."

"I am a Lord of the Realm," Kit said through clenched teeth.

"Then I suggest you do what other titled lords do when they suffer financial difficulties—marry an heiress."

After Eaton departed, Kit's thoughts did not linger on his bills; they became preoccupied with the much more pleasant vision of Alexandra.

At that moment Alex was watching Dottie read a letter she had just received from Lord Staines.

My Dearest Dorothy: I deeply regret that I will not be able to spend Christmas with you. My doctor has confined me to bed, insisting that I have suffered a mild seizure. Damned fellow won't be told that my best medicine is you, my love. Yours alone, Neville

Dottie packed immediately. "I know it's only three days until Christmas, but I'm off to nurse Neville, darling. Far preferable to spending Christmas with your brother and the Hardings. Guard your reputation, Alexandra. Rupert must escort you to all the festive entertainments, and Sara must go out with you during the day."

"Don't worry about me," Alex ordered, feeling relief that her forays to Champagne Charlie's would go undetected.

Chapter 20

On the front lines in France, the Royal Horse Artillery had no time to celebrate Christmas. Captain Nicholas Hatton's men were in pursuit of Soult's army, while other divisions had been given the safer task of blockading Bayonne.

Slowly but surely, they took one hill after another, forcing the enemy to retreat and reform its line of defense farther back. They drove Soult's army from Gave de Pau to Orthez, then they captured that position also. The terrain had treacherous mountain passes and raging rivers, and more than one of Nick's men drowned. He shepherded them as best he could, but he now had command of an entire battalion of a thousand soldiers and could no longer give them all his personal attention.

With each victory, Nick grew more confident that the end was in sight. At night he moved among the campfires, encouraging his men and restoring their flagging morale. "In every village we pass through, I see more and more deserters from the enemy army. I can spot them a mile off with their cropped heads. Half of them are barefoot, and an army without boots is staring defeat in the face!"

Nick silenced rumors that were negative and repeated those that fostered hope. "Our scouts estimate there are more than five thousand deserters scattered over the countryside. Marshal Soult is mounting his last possible defensive. He knows the end is close!"

Captain Hatton's men began to believe him when they captured St. Sever. Soult's troops retreated so quickly they had no time to destroy their magazines. More and more, the soldiers' talk turned to victory and what they would do when the war was over and Napoleon defeated. Most wanted to leave the army and return to England. Some, to Nick's amazement, wanted to become career soldiers. There was another war raging in the United States and the American continent held a fascination for many. Nicholas Hatton wanted nothing more than to return home. When the war was over, he would resign his commission and leave the army. First, however, Nick knew he must remain alive long enough to seize victory.

Early in the new year, Alex went round to Coutts Bank with money. Dottie was still in the country with Neville Staines, so Alex decided she would take over their financial difficulties. She learned that her grandmother had borrowed five thousand pounds and was already in arrears for three hundred pounds interest. She handed over the money she had made from Champagne Charlie's and realized, with a sinking heart, just how long she would have to keep on performing if she were to pay off the actual loan and not just the interest. Alex knew she had no option; Dottie had assigned the deed to Longford Manor as collateral.

When she arrived home, she was surprised to learn that Kit Hatton had called and left a note for her. When she read it she was even more surprised that he was inviting her for an evening at the theater tonight. He apologized for the short notice and sounded eager for her company. She scribbled her acceptance and had a footman take it round to Curzon Street.

They saw a Sheridan play, and Alex found that she enjoyed herself immensely. Then Kit took her for a late supper.

"I went home to Hatton Hall for Christmas, but it was so gloomy, rattling round the place alone, I couldn't wait to get back."

Alex was flattered that he gave her his undivided attention, but at the same time she suspected it was because he had seen her with Hart Cavendish and it had aroused, not jealousy exactly, but rivalry perhaps. Kit assumed Hart was competing with him for her hand. She hid her amusement and did not disabuse him of his assumption. "I don't suppose you've seen much of Rupert lately?"

"Well, over Christmas he was busy with his new family, but truthfully, marriage hasn't cramped his style at all. Being a husband hasn't curtailed our outings together; I'm starting to view marriage in a different light."

Alex searched his face for any sign of mockery, but his gray eyes held only sincerity. Her gaze lingered on his dark, heavy brows and slanting cheekbones, then her glance lowered to his square chin, with its deep cleft. *He really is one of the handsomest men I've ever seen in my life. If only I were starting to view marriage in a different light.*

A few hours later at home in her bedchamber when her dream began, the face with the dark, heavy brows and slanting cheekbones played a prominent role. He was so close Alex could feel the heat of his body and see the blue shadow on his square chin. She reached out a finger and dipped it into the deep cleft with a delicious shiver. But the man who dominated her dream was not Kit Hatton, it was his twin, Nicholas.

In St. Sever, Nick Hatton had little time to sleep, let alone dream. Wellington had given his troops orders to press on relentlessly and assured them that their northern allies were poised to take Paris.

Captain Hatton discussed strategy for taking their next stronghold with his lieutenants. Mont de Marsan was extremely important because it served as the enemy's great central depot. Snow fell heavily all day and helped to conceal their advance. By late afternoon, the battalion had accomplished its goal and captured Mont de Marsan. But before Nick had time to praise his men for their victory, there was a massive explosion as powder magazines blew up, filling the air with acrid, black smoke and the sky with orange flames. The number of casualties was great; the dead were dismembered, and the living received horrendous wounds.

Hatton ordered a field hospital be set up, and himself picked up and carried in casualties, all the time raging and cursing at the Gods of War. Seeing his men burned black sickened his soul. Within days, they had orders from Wellington himself to move on. The great man, who was suffering from a heavy cold, rode Copenhagen through the March snowstorm to bring General Hill word of Marshal Soult's position on the River Aire. They stormed the enemy's position *en masse* and forced them to fall back wearily toward Toulouse.

Wellington was relentless. In less than a fortnight he had gathered all his generals and their troops and ordered them to attack Toulouse. Soult decided to stay and fight, making a last vicious stand. The ensuing bloody battle left the wounded and dead from both sides lying everywhere. Captain Nicholas Hatton, buoyed by the courage of his men, felt immense satisfaction when he saw them fight, using the defensive tactics he had taught them. Late in the day it became obvious to British and French alike that Soult's resistance was useless. The defeated army began to flee.

Nick turned quickly in the saddle to see a dragoon riding him down, intent on decapitating him with a flailing saber. Nick fired his pistol point-blank, which saved his life, but the Frenchman and his mount barreled into him, knocking him from the saddle. Nick was momentarily stunned by the fall; as he got to his feet he heard Slate screaming. He stared in horror as his gray writhed on the ground, his guts protruding through a gaping gash in his underbelly. In a flash, Nick cocked his second pistol and put a bullet in Slate's brain.

The battlefield had no shortage of riderless horses, but before he grabbed the trailing reins of one, Nick laid a loving hand on Slate's still-warm flank, and the lump in his throat threatened to choke him. He looked about him and realized that the fighting was done, the battle won. As he picked his way through the carnage, Nick took little joy in the victory. Their casualties were heavy, and the enemy had fled, leaving behind hundreds of wounded men.

It was midnight before he had checked on the men in his battalion. As he lay in the darkness, physically, mentally, and emotionally exhausted, blessed sleep eluded him. Nick railed against a God thirsty for blood and vengeance. *When I came here, everything in the world had been snatched away, except Slate. You weren't satisfied until you took that one last thing from me!* He felt raw, sapped, desolate, a breath away from madness. But as he lay there in the dark, a strange transformation began to take place. Slowly, gradually, peacefully, a calm descended and his sanity returned. Nick knew that, except for Slate, he had no regrets. The adversity of war had taught him things he could not have learned anywhere else. Though he was more cynical, his belief in himself and his abilities was now unshakable, and his self-worth had doubled. He closed his eyes and dreamed of home and Alexandra.

"The extra five shillings a week you've given me since Christmas has made a world of difference, mistress." Sara bobbed a curtsy.

"Call me Alex, and please don't genuflect to me, Sara. I am no saint." Alex had promised her a raise when she thought her grandmother was a wealthy dowager, so she had had no option but to give Sara a little of the money she earned at Charlie's.

"I just want you to know how much I appreciate it. I'm able to buy my mother a few luxuries she's never had before."

"How is your mother, Sara?"

"She was well the last time I went round. The winter's not been kind to Maggie, though. She's been very poorly. Spring is in the air today, so let's hope she starts to improve."

"You are right, spring is in the air. Why don't we take a walk and go to visit them, Sara?"

"Oh, could we? I'll take her some tea; it's so expensive."

Alex reflected on the high price of the imported luxury and gave thanks that dear Neville Staines footed the food bills at Berkeley Square. She sent up a quick prayer for Neville's full recovery. Dottie had returned from nursing him a fortnight ago, and reported that he was vastly improved, but yesterday she had gone back for a few days, just to make sure.

Outside, the pale sunshine reflected in the windows of

the houses they passed. When they neared Regent Street, they saw that the lovely weather had brought all the vendors out to peddle their wares. Old women selling spring flowers tempted Alex to part with her money, but she resisted, knowing she must buy Sara's mother something more useful. They went into a shop, where Sara bought two ounces of tea and Alex selected a pot of honey. Then impulsively she picked up a second pot for Maggie Field.

As they walked toward the squalid streets, Sara warned, "Better hide these things or they'll be snatched from our hands by the first raggedy little bugger who runs past us." She slipped the tea into her pocket, and Alex followed suit. The houses in the slum seemed more dilapidated than Alex remembered, and the warm day brought an unbelievable stench to the entire area.

Inside, Alex explained to Sara's mother that when she had visited last time, she had been dressed in her brother's clothes. They all enjoyed a good laugh, and when the older woman saw the tea and honey they had brought her, she was overwhelmed. Alex moved apart to give them some privacy and pretended not to notice when Sara slipped some shillings into her mother's hand. They stayed for half an hour, then said their good-byes and knocked on the door across the hall.

"I heard her say come in," Sara said. She lifted the latch, and the two young women stepped across the threshold. "It's Sara. Are you feeling any better?"

Maggie was reclining on a narrow horsehair sofa, and she struggled to sit up. When she saw that Sara had someone with her, the smile of welcome faded, and her sunken eyes went wide with horror. "No . . . no . . . get her away," she gasped.

"It's all right, Mrs. Field. I came before with Sara. I was dressed in my brother's clothes." Alex touched her hair self-consciously as Maggie stared at its color as if she couldn't believe her eyes. "I brought you some honey."

"Alexandra . . . get away from me," she gasped.

"She's afraid you'll catch her consumption," Sara explained.

"She knows my name!" Alex was surprised. "Maggie, do you know me, or perhaps my grandmother?"

"No!" The denial was too swift. Too painful.

Maggie Field, you do know me. Margaret Field . . . Margaret . . . Alex's hand covered her mouth, then it slipped down over her heart.

"Your name is Sheffield . . . Margaret Sheffield, isn't it?"

The woman fell back on the couch. "Go away . . . don't look at me!"

Alex stepped back. "I'm sorry. I didn't mean to upset you."

"We'd better go," Sara said.

Alex nodded and followed her outside.

"Your face is as white as a sheet. Do you know Maggie?"

"I knew her once." Alex pressed her lips together. As her feet moved swiftly, carrying her away from the decaying streets, she could not bring herself to discuss the matter with Sara. She needed to sort out her tangled emotions. Her thoughts were in disarray, her feelings were in chaos, and her tranquility was completely shattered.

As Alex distanced herself from the slums and walked through Soho toward Mayfair, her thoughts became clearer. When they got to Berkeley Square, she turned to Sara. "I'm not coming in; I have somewhere I must go."

Sara hesitated. "Would you like me to come with you?"

"No"—Alex shook her head—"but thank you." She carried on walking to Curzon Street, then turned the corner into Clarges. She was admitted into the town house by the usual servant. "Is my brother at home?"

"I am, Alex, but not for long." Rupert, dressed in his driving coat, came down the stairs into the entrance hall.

"You are going driving; that fits into my plans perfectly."

"Unfortunately, you don't fit into my plans. I'm off to the spring meet of the Four-In-Hand Club."

"They'll have to manage without you," Alex said decisively. "I need you to drive me somewhere, Rupert."

"Do you indeed, Miss Bossy-boots? Would you mind telling me what's going on?"

"I can't tell you . . . it's something I have to show you."

Olivia emerged from the drawing room. "Hello, Alexandra." She looked from one to the other. "If you're taking your sister driving, Rupert, I shall come too. A carriage ride is the very thing to start the baby coming."

Alex looked aghast at Olivia's expanded belly. "No, you cannot possibly go racketing about town in an open carriage in your condition. Come, Rupert!"

As he followed his sister through the front door, he said through his teeth, "You're getting more like Dottie every day."

"I shall take that as a compliment."

A groom, standing with the carriage and matched pair, handed the leader's reins to Rupert, and Alex climbed up without assistance.

As her brother released the brake, she directed, "St. Giles."

"St. Giles?" Rupert shouted with disbelief. "I'm not driving my cattle into St. Giles! Have you taken leave of your senses?"

"Then get out and I shall drive them myself."

Rupert stared at her, and she gave him a level look back. "I wouldn't ask you, Rupert, unless it were absolutely imperative."

He saw the look in her eyes that told him he had no choice. "I can see that you are serious."

"Never more so in my life."

He took a corner carefully, and looked over at his sister. "I read your article in the *Political Register* about climbing boys." He glanced at the road, then back to her. "It's most admirable to champion a worthy cause, Alex, so long as you don't fall into the habit of doing it on a regular basis."

Alex held her tongue, not without difficulty.

Rupert turned the horses onto Oxford Street. "Look here, if this is one of your misguided missions to save some downtrodden wretch, I think you should know that charity begins at home."

"Meaning?"

"I think it's time you knew that Dottie is not the wealthy dowager you think her. You can't go wasting her money on charity cases; she doesn't have any."

"I am well aware of our financial difficulties. Each of us must deal with it as we think best."

"Are you condemning me because I married for money?"

"Oh, God, Rupert, of course not!" She reached over and touched his hand. "Before the year is out, I'll be doing the same thing."

"Damn it, Alex! Marrying Kit Hatton is not the same thing. You've known each other since you were children. It has always been understood that you would marry."

"Turn down this street."

"It's too narrow. . . . Good God, no wonder it stinks—this is the Rookery! Alex, it absolutely wasn't necessary to show me; you could have simply told me."

"Stop just along here."

Rupert was driving slowly, and the horses stopped when he pulled back on the reins. He set the brake on the phaeton, then threw up his hands in resignation when Alex got down and expected him to follow her.

Alex went into the building and, without knocking on Maggie's door, lifted the latch and walked in with no hesitation. She hurried over to the sofa and knelt before the coughing woman.

Her brother was right behind her. He looked down at the woman and tried to hide his distaste. "Who is this person?"

"She's our mother, Rupert."

Shocked silence filled the air for a full minute. Then he stepped back and murmured, "You are mistaken, Alex. Mother is in her forties; this woman must be in her sixties."

"There is no mistake, Rupert. I shall get a blanket, then I want you to carry her out to the carriage. I'm taking her home."

On the drive home, Alex sat in the back with her mother so she could not answer the questions that she knew Rupert must have. Maggie, or Margaret as Alex thought of her, didn't seem to have the strength to protest being taken from where she lived, though between coughing bouts her face looked racked with worry. "Please don't be distressed. I want you to get well. You can't be alone anymore; you need someone to take care of you."

When the carriage stopped in Berkeley Square, Alex alighted and spoke with Rupert. "I think you should carry her."

"Alex!" Both his face and his voice were filled with alarm. "Does Dottie know about all this?"

"Not yet," Alex temporized, refusing to let doubt sink its teeth into her.

"I'm not going in there! She'll put the entire blame for this on me . . . she'll savage me!"

"Dottie isn't home; she's away in the country."

The relief on Rupert's face would have been laughable if Alex had not shared her brother's fear of their grandmother's wrath.

Then another worry raised its ugly head. "Whatever will I do when the Hardings find out about this?" he muttered.

"You need not even discuss it with them. It is our business, and our business alone, Rupert."

He carried the frail invalid upstairs and, as Alex directed, put her in the handsome bedchamber he had vacated when he married Olivia. He tried to ignore the gaping servants, but Hopkins followed him upstairs and handed him a note.

"A footman delivered this, my lord; you are needed at home."

When Rupert read the note, a look of panic came into his face. "It's Olivia . . . the baby . . . I must get back. You'll have to excuse me, Alex."

After Rupert left, Alex took Sara aside and explained that Maggie Field was her mother. The maid was astounded at such a revelation, but she was thankful that the woman who had made it possible for her to leave the Rookery had been rescued by her daughter. "What can I do to help? Perhaps I should bathe her?"

"The bath can wait, Sara. I think she needs something nourishing inside her. Would you go down and ask the cook to warm some broth and perhaps ready some bread and cheese? I'll make up Rupert's bed with some fresh linen. Later, I am going to find her a doctor."

They heard a door slam downstairs and a raised voice. Dottie was home, and by the sound of it, she was in a temper. Alex went down to greet her with her heart in her mouth.

"Thank God I'm back to a sane environment! Lord Staines's niece descended, and until I packed her off with a flea in her ear, it was barely controlled chaos!"

Hopkins took Dottie's traveling bag and threw Alex an accusing look that clearly said, *You are about to give your grandmother apoplexy!*

"If there is one species I cannot abide, it is ingrates; parasites disguised as female relatives who descend like vultures at the rumor of a fatal illness. Makes one want to seek out their nest and crush their eggs!" Dottie started up the stairs.

Alex followed her. "How is Lord Staines?" she asked with genuine concern.

Dottie pierced her with a fierce glance. "He may have gone from rampant to stagnant in one fell swoop, but I assure you he is not ready to stick his spoon in the wall." She spotted Sara, who had a guilty look on her face. "Why is everyone hovering about?" She lifted her head as she heard a wracking cough coming from Rupert's bedroom. Dottie stalked into the chamber and stood stock-still, staring.

Alex wrung her hands. Her grandmother's face looked as if it were carved from stone. Alex licked dry lips and opened her mouth.

"Leave us," Dottie ordered; her tone brooked no disobedience.

Alone, the silence stretched between the two women for long, drawn-out minutes, then Margaret whispered, "Forgive me, Mother?"

A heartbeat later, Dottie, fighting back tears, gathered her daughter in her arms. "There is nothing to forgive, my dearest, other than the fact that you didn't come to me sooner."

Chapter 21

As the white cliffs of Dover came into view, Nicholas Hatton rejoiced. He stood at the ship's rail, reflecting on the events of the past month. After the victory at Toulouse, that city, as well as Bordeaux, had welcomed the occupying army with open arms. Then they received the welcome news that Napoleon had abdicated at Fontainebleau, and he was quickly packed off to the Island of Elba under armed guard. Wellington was declared a conquering hero.

Though Nick had been offered his choice of policing duty in France or a transfer to the war in America, he chose neither. He'd had a bellyful of war, so he cashed out his captaincy. Nick was very certain of what he wanted to do. He would offer his twin the pay he had earned as an officer as a down payment on Hatton Grange. He would live at the Grange and breed horses. Nick gazed at the white cliffs. *All I want is peace . . . a peaceful life . . . a life filled with peace.*

Alexandra's heart overflowed with joy when she learned that the war was over. *Nick will be coming home!* was her very first thought. Then another intruded, and cast a cloud over her joy. Olivia had been delivered of a baby girl. Everyone agreed that the baby had her mother's lovely dark coloring, and Rupert seemed filled with fatherly pride when he announced that they were naming their daughter Amanda. But Alex could not forget the icy tone of her brother's voice when he had accused Nick of being a coward and bolting with his tail between his legs. *I hate you, Nick Hatton!*

London went wild with the news of the British victory, and the defeat of the madman Napoleon. Celebration parties were planned by every hostess, and London's pleasure gardens announced festive entertainments to commemorate England's glory. The Prince of Wales would preside over the most fashionable celebration at Vauxhall. It would last for three nights in succession with victory parades around the Rotunda, culminating in a magnificent fireworks display, the likes of which had never before been seen.

Alexandra accepted invitations from both Hart Cavendish and Christopher Hatton, persuading each to take her on subsequent nights. Both men were disappointed that she refused to go on the final evening, which would of course be the most spectacular. Alex knew she must perform at Champagne Charlie's on Saturday because the money was needed more than ever now that her mother had been found. She shared the nursing duties with Dottie and Sara but could not avoid the expense of a doctor. Alex was determined to pay off an entire year's interest on the Coutts Bank loan before they returned to Longford Manor.

"I have it all worked out, darling." Dottie told her granddaughter. "I shall strip the two wings of the manor of every piece of furnishing that is left and close them up tightly. We shall have one luxuriously appointed reception room where we can receive guests, and none will be the wiser. Not Annabelle and Olivia, the twin spirits of mirth and harmony, and most assuredly not Christopher Hatton when he pays court to you. If I'm not mistaken, and I never am, Lord Hatton seems rather keen these days."

In actual fact, Lord Hatton was becoming desperate. In a futile attempt to restore some of his money, he and Rupert had spent every night of the last two weeks at White's. His reckless gambling had not paid off, however, leaving him deeper in debt. He handed out markers with feigned casualness, knowing he must keep his financial difficulties from his friend. Marriage to Rupert's sister was his last hope, when all else failed.

To make matters worse, Nick would be coming home now that the war was over. Kit knew he didn't have a chance in hell of keeping his shocking financial situation from his twin. Nick was far too shrewd. His only hope was to rehearse a plausible explanation for his reckless spending and have a solution ready. Each night after Rupert left him in Curzon Street, Kit drowned his sorrows with whiskey and soothed his nerves with opium.

Nicholas Hatton stabled his horse in the cobbled coach house behind Charlie's in Pall Mall and grinned into the darkness. It seemed only fitting that the first place he visited upon arrival in London was where he spent his last night almost a year ago.

He walked into the gilded reception room, and though his hair was long and he sported a black beard, Charlotte King knew immediately that the man in the well-worn uniform was Nick.

"Hazard Hatton, as I live and breathe! The conquering hero returns. By God, it's good to see you."

"Hello, Charlie. You are a sight for sore eyes—still the most elegant woman in London. No, don't touch me; I need a bath and a shave."

"I bet that's not all you need!"

"Where the devil is everyone? Don't tell me business has fallen off?"

"Saturdays have never been better. The clientele is all in there watching Caprice." She indicated a closed door. "Take a gander and tell me what you think."

Bemused, he opened the door, found the room in semidarkness, and stood at the back. The silence struck him as his eyes adjusted to the diffused light emanating from the stage. The sound of men breathing but making no other noise seemed unnatural. And then he saw her. The female was ethereal. The gauze curtains combined with the gaslight gave her a golden glow. Everything about her excited him, her elegance, her youth, her innocence, and her luminous beauty. Her delicate loveliness was the sort that evoked instant yearning in a male.

Nick gave her his rapt attention as she sat and lifted one slim leg. Slowly, she removed a garter, then she posed again with the other leg elevated. His mouth went dry. Surely, she had the longest legs he'd ever seen in his life. When she held her leg motionless in the air and slowly inched a striped stocking along its length, Nick's cock went so hard he could have cracked walnuts with it. *It's because I haven't had a woman in a long time. It's the illusion she's creating, revealing all, while remaining untouchable.* He looked at the men seated in the semi-darkness. *It's not just me; they are just as mesmerized as I am. She holds them in thrall.* He was amazed at the intense desire she had aroused in him by merely pretending to be in her private chamber.

He cursed beneath his breath. Her price would be high; she was obviously the specialty of the house. There was no way he would waste his hard-earned officer's pay on a whore, no matter how delectable. Nick laughed at himself. A sexual male animal, fully potent, such as himself, was a bloody fool to even watch her. He turned, eased the rough material that stretched taut over his erection, and quit the room.

Charlie sauntered over to him. "What do you think?

"Quite a drawing card you've got there."

"Caprice is more than that. She makes the men who watch her so randy that some of them order two girls at a time."

He shrugged. "A fool and his money . . ."

She took a step closer and looked up into his dark face. "Go on up to my private suite; I'll order you a bath."

The moment the lamps were snuffed, Alex gathered up her clothes. She had become efficient at making a quick exit through the door and up the stairs. Charlie allowed her to dress in her rooms, then Alex departed still cloaked and masked. As she emerged from the stairs, she dropped a slipper and bent to retrieve it. When she straightened, she saw that she was not alone. The tall figure of a man came down the hall toward her, and she noticed he was wearing some sort of faded uniform. His hair was long, his face covered by a black curly beard.

In a flash of recognition, Alex knew it was Nick. She felt the walls move in to meet her, and she almost fainted. She drew in a steadying breath and focused on one thought: *Under no circumstances must he learn my identity!*

His mouth curved in a slow smile. "Caprice." He spoke her stage name as if he were testing its texture and flavor. "May I say you are one long-legged filly?"

"Non!" She put up a forbidding hand. "I do not speak weeth customers!" She desperately hoped that the heavy accent would disguise her voice.

His amusement increased. "No intercourse at all?"

You are a devil, Nick Hatton! Your wicked play on words is meant to fluster me. "Let me pass, *m'sieur.*"

He took a step closer and towered above her like a raptor closing in on its prey. His nostrils flared as her fragrance stole to him. *Breast-high scent.* The hunting term came to him in all its sensuality. He fought his desire before it got the better of him. *I have captured so many French, they no longer interest me.* He bowed and allowed her to escape.

To her consternation, he opened the door to Champagne Charlie's private suite and disappeared inside. Alex moved down the hall and opened the first door that presented itself, hoping fervently the room was unoccupied. Her hands were trembling as she donned her clothes with the utmost speed. *You dissolute rakehell! How could I ever have imagined I was in love with you?*

The next morning when Nick arrived in Curzon Street, he was bathed, shaved, and his hair, cropped to a fashionable length, was brushed back in its usual style. He stabled his horse behind the town house and examined the shiny perch-phaeton and the pair of chestnut carriage horses. The servants were overjoyed to see him and welcomed him back with genuine affection. He took the stairs two at a time, eager to shed the shabby uniform and put on his riding clothes. He quietly opened Kit's chamber door a crack, expecting him to be still abed, for he was ever a late riser. Nick's lips curved fondly when he saw the dark head of his sleeping brother. He closed the door softly so he wouldn't disturb him and went into his own room.

When Nick emerged, he was clad in gray buckskin riding breeches and a dark green hacking jacket. When he donned the buckskins he found them loose about the waist but tight around the thighs, and he realized that his thigh muscles bulged from so many hours in the saddle. As he collected his mount from the stable, he ran his hand along the mare's glossy coat and marveled. This was the horse he'd found on the battlefield. He'd been amazed that the animal was a mare rather than a gelding. She'd been bred for stamina and strength rather than beauty, but once he had washed the blood and dust from her, her coat shone like black satin.

He rode in Hyde Park, delighted at how lushly green everything was from the turf to the treetops. There were swans on the Serpentine and larks rising in the morning sky. Nick had never appreciated an English spring as much as he did at this moment. He nodded cordially to the gentlemen who rode past and doffed his hat to the ladies in their carriages. Most probably mistook him for his twin, but that was inconsequential, he realized happily. He was home, and nothing could diminish the joy he felt in his heart.

By the time Nick got back to Curzon Street, Kit was up and dressed. When the servants had told him his brother was home, Kit felt panic and decided on the spot that he would return to Hatton. Nick found him in the breakfast room. When he looked into his twin's face, identical to his own, Nick threw back his head and laughed, then he thumped Kit on the back. "I had forgotten what a handsome devil you are."

Kit laughed. "Well, war hasn't changed you either."

It has, I'm afraid. "It taught me the importance of home and family. I have a proposition for you, Kit. I'd like to use my officer's pay as a down payment on Hatton Grange. I'll live at the Grange and raise horses." He stole a sausage from his twin's plate.

"How much?" Kit asked avidly.

"It's less than two thousand, but once I start to sell the horses I breed, I'll give you fair value for the Grange."

"Two thousand? That's all they paid you for fighting

a bloody war? I lost more than that at White's last night!" Kit bit his tongue. Why the devil had he let that slip?

Nick refused to take offense at the blatantly insensitive remark. "Your bad luck at cards is legendary. Be thankful you have more good sense than to make a habit of it."

Kit suddenly realized he wanted to confess. "Actually, I have been making a habit of it. I've been tossing out markers like confetti."

"Damnation, you should know better!" Nick felt as if he were addressing one of his young recruits. "You must always pay your gambling debts with cash. That way you don't get in over your head." He clapped Kit on the back. "I refuse to let you ruin my good mood. Just be thankful you are a wealthy man. Why don't I come with you tonight and try to win some of them back?"

"I was on my way home to Hatton . . . the valet is packing for me now . . . but I think it's a damned good idea for you to win some of them back. I'd truly appreciate it, Nick."

Nick shook his head in disbelief. Nothing had changed. *Kit still expects me to get him out of every difficulty. If he knew how badly I want to go home to Hatton, he wouldn't ask this of me.* "Let me have a list of your markers," he said with resignation.

An hour later when he saw Kit drive off in his perch-phaeton, Nick's attention was drawn to the chestnuts. He hoped his brother hadn't paid a high price for them, since they were not a matched pair. *I mustn't criticize everything he does; Father did that.*

That night as he donned his evening clothes, Nick looked in the mirror to assess their fit. He looked into the reflection of his own gray eyes. *I know, I know. I swore never to set foot in White's Club again, and already I'm compromising my principles.* A mocking voice answered, *War taught you that only a fool has principles!* Since he wasn't a member of the club, he would have to pose as Christopher anyway. He heard Rupert arrive and decided to put the imposture to the test. "You're early," he called down, then delibertly brushed a curl to fall forward on his brow.

"No, I'm not. You're late, as usual."

As Nick descended the stairs he thought Rupert looked much thinner. "You'd think after all these years I would mend my ways."

"I don't expect pears from an elm tree. You'll never change."

"A literary allusion." Nick put on his top hat. "Don't tell me you've been reading, old man?"

"No fear of that; it's one of Dottie's expressions. Oh, and speaking of the devil, she wants me to drop you a broad hint that Alexandra is attending the rout at Burlington House tonight with Hart Cavendish."

Rupert's words aroused Nick's envy. "Really? I suppose we could drop in at Burlington House after we've been to White's."

Rupert opened the door and said over his shoulder, "Suits me! M'wife and her mother have turned the house into a damn nursery."

You're married? It was a good thing Nick was behind Rupert as his face registered his astonishment. *Who is your wife?*

"Olivia's mother has taken over since we had the baby. Annabelle couldn't get me out of the house fast enough tonight."

You're married to Olivia, and you already have a child? As they climbed into the carriage, Nick was baffled. When he left, his brother had been keen on Olivia. Nick's suspicious thoughts sprang to the obvious conclusion. *That's ridiculous! If my brother got her with child, he would do the honorable thing.*

At White's, the usual gambling addicts were present, three of whom held markers from his twin. Nick was in a dangerous mood. He marked his first prey and sat down at the baccarat table opposite Lord Brougham.

"Ha, young Hatton! Back for more, eh?"

"Back for considerably more." His gray eyes bore into his opponent's with supreme confidence. Nick was using his own money, and there was no way on God's green earth he was going to lose any of it. As he bluffed his way through every hand, the pile of *rouleaux* in front of him grew apace with his deadly determination. In the process he cleaned out Brougham. Nick stood and gathered in his counters. "I know I may rely upon you to tear up my marker, my lord."

Nick asked Rupert to cash in his winnings and walked a direct path to the whist table, a game he loathed. He slanted a dark brow at the Earl of Bingham. "I am here to change your luck, my lord." In slightly more than two hours, three of Kit Hatton's markers were history, and Nick was richer by more than a hundred guineas. "I seem to have done all the damage I can do here," he informed Rupert. "I'm more than ready for Burlington House."

When they arrived at the mansion in Piccadilly, Rupert went to pay his respects to the hostess. Nick did not go directly to the gaming room that had been set up but took a leisurely stroll through the reception rooms, searching for a glimpse of red hair. When he did not see Alexandra, his disappointment was more acute than he expected. He lingered in the ballroom until he was certain she was not dancing, then headed to the card room.

When he saw her playing cards, sitting beside Hart Cavendish, a burning streak of jealousy ripped through him. Nick was completely aware of the violence of his feelings, and it surprised him. He prided himself on being in control of his emotions. He was usually calm, cool, and unruffled, no matter the provocation.

When Alex glanced up, saw him, and gave him a fleeting smile, it was almost impersonal. The lion within roared its fury and refused to be dismissed. The game they played was *vingt-et-un,* and he immediately sat down at the table. It was only after he had taken his seat that he saw the Earl of Carlisle; by the pile of counters in front of him, their host was obviously winning. Since it was permissible for any player who wished to shuffle and cut the cards, Nick held out his hand. When the deck was passed to him, he turned to Carlisle. "I'll cut you for the amount of the marker I gave you last week."

"You play for high stakes, Hatton!" Carlisle declared loftily.

Nick knew they were the center of attention. He narrowed his eyes. "You are not dallying with a young boy, you know."

Alexandra blinked. Was Kit blatantly referring to Carlisle's predilection for young men? She glanced quickly at their host, saw him flush and cut the cards. It was a two, and any card in the deck would beat it. She saw Kit nod curtly and hand the cards back to the dealer without even bothering to cut them.

Even though he pretended otherwise, Nick was acutely aware of Alexandra. After she lost the next two hands, she stopped playing and watched Hart Cavendish. Nick decided then and there that the duke had had enough of her attention. He rose and casually walked around the table until he stood behind Cavendish. He placed a firm hand on Hart's shoulder. "I'm stealing Alex for a dance. I'm sure you won't object."

Startled, Hart replied, "Of course not." Though he actually objected strenuously, he was too civilized to say so.

Alex too was startled. Politely, she excused herself from Hart and with a quizzical expression accompanied Kit Hatton from the card room. "I thought your mourning barred you from dancing?"

"I have decided my mourning period is over, as of tonight."

His voice was so deep it sounded like a soft growl. His words were pointedly decisive. Was he telling her by implication that now he was out of mourning, his wooing would begin? She took a deep breath and refused to panic. Questions arose in her mind, and thoughts of Nicholas intruded. She wondered why Christopher hadn't mentioned that his twin was back. "Is Nick home yet?"

He nodded. "He's enjoying being back in London so much, I haven't seen a lot of him."

Alex closed her eyes, and cursed herself for even mentioning the libertine's name.

The moment they entered the ballroom he swept her into his arms. Alex caught her breath and focused on the waltz music so she would not misstep. She had no need to fear. Kit, it seemed, was an exceptionally confident dancer. He held her securely and firmly took the lead, boldly swirling her, then bringing her close on every third beat of the music. She gave herself up to the movement of his body, swaying with the gentle pressure of his powerful arms.

The rhythm of the dance insinuated itself inside her, and with half-closed eyes, Alex began to pretend it was Nicholas who held her so possessively. She was lost in a sea of warm sensation, yielding her softness to his hard, demanding length.

As he watched her face and felt the brush of her gown against his thighs, the ache inside him became unbearable. He pictured her in his bed, beneath him, her half-closed eyes languid with love. He looked down hungrily. "Why do you never flirt with me?"

Her eyes opened slowly. *I've been flirting with you for years.* Suddenly, she realized it was Kit with whom she danced; Kit who asked the question. She was flooded with guilt about daydreaming over Nicholas. "We—we are old friends; I feel no need to flirt."

His lips curved sardonically. "Not a flattering answer." He knew if he held her one more minute, he would crush her to him and devour the soft pink mouth that tempted him beyond endurance. "It's hot in here, and such a lovely spring night; would you mind if we went out for a breath of air?"

She murmured her assent and followed him from the floor. He took her out the front entrance of Burlington House to Piccadilly. The building was well lit, and they moved into the shadows cast by its tall columns. When Kit seemed content with the silence, Alex decided this might be a good time to reveal that she had found her mother. As he listened, he slowly began to stroll past the waiting carriages, and Alex matched her steps to his. She expected him to thoroughly disapprove, but his reaction surprised her.

"And you took her home and made peace between Dottie and the daughter she had disowned? That was a generous, heartfelt thing to do, Alex." The look of admiration he bestowed upon her made her feel special.

"You are as lovely on the inside as you are on the outside, Alexandra."

His understanding and praise pleased her. Perhaps he wasn't shallow after all. "Thank you, Kit." She searched for another topic. "I hope the Canaletto you bought wasn't a fake," she said earnestly.

"Canaletto?"

"When you bumped into Hart and I at the opera, he seemed to think he already owned the painting you had just bought."

"Just a misunderstanding." Nick dismissed the topic but tucked away the information. "Hart Cavendish escorts you quite frequently." He tried to keep the resentment from his voice.

"I enjoy his company," Alex said lightly.

"That's perfectly understandable; any lady would enjoy being escorted by a Duke of the Realm."

"It has nothing to do with his title," she insisted.

"His dukedom makes him a leader of the *beau monde* and bestows deference not accorded to others. He has more wealth and privilege than royalty; don't deny that you enjoy these things, Alex."

"I do admit that I enjoy them! What pray is wrong with that?"

"There is nothing wrong with that, unless you expect him to make you his duchess. Hart is not looking for a wife, Alex. He is looking for a mistress, and I don't want you to get hurt."

The truth of his words touched her vanity, and she wanted to fly at him and scratch his face. Instead she used words to wound him. "Hart has been completely honest with me, Kit. He has made it quite plain that he wishes to be my lover."

Nick halted and took forceful hold of her shoulders. "I'll take a horsewhip to him!"

She looked up into the dark, dangerous face and shuddered. She pulled out of his grip and kept walking. "I don't need a keeper; I'm perfectly capable of looking after myself."

He took two strides to catch up with her. "I don't want you to go out with him again, Alex!"

"You are jealous of him!" she accused incredulously.

"Why would I be jealous of the wealthiest duke in England, who has the physique and looks of a golden god?"

She stopped beneath a gas lamp and looked up at him. She gazed at the fathomless gray eyes above the slanting cheekbones, then her glance lowered to his beautiful mouth and the deep cleft in his chin. "You are one of the handsomest men I have ever laid eyes on in my life." She glanced around and saw that they were now walking on Berkeley Street, which opened into Berkeley Square. She threw back her head and began to laugh.

"What's so bloody funny?" he growled.

"You deliberately stole me away from Hart Cavendish and escorted me home, you devious devil!"

His mouth curved. "I admit it. My rival doesn't stand a chance." His glance licked over her lovely, laughing face. "That amuses you, Alex?"

"I am amused because Hart Cavendish isn't your rival—never has been and never will be. Your rival is your own twin. I was infatuated with Nicholas for years."

"Was?"

She heard the intensity in his voice and could not bring herself to hurt him further. "Not any more, of course. It was a young girl's fancy. Before he went away, Nick made it plain that he thought of me as a sister."

"Nick is a fool. He always did have an exalted sense of honor." He drew her into his arms and captured her lips with his. He felt her stiffen but refused to let her pull away. His possessive mouth moved on hers, coaxing, savoring, wooing her to soften toward him. He was exultant when he felt her lips cling to his and took pleasure from the physical, intimate contact.

Alex was reluctant to have Kit kiss her, but found him as competent at kissing as he was at dancing. When she closed her eyes, it felt exactly like she was kissing Nicholas, and her reluctance melted away. Delicious sensations spiraled through her body as she gave herself up to him and clung to the demanding mouth that was giving her untold pleasure. "Nick," she murmured against his lips. Her eyes flew open and she pulled away quickly. "Good night, Kit." Alex ran the short distance to her house, hoping he hadn't heard her say his twin's name.

Nick watched Alex go, giving thanks that she had whispered his name, yet feeling guilty at the same time. He stood at the corner of Berkeley Square a long time after she had gone, wondering how he would solve the dilemma that raged within.

Chapter 22

When Nicholas returned to Curzon Street, he found the butler still on duty. "There's no need to wait up for me, Fenton; your day is long enough. I'll lock up and see to the lights."

"Yes, sir," Fenton replied. He moved down the hall, then turned and came back hesitantly. "I hate to trouble you, sir, when you've just returned from France. I hoped Lord Hatton would take care of the matter before he left . . ."

"What is it?"

"It's the wine merchant, sir. He left this account two days ago and said he'd be back tomorrow. When I gave it to your brother, he threw it in the wastebasket."

Nick took the bill and read it. "Three hundred pounds for whiskey? That's outrageous! There must be some mistake."

"The bill is most likely padded, sir. The wine merchant has a rather threatening way about him. I would have paid him something on account, except . . . I haven't received my wages yet."

"You've been owed wages since December?" Nick was angry. *What the devil is Kit playing at?* "None of the staff has been paid?"

"I'm afraid not, sir."

Inside, Nick was livid, but he did not display his temper in front of the servant. He took out his winnings. "There is more than a hundred pounds here. That should take care of it. Please give my apologies to the staff." He waved the bill for the whiskey. "Don't worry about this, Fenton. I shall go and see him tomorrow."

Nick went upstairs to Kit's room and opened the desk, looking for the household account book. He uttered a foul oath when he found it stuffed with overdue bills. Kit had not made a single entry in the book. There was one receipt from an art dealer for a Canaletto; it was for nine thousand pounds. *Jesu!* He remembered Alex's words about a fake Canaletto. Nick's glance swept the chamber, then he looked beneath the bed. Nothing! He opened Kit's wardrobe, swept aside the garments, and found the painting.

He took it and the receipt to his own room. He undressed and opened the casement window. *Kit needs a bloody keeper; he is totally irresponsible!* He thought of the markers he had retrieved tonight. *No wonder he ran home to Hatton, before I found out about all this!* As he filled his lungs with the spring air, Nick knew he would have to take matters into his own hands. His resolve hardened. Tomorrow, he would start with the art dealer.

Early the next morning, Nick paid a visit to Spinks & Co. The old art dealer was one of the shrewdest men in the business, and Nick guessed he would know what went on, on both sides of the law.

Spinks glanced at the name and address on the receipt. "That's not his real name. It's Wicklow. Shuts up shop and moves every month. Try Warwick Lane, by St. Paul's."

Nick knew he had found Wicklow when the man immediately dodged into the back room. In a flash, Nick strode into the huge storage room and confronted him. Two boys at a worktable fled out the back door. "You sold me a fake Canaletto. I am here for my money."

"You have no proof," he countered. "Choose another painting."

Nick selected an oil painting, struck a match, and set fire to it. "My money, or by morning this place will be ashes."

"Christ, stop!" Wicklow stomped on the flaming canvas. "Come into the shop, my lord. We've both been the victims of a fraud. Let's split the difference."

Nick Hatton stepped close, towering above him, his

dark face threatening, his gray eyes cold as steel. "You dare to bargain?"

Wicklow tried to mask his fear but failed. He opened a cast-iron safe and counted out nine thousand pounds.

"A thousand pounds interest." Nick's voice was implacable. Before Wicklow could hesitate, he added softly, "Did I mention that your bones would be found among the ashes?"

Within five minutes, Nick was on his way to the wine merchants in Thames Street. The small shop was part of a large warehouse on the docks. He produced the bill. "I'm here to settle my account." Nick knew there wasn't a business in London that wasn't on the take. "I have reason to believe this bill has been padded." The offensive tactic worked; they knocked a hundred off the bill.

By the time Nick got back to Curzon Street, he knew he had little choice. Tomorrow, he must go to Hatton and confront his twin. Lord Hatton or no Lord Hatton, Kit could not be allowed to conduct Hatton affairs in this careless, irresponsible manner.

Dottie knocked on her granddaughter's bedchamber door and opened it softly. "Darling, I have to talk with you."

"Please come in. I was just working on my newspaper article." In reality, there was no newspaper article. Alex had been working out the amount of interest she must take to the bank tomorrow.

"It's about Margaret. Though we pretend otherwise, you and I both know that her condition is deteriorating. We should take her home to Longford so she can sit in the sunshine in the garden. It may not help, but she will be surrounded by beauty and serenity."

"That's a splendid idea. I'm so glad that you don't regret that I found her and brought her here."

"Darling, it was meant to be. How many of us get the chance to forgive—and be forgiven?"

Alex knew she could not afford to hire a carriage. "I'll go and ask Rupert tomorrow."

The next morning, Alex made her way to Coutts Bank and paid a whole year's interest on Dottie's loan. Though she was unable to pay off anything on the principle, she hoped it would postpone them from foreclosing and taking Longford Manor. To save money, she walked all the way from the bank to Clarges Street. When she arrived at Olivia and Rupert's, she found them in the midst of packing up for their removal to Harding House for the summer. Rupert held Amanda, while Olivia directed the maids, who were running up and down stairs, carrying baby paraphernalia.

"I need to speak with you privately, Rupert."

"Come, we'll sit in the drawing room where we'll be out of the way."

Alex sat down, glad to take the weight off her aching feet. "May I hold her?" she asked softly. When her brother put the child in her arms, she looked down in wonder at the beautiful baby girl. All the ugly suspicions she'd had about the baby's paternity melted away. None of it mattered! A wave of maternal instinct swept over her. *Oh, how I wish this child were mine!* Then she said the words aloud. "She's so precious; I wish she were my daughter."

Rupert smiled and said wisely, "The sooner you marry, the sooner you will have children of your own, Alex. When Kit came looking for you at Burlington House the other night, you disappeared with him. Has he begun to court you?"

"I rather think he has." Alex quickly changed the subject. "We need transportation to Longford, and I can't afford to hire a carriage. Dottie thinks Mother will be better in the country."

His mouth hardened. "You and Dottie seem to have forgiven Margaret Sheffield. . . . I don't think I can."

Alex laid the baby back in her brother's arms and looked deeply into his eyes. "Yes, you can, Rupert; you have a forgiving nature. Margaret is dying, she likely has only another year left. She's suffered enough for her sins."

"I'm sorry that you have to carry the burden. Of course I'll move you back to Longford. And I want you to hire a couple of servants. You and Dottie can't do it all alone. I'll pay their wages; I know you are struggling financially."

"Thank you, Rupert; that is most generous of you."

She knew it was Rupert's way of both showing and asking forgiveness.

Nicholas packed some of his favorite clothes and his flintlock army pistols, then went down to saddle his mare, Satin. He walked back to say hello to Kit's Renegade and found him restive and mettlesome, kicking his stall. "Hello, old man. Looks like you need more exercise." Nick spoke to the stable boy about it.

"I just keep 'im clean, sir. I don't dare ride 'im."

Nick decided to ride him to Hatton. He put the saddle on Renegade and fastened a lead rein to Satin. The six-mile gallop was just what the Thoroughbred needed, and by the time Hatton land was in sight, he was responding instantly to Nick's calm voice. He decided to breed the two black horses; the colt wouldn't be a Thoroughbred, but it would have good bloodlines.

In the stable courtyard he encountered Kit, who had been out shooting and was just returning with a brace of pheasant over his shoulder. Kit's look of dismay made it obvious that he was not pleased to see his twin, and he took the offensive immediately.

"I would appreciate it if you respected my property," he said pointedly, indicating Renegade.

"Respect must be earned." Nick's voice held a warning. He thought of Slate and wished he was bringing him home to Hatton. "If you valued this animal, you would exercise him."

Kit turned his back on him and headed toward the kitchen door.

The moment he opened it, a black streak dashed past Kit, almost knocking him over, and bounded toward the man in the saddle.

"Leo!" Nick dismounted and the dog stood on his hind legs, resting his front paws on the tall man's shoulders. Joyful barks were interspersed with long, wet licks. Nick buried his face in the thick black fur. "I love you too," he growled. The wolfhound followed him into the stable and sat, thudding his tail on the flagstones, while Nick unsaddled Renegade and watered both horses.

When he went in through the kitchen door, Meg Riley began to laugh and cry at the same time. "I thought it might be you, when the dog rushed out like a scalded cock. I prayed for you every night. I'm so thankful you're home safe and sound."

He set down his saddlebags and put his arms around her, holding her close. "Thanks, Meg; dry your eyes and let me hear you laugh."

Mr. Burke shook his hand. "Welcome home, Nicholas."

"It feels so good to be back at Hatton."

"This is where you belong," Mr. Burke said from the heart.

When Nick went in search of his twin, he found him in the library, cleaning his gun. When trouble brewed, he knew it was Kit's way to retreat, while he preferred being direct. From his saddlebag Nick withdrew the list of names to whom his brother had given markers and placed it on the desk before Kit. Four of the six names were crossed out.

"You always did have the luck of the devil." Though Kit's words were grudging, he looked relieved.

Nick pulled out the sheaf of unpaid bills and set them on the desk without a word.

Kit immediately fell back on another favorite tactic that had always worked. He threw himself on his brother's mercy. "Nick, I swear this isn't my fault. It was my understanding that John Eaton would take care of these financial obligations, so I spent the money on a Canaletto painting that turned out to be a fake. The art dealer defrauded me, and I will need your help to find him."

"I found him . . . and I got the money back, plus interest."

"How did you find out about the painting? How did you get the money back from the swindling swine?"

"It doesn't matter, Kit. What matters is that you stop being irresponsible with the money that was left to you. That money is for the upkeep of Hatton. An estate this size has a lot of expenses. You must take things more seriously and learn how to manage it all."

"You are right! God, Nick, it's such a relief to have the money back." Kit reached for the whiskey. "This calls for a drink."

Nick pushed the decanter out of his reach. "I think

not. I just settled a three-hundred-pound account for whiskey; we don't need another. I also took care of the London staff's wages."

"By God, Nick, you're a wonder! What the devil would I do without you?" Kit's sullen mood seemed to have vanished.

"You would end up in Fleet Prison for debt."

"You are right! Every word you say is gospel! I've learned my lesson. Running Hatton is a serious business. From now on, I will take care of my responsibilities and be scrupulous about money."

Nick carried his saddlebags over to the wall safe. "I'll put your money in here, plus my two thousand for the down payment on Hatton Grange. While you're at the desk, you can write out an agreement that you are selling me Hatton Grange and make me out a receipt for the money."

Kit laughed. "You don't trust me!" He took a piece of paper and began to write. "You'll see, Nick. From now on I'll do the right thing. I'll make you proud. As soon as Alexandra Sheffield returns to Longford, I'm going to ask her to marry me and settle down."

Nick felt like he'd been punched in the solar plexus. He carefully schooled his face to reveal none of his inner turmoil. "You didn't tell me Rupert was married and had a child."

"Yes, he confessed to me that he had been in love with Olivia for years. I told him that I understood completely. It made me realize I've been in love with Alexandra for a long time." Kit added, "And it's what Father always wanted for me."

Nick looked away. There was absolutely no denying that their father had always wanted Alexandra to marry his heir. But he was skeptical about Kit's declaration of love. *Has war made me so cynical that I can't even give my brother the benefit of the doubt?* His glance traveled around the library shelves. "Tomorrow I'll be moving into the Grange. I'll take my horse books with me." He picked up the signed agreement and the receipt for his money. "Only the servants know I'm back; I'd just as soon keep it that way."

* * *

The next morning Nick took some of his belongings to Hatton Grange and spoke with Tom and Bridget Calhoun. "I'm moving in. I have decided to purchase the Grange from my brother and breed horses again."

"We're relieved to see you back, sir. Lord Hatton took no interest in the Grange, if ye'll forgive my saying."

"Leo intends to make himself at home too." He glanced at Bridget. "You won't be afraid of him?"

"He's not the ferocious beast he pretends to be; Leo often comes visiting. It'll be grand to have you here, sir. It's a big house; all the chambers upstairs an' half the rooms downstairs are empty. Tom an' me have rooms off the kitchen."

"Bridget's a grand cook," Tom offered.

"I remember. She often fed me when I was too tired to go home," Nick acknowledged. "The colts out there are yearlings now. You've done a good job with them, Tom. We've missed a year, but I'll try to get another couple of mares, and next year they'll all foal."

Nick spent the afternoon walking over the land he loved more than any other place on earth. With Leo at his heels he took flowers to his mother's grave, then walked around the lake. As he covered the acres, he was filled with gratitude that at last he was home. Today, he felt like he was the luckiest man in England.

When Nick returned to the Grange, he lit a fire in the master bedchamber, and as he hung his work clothes in the wardrobe, Bridget put fresh linen on the massive oak bed. After dinner, which he ate in the kitchen with the Irish couple, he went back upstairs to unpack the box of books he had brought from the Hatton library. Some were books on breeding, others were on animal husbandry, and a few specialized in equine ailments, treatments, and cures. Nick picked up a journal he had kept in which he'd recorded the sires and dams of all the colts he'd bred. Then he picked up another journal that looked unfamiliar. The handwriting was not his yet, curiously, the name was: JOURNAL OF CAPTAIN NICHOLAS HATTON, 1662. Fascinated, Nick sat down by the fire to read the words set down a hundred and fifty years before.

For the past two years I have led a secret life of crime. It is over now, thanks to King Charles's fortunes and those of his loyal captains being restored, but I set these words down as a guide to any future Hatton who loses all and finds himself destitute. Survival is possible for a Hatton with guts enough to become a gentleman of the road. Hounslow Heath is the answer to a penniless rogue's prayer!

It all began with a terrible row I had with my father. When the king was put to death and civil war erupted, I was an idealistic youth on the side of the Royalists. My father, for the sake of expedience, chose to side with Cromwell. Our quarrel came to blows so I joined the army and fought for Prince Charles at Worcester. We lost, and I followed the prince into exile in Europe. No words can ever express my longing to be back at Hatton. It took nine long years before Charles was crowned king. When I returned to Hatton in 1660, it was impoverished, and it has taken me two years to fill its coffers and begin its restoration. Now, ironically, the tide has turned; King Charles and his loyal captains enjoy great favor. I no longer need to hold up coaches on Hounslow Heath; I simply attend Court, where money is thrust at me. This is another form of stealing, of course, but one that has Society's stamp of approval.

Nick stopped reading and began looking at the sketches. They were all maps and diagrams of Hounslow Heath, showing the coaching routes, the best places for an ambush, and the spots where a horse and rider could conceal themselves. Nick was amazed that though the maps had been drawn a hundred and fifty years ago, the lay of the land was exactly the same, and even some of the landmarks still remained.

As he set the journal beside his bed, he drew parallels between himself and the writer. Not only did they share the name Nicholas Hatton but their relationship with their respective fathers had been more than strained. Both were captains in the army. Both spent time in Europe, where their longing for Hatton had often been unendurable. There was something else that made Nicholas identify with his ancestor. He had loved Hatton so much he had become an outlaw to restore its fortunes. Nick completely understood the deep and abiding love that had driven the other Nicholas to break the law in order to keep Hatton.

Hours later when he lay abed, Kit filled his thoughts. He had few illusions about his brother anymore. He suspected that by now Kit had likely dipped into both the whiskey decanter and the safe. Not without an inner battle, Nick gradually let go of his resentment toward his twin. Kit had always been careless and irresponsible. He was secretive for reasons of self-protection, but Nick knew that he must share the blame for his brother's behavior. Since they were children, he had always protected Kit by covering up the things he had done as well as the things he had left undone. Nick now believed it was his fault that Kit had never been held accountable. Unwittingly, Nicholas was once again excusing his twin by taking the blame upon himself. *I had to excel at everything! I loved the attention it brought me! I had to be the leader, overshadowing Kit in everything we did.* Nick thought about Alexandra. It had always been understood that she would marry Kit. Was that the only reason he wanted her? Was this insatiable attraction because she was the only female he could not, *must not,* have? He fell asleep without knowing the answer, and almost immediately his dream began.

Nicholas sat astride his horse in the ink-black darkness, waiting, listening. He exercised infinite patience, for he knew that sooner or later the coach must pass this way. It was inevitable. The hint of a smile touched his mouth as he heard the faint rumble of wheels. Recklessly, he waited until the last possible moment to emerge from the trees. Risk made the game so much sweeter!

Nick touched his knees to the black hunter, drew the pistols with the deadly twelve-inch barrels from the saddle holsters, and lunged into the path of the coach. "Hold!"

As the coachdriver hauled back on the reins, Nick leveled the pistol at his head. "Throw down your gun." He was too cautious to ever take the chance of a concealed weapon. He urged his mount close to the coach door and kicked it with a booted foot. The door was opened from within, and he looked into gray eyes, identical to his own. "Sorry for the change in plans, my lord." He holstered one of the guns, then raised his black-gloved hand and beckoned once. She came to him quickly, silently, defiance etched on her proud face. He lifted her before him in the saddle, raised the pistol, and shot it into the air. The startled horses lunged forward; the coach door swung shut. He tightened his arm about his prize and set his spurs to his mount.

"I only came so you wouldn't kill him, Highwayman!"

"No, sweet liar. You came because you know my identity."

Nick awakened slowly, without opening his eyes. He could feel the curve of her back against his chest, feel the velvet flesh of her breasts cupped in his palms. A tendril of her hair brushed against his lips, and he buried his face in the tumbled mass of curls. Instantly his cock stirred and lengthened against her bottom cheeks. When he opened his eyes, he could not believe that she was not in the bed with him. He mocked himself for a fool. Only in his dreams did he have the will to steal her from his twin.

Chapter 23

Christopher Hatton knew he was in a race against time. His twin was an extremely shrewd man, and Kit knew if he was to keep his brother from learning of the true state of Hatton's depleted wealth, at least until he had secured his heiress, Kit would have to keep his wits about him.

Kit left the decanter of whiskey in the library untouched and decided that under no circumstances must he take any of the money that his twin had put in the safe. He wanted to restore Nick's trust in him; if his brother was suspicious and came to check on the money or the liquor, he would find them undisturbed.

The next morning, Kit donned buckskins and riding boots and went to the stables to saddle Renegade. He purposely rode over to the Grange to show Nick that he was giving his hunter exercise.

Nick, surprised to see his twin up and about so early, greeted him warmly. "Kit, I brought this mare back from France. She's no Thoroughbred, but she has great stamina and perhaps decent bloodlines. Would you let Renegade cover her?"

"I have no objection, but he might; she's rather ugly."

"A marriage of convenience," Nick said, laughing.

Kit looked at his twin sharply, suspecting a jibe about his own marriage plans. Then he too laughed. "Feel free to come and get him anytime. Well, I'd better be off; I need the exercise as much as Renegade."

Nick waved him off. *He made a point of riding over*

here to show me he's following my suggestion. I wonder what he's up to?

Kit was satisfied that his twin suspected nothing so far. He knew he was lucky that Nick had a soft spot for him that always gave him the advantage. Kit galloped across the field, then along the banks of the River Crane. When he skirted the Harding property, he was surprised to see Rupert tooling his carriage down the long, yew-lined driveway. Kit waved and called out to him, and Rupert reined in his horses. "I had no idea you were back."

"Brought the family yesterday; now I'm off to London again to get Dottie and Alex."

"That's marvelous news! I don't suppose it's necessary between the two of us but, strictly speaking, custom demands that I ask your permission before I pay my addresses to your sister, Alexandra."

"And, by God, not before time! Hart Cavendish has monopolized so much of her time lately, I feared she'd end up a duchess!"

Kit threw back his head and laughed. "Rupert, you are such a loyal friend. No other man in England would prefer that his sister marry me rather than the Duke of Devonshire."

"There's something I should tell you. A few weeks ago, Alex found our mother. She's in extremely poor health, and Dottie and my sister are bringing her to Longford. Nobody knows about it, but I didn't want you to be caught off guard when you visit them."

Though the thought of Margaret Sheffield living at Longford was repugnant to him, he was glad Rupert had warned him. "Thank you for confiding in me."

"Well, since you are planning to be part of the family, I didn't see how I could do otherwise," Rupert said ingenuously.

Dottie dosed Margaret with laudanum for the carriage ride to Longford. She also asked Sara to come for the summer. Though Neville Staines would be paying her wages, Dottie knew he would have no objection. When they arrived, Rupert carried a sleeping Margaret up to his old bedchamber. Then he dutifully helped carry in their luggage while Alex went to stable Zephyr.

"Oh, before I forget, Christopher's back at Hatton. This morning I told him I was bringing you from London, so don't be surprised if he rides over to welcome you home."

"Death and damnation! We're not ready for him!" Dottie cried.

"But he's coming as a suitor! Don't tell me you've changed your mind about wanting Alex to become Lady Hatton?"

"Of course not, you corkbrain, but to receive a lord, we must have a decent reception room. Well, take off your jacket and roll up your sleeves; you have a deal of furniture to move."

"Dear God, every time I come near you, you put me to work. Do I resemble a mule, Dottie?

"A mule's the same as a jackass, isn't it? By the way, we need a cook. Sara and I will nurse Margaret, but we must have a cook."

"I'll take care of it, if you ever release me from hard labor."

"Oh, I trust you'll go hunting soon. A cook will need something to cook, after all."

It took the best part of two hours, but when Alex, Dottie, and Rupert stood back to survey their efforts, they declared the reception room fit to entertain a queen. "If we *had* a decent queen," Dottie added. "No one need know Longford has two empty wings."

"Speaking of wings, you've been an angel, Rupert." Alex helped him into his coat and kissed his cheek. "Thank you, love."

No sooner did Alex go upstairs to take a bath and wash the dust from her hair, than Christopher Hatton arrived.

"Lord Hatton, do come in." Dottie led him into the luxuriously furnished reception room and waved a hand. "As you can see, we are all at sixes and sevens, having only just arrived."

"I wanted to ride over and welcome you home, Lady Longford."

"Pretty manners indeed to welcome a dowager home." *You're too handsome for your own damned good. My granddaughter must marry you if we're to save*

Longford Manor, but don't think you can stroll in here and take Alexandra for granted.

Kit bowed gallantly. "Is Alex about?"

Dottie raised her eyebrows, then lifted her lorgnette to examine him. "Alexandra isn't receiving this afternoon. If you'd care to leave your calling card, I'll apprise her of your visit, m'lord."

Kit was taken aback. He had no calling cards with him. Such formality must stem from her wealth. He thought it had all been arranged between his father and Dottie Longford but it suddenly dawned on him that she would have to approve him before she gave her permission for him to court Alexandra. "My lady, would it be permissible for me to call again tomorrow?"

"Ah, by all means, dear boy. Y'know, in my day, when a gentleman called, he didn't come empty-handed. A gift wasn't necessary, just a token of game or a brace of birds. Do you hunt, Lord Hatton?"

"Indeed I do, Lady Longford. Until tomorrow, then?" *The old bitch intends to put me through my paces, begod!*

The next morning, there wasn't a cloud in the sky. The roses were in full bloom in the Longford garden, and Dottie declared that Margaret would benefit from the warm sunshine. Alex helped her mother downstairs and took her out to the lawn where she and Sara had carried a wicker *chaise longue* and pillows. Alex sat down on the grass beside her to keep her company.

"We need to talk," Margaret whispered.

"But talking makes you cough—"

"It doesn't matter." Margaret drew in a labored breath. "I made terrible choices and ruined my life. I broke Mother's heart, and worse, my selfishness hurt my children." She began to cough and covered her mouth with a heavy linen handkerchief.

"That's all in the past; there is no need to castigate yourself and catalogue your sins."

"There is every need . . . I don't want you to make the mistakes I made." She pressed the linen to her mouth and breathed slowly. "I refused to marry the man Dottie chose for me. I ran off to London and behaved shamelessly. Duty meant nothing to me. In open defiance I married a commoner, who made my life hell. He went through all my money, and my parents had to pay off his debts." Margaret became racked with a coughing spell.

"Please don't talk anymore. I know what happened next."

She took some slow breaths. "All right, but I beg you be guided by Dottie. The way of duty is the way of happiness, Alexandra."

"I have already given my grandmother my solemn promise."

Margaret smiled, then closed her eyes and drifted off to sleep.

Mrs. Dinwiddie, the elderly housekeeper, came out to the garden. "Ye have a gentleman caller, Alexandra; I'll stay with Margaret."

Alex went in through the kitchen door and saw the table held an abundance of game. When she entered the reception room, she found Kit and Dottie laughing at a shared joke.

"Here's Christopher come to call. The dear boy brought enough game for a week."

"Hello, Kit. Dottie no doubt gave you a broad hint."

"Oh, it was more than a hint. I set him a task, a noble quest, and he fulfilled it. He has completely won me over."

"Good morning, Alex. I came to see if you'd care to go riding?"

She swallowed the excuse that rose to her lips and smiled at him instead. "I'd love to. I'll just run up and change."

As she put on a riding dress, Sara brought her boots. "Lord Hatton is so handsome, he makes my knees go wobbly."

Alex immediately thought of Nick, then she dutifully pushed his image out of her mind and went to join Christopher.

In the stables, Kit saddled Zephyr over her protests. "Alex, it gives me pleasure to do things for you." He gave her a sideways glance. "You'd better get used to it."

When he lifted her into the saddle, she looked down

into his face, so darkly handsome. *I'd better get used to everything you do.* As she watched him mount, she realized how unfair she was being to him. *I must not be resentful toward Kit; I must not think of marriage to him a death warrant.* She had always had an affection for him; she must give him a chance to win her heart. "I'll race you to the woods!" she challenged.

Alex was amazed when she reached the trees before him. Nick would never have allowed her to win. Her heart softened toward Kit for being gallant. Laughing together, they walked their horses through the leafy glade, and when they reached the river, he lifted her from her saddle. As the horses drank, he invited her to sit on a fallen log so they could talk.

"Alex, when I asked Rupert if I could pay my addresses to you, he was delighted. I also believe I've smoothed the waters with your grandmother—no easy task. Now, I need to hear it from you."

Her eyes danced with mischief. "You're asking to court me?"

"No, I'm asking to marry you!"

The mischief left her eyes. "Oh, Christopher, surely the courting comes first?"

"Damn it, Alex, there's been an understanding since we were children that we would marry. Rupert wants it, Dottie wants it, and my father wanted it. Do you deny it?"

"No, but it has to be what you and I want, Kit."

"You're saying you don't want me, is that it?" he demanded.

"No, no, I didn't say that." Alex covered his hand with hers, mortified that he had sensed her rejection. *Oh, Kit, why don't you just take me in your persuasive arms, as you did in London?*

"For God's sake, Alex, don't play games with me. I want this settled. If I don't get your promise, I'm afraid I'll lose you."

"Kit, I need a little time before I can give you my promise."

"Of course; time we'll spend together. I'll take you for a drive in my phaeton tomorrow. And I want to have a dinner party; just a family affair to let them all get used to the idea that you're going to be Lady Hatton. You don't have to set a date yet."

I cannot go for a drive tomorrow; I have to perform at Charlie's tomorrow night! "You may take me out in your phaeton on Monday, and dinner another night next week, perhaps—if you insist."

"I do insist. Tuesday night. Alexandra, you'll never know how happy you've made me!"

Alex saw how quickly his moods changed and told herself she should not be surprised; Christopher had always been this way. He was sensitive and took offense easily. She would have to guard against hurting him.

On the ride back to Hatton Hall, after he'd returned Alex to Longford Manor, Kit gave vent to his temper. *Not only did I have to cater to a madwoman today, I had to grovel at the feet of her high-and-mighty granddaughter, who thinks she's too bloody good for me!* Marriage was anathema to Kit. He feared it, because he had always thought of it as the ultimate trap. But he knew his back was against the wall, and he had no other way out. The thing that deeply galled him above all else was the knowledge that this marriage was what his father had always planned for him. Henry Hatton was finally getting what he wanted!

Kit went straight to the library and picked up the decanter. He needed a drink. Badly. Yet he knew that if he poured one, he would keep at it until the whiskey was gone. His hand trembled as he set the decanter back down. He heard someone enter the library and spun around guiltily.

"Your mail, sir." Mr. Burke handed him two envelopes.

When Kit saw that one was from Barclays Bank and the other from John Eaton, a wave of nausea washed over him. He knew he could not face reading them and threw them negligently on the desk. "Mr. Burke, you are just the man I need. I want you to plan a dinner for Tuesday evening. It will be a select affair . . . just a few guests: Alex and Lady Longford, Rupert and his viscountess, the Hardings, Olivia's brother, Harry, and Neville Staines. I want it to be formal, elegant, something special. It's an engagement party, Burke. Alexandra has consented to become Lady Hatton."

"Congratulations, sir. The lady will be a most welcome addition here at Hatton. Is Nicholas to be invited?"

"Good God, no. He doesn't want anyone to know that he is back. He intends to keep to himself at the Grange." Kit knew that within minutes Burke would inform the staff about the engagement. Perhaps the news would spread to the servants at Longford Manor and Harding House. The more who knew about the engagement the better. That way, Alex would find it difficult to refuse him. At the dinner he would present her with one of the rings that had belonged to his mother. That would make it official in everyone's eyes.

Kit looked longingly at the whiskey, then he cursed all the people who had brought him to this sorry pass. He snatched a hunting rifle from the library gun case. He knew that if he didn't hunt something down and kill it, he would explode.

The moment the gas lamps dimmed, the applause exploded. Alex quickly gathered her clothes from the screen and headed for the stairs. Tonight her posing vignette had included taking a bath in a delicately painted porcelain bathtub that contained imaginary water. She wished with all her heart that she didn't have to perform at Champagne Charlie's anymore. *All you have to do is marry Christopher Hatton,* an inner voice said. *You've already promised Dottie that you would!*

As she rode in the hackney cab back to Berkeley Square, her inner voice was still talking to her. *Once you've married him, you'll have to confess that Dottie's wealth is a myth. That shouldn't matter,* she reassured herself. *His father left Kit everything; he certainly isn't marrying me for money.*

As Alex lay abed, she schemed about taking the thousand pounds Dottie had set aside for her dowry and paying it toward the loan. That would postpone for some time Dottie's financial difficulties. Rupert had no money worries these days; perhaps he too would contribute.

Alex had told her grandmother that she was earning money at the newspaper and the sojourn to London was necessary, but she worried about how much longer she would be able to pull the wool over Dottie's eyes. There seemed to be no answers to her dilemma, and Tuesday there was the dinner party at Hatton Hall to face. That would bring yet another question to which she had no answer.

The ride home to Longford, early the next morning, lifted Alexandra's spirits considerably. The English countryside was so lovely, and she acknowledged how lucky she was to live there. As the weather warmed, London left much to be desired, even in the better areas. The Thames stank, and the vast slums teemed with people who would never experience anything beyond hardship, poverty, and misery.

She lived a life of privilege, thanks to her beloved grandmother. She had beautiful clothes, her own saddle horse, and servants, and she lived in a country manor. Her suitor was not only wealthy and titled, he was one of the handsomest men breathing. Best of all, she had known him since childhood. He had been extremely gallant when he had proposed on Friday, allowing her time before she made her decision. If she agreed to marry him, she would move from Longford Manor to Hatton Hall, the most magnificent estate in the entire county. Her mother's words danced before her on the morning breeze. *The way of duty is the way of happiness.*

At Hatton Hall on Tuesday, preparations for the dinner had been underway all afternoon. Mr. Burke had planned the special menu. The smoked trout came from their own river, the spring lamb from their home farm, and the fruit from Hatton's own orchards. Even the flowers that decorated the table came from the hall's conservatory.

Christopher Hatton spent the afternoon hand-painting place cards with intricate Celtic symbols that matched the elegant invitations he had sent out three days before. He brought them down to the dining room and surveyed Mr. Burke's handiwork with approval. Tall, scented wax tapers graced the long refectory table and the mantelpiece. Crystal water goblets, wineglasses, and monogrammed Georgian silver gleamed against the heavy damask linen tablecloth.

"I have the champagne cooling, but would you select the dinner wines, sir?"

"I am no connoisseur of wine. You had better come down to the cellar and give me your guidance, Mr. Burke."

The two men descended the stone steps that led from the kitchen to the cellars and made their way into the older foundation where the wine cellar was housed. As Kit brushed away cobwebs, he realized that no one had been down here since his father's death.

"For the fish course, I suggest the white Burgundy; these bottles were from a vintage crop of Chardonnay grapes. With the main course, I'd serve this Languedoc earthy-red Bordeaux."

"I bow to your expertise, Mr. Burke." Kit moved down the wooden racks. "Hello, what's this? Judas, I believe it's brandy!" He plucked two bottles from their shelf. "Harding enjoys brandy." Kit walked down to the end of the row to see what else he could spot. He glanced up at the heavy door in the ancient wall, and he recoiled at the sharp memories it evoked. Behind the door was an underground tunnel that led to the stables. He and Nick had discovered it when they were about six. They hadn't dared venture inside more than three or four feet because it was pitch-black. But their father had caught them playing there and had locked them in as punishment.

Kit remembered the paralyzing fear even now. He had clung to Nick and cried like a baby. When he heard the scurrying of rats in the blackness, he had trembled uncontrollably then wet himself. Nick wanted them to go down the tunnel and find their way out, but Kit clung to the door and wouldn't let go. When his twin left him, and he knew he was alone, he felt bereft. Panic set in, and he clawed at the door until his fingertips were bleeding. His imagination created demons from hell, who sucked the breath from his lungs to keep him from screaming. Then his twin returned with a lantern from the stables and saved his sanity.

Kit made his way back to Mr. Burke, whose arms were laden with wine bottles. "May I help you?" he asked breathlessly, as the pressure in his chest tightened.

"I have them secure, sir."

Kit gripped the brandy and hastily made his way back to the stone steps that led up to the kitchen. He took a deep breath and felt a trickle of sweat run down between his shoulder blades. He checked the time and, though it was still more than two hours before his guests were to arrive, he went upstairs to bathe. In his bedchamber, he saw that the valet had laid out his evening clothes. He set the two bottles of brandy on his bedside table, then opened the drawer and took out the small box that held his mother's ring.

As he looked down at it, his father's words echoed in his head: *I spoke with Dottie Longford, and we reached an understanding about a betrothal between you and Alexandra. I think we should announce it tonight at the hunt dinner. You may present her with your mother's diamond and sapphire ring.*

"Are you satisfied, Father? This marriage is what you always wanted; what you planned for me!" Kit ground out through clenched teeth. "Even this bloody ring was your choice!" He flung the ring box on the table beside the brandy. "This marriage was the reason we argued the day of the fatal shooting. Your death brought an end to your plans for me. That day I won, and you lost, Father!"

Kit unfastened his tight neckcloth and stripped off his shirt. It was as if Henry Hatton would not be denied. He felt his father reaching out from beyond the grave to bend him to his will. There was no way out of the trap. When he married Alex, his father would win! Kit twisted the cork from the nearest bottle and lifted the brandy to his lips.

Chapter 24

Two hours later, Mr. Burke knocked on the door of the Grange. When Nicholas saw his worried demeanor—a sharp contrast from his usually calm, capable manner—he knew something was amiss. "Come in, Mr. Burke."

"Sir, perhaps you know that his lordship planned a dinner party for this evening?" Burke began tentatively.

"No, I wasn't aware of it, Mr. Burke. I've been too busy to keep abreast of my twin's plans."

"All is in readiness, sir, and the guests will start arriving any moment . . . but . . . Lord Hatton is under the weather."

"Kit's drinking is nothing new. You'll simply have to make his excuses to the guests, Mr. Burke. You and I are well versed in making excuses for him."

"Sir, you cannot be aware that this is a very special evening. The guests are Lady Longford and Lord Staines, the Hardings, Rupert and the viscountess. Lord Hatton planned this intimate family gathering as an engagement dinner for Mistress Alexandra."

Nick felt his heart skip a beat. Did Alex know about this, or was Kit about to spring a surprise upon her? "I'd better come and speak with him, Mr. Burke." When he saw Burke's doubtful look he added, "Perhaps douse his head in cold water."

As they passed the dinning room, Nick caught the scent of flowers and the gleam of crystal and silver against damask. The air was redolent with the delicious aromas of roasting lamb, mint sauce, and piquantly spiced cherries flambée. They ascended to the third floor, then down the east wing to Kit's chamber.

Nick found his twin lying on the floor beside two empty brandy bottles. "I'm afraid it's beyond the cold-water stage, Mr. Burke."

"Yes, sir," he said quietly. "The dinner needs a host."

"Oh, no, don't look at me!"

"No one need ever know; you are Lord Hatton's only hope, sir. It pains me to think of his disgrace and Mistress Alexandra's disappointment. You and I know that she is the rightful future Lady Hatton. . . . This ought to be one of the happiest nights of her life." Burke looked into Nick's clear gray eyes. "The guests should start arriving any time, sir. I'll get you hot water so you may shave."

Nick's resolution wavered as he thought of Alexandra. He cared about her happiness as much as he cared for his own. She had been brought up to believe that she would become Lady Hatton, and if that was what she wanted, then he wanted it too.

He had misgivings about Kit making her a worthy husband, but he admitted that he would think the same of any other man. If the choice of a husband for Alex was up to him, he would selfishly choose himself. But the decision was not his; the decision was hers alone. He acknowledged that if she married Kit, it would not simply bring her a title, it would bring her Hatton Hall with all its wealth and property. The thought that it would be hers to pass on to her children seemed right and brought him a sense of satisfaction. *Mr. Burke is right; when a lady becomes engaged, it should be one of the happiest nights of her life!*

Alexandra sat at her dressing table while Sara pinned up her now long tresses in fashionable swirls; red-gold tendrils decorated her temples and the nape of her neck. She was wearing her oldest yet most feminine gown of palest blush pink. The skirt was designed from chiffon scarves, whose points floated when she moved. Around her neck she wore a single strand of tiny seed pearls.

Alex picked up the invitation and traced the intricate swirls of the Celtic pattern with the tip of her finger. It dawned on her that the design Christopher had painted was a marriage knot! It told her that tonight he would again press her to marry him, this time in public, and she was still not ready to give him an answer.

"Why, Sara, you've turned her into an innocent debutante; how did you manage such a feat?"

Alex gave her grandmother a wistful smile. "And you look like an extremely wealthy dowager in that lovely silvery-gray gown. However did you manage to find a wig to match it so exactly?"

"This isn't a wig; it's my natural hair, you cheeky young monkey. Neville is here; he's brought the closed carriage so we shan't be blown to bits. Do drag yourself from the glass, darling; it's too late to do anything about your virginal look now."

"I'll be right down. I'm just going to show Mother."

Alex and Sara moved down the hall to Margaret's bedchamber.

The eyes of the woman in the bed filled with tears, but they were happy tears. "You get your great beauty from your grandmother, Alexandra. I can feel magic in the air tonight."

Alex blew Margaret a kiss and hurried down to the waiting berline coach for the short drive to Hatton Hall. When it drew up in the courtyard, they saw that the other guests had already alighted from their carriages and were heading to the front door of the hall. "As it should be—the best for last," Dottie declared as she accepted help from Neville.

The first guests were greeted by Mr. Burke, who took the ladies' wraps and showed them into the drawing room, which was beautifully lit by scented candles. Their host turned at the same moment that Alexandra came into the room. Their eyes met, and Alexandra's breath caught in her throat; in his formal evening clothes, Christopher Hatton was an arresting figure. He seemed taller, darker, more commanding than other men. He seemed totally different from the Kit she knew. Tonight he looked so much like Nick, he set her pulse racing. Alex watched with fascination as he easily took charge of his guests. He singled out Dottie first, bringing her hand to his lips. He murmured something outrageous for her ears alone and won her approval in a heartbeat. He turned to Annabelle. "Lady Harding, would you help pour us all champagne?" Alex watched her preen at being chosen unofficial hostess.

Alex saw him bow before a frozen-faced Olivia. He placed an affectionate hand on Rupert's shoulder. "There is no need for me to tell you that you chose the most worthy man in England." Alex saw Olivia begin to thaw. He gave a friendly nod to Harry, shook Lord Harding's hand, and murmured confidentially, "You'll find whiskey in the library, my lord."

He took Lord Staines's hand between both of his in a heartfelt gesture. "I am pleased to see you looking so robust, my lord." Alex watched him listen attentively as Neville spoke of his recent illness and gave Dottie credit for his complete recovery.

When their host saw that everyone had been served champagne, he turned his full attention upon Alexandra. Without taking his eyes from her, he said, "I would like everyone to join me in a toast to Alexandra, my guest of honor. She and I have been devoted friends since we were children. I have watched her grow into the loveliest of ladies, and it is my dearest hope that our friendship will deepen and continue forever." He raised his glass. "To Alexandra." His words were so heartfelt that Alex thought it could have been Nick who was speaking. How could she have missed this very attractive side of Kit before?

The genuine affection he felt for her was perceptible to everyone in the room, especially Alex. His words were tangible; she felt them touch her, as warmly as his glance caressed her. Fleetingly, she wondered if her obsession with Nicholas had blinded her to Christopher's innate charm.

Amazed, she watched his deft touch at play with his other guests. He held them in the palm of his hand with an easy camaraderie that made the atmosphere pleasant and encouraged them to converse with one another in a civilized manner. He then again turned his undivided attention upon her, making her feel special. Kit's words and actions were so like Nick's, she was spellbound.

When dinner was announced, he ushered them all into

the dining room and seated Alexandra beside him at the head of the table. The name cards placed the other three couples opposite each other, with young Harry Harding at the foot of the table. Alex smiled inwardly at the clever arrangement. Neville Staines, who thought the world of her, sat on her left, while Dottie took it as a compliment to be seated on the host's right.

The food was delicious; the chosen wines complemented each successive course, and Mr. Burke's service was impeccable. The conversation was congenial, covering a score of topics which they all lively debated. Alexandra saw clearly that this was due to the adroit skills of her dinner partner. The guests were all enjoying their dessert when their host, as if by design, introduced a topic upon which none of them agreed: politics.

Alexandra saw her partner smile as he plucked a blush-pink rose from the table arrangement. He presented it to her, then stood and pulled back her chair. "I am sure you will all excuse us." He slipped a powerful arm about her waist and swept her from the dining room. When they reached the door, his other arm slipped beneath her knees. He lifted her against his heart and carried her outside. "There's something I want you to see, Alex."

"We can't just leave," she protested breathlessly.

"Of course we can. They are talking politics, and soon their arguments will become so heated they won't even notice that we have left. My obligation as host is to make certain my guests enjoy themselves. Now they are doing so, at the top of their lungs, and my duty has been fulfilled. My sole responsibility now is to focus on you."

His hypnotic words enchanted her. Tonight he spoke and acted so much like Nick, she was enthralled. Alex could feel the hard muscles of his powerful arms through the thin material of her gown, and she experienced a tingle of excitement. She lifted the rose and breathed in its fragrance, then lifted her lashes and looked into his shadowed gray eyes. "What is it you want me to see?"

"I want you to watch the moon as it rises above the lake. Alex, if I had my way, I would carry you out to see the moon rise every night. It rises pale at first, then as it sails higher, the sky turns into dark velvet, and the moonlight touches Hatton with a silver-edged magic."

His words were so romantic, her breath caught in her throat. She brushed the petals of the rose over the shadowed cleft in his chin, and he bent his head to brush his lips softly over hers. "As darkness falls, the lingering warmth from the departed sun fills the air with the fragrance of lilies, and roses, and night-scented stocks. Their loveliness always reminds me of you." He set her feet to the lawn and clasped her hand, enfolding his fingers around hers. A haunting call of a night heron came from the lake. "Can you feel the mystic power of the water drawing us closer? Come with me, Alex."

His voice, low in the dark, throbbed along her spine. His romantic words, reminding her so much of Nick, mesmerized her. As they strolled toward the lake, handclasped, Alex was surprised at the pleasure his touch brought her. His hand felt strong and protective, and his fingers curling about hers made her aware of their possessiveness. His presence silently overwhelmed her, as if he wove a spell about her that deliberately heightened her senses. She became acutely aware of the flutter of her gown against her legs, and against his legs too, as they moved together through the moonlight. She felt the soft night air upon her skin and breathed in the intoxicating perfume of the flowers. It seemed as if Christopher had created the romantic atmosphere for her alone, and Alex had never felt more feminine than she did tonight. She leaned her head into his shoulder, savoring the moment. "*You* have the mystic power to draw me closer."

As Nick looked down at her, he saw how small she was beside him, and a wave of protectiveness washed over him. Her beauty was so delicate and luminous in the moonlight that it made his heart ache with tenderness. When they reached the edge of the lake, the familiar wooden punt beckoned to them. She made no protest when he picked her up and carried her into the small boat then set her down beside him.

Alex sighed as he rowed them out onto the lake and ripples moved out in widening circles. "Hatton must be the loveliest place in all England. To know that it has been here for almost two centuries must make you feel so proud."

"I love it with all my heart and soul."

His voice, low and passionate, sent a thrill shivering down her spine. *A woman would give much to be loved with such deep devotion.*

"Alex, could you learn to love it?"

"I already love it, have always loved it."

"I want to give you the moon and the stars!"

She pointed to their glittering reflection in the water. "Tonight, you have given them to me."

"Look at me, Alex, while I tell you what is in my heart." He brushed the back of his fingers over her cheek with reverence. "I desire no other lady but you to be Lady Hatton, the *châtelaine* of Hatton Hall. I want its beauty and permanence to wrap its strength about you and keep you secure. I want to see your children running and laughing across Hatton's lawns. Then I want it passed down to your grandchildren, and I hope the future generations cherish it with the same deep and abiding passion that I feel."

Alex knew that he was baring his heart to her. She realized too that he wasn't just speaking of his feelings for Hatton. He was making it plain that he also cherished her with a deep and abiding passion. He was telling her that he loved her! The magic spell he wove around them was so perfect, she forgot altogether that she was with Kit.

He reached into his pocket and took out a small box. When he lifted the lid, the moonlight glinted off the diamonds and sapphires, reflecting the fire within the jewels. "Alexandra, this ring is precious to me, not because of its stones but because it belonged to my mother. If you would accept this ring, it would fill my heart with happiness."

"Ohhh . . ." Her breath came out in a heartfelt sigh. "I will be honored to wear her ring. I will treasure it always." Alex held out her hand, and he slipped it onto her finger. Deep within her heart she knew that Nicholas was her true love, and she believed it was Nick to whom she pledged herself.

"You accept the engagement?" Nick held his breath as he awaited her answer.

"Yes," she said softly.

Nick cursed himself, knowing he had seduced her. He refused to press her about setting a date for the wedding; his twin would have to do that for himself. "Perhaps we should return to the house before our guests annihilate one another?"

Alex laughed. "My money is on Dottie." She was relieved that he had not spoiled the moment by insisting they marry immediately. She sensed that he would be attuned to her wishes and desires, and her heart overflowed with gratitude that his goal seemed to be her happiness. She welcomed his arms as he lifted her and carried her from the boat, then he stood looking down at her for a long, drawn-out moment, as if he couldn't bear to let her go. Finally, he set her feet to the grass, and his possessive arm drew her close against his side as they slowly made their way back to the hall.

Early the next morning, Nick walked over from the Grange. "Mr. Burke, when my brother comes down, would you tell him I'm in the library?" While he waited, Nick glanced idly at Kit's gun collection and noticed a new set of duelling pistols with silver butt caps engraved with a double H, presumably for Harm Hatton. Nick was not amused at the way Kit indulged himself. He sat down at the mahogany desk and reflected on the words of the dinner guests when he and Alex had returned to the hall. Clearly, they were all anticipating the engagement, for the moment they reappeared he was heartily congratulated and Alex forced to show off the ring. He took the empty ring box from his pocket and set it on the desk.

When Kit came into the library, he looked repentant. He sank down in a chair and ran his hand through his hair in a boyish gesture. "Burke told me that you took my place and hosted the dinner last night. Nick, I'm so sorry about what happened; it was unforgivable. Going to the cellar is what did me in. When I saw the door to the underground passage, I relived the horror of being trapped in the dark as a child. I needed a brandy to settle my nerves and give me courage to ask Alex to marry me."

Nick pushed the small velvet box toward him. "You are officially engaged. The rest is up to you," he said curtly.

"Nick, how can I ever thank you—"

"Don't thank me," Nick growled. "I didn't do it for you, damn it! I did it for Alexandra! When a lady becomes engaged, it should be one of the happiest nights of her life. If I hadn't stepped in, it would have been a disaster. But let me make it plain, Kit: This is the last time, the *absolute* last time, that I pull your bloody coals from the fire!" Nick slammed his fist down on the desk.

Kit looked at his twin's clenched fist and saw that it rested on two envelopes. Seized by panic, he jumped from the chair and lunged for the letters. "What the hellfire are you doing, reading my personal mail? You are forever sticking your nose in where it isn't wanted. It seems you need a reminder that *I* am Lord Hatton, and you are here on my sufferance!" he shouted desperately, as he tried to snatch the letters from beneath his twin's clenched fist.

In a flash, Nick picked up the letter opener and jabbed at his brother's hand. Kit drew back his fingers immediately, and Nick proceeded to take the first letter from its envelope and read it. It was a letter from Barclays Bank informing Lord Hatton that once again his account was overdrawn.

Nick looked at his twin blankly. "Kit, what does this mean?"

"What the hell do you think it means? It means the money is gone . . . spent . . . every goddamn shilling!"

Nick's words were low, deliberate, soft. "You mean that you have spent all the money you inherited in the year I've been gone?"

"It wasn't my fault, Nick!" his twin cried. "That bastard Eaton forced me to sign an authorization giving him the power to make all my financial decisions!"

"Forced you?" Nick's voice was quiet, deadly.

"I was in over my head, Nick! He loaned me money for lucrative investments, then lost it all and told me Father's stocks were worthless. He defrauded me, when my back was against the wall! You were right, I never should have trusted him!"

Nick put up his hand in a commanding gesture to stop Kit's words. "Let me understand this correctly. Not only did you go through the money in the bank, you lost all the investments too?"

Nick took the second letter from its envelope. It was from John Eaton informing Hatton that his loans were due. *As you know, I hold the title deed on Hatton Hall, and unless the loans totaling more than fifty thousand pounds are repaid in full by the end of this month, the property is legally forfeit to me.* Nick raised his eyes from the letter. They were no longer gray. They were obsidian black. He stood up from the desk and advanced slowly toward his twin. "You gave him the deed to Hatton Hall." It was not a question.

Kit took a step toward him in supplication. "I'll be able to pay off the loan with Alexandra's money!"

The first blow smashed into Kit's cheekbone, lifting his feet off the carpet; the second thudded into his gut, doubling him over. As he rolled on the rug in a fetal position, the dregs of the brandy he had imbibed the night before came spewing forth in a torrent.

Nick looked down at his twin with contempt. "You are pathetic." He strode to the window and flung it open, staring with unseeing eyes at the garden beyond. He saw the young men who had served under him, honorable men, courageous men, fighting for their country, dying for their country, while a profligate young buck like his twin had debauched away a fortune.

Mr. Burke came to the library door. He was horrified at the scene that met his eyes. "I'll fetch a bucket and mop, sir."

"You may bring water, Mr. Burke," Nick said implacably, "but from now on Christopher Hatton will mop up his own spew."

Chapter 25

Nick strode to the wall safe and opened it. Miraculously, he found the money he had put there intact—almost twelve thousand pounds. He removed it and went upstairs to his bedchamber to pack a bag; he wouldn't need much, for most of his dress clothes were in London. He had not yet formulated a plan of action, but obviously he couldn't hide out at the Grange. One thing was certain: Eaton would not get his greedy hands on Hatton Hall. Nick would die first.

He would take the money with him; he dared not leave it here, for there were too many temptations close at hand. There was Epsom, with its horse races; Chiswick, with its boxing matches; and even closer was The Cock and Bull in Hounslow, where cockfights were held twice a week in the inn yard. Nick decided that he would deposit the money in Coutts Bank, where neither Kit nor Eaton could get their hands on it. When he opened his drawer and saw the black leather mask, half a dozen reckless schemes flashed through his imagination. He dismissed them out of hand, yet some perverse whim made him stuff the mask into his bag.

On his way out, Nick paused on the library threshold. His brother had managed to pull himself up into a chair, and Meg Riley bathed his face. When Nick saw that Kit's cheek was badly bruised and his eye swollen closed, he felt a surge of deep satisfaction.

"You can't leave!" Kit shouted, then winced from the pain. "I cannot let Alexandra see me like this."

"I suggest you send Alex some flowers and a note

of apology telling her you have unavoidable business in London. That should give you a week to crawl to your bed and lick your wounds."

When he arrived in London, Nicholas immediately went to Coutts Bank and deposited most of the money under the name Flynn Hatton. He kept one hundred pounds for gambling, knowing a game of chance was likely the only way he would get his hands on more money quickly. At Curzon Street, Nick stabled his horse and went straight upstairs to his twin's chamber. He methodically emptied the contents of Kit's desk and finally found what he was looking for. It was the list of investments that John Eaton had sent the day before Nick had left for Spain.

As he read the list, suspicion reared its ugly head. Not only did the list appear to be inadequate but the investments seemed improbable for a businessman like Henry Hatton. He could well believe that his father had invested in shipping, but the vessels would not be American; they would be British. Nick also doubted that his father would sink money into crops such as tobacco grown in the Colonies, when England was at war with America. British manufacturing was at its height, and her factories produced everything from guns to machinery that wove cloth for uniforms. It was inconceivable that his father had not taken advantage of the opportunities available in times of war. He folded the list, tucked it into his pocket, and decided to pay a visit to Tobias Jacobs, his father's former solicitor, in Chancery Lane.

There were a great many law offices in the area, but he finally managed to locate Jacobs's place of business in an ancient building with wooden stairs. He went through a door marked SOLICITOR AT LAW and was surprised to see a young man with a familiar face. Nick's brows drew together as he searched his memory for a name. "Jake . . . Jacob Smith . . . do you work here?"

The young man was grinning from ear to ear. "Captain Hatton, sir, the Jacob part is real enough, but my name was never Smith. Remember I told you my father wanted me to be his clerk, so I ran off and joined the army?"

"I do indeed. Don't tell me your father is Tobias Jacobs?" Nick asked in disbelief.

"Yes, he is, sir. After I had a taste of what real war was like, I was damn glad to come home and be a law clerk. I'll get Father."

Tobias Jacobs emerged from an inner office. "You're Captain Hatton? The man who dug the bullet from my son's arm and took him under your wing? But you're the twin, the one who inherited a great estate. Why did you join the army?"

"I am the other twin, Mr. Jacobs. I'm Nicholas, the one who was disinherited." Nick handed him the letter that he had made Kit sign allowing him to handle his affairs.

"Ah, it begins to make sense. I don't believe I can help you, Captain Hatton. Though grossly unfair, your father's will followed the letter of the law scrupulously."

"I'm not here about contesting the will, Mr. Jacobs. I strongly suspect that my father's financial advisor misrepresented the investments my twin inherited. I am hoping against hope that when you prepared my father's will, you made a list of the investments he had with John Eaton."

"It is most probable that I did, knowing that I would need to prepare a statement of assets and liabilities of the estate for probate. Let me locate your father's file."

Within ten minutes, Jacobs provided Nicholas with the list he was seeking. Nick took Eaton's list from his pocket and began to compare them. He saw immediately that they were totally different. "Shares in coal, lead, and copper mines seem far more likely ventures for Henry Hatton," Nick said. He read the complete list of investments, which included northern factories that produced not only guns but copper pipes to carry water and gas.

"I remember thinking he had great foresight to invest in gas. At the time, gaslight in the streets was only an experiment, but now there are plans to light half of London, and I predict it will eventually illuminate every city in England."

"I need this list," Nick said decisively.

"My son will make you a copy, which I shall certify. If you are considering litigation, Captain, please keep us in mind."

"I hope it won't come to that, Jacobs; lawsuits cost money. But I sincerely thank you both for your help in this matter."

"Nay, Captain, it is we who give thanks to you."

Nick descended the wooden stairs two at a time. Now that his suspicions had been confirmed, a hot, burning anger ignited in his gut and threatened to flame out of control. He had long known that Eaton was a greedy, avaricious swine; now he was convinced that the financier was corrupt. Nick knew he would not have a moment's peace until he confronted the thieving bastard. He strode down to the Strand and took a hackney cab to Jermyn Street. When he saw that number 10 was a brick town house, Nick concluded that John Eaton must conduct business from an office in his home. He knocked loudly, twice, before the door was opened by a man wearing spectacles, who seemed distracted.

"Yes, sir?"

Nick saw the ink stains on the man's fingers and surmised that he was Eaton's clerk. "I have business with John Eaton."

"Sorry, sir, but you're too late. Mr. Eaton has closed this office for the summer and we are in the midst of packing up everything for his transfer to Eaton Place in Slough."

Nicholas banked his anger and masked his irritation. "I'm quite sure Eaton will see me, if you will be good enough to announce me."

"That is impossible, sir. Mr. Eaton had a social engagement and left early. If you will excuse me, sir, it looks like rain, and I must transfer the files to the coach before the deluge starts."

Nick uttered a foul oath when the door closed in his face. His fingers fairly itched to rifle through Eaton's documents. *If I had a gun, I would relieve you of your bloody files!* Then it came to him that at Curzon Street he did have a gun. He also had a mask. Nick crossed the street to observe the house from a discreet distance. He could see that there was indeed a coach at the back door of the house. There were no horses in evidence, however. Nick reasoned that if Eaton had a social engagement this evening, likely he would not journey to Slough until tomorrow. An inner voice told him that it would be a simple matter to break into the coach after midnight and lift the files.

Nick felt a cold drop of rain hit his face. It was barely three o'clock in the afternoon; he had at least ten hours to kill and knew he could put them to better use than standing in a downpour.

Champagne Charlie was observing a game of four-hand bezique, a fast-paced diversion that was becoming quite fashionable. She left the players and with a radiant smile came to greet the tall, dark man. "Since Rupert isn't glued to your side, it must be Nick."

"Hello, Charlie. I came to pick your brains."

"Oh, I thought you might have dropped in for another shave," she drawled with exquisite sarcasm.

"Sorry," he said shortly, "I'm in a dangerous mood. I need money—as much as I can get my hands on. Do you know of any high-stake games going on tonight where the betting will be steep?"

"Well, it certainly won't be here with my bezique players. Actually, there'll be deep play tonight at the Mollies' Club, but that's not in your style. Better wait until Saturday night. The brandy-soaked Prince of Wales, his buffoon-of-a-brother Frederick, and their profligate cousin, the Duke of Gloucester, will be gathering at the Foxhole losing thousands to the wily Dukes of Rutland and Bedford."

"The Foxhole?"

"That gaming hell Charles James Fox opened near Carlton House. It's just a stone's throw from here."

"I thought they closed that place when Fox died."

"Only officially. Prinny offers a melodramatic toast to Fox, dripping with bathos, before every game. They sometimes ask for a couple of my girls, who invariably return convulsed with laughter. That would be your place to make a killing."

He drew her hand to his lips. "Charlie, you never disappoint."

As he walked out onto Pall Mall, he looked up at the sky. It was still only spitting rain, but gathering bruise-colored clouds had stolen the light from the afternoon and darkened the city. Since Curzon Street wasn't that far, it suited Nick's mood to gamble on the weather. As he strode past White's on St. James's Street, the urge to gamble further soared in his blood, and he knew that before the night was out he would risk much more than getting drenched.

He thought about the Mollies' Club, where homosexuals and men dressed as women shared intimate oyster suppers and other decadent appetites in the club's private rooms. Before they withdrew up the stairs for their licentious fun and games, however, they indulged in reckless bouts of gambling in the opulently furnished gaming rooms. When it came to Nick that the Mollies' Club in Piccadilly was just around the corner from Eaton's town house, where he planned to be at midnight, he knew where he would go to play cards.

After Fenton served him a light supper, Nick picked up the *Political Register* to pass the time before he dressed for the evening. What he read only inflamed his temper and made his mood more dangerous. Because Wellington was considered a hero by the public and was fast becoming the most popular man in England, the idiotic Prince Regent was denouncing him with scathing criticism and was doing his best to prevent the government from honoring him at a public reception upon his return to England. Nick flung the newspaper across the room. Come Saturday night, it would give him the greatest satisfaction to spit in Prinny's royal eye, by winning Prinny's royal gold.

When he judged the time to be right, Nick dressed for his night's adventure with care. He put on his black evening clothes, chose a black stock for his throat, then pulled on black riding boots. Only his shirt was white, and he planned to remove it before he ransacked Eaton's coach. He slipped the black leather mask into his coat pocket, then donned his long black evening cape and a black tricorn. They would not only protect him from the rain but would conceal his identity. Before he forgot, he took the list that Jacobs had given him and put it into his wallet; from now on he intended to keep it in his possession at all times.

Nick loaded his army pistols and took them down to the stables. When he had saddled his mare, he mounted the weapons in their saddle holsters. He rode to Pall Mall and stabled his horse in the cobbled coach house behind Charlie's, then he walked to Piccadilly.

At the Mollies' Club, the doorman's bulk was imposing, his pugilist's face intimidating. Nick slipped the man five guineas in lieu of the password and gained entrance. Inside, it was extremely crowded because of tonight's high-stakes betting. He couldn't get near the cloakroom, so he removed his hat and folded his cape over his arm. Nick kept to the shadows, walking the perimeter of the gaming room, focusing his attention on the brightly lit tables rather than on the painted creatures in their garish gowns who were making wagers. The raucous laughter and exaggerated, high-pitched voices were an assault on the ears. He narrowed his eyes against the blue smoke that filled the air as he searched for the table holding the most money. When he found it, he saw that it was a *roulette* table. He blinked to make sure he wasn't seeing things as his glance fell upon a stack of *rouleaux* that must have represented twenty or thirty thousand. His nostrils flared as he was about to walk a direct path toward the spinning wheel of fortune, when suddenly he raised his eyes and saw something that momentarily rooted his feet to the carpet. When he could move, he stepped quickly back into the shadows.

"Joan, dahling, I warrant you'll break the bank!"

"Oohh, Joan, let me rub you for luck!"

"I'll let you rub me for fun, but not for luck!" came the arch reply from the woman they addressed as Joan.

Nick was mesmerized as he stared at the creature in the striking red gown and jet-black wig. *It cannot be possible; my imagination is playing a trick on me!* Yet the longer he studied the woman's face, the more convinced he became that the agate eyes and long arrogant nose bore a remarkable resemblance to someone he knew. Though he could not be absolutely certain, Nicholas strongly suspected that Joan was not Joan at all, but John . . . John Eaton!

"Place your bets, *ladies*!" admonished the croupier. When the wheel stopped, a cheer went up from the crowd, and Nick was jostled aside as a rush of people gathered closer to enjoy the excitement and completely blocked his view of the lucky lady in red.

Nick knew he must leave. If it was Eaton, he could not take the risk of being recognized by him. But if he was right, the knowledge he had just gained would be worth far more to him than anything he could win at the tables. He put on his cape and tricorn and stepped out into the night. He heard the distant rumble of thunder in the west and was thankful that the rain had moved off. He crossed the road and stood in the recessed doorway of the building opposite, prepared for a long vigil. Nick had no choice; he had to prove to himself that the man he had seen in the striking red gown was indeed John Eaton. If he was a *habitué* of the infamous Mollies' Club, Nick knew he would hold the upper hand.

His wait turned out to be shorter than anticipated. Within the hour, Joan came out of the club, escorted by the burly doorman. The black leather satchel she carried obviously held her winnings, and Nick assumed her escort would be armed. He held his breath, half expecting a carriage to draw up and whisk them away. When the pair walked briskly to the corner, his spirits soared. He willed them to turn the corner and make their way to number 10 Jermyn Street. When they were out of sight he controlled his impatience by counting to two hundred before he stepped from the doorway to follow them. He kept a safe distance behind the queer-looking couple, not actually believing his good fortune until Joan entered her town house and her vigilant escort departed.

As Nick watched the lights go on upstairs, his gut ached from holding in his laughter. *What a bloody sight for sore eyes!* He dared not let himself picture Joan as she readied herself for bed. Instead, he focused on the task that lay ahead, estimating that it would be at least an hour before everyone in the household was safely asleep. As Nick sauntered off to retrieve his horse, he hoped his saddlebags would accommodate the files he intended to steal from John Eaton's coach.

* * *

When Nick returned to Jermyn Street, he found the house in darkness. He slid from the saddle, garbed in black from head to foot. The white shirt was in his saddlebag, and the black leather mask covered his face completely. He tethered his mount to a tree and with great stealth made his way to the back of the house.

Judas Iscariot! The bloody coach is gone! He leaned against the wall in disbelief as his brain strove to make sense of it. It took only a minute to realize that Eaton must have gone upstairs to change his clothes, then left for Slough tonight. He untethered Satin and stroked his hand along her withers. "Come, my beauty, we have our work cut out for us."

Nick mounted, removed his mask so it would not impede his vision, and rode along Piccadilly, hoping to catch a glimpse of Eaton's coach. There were not many mounted riders out tonight because of the wet weather, but the carriage traffic was heavy and didn't thin out until Kensington. Nick rode all the way to Chiswick before he singled out a lumbering coach ahead of him that could be the one he sought. "Now, if yonder contraption turns onto the Great West Road, I think we've got our man."

They rode head-on into the rain, which obliterated his view of the coach, but suddenly a flash of lightning lit up the sky, and Nick's mouth curved in a sardonic smile as he saw the coachman turn his horses onto the Great West Road. "The trick now, my beauty, is to get to Hounslow before them."

As he galloped after the coach, amused that the rumbling wheels and booming thunder masked the clatter of his horse's hooves, it all felt strangely inevitable to Nicholas, as if it were preordained. It almost seemed as if he had done it all before, perhaps in another lifetime. The words of an ancient rhyme ran through his head:

What memories those roads bequeath
That traverse Hounslow's dreaded heath,
Where every tree might hold beneath
A masked and pistoled rider.

Nicholas knew exactly where on the wild heath the coach must turn from the Great West Road onto the Bath Road. It was the only way to Slough. And, thanks to his ancestor's journal with its detailed sketches of Hounslow, he knew precisely which black spot best suited his plan. He headed into a wooded stretch at the side of the road and, allowing his mare to set her own pace, guided her in a wide arc that put him ahead of the coach. Once he was back on the road, he urged her into a full gallop and did not draw rein until they reached the crest of Shooter's Hill. The area was heavily treed on both sides of the road, providing perfect cover.

He slid from the saddle and tethered Satin to a tree. The woods were littered with fallen oak branches, which he dragged onto the road at its steepest incline. They were not substantial enough to impede a heavy coach, but Nick knew the pair of coach horses would shy in panic at the unexpected barrier. He quickly remounted, and as he waited beneath a sheltering oak, he calmly donned his mask, withdrew his pistols from their holsters, and made sure that their flashpans were filled with dry powder.

Nicholas heard the pounding hooves and clattering wheels long before he saw the faint yellow light of the coach lamps. In this weather they did little to illuminate the road or aid the coachman in any way; they were, however, most helpful to the man who silently tracked the progress of the coach. He waited with infinite patience, aware of the slow, steady thud of his heart. Nicholas experienced no fear; he was merely righting a wrong. He was not the thief—Eaton was.

The coach rumbled along, passed through muddy Dog's Hollow, then slowed as it started up the incline of Shooter's Hill. Suddenly the carriage horses encountered the branches. They whinnied in fear and reared up, straining in their traces to avoid the strange objects that lay in their path. The coachman cursed and dragged on the brake. "Whoa! Whoa there!" The coach swayed then lurched to a halt. The driver threw aside the reins, jumped down from his seat, and grabbed the leader's bridle.

The coach door swung open. "What the hell are you

about man? Why did you stop?" Eaton's arrogant voice demanded from within.

"Nothin' to worry about, sir. Just some branches the storm brought down."

"Then get them cleared away, you fool!"

The masked rider smiled with satisfaction as the glow of the coach lamps showed him that the driver had left his flintlock musket up on the box. Nick raised his pistols and, with his knees, guided his horse to the open coach door. *"Stand down!"*

The voice—deep, demanding, and dangerous—brooked no disobedience. John Eaton looked down the twelve-inch pistol barrels and knew he had no choice but to obey. The coachman jerked upright when he heard the command, a branch still clutched in his hand. The highwayman silently motioned with his pistol, and the hapless driver dropped the branch and joined his master beside the coach.

"Deliver up your goods." Nick half cocked both weapons.

Eaton pulled a large valise from the coach and threw it to the road. It was not the leather satchel that held his winnings.

"Deliver *all* your goods." Nick took aim at Eaton's head.

With great reluctance, Eaton reached beneath the seat and drew out the bag that held the money. "You'll not get away with this!"

"Are you threatening me?" The question was low, deadly.

Eaton threw the bag on the road beside the first.

"You!" Nick addressed the driver. "I said *everything*!"

When the man hurriedly reached inside the coach for the metal box of files that sat on the floor, Eaton protested, "No, the rest are just personal papers of use only to me."

"Deliver or die!"

The coachman slid the box onto the road with care, never taking his eyes from the cocked pistols. Eaton dared not protest further.

"Now start walking." The voice was implacable.

Before they were twenty-five yards down the road,

Nicholas was transferring the papers and documents to his saddlebags. He secured the leather satchel to his saddlebow, then dragged the valise and empty file box behind the trunk of a sheltering oak. Nick mounted, but before he set his heels to Satin's flanks, he fired a warning shot, then disappeared into the dark, wet night.

Chapter 26

Nick was less than two miles from Hatton Hall. Unfortunately, so was John Eaton, and Nick guessed that would be his destination, once he and his driver returned to their coach. Like a black phantom in his billowing cape, he rode into the wind, never slowing his pace until he reached the Hatton stables. He led his mare into a box stall at the back of the stables and covered her with a horse blanket. He lit a shuttered stable lamp, then brushed aside the piles of straw that concealed the fact that half of the wooden floor was a hinged door. Within minutes, both horse and rider had disappeared into the tunnel that led to Hatton Hall's cellars.

When they reached the far end, under the ancient foundations, Nick relieved Satin of both saddlebags and Eaton's leather satchel. Then he removed her saddle with its holsters that held his pistols. He gave her a rubdown with his once-white shirt then covered her again with the warm horse blanket. He scratched her ears and murmured affectionately, "I couldn't have done it without you, my beauty."

After Nick tended his horse, he proceeded to make himself more comfortable. He removed some of his wet garments, then sat on the floor with his back propped against the wall. He set the lantern down beside him, opened his saddlebags, and began to carefully examine the files he had stolen from Eaton's coach.

Within the hour, John Eaton was pounding on the front door of Hatton Hall. Mr. Burke threw on his clothes and went to answer the urgent summons. He immediately recognized Henry Hatton's cousin and with a puzzled frown inquired, "May I help you, Mr. Eaton?"

"It would help if you stopped blocking the doorway." He pushed his way past Burke. "I demand to see Hatton immediately."

"Lord Hatton is indisposed, sir; he retired early."

"He will be more than indisposed when he sees that I have followed him to his lair! An hour ago, my coach was robbed by a highwayman not two miles from this hall! Get Hatton now!"

"As you wish, sir, but I assure you that Lord Hatton has been at home all evening." The long-suffering Mr. Burke went to inform Christopher that he had an irate visitor who demanded his presence.

Kit Hatton, garbed in a hastily donned bedrobe, descended the stairs and followed Mr. Burke to the entrance hall. "What the devil is this nonsense about being robbed? There've been no highwaymen riding the heath for a decade!"

The sight of Christopher Hatton, fresh from his bed, nursing not only a bruised face but a debilitating hangover, did much to allay Eaton's suspicions. "I tell you my coach was held up and I was robbed! We went straight to the inn at Hounslow, asking them to summon the authorities, but they refused to do anything before morning."

"The Cock and Bull Inn?" Kit snorted. " 'Tis a hotbed for criminal activities. Most likely their cockfight was canceled because of the storm and your coach was robbed by a disgruntled gambler desperate for money."

"Summon a groom to stable my coach horses. My driver and I will stay here for the night and inform the authorities in the morning."

"I have no bloody grooms, thanks to you, Eaton! You have one hell of a nerve, arriving here in the middle of the night, throwing your orders about as if you own the place!"

"I shall own the place soon, Hatton. Surely it hasn't slipped your whiskey-soaked brain that I hold two outstanding loans on Hatton Hall, which are due at the end of this month?"

"Then I suggest you continue your ill-fated journey to Slough and return at the end of the month," Kit replied with exquisitely polite sarcasm. "Show him out, Mr. Burke."

Eaton once again took out his temper on his coachman. "The bloody highwayman would be lying dead out on the heath, if you'd done the job I pay you for! Before we go, I intend to have a look inside Hatton's stables. A wet horse is all the evidence I need to return tomorrow with the authorities and lay criminal charges."

The driver climbed down from his box, his weapon belatedly clutched in his hand, and followed Eaton through the courtyard to the stables. Inside, they groped about for a lantern, finally found one, then had the devil's own time lighting it. The yellow glow from the lamp showed them that the huge stables held only three animals. Renegade occupied the first stall, and Eaton ordered his driver to examine the high-spirited black who was moving about restlessly.

"Dry as a bone, sir. Never so much as had his nose outside all day." The coachman took a look at the pair of chestnut carriage horses and the phaeton. "These cattle are dry too, along with the rig. They'd have mud splattered up to their arseholes if any of 'em had traversed Hounslow Heath on a night like this."

"Well, there's nothing further we can learn here tonight. No doubt the brigand was being protected by the owner of the inn. I shall demand the names of all the patrons who were there tonight. Get me home, and don't spare your whip on the horses!"

"I'll have ye home in a trice, sir. Slough is only a league up the Bath Road."

An hour after the unwelcome visitors departed, Mr. Burke went down into the cellars and unlocked the door to the underground tunnel. "Thought it might be you, sir," he said calmly.

Nicholas, still sitting on the floor amidst a pile of papers, looked up in surprise. "How the devil did you know I was here?"

He stabbed a thumb into the air. "My quarters are just above here, and you're the only one who ever ventured into the tunnel." Though it was obvious that Nick Hatton was the highwayman who had robbed John Eaton's coach tonight, Mr. Burke made only one comment. With a sigh he picked up the filthy evening shirt and said, "Really, sir, it will be impossible to get this linen white again."

Nick grinned. "Give me a hand, Mr. Burke. I need to take all this up to my chamber."

"I trust you don't expect your mare to navigate the stairs?"

Nick's grin widened. "Before first light I'll take her over to the Grange and feed her. She earned her oats tonight, Mr. Burke. Did you by any chance have an unpleasant visitor?"

"Indeed we did, sir. John Eaton came pounding on the door with some preposterous tale of highway robbery, but when your twin stumbled from his bed, looking like death warmed over, Eaton's suspicions melted like snow in summer. When Lord Hatton refused him hospitality, Eaton and his lackey departed for Slough."

"Poor Kit, his day went from bad to worse! I intend to make it up to him, but not tonight, Mr. Burke; best let him sleep."

By the time Nicholas gained his own chamber, he had never felt less like sleeping in his life. The two hours of sifting through letters and documents had certainly paid off. He had wanted to cheer with triumph when he unfolded a crumpled document and found that he was holding the original Hatton deed, complete with its legal seals. From that moment he no longer felt the discomfort of the soaking wet garments that were rubbing his skin raw nor the cramps that assailed his limbs from crouching on the damp floor. It was like cream on the cake when he found the paper that Kit had signed, authorizing Eaton to handle all his financial affairs. Nicholas carefully placed the two documents in his desk and locked the drawer. He removed his wallet from the inside pocket of his coat, then stripped off his clothes and lit a fire in the grate. Not until after he had enjoyed a warm bath did he open the leather satchel to count Joan's winnings from the Mollies' Club.

Nick whistled as he pulled out four bundles of twenty-pound notes, each more than three inches thick. When he counted them, they totaled more than forty thousand pounds. Without a doubt, they were the loveliest ill-gotten gains he had ever seen. He could only imagine the tumult and fury Eaton must have experienced when he had been forced to hand over the bag. Until he could deposit the money in London, Nick decided to lock the cash in his desk along with the two all-important legal documents.

There was little more than an hour of darkness remaining, and Nick knew he was not yet finished his night's work. Before the first flush of dawn touched Hounslow Heath, he intended to return the remaining papers to Eaton's metal file box, along with the empty leather satchel from the Mollies' Club.

Nick glanced in the mirror, wondering if he had time to shave, and saw his own gray eyes, brimful of laughter. "All in all, Hazard Hatton, I'd say you had an enjoyable night!" He rubbed his fingers along the dark stubble of his jaw and grinned. "But not nearly as much fun as I intend to have before I'm done!"

Alexandra opened her eyes as the first rays of sunshine filtered into her bedchamber. Yesterday's rain had kept her a prisoner indoors, and she couldn't wait to saddle Zephyr for a morning ride. Instead of throwing back the covers, however, she lay still, trying to recapture the details of the dream that still floated about her. It had been a compelling dream about the Hatton twins; the thing that stood out most vividly was that she could not tell them apart. When the twins appeared together, she was both confused and confounded. When she was with Christopher, she thought he was Nicholas.

When you are with Christopher, you want him to be Nicholas, an inner voice whispered. *That is a lie! When Kit took me to the lake the other night, he was far more romantic than Nick could ever be. When he gave me his mother's ring, it touched me deeply, and when he said he desired me to be Lady Hatton, I knew he meant every word. He spoke of his deep and abiding love for Hatton Hall, and he stole my heart. I felt a oneness with Christopher that I never felt before. When he kissed me, I didn't want him to stop!*

Alex slipped from the bed and picked up the note Kit had sent yesterday. Her mouth curved in a soft smile as she read his words.

My Dearest Alexandra,
My head was so filled with your lovely face when I arose this morning that I walked straight into my bedchamber door. Since I don't want you to see my black eye, I shall refrain from visiting you for a few days. When I look more presentable, I hope you will come with me to the church so we can set a date for our wedding. Love, Christopher

Alex decided that though Kit would refrain from visiting her, she had no such qualms. She would ride over to see how he was and to decide on a date when their banns could be read in the Hatton church. Now that she and Christopher were officially engaged, there was little point in postponing the wedding. She looked down at her beautiful ring and smiled a secret smile. It announced to the world that she was his, and it reminded her of how possessive he had been the night he had stolen her away from Hart Cavendish and danced with her at Burlington House. The memory was so tangible that when she closed her eyes, she could feel their bodies swaying to the music.

While Alex was taking her bath, she made an important decision. On Saturday, after her performance at Champagne Charlie's, she would tell Charlotte King that she would not be performing again. Alex felt relief wash over her. She had no regrets about what she had done; it was the only way she had been able to earn money to help Dottie and her mother, but she was glad that she would not be going to Pall Mall again after Saturday night.

She put on a pale gray riding skirt with a yellow jacket to match her sunny mood, grabbed a quick breakfast, and hurried to the stables. She was surprised to see Dottie there before her, talking with Rupert, who had two other men with him.

"Sirrah! We are a household of ladies here at Longford. It is preposterous that you suspect one of us of highway robbery out on the heath! No, I emphatically refuse you permission to search my home and stables!" she announced in withering tones.

"Dottie, he doesn't suspect any such thing," Rupert assured her. "Officer Thorpe merely wants to look in the stables to see if the robber is hiding there without our knowledge. He has already searched the Hardings' stables, and I came over here with them so that you wouldn't be alarmed."

Dottie lifted her lorgnette for a more thorough inspection. "You profess to be John Eaton's coachman? My condolences!" She swung around to Thorpe. "And you are the authority from Middlesex County?" The moment Thorpe nodded in the affirmative she said, "There you are, then: This is Bucks County, and you have no jurisdiction whatsoever!"

"Lady Longford, would you prefer that the Bow Street Police of London be called in? They would overrun the entire area and leave you no privacy whatsoever."

"The London authorities have more good sense than to waste their time chasing phantom highwaymen. I suggest you need look no farther than The Cock and Bull Inn in Hounslow. No doubt you will discover it was nothing more than drunken horseplay!"

Rupert finally realized that Dottie wanted him to get rid of her unwanted visitors. "Gentlemen, I know the owner of the inn. Why don't we go there and get to the bottom of this matter?"

Before they were safely out of earshot, Dottie remarked to Alex, "Deliver me from the country bumpkins of Slough!"

Alex laughed. "I'm off to Hatton to see how Kit is faring. If I discover a highwayman hiding in Zephyr's stall, I shall run him through with a pitchfork!"

"No, darling, send him up to the house. I wouldn't mind an encounter with a dark and dangerous night rider."

As Alex rode the short distance to Hatton, she thought of the masquerade ball. A picture of Nicholas disguised as a highwayman came full-blown into her mind. It was so compelling that it took her breath away.

I was so madly in love with him that night. It is nothing short of a miracle that I got over my feelings for him. As Alex cantered across the lush meadow of Hatton Grange she saw a man standing beside a black horse. Suddenly, her heart began to hammer. *It cannot be Nick! My imagination is conjuring his image because I am thinking about him!* Then again, it could not be Kit, who never cared to work with the horses. She closed the distance between them, and when her eyes told her she was not imagining him, the ground came up to meet her and she swayed in the saddle.

"Alex!" Nick caught her before she fell and held her secure in strong arms until her eyes fluttered open. "Are you all right?"

"Yes," she replied breathlessly. *Dear God, no, I'm not all right!* "I didn't expect to see you." *I've been longing to see you!* "Kit told me you were safely back from France." *I saw you with my own eyes at Champagne Charlie's! Dear God, I thought I was over you, but now I know that I shall never be over you!*

Nick carefully set her feet to the ground, cursing himself for causing her to feel faint. "Can you stand, Alexandra?"

"Of course." She saw that he had been washing mud from the mare's legs. *When Hounslow Heath is all afire, then Hounslow's roads are naught but mire.* The words of the old rhyme ran through her head. *My God, Nicholas, are you the highwayman?* She knew he needed money. His father had left him penniless, and army pay was a disgraceful pittance. She also knew he was reckless enough to risk his neck. Her heart turned over in her breast. If aught happened to him, she would die. "I . . . I came to see Christopher."

Nick frowned. "Didn't you get his note?"

"Yes . . . he told me he walked into a door . . . I have to see for myself that he is all right." She hesitated. "We are engaged."

"I know." He took her hand and looked down at her ring. "Alex, more than anything in the world, I want you to be Lady Hatton."

"Thank you." She lowered her lashes so he could not read the pain in her eyes. "I'd better go." Her lashes flew up as he drew close. "No, no, please don't lift me into the saddle; I'll walk Zephyr." She felt so brittle that she feared she would shatter into a million shards if he touched her.

As she slowly walked toward Hatton Hall, her thoughts were in chaos, her emotions tangled up in knots, and she now felt reluctant to visit Christopher. She had a sudden impulse to mount Zephyr and ride away, yet she knew that if she gave in to the urge, she might never return. Alex chided herself for being a coward. She had a duty to Christopher and to her family; she must not play fast and loose with her promises. She tethered Zephyr's reins and knocked on the hall's magnificently carved door.

"Good morning, Mistress Alexandra. Lord Hatton is in the breakfast room. I shall bring you a cup of chocolate."

Mr. Burke's cheerful welcome did much to calm her agitation, and the moment she saw Kit's bruised face, her reluctance to see him fled. "I know you said you couldn't see me for a few days, but I wanted to make sure you were all right. Is it very painful?"

"Only when I breathe." His words, which could have been meant as a jest, sounded petulant and filled with self-pity.

Mr. Burke brought her a cup of chocolate, and she noticed that Kit did not speak again until he had left the room. She took a sip and broached the subject of their wedding. "Your note mentioned going to the church to arrange a date for the ceremony. As I understand it, the banns are read three Sundays in succession, so it would be possible to have the wedding in a month, if you wish."

"No, that's not soon enough!" he said sharply. "I'll get a license so we can dispense with the banns. Alex, surely a fortnight is long enough to wait?"

She felt dismayed that he was behaving so differently today. Yet she had known all her life that Christopher could be moody and sensitive at any hint of rejection. She did not wish to argue with him. "Arrange for the license. You are right; two or three weeks is long enough to wait." At least this way there would be no time to plan a costly wedding reception, inviting half the county. She set her cup down and gave him a radiant smile. "Kit, why don't we go for a gallop in the sunshine? I'm sure it will make you feel better."

"Alex, I have such a headache. I thought I'd go out by the lake and do some painting today. You understand my need to be alone?"

"Of course I do! My own sketching brings me both pleasure and tranquility. Solitude is exactly what you need. I'll see you in a few days when you are feeling better."

As Alex galloped along the river, she pondered over how withdrawn and unwell Kit had seemed. And yet, at the same time, he had insisted that they waste no time in getting married. Alex sighed. She should never have invaded his privacy. His note had said that he didn't want her to see him with a black eye. Now she wished with all her heart that she had not ignored his wishes. If she hadn't gone to Hatton this morning, she would not have discovered that she was still madly, hopelessly in love with Nicholas.

Nick Hatton was in no great hurry to see John Eaton, and he deliberately waited until after lunch to set out for Slough. He surmised that at first light Eaton would have informed the county authorities that his coach had been robbed on Hounslow Heath, and that they would have dispatched an officer to investigate. When Eaton's baggage and files were recovered in Dog's Hollow, they would have returned them to him; for his own perverse pleasure, Nick wanted to arrive after the fact.

When he rode into the courtyard at Eaton Place, he hid his amusement and nodded politely to the driver he had encountered last night who was now washing the mud from the black berline coach. At the stables, Nick turned his gray yearling over to a groom then proceeded to the front door, which was opened by Eaton's liveried majordomo.

"I am sorry, sir, Mr. Eaton is presently engaged."

"I'll wait," Nick said implacably and took a seat in the luxuriously furnished entrance hall. When the servant withdrew, Nick could hear voices coming from Eaton's office, and he smiled with satisfaction, knowing he had timed his visit perfectly.

"I have concluded that your unfortunate encounter was nothing more than drunken revelry, Mr. Eaton. I believe it was a practical joke perpetrated by young bucks gathered at the inn on Hounslow for a cockfight. Such behavior is reprehensible, yet not uncommon."

"In other words, Thorpe, you failed to turn up any suspects?"

"You have no witnesses, sir, and I recovered your baggage at the precise spot your coach was stopped, which lends weight to the probability that it was no more than drunken horseplay."

"You may have recovered my valise and my files, Thorpe, but this leather satchel contained a great deal of money! I was robbed—robbed blind—yet you seem reluctant to pursue the matter!"

"Sir, do you have proof of how much money was in the satchel?"

"Proof? Do you not realize that I am financial advisor to the Duke of Devonshire, among others? My word should be all the proof that is necessary!"

"I am not questioning your word, sir. Nevertheless, the fact remains that the satchel lay out on Hounslow Heath all night where any who passed by were free to help themselves."

"Your incompetence is staggering! I shall report you to your superiors, Thorpe. I should have gone to the London authorities straightaway."

"I have reason to believe the London authorities would not waste their valuable time chasing phantom highwaymen on Hounslow Heath. In my opinion, such a tale could make you a laughingstock and cast doubt on your own competence to handle the money of others. I bid you good day, sir."

The officer left and Nicholas was shown into the office. Eaton's blood was already boiling with anger, and Nick knew this put the financier at a disadvantage. "Good afternoon. I am here on behalf of my twin, Lord Hatton." Nick spoke with the same air of authority he had used as Captain Hatton, when he had commanded more than a thousand men. He reached into the breast pocket of his blue superfine coat and brought out the letter that Eaton had sent to his brother and laid it on the desk. "What exactly is the meaning of this?"

Eaton snatched up the letter and scanned it. "It's simple enough!" he shouted. "He cannot repay the loans I made him. Since I hold the title deed on Hatton Hall, it is forfeit to me."

Nick's mouth curved. "Surely you jest. My twin is far too shrewd to forfeit our ancestral home to anyone."

"Shrewd?" Eaton sneered. "It may come as a shock to you to learn that he has squandered his inheritance along with Hatton Hall. I have his signature and all the necessary documents in my possession."

"It may come as a shock to you to learn that you *do not*. My twin would never let the deed for Hatton out of his possession."

Eaton glanced quickly at the metal container of files that sat on his office floor where Thorpe had laid them, then he hesitated, suddenly unsure of himself. Some of the high color left his face, as doubt insinuated itself into his mind and uncertainty drained away his bombastic confidence.

Once more, Nicholas Hatton reached into his breast pocket and withdrew a sheet of paper. Again he laid it on Eaton's desk. "This is the real list of my late father's investments, notarized by Tobias Jacobs, his solicitor at law. Lord Hatton wishes to withdraw them from your administration."

Eaton went purple and opened his mouth to vilify him.

Nick held up his hand. "Before you protest, let me give you the reason, *Joan, darling*. Lord Hatton refuses to do business with a deviant financial advisor who is a member of the decadent Mollies' Club. I doubt very much if our good friend Hart Cavendish will keep you in his employ either, once he learns what your nickname, the Corkscrew, really stands for."

Suddenly Eaton was sweating, and a gray pallor had replaced the alarming color of his face. Nicholas smelled victory. When you had a man by the balls, his head and his heart soon followed.

"I am a reasonable man, Eaton, with the patience of

a saint. I shall sit quietly while you get my twin's stocks and bonds from your vault. In return, I shall forgo the pleasure of revealing your scandalous secrets to every newspaper in London."

Chapter 27

Nick was filled with triumph as he rode back to Hatton. When the property came into view, he realized that the hall, with its verdant pastures and tranquil lake, had never looked lovelier nor meant more to him than it did at this moment. He had overcome the threat of its loss and firmly believed the risks he had taken to keep it safe were not only worth it but completely justified.

Nick couldn't wait to share the wonderful news with his twin and put Kit's mind at ease about losing Hatton Hall to John Eaton. He knew they would have to have a serious discussion about the investments and choose a new trustworthy financial advisor who would keep a tight rein on his brother's spending, but Nick decided that could wait. Today, he simply wanted Kit and himself to savor the moment and celebrate their good fortune.

"Kit, are you home?" Nick called the moment he opened the door.

"He's been outdoors, painting, most of the afternoon. He'll return when the light starts to fade," Mr. Burke predicted.

"I have excellent news, Mr. Burke. We can stop worrying about John Eaton; I don't believe he will be favoring Hatton Hall with his presence any time soon."

"I was never worried, sir. I knew Eaton was no match for a man who defeated Napoleon."

Nicholas threw back his head and laughed. "Wellington gave me a little help with that one, Mr. Burke." He ran upstairs and removed the stocks and bonds from his saddlebags. As he looked at the valuable certificates,

Nick admired their father's shrewdness; his only mistake had been in trusting his cousin. The investments, and Kit's vulnerability, had proved to be too much of a temptation for a miscreant corrupted by greed, as Eaton was.

He unlocked his desk and placed the investment certificates in the drawer along with the forty thousand pounds. Before he relocked the desk, he removed the title deed to Hatton Hall, along with the paper Christopher had signed, authorizing Eaton to make all financial decisions for him. Nick's mouth curved as he anticipated his twin's surprise when he handed it to him. He hung his blue coat in the wardrobe, removed his starched neckcloth, and unfastened the buttons on his embroidered waistcoat. When he heard his brother below, he picked up the two precious documents and hurried downstairs to share the good news.

"Let's go into the library for a minute, I have a surprise."

Kit set down his canvasses and followed him warily. "I remember the surprise you gave me last time we were in the library!"

Nick laughed. "I'm sorry I thumped you; I can never remember being that angry with you before." His eyes examined Kit's face, and he was relieved to see that the bruise had almost disappeared. "Christopher, if you could have one wish for anything in the entire world, what would it be?"

Kit's eyes became wistful. "Do you want the truth?"

"Always." Something told Nick he shouldn't have asked.

"I wish I could go to Italy and study painting. Did you know that most of the world's finest art is in the city of Florence?"

"Italy? What about Hatton?"

"Hatton has become a millstone about my bloody neck. Sometimes I hate the damn place!" Kit said passionately.

Nick was dismayed and wished he'd told him the good news immediately. "John Eaton no longer has possession of the title deed to Hatton Hall; we do! It will never be a millstone again."

Kit stared in amazement at the deed with its red seals. "How on earth did you get it back from the thieving swine?"

"I robbed his coach on the heath."

"*You* are the highwayman?" Kit asked in disbelief.

Nick grinned. "That's not the only document I retrieved." He handed his twin the authorization he'd signed. "I thought you might relish the pleasure of burning this paper."

Kit let out a whoop of joy. "Christ, Nick, you are amazing! If you hadn't left to join the army, I never would have gotten into such a bloody mess. Together, nobody can beat us!" He lit a candle, held the paper to the flame until it ignited, then tossed it into the empty fireplace.

"I'm taking Hatton Hall's deed to London, and putting it in a bank vault, where no one can get their greedy hands on it again."

"You are an arrogant bastard, Nick. Have you forgotten that I am Lord Hatton and the deed belongs to me?"

"Are you prepared to fight me for it, Kit?" Nick slipped the deed inside his shirt. "I assure you, *my lord,* that is the only way you will get it."

Gray eyes stared into gray for a long, drawn-out minute. "I was only jesting. Damn, this is such a load off my mind; I think I'll join Rupert at the Epsom races this weekend to celebrate!"

Nick immediately decided that it was not the best time to tell his twin about the investments he'd recovered. He also concluded that it was high time he removed everything from his desk and got it safely to London. "I won't join you. I have some unfinished business in Town."

"In that case why don't you try out my phaeton? That pair of chestnuts I bought are a bit of a disappointment. Their gait doesn't seem to match. Perhaps you can solve the problem."

The problem is that they are not a matched pair. "All right, I'll give them a run and take a look." Nick hesitated, more than curious about Alexandra's visit this morning. "By the way, did you decide on a date for the wedding yet?"

"I told Alex it would have to be in the next two weeks, thinking I'd need her money to save Hatton, but thanks to you I can now give her the month she asked for."

"Did you tell her about your financial troubles?"

"Good God, no! I don't want her to think I'm marrying her for her fortune. She'll find out soon enough."

Nick clenched his fists and vowed to replace the money his twin had squandered. He would do everything in his power to make sure that when Kit married Alexandra, it would not be for her money.

The next morning, while Kit still slept, Nicholas transferred the stocks and bonds, as well as the four bundles of twenty-pound notes, from his locked desk into a valise. In a separate bag, he packed his black clothes, which Mr. Burke had meticulously cleaned, tucked in the black leather mask, and added his army pistols. In the stables, he harnessed the chestnuts to the phaeton, tied his mare's reins to the back of the carriage, and was on his way to London before his twin even opened his eyes.

As Nick tooled along the Great West Road, he watched the chestnuts' gait closely and saw that every now and then, the lighter horse fell out of step with the leader. He theorized that if he put blinkers on it, so that it couldn't see the leader, it would have to rely on the other animal's rhythm and would find it easier to keep pace. He reflected that it was rather like what he was doing with Kit, keeping him in the dark about their finances to keep him in line. His mind then moved on to what lay before him.

Alexandra put off telling Dottie that she had agreed to marry Kit in two weeks time. Then, on Friday, she received Kit's note, giving her a short reprieve.

My Dearest Alexandra,
Please forgive me for the way I behaved when you came to see me. I am more than happy to concede to your wishes and have our banns read in church. A month may seem forever to an impatient bride-

groom, but I do understand that a bride needs time to prepare for her wedding.

Love, Christopher

P.S. Rupert and I are off to Epsom races on Saturday.

Struggling to push aside all thoughts of Nicholas, Alex went out to the garden to convey her news to Dottie and Margaret. "Christopher and I have decided to get married in a month. Our banns are to be read in Hatton church the next three Sundays, and the wedding will be the following Saturday."

"Oh, darling, that's wonderful. You must have a new gown."

"We cannot afford such an extravagance," Alex protested.

"Fiddle-faddle! You are to be Lady Hatton; you cannot go to your husband in rags! Ride over and tell Rupert he must drive us to London tomorrow."

"Rupert and Christopher are going to Epsom races, I'm afraid. I shall ride to Town as I did last weekend. I have to deliver my article to the *Political Register,*" she improvised quickly.

"You cannot ride into Town alone; 'tis most improper! I cannot understand what I was thinking of to let you go last week."

"I'll wear Rupert's clothes and a tie-wig. No one will know I'm a female, and it will be the very last time, I swear! We did have an agreement, Dottie. You promised me complete freedom if I agreed to become Lady Hatton; I have kept my part of the bargain!"

"Mmm"—Dottie cast an accusing glance at Margaret—"I do know what happens when a young woman is forbidden to do something. Since I don't want you running off with an untitled lout, I suppose I had better let you have your last taste of 'complete freedom' as you call it. I shall be most interested in reading your article."

Alex swallowed. "It's not finished yet; I'd better get to it."

When she put pen to paper it was simple enough to write a scathing article about the Prince Regent and his disgraceful attitude toward England's new hero, Wellington. It was no secret that the Iron General had shouldered most of the cost of war during the last year, with little support from the government or pudding-witted George, who had been deliberately penurious with both troops and funds. Then, when Wellington had won victory for England, Prinny was so jealous and afraid that he had stripped him of his power and sent off his Peninsular Army directly to America, out of his control. Now the Regent was offering him the insulting post of Ambassador to Paris to keep him away from England.

Alex pointed out that the Prince of Wales was reluctant to reward Wellington with a decent pension, yet he and his brandy-soaked friends dropped thousands of pounds at the races and the gaming tables on a weekly basis, and he had just paid a fortune to an artist called Thomas Rowlandson for some pornographic sketches. To add insult to injury, the rotund Regent had persuaded the government to spend hundreds of thousands on a collection of Dutch artwork. She ended the article by demanding reform. Government abuses had been overlooked because of war, but now that the war was over, they should and would no longer be tolerated.

Alexandra was so pleased with the article that she decided to take it to the *Political Register* in the morning and try to get it published. Then she drew a caricature of Prinny and his cronies at a gaming table, groaning beneath a mountain of money.

On Saturday morning, Rupert drove his phaeton to Hatton Hall, picked up his friend Kit, and headed south to Epsom for the races. This weekend was the annual Oaks race, second only in importance to the Derby, and Epsom's close proximity to London guaranteed a large attendance by titled young bucks. It also attracted opportunists such as prostitutes, pickpockets, and peddlers who sold everything from fruit to flesh. Since drink was the foremost vice of the nobility, tents had been set up with the expectation of doing a brisk business in the sale of wine, whiskey, and blue ruin.

Christopher carefully avoided any mention of his financial difficulties to his future bride's brother, yet thought nothing of sponging off his friend, taking full advantage of his generosity. Rupert laid out the money for their bets on the first race, and when Kit won he pocketed the winnings without a thought. When they encountered the Duke of York with his latest mistress on his arm, Kit tipped his hat with great deference, hiding his jealousy until His Royal Highness was out of earshot. "Fat Freddie is addicted to the turf! The lucky swine always wins obscene amounts of money. No wonder the fat pig has women panting after him. Let's put our money on whatever he's backing in the next race."

Their enjoyment of the day increased apace with the guineas they won, and their laughter grew louder each time they repaired to the refreshment tent. It was mid-afternoon before Kit had a sobering encounter that effectively wiped the smile from his face. Rupert had just left to place their bets on the next-to-last race, while Kit lingered behind to finish his whiskey. Suddenly, he heard a voice that sent a cold shiver down his spine.

"Hello, Harm; thought I might run into you at Epsom."

"Get the hell away from me, Jeremy Eaton. You and your fucking father have sucked me dry!"

"I doubt that, cousin. You are adept at worming your way out of any difficult situation that may arise. We have much in common, you know. Trouble with our fathers must run in the family. Mine has kicked me out of the ancestral home. It's a good thing I prefer London to Slough; so much more convenient to White's."

"Can you not get it through your thick skull that my money is all gone? Even a leech like you cannot suck blood from a stone!"

"Harm, did I mention anything about money? What I have in mind is accommodation. As I recall, isn't your town house on Curzon Street within walking distance of White's? A year's free lease would suit my needs perfectly."

"You had better have a care," Kit threatened with deadly menace. "If my twin learns that you are blackmailing me, he will take you down so hard, you will never get up again!"

Jeremy laughed in his face. "You are so droll. Your

twin is just as guilty of perpetrating a criminal fraud on the authorities as you are. The two of you conspired to lie about your father's death. I am sure the gallant captain would never forgive you if you allowed this to get out. Think it over, cousin; 'tis a small price to pay for my silence. I shall be at White's on Tuesday."

Kit watched him stroll off to enjoy the last race. *I shall never be free of him! The son of a bitch will blackmail me until the day he dies!* As he went in search of Rupert, one scheme after another went through his mind to rid him, once and for all, of the bloodsucking swine. Each plan he visualized ended by his putting a ball in Jeremy Eaton's brain. Kit dismissed each plot as too risky; then it suddenly came to him that there was a way to shoot his cousin—and get away with it. Without a doubt, the perfect answer to his dilemma was a duel!

"Damn, where have you been? You just won the last race and weren't even here to watch it," Rupert informed him.

"How much?" Kit asked absently, his mind on bigger fish.

"Odds of twenty-to-one gives you a win of two hundred guineas!" Rupert said happily.

"I warrant my luck has changed," Kit declared. "Why don't we go to London for a couple of days next week and make the rounds of the clubs? Sort of a last fling before I become leg-shackled!"

Alexandra, wearing her male attire, went directly to the newspaper office when she arrived in London. The editor of the *Political Register* was so pleased with the article and caricature that he paid Alex ten shillings. It was more than she had ever received for her writing, and it made her feel good inside. The country was sadly in need of reform, and if her efforts helped, even in the smallest way, it was worthwhile. Perhaps after they were married she could persuade Christopher to take an interest in the government. As a Lord of the Realm he had a voice and should use it to help bring about changes to unjust laws and petition the Regent for reform.

She stabled Zephyr at Berkeley Square, then went upstairs to change from her male attire. When Hopkins served her a light lunch he asked after Sara and Mistress Margaret, as he called her mother.

"I believe Margaret enjoys being back at Longford Manor. Sitting in the garden every day seems to have done her good. Sara likes the country too; the sun has brought out her freckles, and I've been teaching her how to ride." Alex took a deep breath, then plunged in. "Hopkins, I want to thank you for your unfailing kindness to me on my visits to London. Whether I dress as male or female, and no matter what strange hours I keep, you never raise an eyebrow or show the least disapproval. After this visit I probably won't be back at Berkeley Square for some time. I am to be married shortly."

"I wish you every happiness, Mistress Alexandra. If the lucky gentleman is Christopher, Lord Hatton, I know your grandmother will be most pleased with your choice of husband."

"Thank you, Hopkins. Before I left Longford, Dottie made me promise to visit Madame Martine's in Bond Street and at least look at new gowns, but it seems such an extravagance."

"Every bride should have a new gown for her wedding, Mistress Alexandra; 'tis a tradition, not an extravagance."

"You've convinced me, Hopkins. I'd better go now, while the mood is upon me, before I change my mind."

As Alex walked up Bruton Street on her way to Bond, she decided against white for practical reasons. By the time they married, Christopher's mourning period would be officially over, and since social invitations would begin to arrive for Lord and Lady Hatton, Alex decided that a new ballgown would not be amiss. She would put it on Dottie's account, and somehow, someway, pay for it later.

Alex did not mention her upcoming wedding to Madame Martine, since she did not want the Frenchwoman telling her that her choice was unsuitable for a bride.

"I weesh to thank you verrry much for recommending my shop to the Duke of Devonshire's sisters. Both Lady Granville and Lady Carlisle came in to buy cashmere shawls, like the one you chose, and ended up purchasing many other garments."

"Oh, I'm so glad they brought you their business. Today I came to look at gowns, and perhaps I'll take a cashmere shawl for my grandmother; she loves beautiful things."

When Madame Martine brought out a gown of palest sea-foam green muslin, Alex knew she had to have it. It had long, diaphanous sleeves that fell in points, and the low-cut bodice was decorated with rosebuds and leaves of green silk love knots. When Alex tried it on, it fit her to perfection. "Oh, it makes me feel so feminine; I cannot resist it!" When she looked at the shawls, one stood out from all the rest. It was cream cashmere with a black silk fringe, and she knew Dottie would adore it. "Wrap them up, please; I shall take them with me."

As she strolled back to Berkeley Square, enjoying the sights and sounds of the London afternoon, she refused to dwell upon what lay ahead of her in just a few short hours.

Only when the clock chimed seven did Alex begin to prepare for what would be her final performance at Champagne Charlie's. To her horror, the flesh-colored net garment that had been washed so often suddenly fell apart. Reluctantly, she knew she would have to perform naked this one time. Alex dressed quickly, feeling great relief that this would be the last time, and hoped fervently that Charlotte King would not be angry when she found out that Caprice would not be back. As Alex walked along Pall Mall, she had to admit that Mrs. King had always dealt generously with her, allowing her to use her private bedchamber to dress after her performance, and always coming upstairs with her hundred guineas before she left. Alex took a deep breath, lifted her chin high, and walked into Charlie's. *Only three more hours and I'll be back in Berkeley Square, without anyone ever knowing my wicked secret!*

Chapter 28

When Nicholas Hatton arrived in London, he deposited the money in the Coutts account he had opened in the name of Flynn Hatton, which now had a satisfying balance of more than fifty thousand pounds. Under the same name he rented a safe-deposit box in which he placed the title deed to Hatton Hall. He also put in the stocks, bonds, and investment certificates for safekeeping until he could find a financial advisor in whom he and his twin could put their trust.

Next, he sought out his friend Hart Cavendish, who was in a better position than anyone he knew, to recommend a financier.

"Nick, I heard you were back from France. I truly envy you your courage. Were conditions over there as bad as reported?"

"Probably worse. Wellington snatched victory from defeat, one bloody battle at a time. He is a military genius; the odds were overwhelmingly stacked against him."

"I have recommended to the Prince Regent that Wellington be rewarded with a dukedom for his service to the Crown, which was consistently above and beyond the call of duty."

"I'm afraid your recommendation falls on deaf ears. I believe the government fears it will have a military dictator on its hands, and George of course is riddled with petty jealousy."

"Is it any wonder? The people of England worship a hero, and Prinny could never be that to them. He is nothing more than a figure of fun, whom the people ridicule for his excesses."

"His excesses are fast becoming an embarrassment. I understand his losses at the gaming table are so out of control they must be conducted in private at the Foxhole."

"That is true," Hart confided. "I was invited to dine at Carlton House, then join them at Fox's old gaming hell, but I declined and used the excuse that I was off to Chatsworth in Derbyshire. I know Prinny too well! Once he loses his own money, he takes it for granted that I will lend him mine; then George conveniently forgets he is in debt to me."

Nick tucked away the information that the Prince Regent had invited his cronies to dine at Carlton House; then, most likely cup-shot, they would make their way to the Foxhole, just as Champagne Charlie had told him. "Speaking of money, I wonder if you could recommend a good financial advisor? My father's cousin, John Eaton, has proved most unsatisfactory. Confidentially, both he and his son spend far too much time at the gaming tables themselves."

"Really? Come to think of it, Jeremy Eaton does seem to be a permanent fixture at White's these days. Most of my investments are in the hands of James Balfour, who is a trustee with Lloyds of London. They have offices in all the large industrial centers like Birmingham, Manchester, and Sheffield, as well as London. If you like, I'll drop Balfour a note and tell him to expect you."

"Thanks, Hart. I appreciate your help." Nick stood up and shook the Duke of Devonshire's hand with sincere gratitude for the helpful information he had just shared.

It was a short walk from Devonshire House to Carlton House, and Nicholas strolled around back to the stables and courtyard where the Regent's carriages were kept. Pretending that he and the Duke of Devonshire would be dining at Carlton House, he enquired if there would be room for their carriages. He learned that indeed there would not be room, since the Duke of York and the princes' dissolute cousin Gloucester would arrive in their own carriages. With a few casual questions, Nick also learned that the Regent's party always left in time for their weekly, nine o'clock card game.

From Carlton House he walked to the Foxhole and estimated that it was less than half a mile away. Nick's plan was simple yet extremely bold. He knew he would have only minutes to carry it out, and an escape route through nearby St. James's Park was essential if his plan was to succeed. He traced his steps half a dozen times, then feeling a confidence known only to those born under the sign of the lion, he returned to Curzon Street to wait for darkness to fall.

A few minutes before eight, Alexandra entered the room that held the stage where she performed. Though no one was in the room yet, she averted her eyes from the empty chairs and focused her gaze on Charlie's red-and-black Axminster carpet beneath her feet. Once she went through the curtain that separated her from her audience, Alex was usually able to relax a little, but tonight, because she knew she would have to perform naked, the tension did not leave her.

As always, she checked the props on the stage and saw that it held both the bath and the bed. Since it was to be her last performance, it seemed as if fate had decided that she give her audience its money's worth. She looked to make sure the hairbrush was on the dressing table, and adjusted the angle of the screen on which she hung her garments once she removed them.

As Alex positioned herself just inside the stairwell door at the side of the dais, she could hardly breathe. It was an extremely warm night, and the layers of clothing she wore, topped by the flowing cape, felt suffocating. The palms of her hands were damp as she listened for Charlie's male clientele to file into the room, and as she tied on her mask and made sure her long wig was in place, she felt her hands tremble. The moment the gas lamps were lit, Alex was assailed by a wave of nausea and feared she might be sick. *What the devil is the matter with you? You've done this two dozen times before,* her inner voice scolded. *That doesn't make it easier; it makes it harder,* she replied. *The sooner you begin; the sooner it will be over!* She steeled her nerves, turned the doorknob, and stepped onto the illuminated stage.

* * *

Nicholas left Satin in her comfortable stall. A horse could be easily traced; tonight he would work on foot. It was such a hot night that he wore neither coat nor shirt beneath his black cloak, and the freedom of movement it gave him added to his confidence. Since he had no intention of shooting anyone, he carried only a single pistol tucked into his belt, along with the leather mask.

Nick stationed himself in the shadows of the Carlton House courtyard, which now held three closed coaches, each with its own matched team of magnificent horses and their attendant coachmen and grooms. He affixed his mask with steady hands, knowing that, garbed in black from head to foot, he was invisible in the darkness. Nick knew that the trio of fat royals would not walk, even though it was less than eight hundred yards to the Foxhole; they would not be steady enough on their feet after their two-hour dinner debauch. He calculated that they would ride together in a single coach, accompanied by one of the Regent's equerries.

Before nine, the French doors opened and Their Royal Highnesses—George, Frederick, and cousin William—stepped out onto the well-lit terrace, then descended the stone steps to the courtyard and the waiting coach. The Regent, unmistakable in pale blue satin, was accompanied by an officer of the Horse Guards carrying an attache case. Nick's mouth quirked with contempt; the members of the Prince's own regiment were nothing more than pampered youths who made perfect lackeys.

It took several minutes for the portly princes to climb inside the heavy coach, then the driver shut the door, climbed to the box, and took up his reins. The coach made a wide turn out of the courtyard, then straightened. Nick's strides easily kept pace with the vehicle, as the horses fell into a slow trot for the short drive. When the closed carriage was about four hundred yards from the Foxhole, Nick, taking great care that the driver did not see him, opened the coach door and swung inside.

Before the occupants could gasp their surprise, the twelve-inch barrel of a pistol was pressed against the Prince Regent's heart.

"Not one word, gentlemen." The voice was polite but

deadly serious. "I bring you a message from Charles James Fox: *Don't risk it, Your Royal Highness; play it safe.*"

The Duke of York was too intoxicated from his day at Epsom and evening at Carlton House to know what was going on. Gloucester moaned softly, and the Regent actually whimpered as a tear rolled down his florid face.

"Take the money from the attache case and put it in here." Nick held out a black velvet bag and watched the officer as he opened the leather case and removed what looked to be about twenty thousand pounds. Then Gloucester opened his purse and emptied its contents into the velvet bag. When Frederick made no move, but sat there like a bloated toad, his cousin William quickly divested him of his Epsom winnings and dropped them into the bag.

"Gentlemen, it has been an honor and a privilege." Nick opened the coach door and swung to the ground while it was still moving, just before it reached the Foxhole. He was headed toward St. James's Park by the time the carriage stopped and the Guardsman jumped out, shouting, "Stop, thief! Stop, thief!"

Suddenly, coming out of the park directly in front of him, was a mounted rider from the Bow Street Mounted Patrol. Nick could have shot him, but his own personal code of honor prevented such a callous act. Instead, he cursed his luck, swiftly turned on his heel, and headed in the opposite direction toward Pall Mall. The mounted constable, however, had no such qualms about using his firearm. Nick heard a shot ring out, then almost instantly he felt a searing, scalding pain burn into the back of his head. It almost drove him to his knees, but in spite of the hurt, he kept running, knowing that if the ball had entered his brain, he would be dead. He could feel his own warm blood begin to trickle down the back of his neck and prayed that his cloak would soak up most of it so that he wouldn't leave a trail.

Nick turned the corner onto Pall Mall and automatically his long legs carried him along the familiar path toward Champagne Charlie's. His hat was already gone, and he whipped off the black leather mask as he burst through the door and stuffed it into the velvet bag that was still clutched in his hand.

A bevy of beautiful whores watched open-mouthed as the Hatton twin dashed through the reception room and headed toward the stairs. At that moment, Charlie, garbed in burgundy brocade, was on her way downstairs. The applause for Caprice's stage show had just begun and was Charlie's cue to come down and greet her clients as they emerged from watching the titillating performance.

"They're after me," Nick warned her, as he passed her on the staircase.

"My God, you're wounded!" Charlie immediately followed him back up the stairs and along the hall toward her private rooms.

They hurried inside and shut the door. Nick slung the velvet bag that held the money, along with his pistol, under the big bed then removed his black evening cloak, the back of which was now soaked with blood.

Alex was trembling all over by the time her performance was finally over. Her poses usually lasted about an hour, but tonight had seemed twice that long. When the gas lamps were extinguished and the applause began then rose to a crescendo, she was weak with relief that the nerve-racking ordeal was over and done with. She pulled her cloak about her nakedness, shivering with cold, and wondered how on earth she had thought it a warm night. As she gathered her garments, her knees felt like wet linen, and she kept dropping things. She bent to retrieve a stocking from the floor, then hurried through the door that led into the lighted stairwell. She paused for a moment to make sure she had everything, then took a deep breath before she attempted the flight of stairs.

Alex reached the top without incident and ran the last few steps to Charlie's private bedchamber. She flung open the door, hurried inside, and almost fainted at the sight that met her eyes. Nicholas Hatton, naked to the waist, and Charlotte King, looking more beautiful than any woman had a right to, were standing so close that their bodies were almost touching. Her wide bed, so decadent and inviting, was less than a foot away.

"It's only Caprice!" Charlie almost sagged with relief.

"No, it isn't Caprice!" Alex dropped her clothes in a

heap and tore off the mask and blond wig. As her red-gold curls tumbled to her shoulders, she stared defiantly at the wicked devil who caused her continual heartache. "It is Alexandra!"

Nick stared back at her as if he were mesmerized. He honestly believed that his loss of blood was causing him to hallucinate.

"Oh, good, you know each other! Quick, get into bed, both of you. I'll go down and see if I can dissuade them from searching."

"Alex! What in the name of God are you doing in this place?" Nick demanded. His hand went up to clutch the back of his head in an effort to stem the tidal wave of pain that washed over him. When he took his hand away, it was covered with bright red blood.

"Oh my God, Nick, you're wounded!" Her outrage vanished instantly and was replaced by heart-wrenching concern for the man who meant more to her than life.

"I was shot. You must hide, Alex; the law will be here to arrest me any minute."

"Nick, you are bleeding to death!" she sobbed.

"No, no, the bullet badly grazed me . . . scalp wounds always bleed like the very devil. Do as I bid you; get the hell out of here and hide somewhere." He swayed on his feet.

Alex grabbed up his discarded cloak and wiped the crimson blood from his hands and shoulders. Then she threw back the cover on the bed and pushed him down onto the black satin sheets. "Press your head back into the pillow . . . the blood won't show on black satin." She discarded her cape, climbed naked into the bed, and covered him with her body. Her heart was thudding so loudly she thought it was someone pounding on the door. She pressed her fingers to his lips. "Hush, my love, please don't speak . . . I'll do the talking." Alex knew she could conceal her love for Nick no longer. Her words and actions in the face of such heart-stopping danger were revealed for him to see, and she was glad.

Seconds later, the door opened and the Bow Street policeman who had shot Nicholas stepped over the threshold and pointed his gun.

Alex raised herself up and gave him a seductive glance from over her shoulder. "You'll have to wait your turn, luv, though I do like a man with a big weapon."

Without lifting his head from the pillow, Nicholas fixed him with a steely gray stare. "What the hell is going on?" he demanded in his most arrogant drawl. "I've bought her for the night."

The constable stared at the naked couple in the bed, noticed the man's possessive hand on the girl's deliciously round bottom, then gave the room a cursory glance. He nodded. "Carry on, my lord."

When he withdrew, Alex collapsed onto the man beneath her. "Oh, Nicholas, whatever did you do?"

"I robbed Prinny's coach, but more to the point, Hellion, what the devil are you doing in a brothel?"

"I've been earning money."

"Earning money!" His grip became so painful she knew he was in no danger of dying.

"Oh, Nick, not this way." She gestured to her body pressed against his hard length. "I'm a posing girl."

"Caprice!" he said through clenched teeth. "I've seen your scandalous performance! I should have put you across my knee and thrashed you years ago, you willful little bitch."

As Nick looked up at her, he realized that it was useless to pretend any longer. "Oh God, Alex, I love you so much! Risking your safety and your reputation to protect me touches my heart." He tenderly caressed her cheek with his fingertips.

"Nick, I've loved you always. There's no room in my heart for anyone but you. . . . You must have known that!"

"Of course I knew. But you were promised to Kit, and I hoped you'd get over me, though I knew I would love you forever."

She longed to believe his protestations of love, but feared the wound was making him delirious. Alex kissed her fingers, then pressed them to his lips. "Please lie still, my love."

Charlie entered the room and closed the door. "He's left for now, but he could be back, so you'd better stay put for awhile."

"He's lost a lot of blood. It won't stop until it's stitched."

"Don't look at me," Charlie protested, "I'm not the domesticated type, and I'm not exactly running a sewing circle downstairs."

"Oh, I'll do it, if you can find me a needle and thread."

Nicholas groaned and closed his eyes. "I can't believe you two know each other!"

"And a damn good thing we do, Hazard Hatton!" Charlie retorted. "The two of us just saved your bloody balls. I'll be back with needle and thread."

The moment the door closed, Alex slipped from the bed and pulled on her shift. She turned up the lamp and brought it to the bedside table. "You'd better let me have a look."

He sat up gingerly. "Tell me what you see."

Alex steeled herself to examine the wound. His beautiful black locks were saturated with blood, which was still bubbling forth from the gash the ball had opened. As her fingers separated and lifted his hair, the flesh of his scalp lifted with it, and she clearly saw the white skull bone beneath. She grabbed up the pillow and pressed it to the wound to staunch the flow of blood. "It's not as bad as I thought." *My God, it's much worse than I thought!* "The ball made a furrow of about two inches." *It's at least a three-inch gash, and deep too!*

"How the hell did you learn of Champagne Charlie's?" Nick demanded. "And why are you taking off your clothes for money?"

"Nick, if you don't stay calm, the bleeding will never stop. The more you shout at me, the faster it spurts out, and you've already lost far too much!"

"All right, I'll shut up for now, but you've got one hell of a lot of explaining to do, Alexandra."

"Oh, and you think you don't!" She stared angrily into his eyes.

Nick, as always, saw the humor in their situation. "We make a fine bloody pair; the Hellion and the Highwayman. Thankfully, it seems to be more farce than tragedy!"

Charlie returned with a needle and a spool of black thread. She set them down on the bedside table and went to pour Nick a double measure of brandy. "Drink this; it will help."

The corner of his mouth lifted. "It won't really. It might take the edge off the pain, but I've lost blood and should be drinking water. My mouth's as dry as the desert."

Nick downed the brandy anyway, while Alex threaded the needle, and Charlie brought a jug of water from her dressing room. "The officer is searching other establishments along Pall Mall, so I'm pretty sure he didn't actually see you enter my place."

"Hold still, Nicholas. This will take a little time, and the ordeal won't be pleasant," Alex warned as she knelt on the bed behind him.

"Ordeals seldom are, my love," he replied solemnly.

"You two know each other rather well," Charlie observed.

"Since we were children," Nick acknowledged.

"He still thinks I'm a child," Alex accused, as she set the first stitch and agonized over the pain she was causing him.

"The evidence of my own eyes proves beyond a shadow of doubt that you are a woman, Alex, though unfortunately not a lady."

"And the evidence of my eyes proves beyond a shadow of doubt that you are a man, Nick, though no longer a gentleman."

"Not any more, my sweet, I promise you."

Charlie watched Alex make the last stitch then tie off the thread. "I've ordered you your usual bath. It's become such a ritual, the maid puts the water on to heat as soon as she sees you come through the front door," Charlie said dryly. "Let me take these bloody sheets from the bed. You'll find clean ones in the dressing room," she told Alex. "Nick, I have a business to run, so I shall leave you in the capable hands of your lady love."

"I am not his lady love," Alex protested, as Charlie carried out the bundled sheets and closed the door.

"You are, you know."

The deep voice behind her sent a shiver down Alexandra's spine.

Chapter 29

Nicholas sat in Charlie's hand-painted slipper bath while Alex stood behind him and gently washed his blood-soaked hair. His admonition that she was his *lady love* had thrilled her to her very core, but at that moment the servants had brought in the hot water for his bath and it had given her time to realize that it was probably the brandy talking. Alex concentrated on cleansing the back of his head, making sure that the wound was no longer seeping blood. "It looks good, Nick . . . the bleeding has stopped. Here"—she handed him the jug of water—"finish drinking this, so I can use it to rinse you."

"Thank you, sweetheart." He reached behind his head to take her hand and squeeze it. "This is like the fantasies I had about you while I was in France, except we were bathing *together.*"

Alexandra flushed a rosy pink. "You've had too much brandy."

"No, love, I'm wondrously sober."

She wanted to believe him. Desperately. *I shall believe him, just for tonight; how can it possibly hurt?* She took the empty jug from his hands, smiled into his eyes, and began to pour water over him to rinse off the soap. His muscles glistened wetly as the water cascaded down his broad back and over the tight black curls that adorned his chest. *His body is so magnificent, so powerful. It makes me weak with longing.* She set down the jug and reached out to run her fingertips along his collarbone. Suddenly, his cock stood up straight and poked its velvet crown above the water. "Oh!" she gasped then lowered her lashes. How could he become aroused when he was wounded? "Has your pain lessened a little?"

"The only head I am aware of at this moment is the one between my legs, and it aches like the very devil," he admitted ruefully.

She suddenly longed to cradle it in her hand to ease the ache. She reached out, then quickly drew back her hand, shocked at her own wanton behavior.

At just the thought of her touching his cock, Nick almost came out of his skin. His mouth curved with anticipation, knowing that she wanted to touch him; all he had to do was overcome her shyness. The blush on her cheeks made his heart sing with joy. Alexandra, in spite of her thirst for worldly knowledge, was still unbelievably innocent, and he savored the thought of her awakening.

In a concerned voice she instructed, "Don't try to get out of the water by yourself. I'll get a towel and be right back."

When she stood up in her skimpy shift, dampened from the bath water, Nick's erection bucked wildly. He wondered if he had died and gone to heaven. A sharp bark of laughter erupted from his throat. Was he not the Spawn of Satan, headed directly to hell?

Alex emerged from the dressing room carrying a set of clean black satin sheets and two thirsty towels. She remade the bed before returning to the tub. She shook out a towel and admonished, "Lean on me. I don't want you to fall."

Nick stood up, but as the water ran off the bulging saddle muscles of his thighs, he made no move toward her. "I've never leaned on anyone in my life; I'm not about to start now. However, I *fell* long ago, I'm afraid, and what's done cannot be undone."

Can he possibly mean that he fell in love with me long ago? A frisson of pleasure made her breasts tingle then spiraled down into her belly and ended between her legs in a sensation very like the burst of exploding fireworks. She watched him step from the tub, pluck the towel from her fingers, and proceed to vigorously rub himself. Her mouth went dry at being privy to such a flagrant, provocative display of male nudity. *If he rubs his head with such vigor, he'll open up the wound!* "I'll dry your hair, Nick." Alex suddenly realized she wasn't tall enough in her bare feet. She spied a foot-stool and ran to fetch it.

When she bent over, her short shift went up to reveal the cheeks of her gloriously round bottom. "Alex, I swear to God you are purposely teasing and tempting me . . . you are a born *coquette*!"

She straightened quickly. " 'Tis you who are purposely teasing me, you devil, just to keep me covered with blushes."

"Blushes are the only thing I want you covered with, my love."

She set the stool down behind him and picked up the second towel. Then she used his shoulders to help her step up onto the stool. "I didn't hurt you, did I?" she asked anxiously.

"Almost brought me to my knees, and no doubt will before you are done with me, Hellion."

"Do try to be serious for a moment," she reproved. "Now, hold absolutely still while I dry the back of your head." She dabbed his wound with gentle fingers, then held the towel still while it absorbed the water from his curling black hair. Finally she pronounced, "There, you are almost good as new."

Nicholas turned to face her, plucked the towel from her fingers, and dropped it to the floor. Then with purposeful hands he lifted her damp shift over her head and dropped it after the towel. He cupped her face, gazed worshipfully into her eyes, dropped a hungry glance on her mouth, raised his eyes once more to hers, then drew her close for a tender kiss. "Alex, I worship you."

His hands and his lips were so gentle, so reverent, it brought a lump to her throat. Slowly, his mouth became more demanding, and his hands dropped from her face and slid around her body, bringing her soft curves close against his hard length. His marble-hard shaft lay rigid between them, and he heard her draw in a swift breath as if he were hurting her. "This will be far more comfortable; trust me." He slipped his erect cock between her legs, so that it lay along her hot cleft. Even with the stool beneath her feet, she had to rise up on her toes to facilitate their intimate position. Nick groaned. "I like you on a pedestal, my love. I swear I'll never be able to look at a footstool again without thinking of you."

Alex tasted the brandy on his lips, but it didn't matter; the kiss made her breathless with longing. Each time her nipples brushed against the curly hair of his chest, she wanted to scream with excitement. His powerful, possessive hands stroked down her back and caressed her bum, drugging her senses. The words he murmured into her ear in his deep voice were becoming husky with desire, and the lids over his smoldering gray eyes were half closed and heavy with sensuality.

Her reaction to Nicholas was cataclysmic, and she knew it had nothing to do with the highly erotic setting of the brothel, with danger hovering close by. She had daydreamed about the dark, dominant twin for more than five years, perhaps even longer. The reality of this romantic encounter was overwhelming, a thousand times more intensely compelling than any girlish fantasy. His touch stole her senses; he was far more potent than any intoxicant. The heat of his body seeped into her flesh, setting her aflame with a raging desire that threatened to burn out of control and consume her. She was panting with need, and her breasts rose and fell against his powerful, muscled chest. Her hands alternately caressed then gripped his shoulders to prevent her body from dissolving into a pool at his feet. His eyes were now the color of smoke, and she prayed his yearning was as intense as hers.

Nick's senses were saturated with the feel of her silken skin, the scent of her red-gold curls, and the taste of her honeyed mouth. "Lord God, how you make me quiver."

Alex came out of her trance, immediately contrite. "Oh, it's not me . . . it's because you have lost so much blood! You should be abed, Nicholas." Her eyes searched his face for any sign of an imminent collapse.

He gazed back at her and said solemnly, "Perhaps I will take advantage of the bed, since we must stay put until after midnight."

She arched her bum away from him, and his erection immediately slid up her belly and touched her navel, sending a delicious shiver up through her breasts.

"Sweetheart, I wanted to carry you," he protested.

She touched his lips with hers. "When you are recovered, you may carry me about all night and all day, if you desire."

"I desire." The tip of his tongue traced the outline of her lips, as if he could not bear even the briefest separation, then he took possession of her hand and helped her down from her pedestal. As he moved toward the big curtained bed, she felt shy and hung back, but handclasped as they were, he compelled her to follow. He drew the curtains closed, then stretched out on the black satin sheets and gently pulled her down to lie on top of him in the dominant position. After one lingering kiss, he murmured, "Sit up, so I can look at you." And look he did. As she rose to her knees beside him, his eyes missed no finest detail as they worshipped her body, as if they were making intimate love to her.

Alex gazed down at the magnificent male who lay beneath her. Against the black satin, his dark beauty, more tempting than sin, aroused a wild passion she had never before experienced. Midnight-black lashes fringed pools of gray so deep and inviting she would willingly drown in them. Everything about him was virile, hard, and overtly male, making her feel delicately soft and feminine.

He slid his knowing fingers around her wrists and exulted in the rapid pulsebeat he found there. "Touch me," he invited.

With his fingers still encircling her wrist, she reached out to stroke the slabs of muscle on his impossibly wide chest. The slight pressure of his fingers drew her hand lower to caress his taut belly and dip into his navel. The swift intake of his breath told her that her touch thrilled him. He drew her hand to his marble-hard shaft, and when she ran her fingertip from its velvet head down along its length, her eyes widened as he became engorged and his size increased. "Now, you take my wrist, and guide me to touch you."

She slid her fingers around his thick wrist and lifted

his hand to touch her lips. Then shyly she lowered it so that his fingers caressed her heart. "Can you feel how wildly my heart is beating?" Her flesh leaped wherever his hand touched, and breathlessly she drew it up so that he could cup her breast. A sigh of enchantment dropped from her lips as he weighed it in his palm then circled her taut nipple with his fingertip. Feeling more bold, she drew his hand to her other breast and received her reward. With great daring, she moved his hand to her belly and shuddered when he drew a circle around her navel then delved inside. She held his wrist tightly, not daring to lower his hand, yet wanting him, needing him, longing for him to touch her mons. Finally, she simply withdrew her fingers from his wrist and allowed him to wander wherever he wished.

Nicholas threaded his fingers through the red-gold curls on her high mons. "Have you the least notion how many times I've done this before in my dreams? I want you to straddle me, love."

Alex could not bring herself to open her thighs wide enough to span his hips, narrow though they were compared to his chest. Instead, she straddled one muscled thigh. As she did so, she felt his heavy sac brush against her knee. His quick groan made her think she had hurt him. "Are you all right?"

"No, my love, I am in an agony of need, but I beg you to leave your knee exactly where it is. Now, lean back a little."

She did as he asked and saw that it thrust forward her pubic curls most impudently. She watched in delicious fascination as he reached out once more to play among the red-gold tendrils and toy with the tiny bud at the tip of her cleft. "Nicholas!" she breathed as a small spring coiled tightly within the folds of her woman's center.

Crying out his name encouraged him to slip a long finger into her hot sheath and delicately stroke her tight honeyed walls. She wanted to protest, but the sensations his finger aroused made her crave more, not less. She began to pant, then writhe, needing more, much more. "Nicholas . . . no!"

He immediately withdrew his finger and cupped her

entire mons with his palm. He squeezed firmly to ease the ache he had caused, then held out his arms to her. "Come to me, love."

She went down to him, and he enfolded her in strong, powerful arms that Alexandra knew would keep her safe forever. She offered up her lips, and his mouth claimed hers in a possessive kiss that left no doubt just how much he wanted her. One hand stroked down her back, while the other cupped a delicate breast, and his arousal pressed into her belly like a hot branding iron. "Nick . . . please!"

He looked down into her lovely face with disbelief at what she was begging him to do. "Alexandra, my beloved, I have no intention of initiating you in a brothel on black satin sheets!"

Alone with Nicholas in the big curtained bed, the world had receded for Alex. In their own warm, intimate cocoon, filled with love and magic, it seemed as if nothing and no one could touch them. Even her ability to think had been stolen by the dark, dominant, dangerous male who lay naked beside her, enfolding her in his arms. Her mouth curved in a secret smile. He had his own rigid code of respect that obviously extended to where he would make love to her. She kissed the cleft in his chin, which had always been irresistible to her. "Who taught you such *honor*?'

"My idea of honor has undergone a drastic change in the past year, about many things, but not about you, Alexandra. Honor is instinctive. No man can give it to you; no man can take it from you. Honor is something you give yourself."

Alexandra pressed closer. His honor had kept her at arm's length for years, because she was intended for his twin and thus forbidden to him. For a blinding moment, she feared he would never make her his. *If he rejects me again, I shall die!*

His hand stroked over her bum so possessively that the fear of rejection melted into a warm pool of pleasure, where she lay floating ever closer to the shores of Paradise. Her mons lay against his hip, and each time he moved, she became more aroused. The slow glide of his lips along her neck turned her blood to molten hot gold, which flowed into her breasts and down into her belly then cascaded between her legs, making her sheath burn with liquid fire. She arched against his hip, then slid down and rubbed her woman's center up and down his muscled thigh.

Her raw sensuality stunned him, and he sent up thanks to the Goddess of Love, who must have bestowed such a rare gift upon them. He decided to keep her in a delicious state of arousal until he was able to lift her into his own bed at Curzon Street. Only then would he release the passion that he had held in check for years. Again he found her lips, traced the seam with an insistent tongue, then entered the dark, hot cave. At the same time, his fingertips separated the red-gold curls and slipped into her pink cleft, unerringly finding and stroking the delicate little rosebud until it unfurled its petals. His tongue thrust in and out in the sensual rhythm in which lovers had indulged since the dawn of time. His fingers pressed firmly into her scalding, dewy cleft, then began a slow, circular motion, designed to arouse her fully.

His mouth and his fingers took her higher and higher, until she was flying to heights that were dizzying and intoxicating and so blissful she wanted him to make love to her with his tongue and fingertips forever, and never, ever stop. She became aware of a fluttering as delicate as a butterfly wing, then an ache deep within began to build, making her arch her mons into his powerful hand as he skillfully lifted her toward climax. Everything, including time, seemed to stop, as she hovered precariously on the brink; then, with reckless daring, she plunged over the edge of the precipice. The sunburst of sensation made her so delirious, she bit his shoulder. She heard a scream and knew it was her own. It was truly the most glorious feeling she had ever experienced. The initial explosion was followed by deep, intense throbs, close together at first, then drawing out to smaller pulsations. By the time they ceased, Alexandra felt boneless and replete.

Nicholas cupped her mons in his hand, enjoying the feel of her pulsations as he took the soft animal cries she made into his mouth. This was the way he wanted her every night for the rest of his life, writhing and frenzied beneath him, while he buried himself deep inside her. He was in an agony of need as he released her lips, dipped his head to her lush breast and licked his tongue around its jewel-hard center, then sucked it whole into his mouth.

As his teeth toyed with her nipple, Alexandra felt hot threads spark to life between her legs, and she realized that he could ignite her again at will. Suddenly, she wanted to know what would make *him* groan with need and cry out with passion. More than anything, her desire now became centered on his pleasure, his hunger, and she wanted to learn ways to satisfy that hunger. *Feminine ways, wicked ways, surely there are more than one!* Alex boldly reached out to touch between his legs, but Nick's powerful hand covered hers and drew it away. "Don't, my love. I'll spend!"

"Don't you want to spend?" she whispered shyly.

"Of course I want to spend, but not now, not here." *How can I explain?* He knew he couldn't. "I need my strength," he improvised.

"Oh, Nick, I'm so wicked, thinking only of pleasure. Is there anything I can do to make you feel better?"

He grit his teeth to hold on to his control and stop his semen from cascading all over her. "Talk to me; that might help. Tell me what in the name of God you are doing at Champagne Charlie's."

Alex took a deep breath and plunged in, instinctively putting her actions in the best possible light. "Nick, you were so right to laugh at my ambition to become a writer; I soon learned that selling a novel was an impossibility. Dressed as a male, I did manage to get a job writing articles for the *Political Register,* but even when I included a scandalous caricature of Prinny, they only paid me a pittance."

"Dressed as a male?" he repeated quietly, as if her sanity should be questioned.

"Well, it was so much easier dressed that way to roam freely about the seedy areas of London, where crime and poverty flourish. You were right about London having an underbelly, and now I understand completely why you didn't want me exposed to it."

"Roam freely where crime and poverty flourish?" He couldn't believe the things she was telling him!

"But the best part was that it allowed me to frequent the haunts of the *ton,* such as White's and Champagne Charlie's."

Nick held her away from him, so that he could search her face. "You came to Charlie's dressed as a male?"

"Well how else could I have an intimate conversation with a high-class harlot?"

"How else, indeed? Do go on, sweetheart."

"It was a revelation to learn how much money a female could earn in a place like this. Up until Charlie's, I'd only seen street prostitutes, usually accompanied by their whoremaster."

"Alexandra, words fail me." *It is a miracle she hasn't been raped or murdered by now!* He held her more tightly. *She truly does need a keeper, if only to protect her from herself!* But a part of him admired her—she certainly hadn't been sitting around sewing doilies while he was off at war!

"Then I found my mother living in the Rookery in St. Giles. She was very ill and needed care. I took her home to Dottie but thought it only fair that I shoulder the medical expenses and whatnot. That's when I came to Charlie with a proposition."

"You propositioned Charlie?" he asked faintly. "The way you tell it, my love, it sounds perfectly reasonable."

"And so it *was* perfectly reasonable. I knew Lady Emma Hamilton had been a posing girl and thought this place might benefit from a similar attraction. Charlie agreed, and here I am."

"Here you are indeed, naked, with a man who doesn't know whether to spank you or bed you, and will likely do both before morning!"

"Oh, I never performed actually naked. I wore a flesh-colored body net that covered me from neck to knees; it belonged to Dottie, as part of her Godiva costume. But it finally fell apart, and tonight I had no choice but to perform naked."

"Then it was providence that guided me to Charlie's tonight."

"I don't believe it was. It was sheer risk and recklessness, Nick Hatton! Did you really rob the Prince of Wales?"

"I did," he acknowledged solemnly, "and Frederick and Cousin Gloucester. My ill-gotten gains are in a bag under this very bed."

Suddenly, Alexandra began to laugh. "We are a matched pair!" Her breasts rose and fell against his chest. "We are a perfectly outrageous couple with far more daring than brains."

From somewhere they heard a clock chime midnight. "Get your clothes and I'll dress you." His mouth went dry at the thought of inching her stockings up her long legs and fastening her garters.

When Charlie looked in on them, Nick had on his trousers and boots, and his female companion was fully dressed. "I can manage without a shirt, but I'm afraid I must impose upon you for a jacket, my dearest Charlotte."

She looked him up and down with appreciative eyes. "It will have to be one of the servant's. I can't purloin a jacket from one of my customers, no matter how anxious he was to rid himself of such an encumbrance."

When Charlie returned with a claret-colored coat, Nick gallantly thanked her. But when she dutifully counted out Alexandra's hundred guineas, Nick looked on grimly. "Caprice will not be back." His tone permitted no argument.

"I surmised as much, and I don't imagine *your* visits will be any too frequent in the future, Hazard Hatton," she said smoothly. "I believe you have met your match!"

Out on Pall Mall, Nicholas entered the hackney first, and when no one rushed forward to arrest him, he signaled to Alexandra, who stood waiting just inside the doorway.

Nicholas Hatton need not have worried, as it turned out. The Prince Regent and his royal companions were quite vexed at both the Guardsman who had cried, "Stop, thief!" and the officer from the Bow Street Mounted Patrol who had fired off a shot then initiated pursuit. Under no circumstances did Prinny wish to draw attention to himself when he was indulging his insatiable vice of gambling. Especially not at the den of iniquity known as the Foxhole, where they were usually entertained by Champagne Charlie's whores. If such a thing got out, the cries for reform could very easily turn into demands.

Chapter 30

Nicholas braced himself in the corner of the carriage and drew Alexandra into his arms. One insistent hand slipped inside her cloak to cup a lush breast. Though the pain in his head throbbed like the devil, holding Alex blotted out most of it, and filled up his senses with pure joy. His lips brushed against her temple, then he kissed her eyelids, the tip of her nose, and finally took possession of her mouth in a lingering kiss deliberately designed to keep her in a delicious state of arousal.

A small sigh of regret escaped Alexandra's lips when the hackney pulled up outside the tall town house in Curzon Street. The dark interior of the carriage had been so enclosing and intimate, rocking their bodies together in such a sensual swaying rhythm, that she wished the ride could have gone on much longer.

When Fenton opened the front door, Nick told him he could retire for the night. Alex stood behind Nicholas in an attempt to keep her identify from the Hatton butler. "I should have worn my mask," she murmured when the majordomo retreated without glancing at her.

"It's a bit late for masks, love. The servants will certainly see you tomorrow, unless I keep you abed all day." He led the way up the stairs, carrying his army pistol and the bag containing the money he had stolen from the trio of royal profligates. He quickly locked away both in his desk, then he turned up the lamp and looked at her. Thoughts of her pledge to marry Kit tried to intrude, but he deliberately banished them. "I swear I must be the luckiest devil in the entire world. When I set out for London, I had no notion the prize that awaited me was you. Fate stepped in and delivered you into my arms. Have you any idea how precious you are to me, Alexandra?"

Her heart sang. "Do you honestly mean that, Nicholas?"

"Before we leave this chamber, I intend to convince you of it, my love." He moved to the fireplace and lit the tapers in the two silver candelabra that stood on the mantel, flooding the room with a warm glow. "Let me look at you; I'll never get my fill."

Alexandra hesitated, torn between love for this man, and her duty toward Kit. She was engaged to marry Nick's brother and the moral dilemma forced her to choose. His voice was so deep and intense, a shiver ran down her spine. Her decision made, Alex unwrapped her cloak, set it on a chair along with her mask and reticule, then shyly lifted her eyes to meet his.

"This time I shall have the pleasure of *undressing* you." He tried to smile, but his dark face was hard with need. He removed the borrowed coat and hung it in the wardrobe next to his faded uniform, then held out his arms. "Come to me, Alex; it feels like I've been waiting a lifetime for you."

She wanted to fling herself into his arms, but mindful of his freshly stitched wound, she came gently. She closed her eyes blissfully as she felt his arms enfold her and press her to his heart. "Nicholas, I love you so much . . . I've always loved you!"

His lips feathered kisses across the tendrils on her brow, then traced a fiery path along her cheekbone. When their mouths met in a fiercely demanding kiss, each was in an agony of longing. Nick was completely aware of the violence of his feelings, and he tried to curb the savage passion that rode him, reminding himself that Alex was relatively inexperienced, regarding the sex act. In her innocence, she imagined that she was completely initiated, but Nick knew she had a long way to go yet. He intended to enjoy every moment of it. He sat down on the bed and pulled her down into his lap, then his fingers began unbuttoning her gown.

Alex had deliberately chosen a gown with an entire

row of buttons so that she could undo them slowly, enticingly, for her performance at Charlie's. Now the ploy turned the tables on her as Nick's fingers enticed and titillated her almost beyond endurance. He bared her shoulders and brought his lips to touch her skin, which shone translucent as a pearl in the warm candle glow. With gentle fingers he bared her to the waist, then cupped a round, firm breast and lifted it to his hungry mouth. He tongued her nipple, turning it into a tiny, erect spear that thrust itself into his hot mouth, where he teased it with his teeth then sucked hard until she moaned with pleasure.

He lifted her from his lap, laid her flat on the bed, and threaded his fingers into her silken curls, spreading them about her shoulders in a glorious red-gold mass. He buried his face in her perfumed hair and inhaled her intoxicating fragrance. When he lifted his head to gaze down into her eyes, the desire he saw etched on her beautiful face stopped his breath in his throat.

Alex reached up with trembling fingertips to trace his dark beauty. She touched his ink-black eyelashes, then stroked along his saber-sharp cheekbone to the corner of his mouth. As her finger glided across his lips, they opened invitingly, and she slipped inside. He began to suck her finger, and a burning thread of desire ran up her arm, shot down through her breast and belly, and came to rest between her legs, where it sparked and crackled like flames of fire. "Nicholas . . . please!"

With both hands, he lifted her bottom from the bed and drew off her garments, leaving her clad in only black stockings and garters. Then he dipped his head and trailed kisses from her throat down across her heart, over her belly, and along her soft thighs on the intimate flesh where her stockings ended. He watched, mesmerized, as she arched from the bed and again cried out his name. His groin throbbed so painfully, he quickly removed the tight trousers that constricted his manhood, and his rampant cock sprang forth eagerly. He managed to remove one garter and stocking, but he knew he could wait no longer to have her beneath him. "Open your legs wide, darling," he urged, "and wrap them high about my back." He reached down and fit his rigid erection against her, so that it lay along her sensitive cleft. Slowly, he brought half of his weight down upon her and kissed her ear. Then he whispered smoldering love words that told her in explicit detail the things he was going to do to her. He told her how it would make her feel, how it would make him want more; he told her how long he was going to make love to her, how many times he would make love to her, and in how many different ways. His hands explored every soft curve until she writhed and moaned and finally screamed her need.

As Nicholas slid his cock back and forth across her wet lips, she gasped and cried out with hot pleasure. He reached down, took his shaft in his hand, inserted the tip, and rotated it in a circular motion around the tiny pink bud of her womanhood, and she arched in frenzied abandon. Her head thrashed from side to side on the pillow, until his possessive mouth captured hers. Then he thrust his tongue deep inside in a rhythm that imitated what his cock was about to do.

Nick pushed the smooth, marblelike head of his long shaft inside her until he felt her stretch, then he withdrew it. He did this over and over with an undulating rhythm, hoping to make her blood sing as his did. Her sheath felt like velvet, and she was so hot she scalded him each time he penetrated deeper. When she was half mad with passion, crying and biting his shoulders with sharp little teeth, he thrust through her hymen until he was seated to the hilt. Then he stopped and held himself still until she became used to the feeling of his engorged weapon sheathed deep within. "Can you bear it, love?" His deep voice was ragged with passion.

So this is what it feels like when a man penetrates a woman and makes her his own. It was like nothing she had ever imagined. His body was so big, so hard and powerful, so totally dominant. In this moment she realized that she could resist or she could submit. The choice was hers, and it empowered her. "Love me, Nicholas!" Alexandra surrendered to him with abandon, giving him control over both their bodies. She clung to him sweetly as he moved in and out, ignoring the pain and focusing on the pleasure. Almost immediately her body matched his sensual rhythm, and he took her with him to the edge of the universe. She felt him pulse deep inside her, then wondered if it were her body that throbbed; with amazement she realized that their bodies pulsed and throbbed together in an age-old mating ritual shared by lovers.

Nicholas cried out as he felt his seed start, and Alexandra joined his cry as he erupted into her. She felt her muscles contract all the way down her long legs, then she melted like hot, flowing lava. Unbelievably, his shudder was ten times more violent than hers as he spilled fully. They clung together in the warm nest they had thrashed out in the big bed, savoring the precious moments that allowed them to lie naked together in their own private world, where no other could intrude.

She sat up slowly and looked down at him, marveling at the intimate, cataclysmic joining they had shared, knowing he had transformed her and she would never be the same again. She smiled a secret smile; *nothing* would ever be the same again! When she saw the red drops of blood scattered like rubies across the snowy sheet, she cried, "You are bleeding again!"

"I think that's your blood, sweetheart."

She blinked. "Ah . . . perhaps you are right . . . I forgot!"

With aching tenderness he gathered her close and held her against his heart, knowing this was *his* woman.

An hour later, safe in the curve of Nicholas's body, Alex slept contentedly. Nick, however, lay wide awake, staring into the dark. He had no regrets about his actions of the last few days. He considered the robberies he had committed as righting injustices, and in any case, since his crime spree was at an end, he refused to waste time on introspection. His conscience regarding Alexandra, however, pricked him sorely. He had violated the code of honor between himself and his twin—something he had never done before in his life—and though he had no regrets about loving Alex, he suffered pangs of guilt.

Nicholas examined honestly his feelings for the woman who lay beside him. He loved her deeply and completely with all his heart and with all his soul, but as well as loving her, he wanted to protect her. Because she was precious to him, and because he put her above all others, he wanted what was best for her. He picked up a tress of her hair and rubbed it between his fingers. Without a doubt, Christopher could give her the things he, Nick, wanted for her. If she married him, it would deprive her of the title and deprive her of Hatton itself, and it was difficult to bear the thought of her sacrificing everything because of her love for him. Nick lifted the red-gold strand of hair to his lips. Though he thought of all the advantages Kit could give her, he knew that he could never let her go. He vowed to cherish her now, and forever.

At Hatton, Christopher slept until noon. When he finally set his feet to the floor and stood up, his hangover almost felled him to his knees. *Was it only yesterday I attended the Epsom races?* He glanced at his bedside table, saw the money he had won scattered across it, and realized that he'd enjoyed some successful wagers. His brow puckered as he tried to recall something unpleasant that hovered just beyond his grasp. Suddenly, he remembered his encounter with Jeremy Eaton, and he sat down on the bed heavily. As everything flooded back over him, he experienced once more the feeling of hopelessness mixed with desperation.

Dog-bitten as he was today, he knew it was too much to cope with, but he swore off the whiskey, realizing that if he was to rid himself of the bloodsucking blackmailer, he would need all his wits about him while he laid his plans. If his head stopped pounding later this afternoon, perhaps he should go shooting. Though he was an excellent shot, practice at hitting a target would not go amiss; a duel left little margin for error.

Kit could not remember if he had broached the subject of going to London in the coming week with Rupert. Since the company of his best friend was an essential ingredient in his plan, Kit decided he had better ride over to the Hardings once the fog that shrouded his brain had lifted. He yanked on the bell-pull and waited, head in hands, until Mr. Burke arrived.

"Mix me some of that putrid stuff you gave Father when he was hungover. Oh, and better lock up the whiskey, Mr. Burke; I've never felt worse in my life!"

* * *

When Alexandra opened her eyes and saw Nicholas looking down at her, she gifted him with a radiant smile. "This is the happiest morning of my life!" She offered her lips, and when he bent his dark head and brushed her mouth with his, she felt her toes curl. "How is your head this morning?" she asked with concern.

"No worse than a hangover, and fortunately the cure is close at hand," he teased. He had been watching her sleep, a privilege he never imagined he'd be fortunate enough to experience. Alexandra's beauty was ethereal. Her closed eyelids were so translucent, he could see their delicate blue veins. Her dark lashes tipped by red-gold formed shadowy crescents on her high cheekbones. Her nose was small and straight, above a full, generous mouth, whose corners tipped upward even in sleep, as if she were dreaming pleasurable secrets.

"I have *always* been the remedy for what ailed you, Nicholas, but you were too unaware to know it."

He gazed down at her. "I've always known it, sweetheart. How do you suppose I got through the year I spent fighting the war? In the darkest hours, thoughts of you made it endurable. Until now you were my heart's secret."

His words thrilled her. She reached up to caress his heart and felt the strong, steady beat beneath her fingertips. "I am a secret no longer. What will we do?"

The corners of his mouth lifted. "Make love, of course, in all the wonderfully wicked ways I described last night."

She lifted her arms about his neck and arched her body to fit his. "I like being a woman, especially *your* woman," she whispered. "Put your brand on me again."

"I intend to, my lovely, long-legged filly."

It was noon before the lovers left the bed; later than Nick had ever arisen in his life. When he rang for hot bath water, Alex concealed herself behind the door and only emerged when the tub was filled. She quickly slipped into the water, then groaned as its delicious warmth relaxed every muscle in her body. "You devil, I had no idea that making love would be so strenuous. I always imagined a female simply lay still."

Nick threw back his head and laughed. "I am enjoying disabusing you of your quaint notions, my darling." He climbed into the water with her, fulfilling another fantasy he'd often enjoyed. "The pleasure of sharing my bed and my bath with you far exceeds the anticipation."

"We don't fit!" she cried with mock alarm.

"That's what you said earlier, but I proved you wrong," he teased, slipping down into the water and lifting her into his lap.

"I was wrong on both counts; we fit together like Welsh love spoons," she murmured happily, wriggling her bottom against the swell of his male arousal.

It was only when it was time to get dressed that she realized she had no fresh garments to don. "I shall have to go to Berkeley Square for some clothes. Where on earth is my other stocking?"

"Look in the bed; you were definitely wearing it the first time I made love to you."

Alex threw back the covers, but in discovering her stocking, she also saw the evidence of their lovemaking on the pristine sheets and realized for the first time that one of his servants would soon be privy to what had gone on in his bed. She looked at him in dismay. "I cannot come back here; I won't be able to look Fenton in the face. Can we move to Berkeley Square?"

Nick gathered her into his arms and, lifting her chin with his finger, forced her to look into his eyes. "Your town house also has servants, Alex. The only difference will be that I'll be sharing your bed, instead of you sharing mine."

"Hopkins never judges the things I do. . . . Well, until now he hasn't." She bit her fingernail. "It's Sunday. Dottie will be expecting me home. I'll get Hopkins to post her a letter, telling her and that I've been delayed and not to worry."

Nicholas sensed that Alex wanted to return to Berkeley Square alone. "I'll pack some of my clothes and join you in an hour at Berkeley Square. I'll bring Satin so we can ride in the park this afternoon." He grinned wickedly. "I don't want to shock Hopkins by taking you straight to bed."

Alexandra blushed, then laughed, though she realized that before long they would be shocking more than Hopkins. She tried not to think of Christopher Hatton and his reaction when he learned what his betrothed had done. Even more daunting was the thought of Dottie. She would run mad when she found out that her granddaughter had committed the ultimate sin and run off with an "untitled lout," as Dottie would graphically call Nicholas Hatton!

When Alexandra arrived in Berkeley Square, Hopkins did not bat an eye that she had stayed out all night. She quickly changed into a riding dress and penned a letter to Dottie. After Hopkins served her a light lunch, she handed him the letter and asked him to see that it was posted immediately. "I don't want Dottie to worry about me. I told her that the gown I bought from Madame Martine needed alterations." The lie she told Hopkins warmed her cheeks, but he took the letter without even a look of censure.

The moment she finished eating, she glued herself to an upstairs window to watch for Nicholas. Already she missed him and longed for him inordinately. Just the thought of him made her pulse race, her heartbeat hammer, and her senses run riot. She was gloriously, head-over-heels in love, and it made her delirious with joy. Alex suddenly laughed. *Now I understand how Caro Ponsonby became so mad about Byron that she gave him a lock of her pubic hair!*

Her heart caught in her throat at the sight of Nick riding Satin. She stopped herself from rushing headlong down the stairs and took a few calming breaths as she wondered what she would say to Hopkins. Then she opened her bedchamber door and walked slowly down the stairs.

Hopkins was there before her, opening the front door. A broad smile wreathed his face when he saw who it was. "Lord Hatton, may I offer my hearty congratulations on your engagement? It is indeed an honor to welcome you to Berkeley Square. I am sure you will do everything in your power to make Mistress Alexandra happy."

Alex rushed down the remaining steps. "Hopkins, he isn't—" She glanced at Nick, who shook his head emphatically to stay her words.

His hand brushed back his hair, using the same gesture that was a habit with Kit. "Alexandra is trying to tell you that I am not supposed to be here in London with her before the wedding, but I think you can understand my impetuous behavior, Hopkins."

"Your secret is safe with me, my lord. I'll take your bag."

"I think I can manage." Nick winked and slipped Hopkins a five-pound note.

Her cheeks scarlet, Alex turned around and hurried back upstairs. When Nick followed her and closed the bedchamber door, she gasped, "Why the devil did you let him think you were Kit?"

"To save him embarrassment. To save you from explaining the scandalous thing I've done. To save your reputation, Alex."

"My God! I have no reputation to save; I threw it into the wind. And good riddance to it. I shall never count the cost!"

Nicholas enfolded her in his arms and dropped a kiss on her bright curls. *If you marry me, there will be a cost, Alex. It will cost you your title, and Hatton Hall.* "Hopkins didn't raise an eyebrow when he thought I was your husband-to-be. Let's leave it that way."

She raised her eyes to his, filled with joy and mischief. "You *are* my husband-to-be, so I shall be happy to leave it that way."

Nick covered her mouth possessively. *For today I am, my love.* "Let's go riding. I can't wait to show you off in the park."

By the time the lovers returned from their ride, the light had gone from the afternoon. She watched Nicholas unsaddle and tend their horses, then they lingered in the stable, murmuring words of love and kissing until it was dusk.

When they went inside, Hopkins announced that supper was being prepared for them, and the delicious smells drifting from the kitchen told them it was special. "Would it be too much trouble to serve it upstairs, Hopkins?" Nick asked with a straight face.

"No trouble at all, my lord. I shall serve it myself, then see that there are no unnecessary interruptions."

Covered with blushes, Alex hurried upstairs. *It is*

amazing how accommodating men are toward each other when dalliance is involved! She smiled a secret smile. *Perhaps I'll wear my new gown for him.* She handed Nick his bag. "You may change across the hall. I wish to surprise you."

"We're *dressing* for dinner?" he asked with dismay. "I'd rather eat in bed. It whets the appetite," he promised.

"Go!" she said, pushing him from the room. Alex stripped off her riding dress and poured water into the bowl to wash her hands and face. Suddenly, her chamber door flew open, and Nick grabbed her by the hand and dragged her into Dottie's room.

"Who the devil painted this?" He pointed to the portrait above the fireplace.

Alexandra's wicked juices began to bubble. "Don't you think it a good likeness?"

"Hellion! I shall have to undress you before I can give you an honest opinion." Before she could squirm from his grasp, he lifted her shift over her head, removed her busk, and pulled down her drawers. No longer angry, his voice turned husky. "I'd like to see you remove your stockings and garters the way you did onstage."

"You strip first!" she bargained.

Nick wasted no time flinging off his clothes. When he was completely naked, she raised one long leg into the air, removed her garter, then slowly, inch by enticing inch, peeled off her black-and-white striped stocking.

Nicholas did not wait for her to repeat the performance with her other leg. Instead, he lifted her high, then let her slide down his body until she was seated on his cock.

"My God, Nick, that painting isn't me; it's Dottie. And I cannot do this with her eyes upon me!"

"Lucky for us your bed is in another chamber." With his hands firmly cupping her bottom cheeks, he walked across the hall.

Chapter 31

On Sunday evening, Christopher Hatton had a two-hour target practice with his duelling pistols. He did not stop until it was full dark, reasoning that the light would be limited in a dawn duel. As he approached Hatton Hall, he reloaded and hit one of the griffins that stood sentinel on the roof directly in the eye. Kit's confidence soared; he felt ready to face the challenge that lay ahead.

On Monday morning he packed a bag, mounted Renegade, and rode over to Harding House.

Rupert greeted Kit with a relieved look on his face. "I was afraid you wouldn't remember that we planned to go to London this week. I am looking forward to being at my own town house without my in-laws."

"And without your wife." Kit grinned.

"Oh, Olivia and I rub along quite well together these days. It's her father and Annabelle who are rather overbearing."

"Never did understand why my father bedded her," Kit remarked with a sneer.

"Perhaps she has an insatiable appetite," Rupert reflected, thinking it probably ran in the family. "I'm all packed and ready. I thought you'd be driving your phaeton."

"Nick drove it to London, so it'll be there if I need it."

As Rupert saddled his horse, he remarked, "You had a good run of luck at Epsom. Are you still feeling lucky?"

"I always *feel* lucky when I sit down to play cards. Fate, being the bitch she is, soon disabuses me, however." Kit glanced at his friend and sowed the first seed of his plan. "That bastard Jeremy Eaton still holds one of my markers. I wish I could persuade Nick to get it back for me; Hazard Hatton never loses!"

"I think fate has been damn good to you, Kit. Your father left you everything, including his title, and now you are about to marry Alexandra. Surely you wouldn't swap all that for Nick's luck?"

"Of course not." *Especially when his luck might run out.*

They covered the six-mile ride to London in short order. Christopher left Rupert in Clarges Street then rode around the corner to Curzon Street. Kit stabled Renegade and bade the stableboy feed and water him. He glanced negligently at his pair of chestnuts. *I hope Nick has solved the problem of their gait. The bloody nags make me a laughingstock!*

Christopher used his key to open the front door and came face-to-face with Fenton. "Is my brother here?"

"No, my lord."

"Do you know where he is, or when he'll be back?"

"I'm afraid not, my lord." Since Fenton didn't particularly like young Lord Hatton, he provided him with no information whatsoever. "Will you require lunch, my lord?"

"Of course I'll require lunch. Have it ready in an hour," Kit directed. "I shall not be dining at home this evening, however."

"Very good, sir."

Kit took his own bag upstairs and carefully removed his duelling pistols, then he went across the hall to his twin's chamber. He immediately searched Nick's desk, but found it empty. *Damn, he must have already taken the deed to the bank. That shows how much he trusts me!* Kit moved across to the wardrobe. There weren't many of his brother's clothes hanging in it. He looked at the faded uniform and imagined himself wearing it, then he closed the wardrobe doors and returned to his own chamber. His nerves were taut and Kit knew he must do something to relieve his inner tension. The need for a drink almost overwhelmed him as he hung up his clothes. Rather than give in to the craving, he opened a drawer in his own desk, took out a deck of cards, and began to shuffle them with infinite care.

That evening when Rupert arrived expecting to visit White's, Kit talked him into going to Boodle's instead. Kit wanted a practice run of some of his card ploys before Tuesday's encounter with Jeremy Eaton.

It was clear from the outset that Kit's luck had not changed. By eleven o'clock, he had lost most of the money he had won at Epsom races. When he began handing out markers, Rupert became concerned. "Let's call it a night; I hate to see all your winnings run through your fingers!"

Though it was still early, Kit agreed to go home. "Damn and blast my luck! Fate truly is a bitch who frowns upon me while smiling upon my twin; Nick never loses, God rot him!"

When he arrived back in Curzon Street, he was happy to see that his brother had not returned. Before he retired, he stood before the mirror, marveling at his outward likeness to Nicholas. He looked into the gray eyes reflected in the glass and smiled at himself. *So far so good,* Kit thought with satisfaction. *Another seed successfully sown!*

In Berkeley Square, Nicholas and Alexandra stood gazing into the mirror. Though Alex was tall for a female, she only reached Nick's chin. She saw his powerful arms steal about her from behind to pull her against him. Alex closed her eyes and made a wish that they could always be as happy as they were at this moment.

Tonight she wore the new pale green gown, and they had eaten dinner actually sitting on chairs with a small table between them, rather than dining in bed as they had the previous evening. Before they had finished their dessert, however, Nick needed to touch her. "Have you any idea how beautiful you are tonight? Let me show you." He scooped her up and deposited her before the oval cheval glass.

She could see his eyes had gone dark gray, smoky with desire. She watched as he undressed her, and when she was naked he began to make love to her with his eyes. His smoldering glance lingered on every intimate part of her, until she felt more feminine than she had ever felt in her life. Her pulses began to race, and her heartbeats became fluttery with awakening desire.

He covered her breasts with his powerful hands. "I love you so much, sweetheart. I'll never have enough of you." He bent his dark head and whispered in her ear. "I want you to watch me make love to you. I want you to see how beautiful you are."

She watched, mesmerized, as he went down on his knees before her. Then she felt his powerful hands cup her bottom cheeks so that her red-gold curls were on a level with his mouth. He caressed her bum and eased her forward into his kisses. She felt his tongue search out the bud at the tip of her cleft, and she buried her fingers in his crisp, black hair, to keep her from screaming with excitement. As his tongue thrust deeper, invading and plundering her, she saw her nails dig into his wide shoulders. Then she saw her own face and realized that what he had told her was true. In that moment she was wildly beautiful, her Titian curls dishevelled from tossing her head in abandon, her green eyes glittering with new-found passion, her mouth full, soft, and sensual. She watched his name form on her lips. "Nicholas!"

He picked her up and carried her to the bed. He never took his eyes from her as he undressed. Then he turned her onto her side and lay down behind her with his long hard body curved around hers. Holding her breasts, he entered her from behind then eased her over until he was on his knees. He waited a full minute so that she could get used to the feel of his cock stretching her sheath from this new position. Then with slow, firm thrusts he began to bring them both to rapture as Alexandra clutched the sheet with her fists and cried out her passion.

Before she slept, Nicholas lifted her glorious hair and kissed the nape of her neck. "We *do* fit together like Welsh love spoons." As he held her against his heart, Nick knew that in spite of all his noble intentions, wanting Alexandra to have the title of Lady and be the mistress of Hatton Hall, there was no way on earth he could give up this woman to his twin brother. She was his heart and his soul.

When Alexandra awoke her heart began to sing the moment she realized Nicholas was beside her in the bed. It was the most luxurious feeling in the world. But, as she turned into his arms, Alex suddenly realized that her conscience was pricking her. She allowed him one lingering kiss, then pulled away while she could still speak coherently. "Nick, we spoke of you being my future husband, but I have a secret I must reveal before we marry."

He didn't even raise an eyebrow. "Nothing you tell me could possibly lessen the love I feel for you, sweetheart."

"I . . . I'm not an heiress, as you've been led to believe. My grandmother's fortune is all gone. She borrowed from the bank and put up Longford Manor as collateral. That was the *real* reason I was earning money at Champagne Charlie's."

He stared down at her in shocked amazement. "If that's true, Dottie is a superb actress."

"She's a superb grandmother! You mustn't tell anyone, Nick; it's Dottie's secret more than mine. Even the town house belongs to Neville Staines. I do have a dowry of a thousand pounds, but it isn't a lot when compared to a fortune."

Suddenly, Nicholas began to laugh until the tears threatened to run down his face. He wiped his eyes. *How bloody ironic!*

"I fail to see anything amusing," Alex said quietly.

Her confession swept away all the guilt Nick felt over snatching her from his twin's arms; Kit wouldn't want her without her money.

He could never tell her, of course; he would never hurt her. "I'm buying Hatton Grange from my brother. I think I can manage to keep the wolf from our door. If I can't, there's always Hounslow Heath!" He went off into another bout of deep laughter.

Though Alexandra's heart overflowed with love that it made no difference to him, she felt far from laughter. Their dalliance must end. "I have to tell Dottie of my plans, and even more to the point, I have to inform

Christopher that I cannot marry him." She slipped from the bed and went to the wardrobe to select a riding dress. As he watched, Alex donned a fresh shift then poured water from the jug into the bowl. Her glance fell on her beautiful betrothal ring. "I shouldn't be wearing this; I have no right."

Nick was beside her in an instant. "Don't you dare take it off!" As he took her hand, the morning sunlight glinted off the diamonds and sapphires, reflecting the fire within the jewels. "Alexandra, this ring is precious to me, not because of its stones but because it belonged to my mother. If you would keep this ring, it would fill my heart with happiness."

Alex stared at him. These exact words had been said to her the night Kit gave her the ring. *It wasn't Kit who gave it to me. It was Nick!* She chided herself, *Don't be absurd! Don't start mixing them up because they are twins.* Her mind flew back to that night on the lake, sitting in the punt. *Kit spoke of his deep and abiding love for Hatton Hall and stole my heart. I felt a oneness with Christopher that I never felt before. When he kissed me, I didn't want him to stop.* Her inner voice insisted, *That's because it wasn't Christopher! It was Nicholas!*

Nick brushed the back of his fingers over her cheek with reverence, and Alexandra realized it was a gesture he did often. He had done it that night on the lake when he said, *Look at me, Alex, while I tell you what is in my heart.*

Her heart now contracted. She pushed his fingers away from her cheek and held out her hand adorned with diamonds. Her fingers began to tremble. "*You* gave me your mother's ring; it wasn't Christopher at all, was it?" Her voice sounded strange, even to her own ears.

Gray eyes looked into green, and he knew it was useless to lie to her. "It was I who gave you the ring, Alexandra."

Her face showed she was appalled. "How could you?"

"The dinner was planned down to the last detail, then Kit became ill that night."

"I don't mean how could you pretend to be Christopher! I mean how could you seduce me into becoming engaged to your twin?"

"Now I curse myself for doing it, but at the time, it seemed the proper thing to do, Alex."

"The proper thing to do? Am I hearing correctly? It was the most highly improper thing I've ever heard of, Nick Hatton!" Alex felt betrayed. Nicholas had actually proposed to her on behalf of his brother. Such a thing would be impossible if he loved her. She felt as if a cruel hand had taken hold of her heart and was slowly crushing it. She used the only weapon she had to strike out and hurt him; she used her tongue. In a mocking voice she threw his own words back at him. *"I desire no other lady but you to be Lady Hatton, the châtelaine of Hatton Hall. I want its beauty and permanence to wrap its strength about you and keep you secure. I want to see your children running and laughing across Hatton's lawns. Then I want it passed down to your grandchildren, and I hope the future generations cherish it with the same deep and abiding passion that I feel!"* With great haste, Alex threw on her riding dress and pulled on her boots.

Exasperated, Nick took hold of her shoulders and gave them a firm shake. "Hellion, will you listen to me?"

"While you ply me with more lies? Take your hands from me!"

"Willful little bitch!" he cursed.

"You are a devil, Nick Hatton! I hate you!"

His first impulse was to stride after her and drag her back, but Nick knew that he was in the wrong. There was absolutely no excuse for what he had done to Alexandra. Perhaps it was best to let her cool down and think things through. When she realized how much he loved her, she would change her mind and come back. Surely she must know how deeply he loved and cherished her? Had he not shown her over and over during the past two days?

When an hour passed and she had not returned, Nicholas gradually began to doubt that Alex truly loved him. He packed his bag, went down to the stables, and saddled Satin. Then he rode to Curzon Street. When he entered the stables that belonged to the Hatton town house, he saw Kit's Thoroughbred, Renegade. The last person he wished to see at this moment was his twin.

Without dismounting, he urged Satin from the stables and headed to Hatton.

Alexandra was almost at Longford Manor before she remembered the gown and the cashmere shawl for Dottie. Her eyes flooded with tears. It would mean more lies, and she was utterly sick and tired of deception.

That evening, Christopher Hatton stood before the mirror in his brother's bedchamber at Curzon Street. He knew if he was to pull off the deception, he must pay attention to the details. He brushed his hair back into the style that Nick favored. Kit was dressed in his best black evening clothes and was carefully fashioning his muslin neckcloth into his twin's favorite style. He spoke to the reflection in the glass as if it were Nicholas. "Our appearance is identical, as is our voice, and I can be every bit as nonchalant as you, while I effect your lion's pride." His eyes narrowed as he assessed himself honestly. "The only thing you have more of is confidence, damn you to hellfire!"

Kit heard the front door open to admit Rupert, then heard his friend bid Fenton a good evening. He ruthlessly crushed a feeling of panic and before the servant said anything further, Kit called down, "Rupert, come up, will you?"

When Rupert saw that Kit's bedchamber was empty, he turned toward Nick's with surprise.

"Kit has talked me into going with you to White's tonight. He wants me to get his marker back from our insufferable cousin, Jeremy Eaton. Since I am not a member of the club, I shall have to go as your guest. You don't object, do you, Rupert?"

"Of course not, Nicholas, but where's Kit?"

"Left for Hatton this afternoon. Said something about wanting to spend the evening with Alexandra."

"Well, that's good, I warrant. Actually, until the engagement dinner I had begun to doubt he would ever come up to snuff and propose," Rupert confided.

"Kit has far more courage than most people realize," he said sharply. He picked up his top hat and cane. "Shall we go?"

When they arrived at White's, they found it rather

crowded for a Tuesday evening and concluded that most of the men had left their wives in the country, while they indulged their town vices.

A quick surveillance of the gaming rooms told Kit that the bloodsucking Eaton had not yet arrived. He cursed under his breath; waiting for the swine would add to the tension of his nerves. Three different men greeted him as Lord Hatton; three times he corrected them. Their responses were almost identical when he said that he was Nicholas. When each congratulated him on serving in the army that had defeated Napoleon and welcomed him back to London, Kit tried not to grind his teeth.

He bought chips from the cashier and strolled toward the faro table, which was Nick's preferred game though certainly not his. He played negligently, both winning and losing, and knew that once Eaton arrived he would move to the *vingt-et-un* table. As the evening dragged on, Kit would have given his eyeteeth for a whiskey, but he politely accepted the glass of claret Rupert brought him, since it was what his twin usually drank when he gambled.

Suddenly, the hair stood up on the back of Christopher's neck, and he realized that his instincts were warning him that his enemy had just entered the gaming room. Without turning around, Kit left the faro table and walked casually toward his game of preference.

Rupert ambled after him and nodded to young Lord Mitford who was a casual acquaintance of the twins.

"H'lo, Harm. Have you been waiting for me?" Jeremy drawled.

"Sorry to disappoint you. It's Nicholas, I'm afraid, but I have indeed been waiting for you."

Eaton was taken aback for a moment, then seemed to recover. "I have business with your twin; where is he?"

"I am here in his stead. You will have to do business with me. I understand you hold one of Lord Hatton's markers. I'm here to win it back." Kit invited, "Shall we play?"

"Ah, the gallant captain riding to his twin's rescue. Well, it isn't the first time, is it?" Eaton sneered. "You are reputed to have the devil's own luck, but I predict that is about to run out."

Rupert stood rooted to the floor behind Hatton's chair as he heard the uncivil exchange.

Kit Hatton caught himself before he ran his fingers through his hair. He knew it was a nervous gesture that could give his identity away. Instead, he kept his hands busy by picking up the deck of cards and dealing them in rotation. Deliberately, he dealt himself the first black jack, which determined that the first deal would be his.

Kit swiftly gathered the cards together and shuffled them for a long time. He turned up the top card, showed it to all the players, and placed it faceup at the bottom of the pack. Then he dealt one card to each player and waited while they placed their wagers. Each player bet two chips, and Kit called for the bets to be doubled, his prerogative as dealer.

With a smirk, Eaton redoubled his bet, then watched Hatton deal each player one card faceup. The smirk left Eaton's face as he looked at the ace Hatton dealt himself.

With a casualness he did not feel, Kit Hatton turned up a king, which added up to twenty-one, and everyone paid him. Without looking at Eaton, he picked up the deck of cards, shuffled them, and again dealt each player one card. Again they made their bets.

And again, Kit dealt himself an ace.

Jeremy Eaton jumped to his feet. "Hatton, you are cheating!"

A deathly hush fell over the table at the magnitude of the accusation. Kit, feigning outrage at the insult, stood up and faced his cousin. "Are you challenging me?"

"Yes! I am challenging your honesty!"

"If you are challenging me to a duel, Eaton, I accept."

Yes! He's swallowed the bait and challenged me before everyone!

The blood drained from Jeremy Eaton's face.

"Rupert, you will act as my second. As the challenged party, I believe I have the choice of weapons, time, and place," Kit stated. "Green Park at dawn. I am used to my army weapons, but I do happen to own duelling pistols. Choose your second."

Through bloodless lips, Eaton asked Trevor Mitford to act as his second and nodded stiffly when Mitford accepted.

Kit Hatton felt his blood surge, and his heartbeat deafened him. He had pulled off the first part of his plan. The die was cast and there was no going back now. He gathered his winnings and strode from the room.

Trevor Mitford looked at Rupert. "Dawn is only a few hours away! This gives us very little time to make the arrangements!"

"We'll need a surgeon." Rupert spoke as if he were dazed.

"I have a friend who's a doctor," Mitford offered. "I'll contact him immediately."

Rupert turned to speak to Jeremy Eaton but discovered that he had already left White's gaming room. A sea of male faces was staring at him; Rupert lifted his chin and stared back.

Jeremy Eaton tasted fear. He had been coerced into fighting a duel with a formidable opponent—not the twin cousin who was a weakling. He scurried along St. James's Street and turned toward Piccadilly, frantically wondering how he could extract himself from the trap he had fallen into. His legs trembled as if they wouldn't hold him up much longer, so he hailed a hackney. "Just drive!"

Eaton's mind was in such turmoil he didn't notice his surroundings until the cabby drove through the Covent Garden area. As he gazed through the window he noticed a sign that said BOW STREET. Eaton instantly recognized that salvation was at hand.

It was past two in the morning before Rupert and Trevor Mitford had inspected the duelling sites in Green Park and agreed upon one that was secluded by sheltering trees. Mitford's carriage dropped Rupert off in Curzon Street, then went to pick up the surgeon. It was almost three when Rupert climbed the stairs to Nick Hatton's bedchamber.

Rupert's eyes widened when he saw Nicholas. He was dressed in his Royal Horse Artillery uniform. It was slightly faded, but emblazoned with his captain's insignia, it lent him a most commanding air. "Won't you get in trouble, wearing your officer's uniform while engaged in a duel?"

Kit laughed. "I'm in trouble anyway, since duels are expressly forbidden by the Crown."

"Too true! You could call it off," Rupert suggested, running a finger inside his neckcloth to loosen it a tad.

For answer, Kit Hatton handed Rupert the leather case that held his duelling pistols. "Facing this uniform will make Eaton piss himself with fear!" His eyes glittered dangerously.

"Y'know, I don't think Kit actually wants you to shoot Jeremy Eaton over a gambling debt," Rupert offered.

"You are wrong. That is exactly what Kit wants."

Rupert weighed the leather case. "I'm not an expert with guns . . . but I gather I am supposed to inspect these."

"No need. I cleaned them earlier. You'll find everything in order. Balls and gunpowder are in the case."

"I suppose in France you were under fire every day . . . but I'm a little unsettled by all this."

"A gun can be your best friend, Rupert." A combination of fear and excitement made his eyes glitter like black diamonds.

Rupert licked his dry lips. "It's getting close to four. Perhaps we had better get going."

The two men walked to the corner of Curzon and turned down Clarges. When Rupert passed his town house, he glanced up at the tall building as if he wanted nothing more than to seek the safety of his own bed. They crossed Piccadilly, entered Green Park, and followed a path that led them to a heavily treed area. They made out two carriages and a small knot of men gathered in the darkness and walked toward them.

Rupert found Trevor Mitford. "Did you get a surgeon?"

Mitford nodded his head in the direction of one of the coaches. "I haven't seen hide or hair of Eaton since he left White's."

"Let's hope he doesn't show! This is all so unreal."

More spectators arrived, confirming that the *ton* was

addicted to blood sport. "May I inspect the duelling pistols?" Mitford requested. When Rupert handed them over, Mitford opened the case and lifted one of the pistols, but the darkness prevented him from seeing much. "Seem to be in order." He handed them back.

Rupert returned to Hatton's side. "Eaton hasn't shown up yet."

"It's a ploy to try my nerves, but it won't work!" Kit snapped, proving that indeed it was working. He began to pace back and forth across the grass, and as the darkness began to fade, he saw that the men gathered were staring at the uniform he wore. He pulled back his shoulders and lifted his head, imitating the pride of a lion and acting as he imagined Nicholas would.

As dawn began to lighten the sky, all present watched Jeremy Eaton arrive alone. Trevor Mitford approached him immediately, and they huddled together, speaking low. Then Mitford beckoned Rupert, who joined them with reluctant steps. Rupert opened the leather case that held the pistols, and after Eaton gazed down at them, he cast a worried look over his shoulder.

Christopher Hatton could wait no longer. He strode over to the trio, selected a pistol, then proceeded to load it with ball and powder. Mitford handed Eaton the other pistol, but when he made no move to load it, Mitford took it back and loaded it for him.

Rupert spoke urgently. "Gentlemen, surely you can settle your differences in a more civilized manner?"

"Absolutely not!" Hatton snarled. "Eaton has impugned my honor. I will have satisfaction."

When Mitford spoke, his voice had risen an octave. "Gentlemen, you will stand back to back and count off ten paces; at the count of ten, you will turn and fire."

The deadly enemies stood heel to heel. Eaton's face was paper-white. Hatton's was flushed a dull red. Trevor and Rupert began to count in unison, "One . . . two . . . three . . . four . . . five . . . six . . . seven—"

Three Bow Street Mounted Patrolmen rode onto the scene. "Stop, in the name of the law!"

On what would have been the count of eight, the duelists turned. Kit Hatton fired his pistol; Jeremy Eaton fell to the ground. One patrolman went to the fallen victim, while the other two lawmen immediately closed in on the man wearing the army captain's uniform. One confiscated his pistol; the other handcuffed him. "Nicholas Hatton, you are under arrest for the suspected murder of your father, the late Henry Hatton."

Kit began to struggle and shouted, "You've got the wrong man!" His protests were in vain, as the two men flanked him and marched him off. "Rupert! Rupert! Find my brother and fetch him to me immediately!"

Chapter 32

Rupert still stood rooted to the spot after Nicholas Hatton had been taken away. *Good God, they arrested him on suspicion of murder. Apparently, they don't believe the shooting at Hatton was accidental!* Nick's shouts still rang in his ears: *"Find my brother and fetch him to me immediately!"* Rupert tried to recall Nick's exact words when he had asked him where Kit was: *He left for Hatton this afternoon. Said something about wanting to spend the evening with Alexandra.* Rupert, suddenly mobilized, strode from Green Park and hurried to Clarges Street where his mount was stabled. He was halfway to Hatton when he realized that he didn't know if Jeremy Eaton was alive or dead.

Reverend Doyle had not slept well. He was an early riser who was at the Hatton church altar by six each morning, and today was no exception. He owed his living to the Hattons and seldom criticized their actions, but he had been shocked when Lord Hatton had not attended church services on Sunday when his marriage banns had been read before the congregation. Christopher's future bride, Alexandra Sheffield, had also been conspicuous by her absence, Doyle reflected. It was his duty to chastise them, and he would have done so immediately, had it not been for the fear of losing his living.

Doyle had allowed two days to slip by, but his conscience was now pricking him so badly, he decided that he must act. With prayer book in hand as a talisman, he closed the church door and with resolution set out for Hatton Hall.

Nicholas Hatton lay abed. Sleep had eluded him all night as he relived the events of the last few days. They all had a surreal quality, as if they were too fantastic to be believed. Yet he actually *had* robbed His Royal Highness, the Prince Regent, and been shot in the head for his efforts. He *had* discovered Alexandra in a brothel, and he *had* carried her off to his bed in Curzon Street. He *had* stolen her innocence, but only after confessing that he was in love with her. He *had* asked her to marry him.

Nick quit the bed with a foul oath and leaned his arms on the windowsill as he watched the sunrise. All evening he had waited for her to come to Hatton. Even now, he stubbornly refused to give up hope. If she loved him, she would come.

When Mr. Burke brought him a freshly starched shirt and neckcloth, he hesitated. Should he don clothes more suitable for working with his horses at the Grange or wear his best in case Alex came? He compromised, and put on the fresh linen Burke supplied along with fawn breeches and tan leather boots. He picked up the book he had tried to read in the small hours of the night and returned it to the library. He was about to cross to the windows when a paper lying on the desk caught his eye. He walked over to investigate and again an oath fell from his lips. It was a special license to marry, made out in the name of Christopher Flynn Hatton and Alexandra Sheffield.

When he read her name, his gut knotted. His heart told him that Alex loved him and would never marry his twin. His head, however, told him that he had neither wealth nor title to offer her. He had also betrayed her trust. Why should she not marry Christopher?

When Alexandra awakened at dawn she reached out to touch Nicholas. One heartbeat later, everything came rushing back and she realized that she was in her own bed at Longford Manor. Alex closed her eyes against the pain of reality and blushed at how closemouthed she'd been with her grandmother, even though circumstances dictated the things she had said and the things she had left unsaid.

"Margaret has taken a turn for the worse, darling, but I think she's determined to hang on until she sees you and Christopher safely wed."

"I must go to her!"

"No, the doctor dosed her with laudanum and she's sleeping peacefully at last; don't disturb her now."

That's when Alex had told her grandmother that the dress she had ordered for the wedding was not yet ready. She had said nothing to dispel the idea that she would marry Christopher. Her hurt over Nicholas had been too sharp and far too personal to share, but today she would have to find the words that would reveal the truth to Dottie. First, however, she would ride over to Hatton and speak with Kit. He and his twin had conspired to deceive her, and she felt an overwhelming need to confront him.

She put on her gray riding skirt but decided against the yellow jacket she usually wore with it. Her mood was not sunny today. Instead she slipped her arms into a matching gray jacket trimmed with black braid. As she brushed her hair, she absently noticed how long it was getting and pushed it back over her shoulders with impatient hands. She knew that food would stick in her throat, so she skipped breakfast and went to the stables to saddle Zephyr.

As she set out for Hatton Hall, she saw a rider in the distance. She stopped and shaded her eyes from the rising sun. Suddenly her heart jumped into her mouth. Only Nicholas rode at such hell-for-leather speed. As her vision focused, however, she clearly saw that it was not Nick but Rupert, of all people. Alex turned her mare and galloped to meet her brother.

"Rupert, what on earth is wrong?"

"I . . . er . . . I must get a message to Kit."

"Something has happened! Tell me!"

"Nick just fought a duel in Green Park, and they arrested him."

"A duel?" Alex thought he must be mistaken. "A duel with whom, for God's sake?"

"With his cousin, Jeremy Eaton. He may be dead."

"Nick?" Without waiting for a reply, she set her heels to her mount and galloped off.

"Stop! Wait!" Rupert thundered after her and grabbed Zephyr's reins. "Nick isn't dead . . . I meant Eaton."

"I must go to Nick if they've arrested him for shooting Eaton."

"They've arrested him on suspicion of murder."

"That's ridiculous! Let me go!"

"On suspicion of murdering his *father,* Alex."

Her eyes widened in disbelief, and her face turned pale as parchment. "None of this makes sense. Where have they taken him?"

"I don't know. Nick asked me to get Kit and fetch him to London. There's nothing you can do, Alex; it's a job for Christopher. He's a Lord of the Realm."

As they stood arguing, the black berline coach belonging to Lord Neville Staines swept past them on its way to Hatton Hall. As they stared after it, Rupert muttered, "Hasty news travels fast." Without another word the brother and sister followed the coach.

By the time they dismounted and tied their horses' reins to a tree, Lord Staines, Colonel Stevenson, and the man with them had entered the hall. Reverend Doyle hurried his steps to catch up with Alexandra before she and her brother went inside.

"Mistress Sheffield, I would like a word with you, if I may."

"Please forgive me, Reverend Doyle; I'm in a dreadful hurry."

His face was set in stern lines. "You did not attend church service on Sunday when I announced your banns!"

Clutching Rupert's sleeve so that he would not leave her behind, Alex replied, "I was unavoidably detained in London, Reverend."

"And Lady Longford?" he pressed.

"My grandmother was busy nursing our invalid mother. Please excuse us; we must speak with Lord Hatton."

* * *

Mr. Burke opened the door to Neville Staines's urgent knock and admitted the three men. "May I help you, Lord Staines?"

"Yes, Burke. This is Sergeant Norton of the Bow Street Police. Kindly announce us to Lord Hatton."

On his guard immediately, Burke asked, "May I tell his lordship what this is about, Lord Staines?"

"Nicholas has been arrested. We will be needed in London."

Mr. Burke knew full well that Nicholas was in the library, therefore it must be Christopher who had been arrested. "I shall inform his lordship immediately, sir."

Burke dashed upstairs, selected an elegant coat made by Schultz, then rushed down to the library. "Lord Staines, Colonel Stevenson, and a Sergeant Norton of Bow Street are in the hall. They insist that Nicholas has been arrested, and wish to speak with Lord Hatton. Obviously they've mixed you up."

Nick frowned. "Did you straighten them out?"

Burke held the coat while Nick slipped his arms into the sleeves. "They wish to speak with *Lord Hatton;* I told them I would inform his lordship immediately."

Burke ushered the three men into the library. "Will there be anything else, my lord?"

"See that we are not disturbed, Mr. Burke."

"Christopher, this is Sergeant Norton from the Bow Street Police. They arrested your twin this morning on serious charges."

Norton spoke up. "At dawn we interrupted a duel in Green Park and arrested your brother on suspicion of murder."

"A duel?" *The bloody fool! Is there no end to his folly?* "There must be some mistake. Why do you think it was Nick Hatton?"

"There is no mistake, my lord. Your brother was wearing his Royal Horse Artillery uniform."

Nick was stunned. *Kit was deliberately impersonating me!* "He killed his opponent?"

"His opponent, Eaton, was wounded in the duel," Norton supplied.

Christ, which Eaton? John or Jeremy? "If his opponent is only wounded, why is he being held on suspicion of murder?"

Neville Staines cut in. "The suspicion concerns your *father's* shooting. Apparently someone informed the police that it may not have been an accident. Since I was the coroner who signed the death certificate, and the colonel is Justice of the Peace of this county, Norton came to notify us. But before we left for London, I insisted we come here to let you know what has happened."

"My father's shooting was an accident." Nick's tone was implacable.

"Of course it was," Lord Staines agreed. "Now, however, there will have to be an inquest to clear your twin's name. In the meantime, they are holding Nicholas at Wood Street Compter."

"That's near the Guildhall, I believe. I shall leave as soon as possible, gentlemen. Thank you for bringing me the news."

"Thank you, Lord Hatton." Norton bowed; Staines and Stevenson nodded. When Neville opened the library door for them to leave, Alexandra and Rupert rushed in, with Mr. Burke on their heels. Reverend Doyle followed hesitantly and stood inside the door.

"I couldn't stop them, Lord Hatton," Burke apologized.

"There was no need to stop them, Mr. Burke." Burke nodded and left the library to see the men out.

Nick's hungry glance swept over Alexandra. Her hair was a riot of wildfire this morning, contrasting sharply with the sober gray riding dress. Her face was pale; her eyes full of apprehension.

"Nicholas has been arrested on suspicion of murdering your father. You know it was an accident. We must go and do something immediately!"

"We?" His hopes soared. She thought him in trouble and was ready to fly to his side.

Rupert spoke up. "I don't want Alexandra involved in this."

"Were you there, Rupert, when my brother was arrested?"

"Yes. Nick and I went to White's to get back your marker from Jeremy Eaton. Suddenly, in front of everyone, Eaton accused Nick of cheating. Nick asked me to act as his second and insisted the duel take place at dawn. When he came to Green Park, he was wearing his army uniform. I tried to get him to call it off, but he wouldn't hear of it. When they were pacing off, patrolmen came to halt it. Nick fired his pistol anyway and hit his mark. I don't know if Eaton is alive or dead."

"He is wounded, according to Sergeant Norton who just left." *It was a deliberate plan to rid himself of Eaton, and if anything went wrong, I would get the blame. Even Rupert believes it was I who provoked and fought the duel.*

Alexandra was staring at her brother in disbelief. *Nick went gambling to White's after I left him, while I rode home brokenhearted? I thought I knew Nicholas Hatton better than any other person in the world. Apparently, I was wrong!*

"Will he go on trial for murdering your father?" Rupert asked.

"Neville Staines says they will hold an inquest into Father's death. If there is evidence of foul play, it will go to trial."

"No!" Alex cried. "They cannot try him for murder; Nicholas is incapable of such evil. Kit, you must go and tell them so!"

Gray eyes bored into green. "Are you in love with Nicholas?"

Alexandra's pale cheeks turned to flame. She tore her gaze from Kit, glanced at her brother, then looked at Reverend Doyle, who stood silent as a church statue, witnessing everything. *I must not alienate Christopher. He is the only one who can help Nicholas.* "No, of course I'm not in love with Nicholas."

Doyle stepped forward to defend her. "She is your *betrothed,* the future Lady Hatton. How can you ask such a thing?"

Nick looked at Doyle, then at Rupert. "Would you excuse us? I would like a private word with my bride."

Alex waited until they were alone, then spoke quickly. "Kit, we must postpone the wedding. Your brother's trouble is far more important right now."

"Not to me," he said quietly.

Alex was shocked. "You *will* go and defend him, and do everything in your power as a Peer of the Realm to prove his innocence and gain his release, won't you, Christopher?"

"That depends upon you."

"Me?" It came out in a whisper, for she sensed what was coming.

"If you marry me, I will try my utmost to prove him innocent."

"I *have* promised to marry you." She tried not to sound evasive.

"Do you mean it, Alex?"

She knew she would say anything to persuade him to help Nicholas.

"Yes, of course I mean it."

He crossed to the library door and opened it. Rupert and the reverend reentered the room, and he summoned Mr. Burke to join them. Nick walked back to the desk and picked up a paper. "I have a special license here, Doyle. I would like you to marry us."

Alexandra's hand went to her throat. The twin standing in front of her somehow knew her heart belonged to Nicholas. He had made it plain that he would only go to London *after* she had married him.

He raised his eyebrows, asking her capitulation. At that moment his presence and his will dominated the room.

"If you will keep your promise to do all you can for Nicholas."

"Trust me, Alex." He held out his hand.

With the greatest reluctance, Alexandra placed her hand in his.

Doyle stepped before them and opened his prayer book. "Wilt thou have this woman to thy wedded wife, to live together after God's ordinance in the holy estate of matrimony? Wilt thou love her, comfort her, honor and keep her, in sickness and in health; and, forsaking all others, keep thee only unto her, so long as ye both shall live?"

"I will."

Doyle then charged Alexandra with the same question.

She moved her lips, but no one heard her whispered "I will."

"Who giveth this woman to be married to this man?"

"I do," Rupert said with solemn pride.

"Repeat after me: I, Christopher Flynn Hatton, take thee, Alexandra Sheffield to my wedded wife, to have and to hold from this day forward, for better or for worse, for richer or for poorer, in sickness and in health, to love and to cherish, till death us do part, according to God's holy ordinance. And thereto I plight thee my troth."

When it was her turn, Alexandra stumbled over the phrase *to love, cherish, and obey,* and her hand trembled like a leaf as the groom intoned, "With this ring I thee wed, with my body I thee honor, and with all my worldly goods I thee endow."

When Doyle pronounced them man and wife, Alex was infinitely relieved that her husband did not try to kiss her.

Mr. Burke stepped forward to shake the groom's hand. "Congratulations, Lord Hatton." He turned to Alex. "Lady Hatton, let me be the first to welcome you to Hatton Hall."

"Alex, I shall leave you in Mr. Burke's capable hands. Rupert, I assume you are coming to London?"

"I'm coming too!" Alexandra's voice was suddenly loud and clear. And brooked no refusal.

Her husband appraised her with a long, steady look. "As you wish, Lady Hatton."

"I have to pack a bag and, of course, tell Dottie about all that has happened. Will you wait for me?" Alex asked stiffly.

"Perhaps Rupert will be good enough to bring you in his carriage. If I ride alone, I can be there in less than an hour."

Rupert pressed his lips together but did not demur. "If you think it best, Kit, I am happy to be of service. Let's hurry," he urged, leading the way from the library.

As she turned to leave, her husband's deep voice stayed her.

"Trust me, Alex."

"You are a devil, Kit Hatton," she hissed. "I shall never trust you again. Neither you nor your twin, Nicholas!"

Chapter 33

It took Nicholas only forty minutes to ride to Curzon Street. He stabled Satin and saddled Renegade. If he was to be Lord Hatton, he must be seen riding Lord Hatton's mount. On the six-mile journey his inner emotions had been at war. He felt elation that he and Alexandra were safely wed; at the same time he felt nothing but despair over his twin's folly.

He rode past St. Paul's to Cheapside, then turned up Wood Street. At the small prison known as the compter, he tethered Renegade and strode inside. He approached a wooden partition and spoke to a warden through a pigeonhole. "I am Lord Hatton. I understand you are holding my brother, Nicholas?"

The warden ran his finger down the admitting register's page. "Right, milord. Nicholas Hatton, arrested this mornin'."

"I wish to speak with him."

"One moment, milord."

It took considerably longer than a moment, but eventually Kit Hatton, wearing the faded uniform, was brought to a barred gate.

"Thank God you're here! Tell them to get these irons off me . . . get me out of here!"

The turnkey who had brought his brother to the gate said, "Easement of irons, one guinea, milord."

Nick fished in his pocket, produced a guinea, and handed it through the bars. The turnkey removed Kit's manacles. "This won't do," Nick said with authority. "I wish to speak with my brother in private. I shall go to his room."

"I'm in a ward . . . with felons!" Kit cried, rubbing his wrists. "They won't believe that I am Lord Hatton!"

"It will avail you nothing to pretend to be me." Nick addressed the turnkey. "My brother is newly returned from France. He was a captain in Wellington's army."

The turnkey was immediately impressed. "Let me shake yer 'and." He offered his hand to Kit, who recoiled.

"Who do I see about getting the captain a private room?"

The turnkey directed him back to the warden. As Nick crossed to the wooden partition, Staines, Stevenson, and Norton arrived.

"Can I get my brother out on bail?"

"No bail," Norton replied.

"They have lodged him in the felon's ward. I've asked for a private room. How long will they hold him here, Norton?"

"Three days maximum. Then he'll be moved to Newgate."

Neville Staines spoke up. "We shall try to arrange for an inquest in the next couple of days. We need to review the evidence and assemble a jury. Stevenson's a Justice; you and I are both peers. We should be able to expedite matters, Christopher."

"He needs fresh linen, a razor—"

"I'll look after getting him into a private room. You go and get what he needs; there's no time to waste."

Within the hour, Nick returned with clean clothes and his twin's toilet articles. He had to slip the warden a ten-pound note to be taken to his brother's room. Then he had to fork over another ten pounds before the turnkey would leave them alone.

"Why in God's name did you plot this duel with Jeremy Eaton?"

"You don't know what a nightmare it's been for me! As soon as you deserted me to fight your stupid war, that scheming swine began to blackmail me. I paid the scurvy bastard what he asked, but he kept coming back for more. That's where most of the money went!

Between he and his corrupt father, they drained me dry!"

"Keep your voice down," Nick cautioned. "Why didn't you tell me? I took on his father and won; I would have crushed an insect like our cousin under my boot heel."

"Ah, the conquering hero," Kit sneered. "Aren't you the one who thought it was high time I fought my own battles?"

"But you didn't fight your own battle, did you? You fully intended to kill him, but you wanted everyone to think it was me who shot him."

Kit ran his fingers through his hair. "No! I knew the uniform would put fear in him, give me an edge. I had to silence him!"

"Why?"

"He threatened to tell the world that I accidentally shot Father, not you. He was about to brand us both as liars and reveal that we had perpetrated a fraud on the authorities."

"Jeremy Eaton must have been watching that day."

"Yes, damn him to hellfire, he saw everything!"

"You were arrested on suspicion of murder."

Kit ran both hands through his hair. "Eaton's taking his filthy revenge. He's the one who has accused me, or rather *you*!"

Gray eyes stared into identical gray eyes until one pair lowered. "Was our father's death an accident, Kit?"

"Yes! No! I don't know!"

"You do know," Nick said quietly. He held his breath, and it felt as if his heart stopped beating as he waited for the answer. Every fibre of his being wanted it to have been an accident.

Kit's fingers stabbed through his black hair. "We were in the clearing, having the devil's own argument about announcing my betrothal. He accused me of being a coward, of having no guts. He fueled my fury to madness. I saw a flash of red; it was Father's blood! I killed him in the heat of the moment."

Nicholas felt his heart constrict, then it resumed its slow, steady beat. *I thought the war robbed me of all my innocence, but I was wrong. I still had some left until this moment. You knew it wasn't an accident when you begged me to say that I shot him. You would have let me take the blame for murder. You intended to murder Eaton and planned it so that once again I would be blamed. We are the same blood, the same bone. How can one twin do that to the other?*

"You've got to help me! You've always been there for me, Nick . . . we're in this together, right?"

Nicholas stared at his twin, then in a measured tone he said, "I have given you the last full measure of my devotion."

"They are less likely to convict a Peer of the Realm. You *must* convince them that I am Lord Hatton!"

"That would be impossible. *I* am Lord Hatton."

As Alexandra rode the short distance from Hatton Hall to Longford Manor, she did not converse with her brother. She rode in silence because the world had receded as her thoughts and emotions consumed her. *Why on earth did I allow Kit to manipulate me into a wedding ceremony?* Her inner voice answered, *Because it was the only way he would help Nicholas. I vowed I would do anything to help Nick; I must not allow myself to regret it.* The voice asked, *How can I trust Kit to keep his word to help his twin?* She answered, *I cannot, but I won't assume my duty as his wife until Nicholas is free and his name is cleared!*

Dottie, emerging from the kitchen, surveyed her grandchildren. "Alex often goes for a dawn gallop, but I didn't think anything short of peeing the bed would prompt Rupert to remove himself from between the sheets at this time of day."

"Rupert came from London. Nicholas has been arrested on suspicion of murdering his father."

"Good God! We must get word to Neville."

"He knows . . . he was at Hatton. He and Colonel Stevenson have already left for London to arrange an inquest. Rupert and I are going too."

"Alex hasn't told you the happy news. She and Kit were just married! They exchanged vows before Reverend Doyle in Hatton's library. I gave the bride away."

"Alexandra, darling, that is indeed happy news. Wise

too, under the dreadful circumstances. Swift and decisive action is ever the best course. *Lady Hatton,* sometimes I despaired I would ever be able to call you that." Dottie embraced her granddaughter with heartfelt happiness, then held her at arm's length. "You have such a stunned look on your face, darling. The shock of marriage does that, but usually to the groom. Shall we go and tell Margaret?"

Dottie and Alex climbed the stairs together, with Rupert just behind them. Sara was helping Margaret drink a cup of chamomile tea when they arrived at the bedside.

"How are you feeling?" Alex asked gently.

"Your news will be a better tonic than chamomile tea. Alex has become Lady Hatton. She and Christopher were wed this morning."

Margaret's face was transformed with joy. "Alexandra, you have made me so happy." Her eyes filled with tears. "You have made up for the sorrow I caused my own mother, years ago."

"Fiddle-faddle, Margaret! I loved you no less for your folly. Run along, Alexandra, and pack a bag for London. As Lady Hatton you will need all your very best clothes."

"I'll help you pack," Sara offered, eager to learn all the details of the impulsive wedding ceremony.

"Lord Staines will be staying in Berkeley Square; I believe I shall come to London with you," Dottie declared. "Christopher and Neville will need all the support we can muster; Nicholas too, of course. The *ton* will be hovering like vultures at this inquest, hoping for a bloodied victim."

Alex knew she couldn't bear to talk about Nicholas or the inquest, even with Sara. "I can manage my own packing, thank you, Sara. Why don't you help Dottie?"

"I shall go home and ready the carriage," Rupert declared.

"Post haste! None of your usual lollygagging."

Rupert looked highly offended. "I'd have been in London by now, if it wasn't for the need to transport the females of the family!"

* * *

Two hours later, they arrived in Berkeley Square. "Just drop me off, Rupert. Alexandra will wish to go straight to Curzon Street."

"No, no, I would much prefer to stay here for now, Dottie."

"Mustn't cling to me, darling; you're a new bride. Conquer those nerves immediately. Hatton men aren't noted for their celibacy."

Alex blanched. "Christopher will be directing all his time and effort to Nicholas today. He won't be at Curzon Street for hours."

"Do come up, then. Rupert, drop your sister's trunk at the Hatton town house before you go sloping off to join Kit."

When Hopkins opened the front door, he was surprised. Not that Dottie was joining Lord Staines, but surprised that she had brought Alexandra with her on this rendezvous. Usually, the pair was more discreet. "Good day, Lady Longford, Mistress Alexandra. I shall announce you to Lord Staines."

"She's *Lady Hatton,* as of this morning, Hopkins."

"Lady Hatton, I am delighted at your news."

Alex pressed her lips together. Hopkins was looking at her with relief that the man who had so recently shared her bed had made an honest woman of her. In hindsight, how fortunate that he had assumed her lover was Lord Hatton.

Neville appeared at the top of the stairs. "Dottie, this is a lovely surprise. I take it you've heard the unpleasant news."

"Not all the news is bad, Neville." She ran upstairs, spry as a girl. "Alexandra and Christopher were married this morning."

"This morning? After I left Hatton?"

"Yes." Alex allowed Neville to enfold her in his arms, and his genuine affection for her gave her a measure of comfort.

No sooner did they go into the drawing room than Hopkins arrived with champagne and glasses. "I thought you would wish to toast the bride, my lord."

"Pour yourself one while you're at it, Hopkins." Neville raised his glass. "I drink to your joy, my dear. I could not be more fond of you if you were my own granddaughter."

"How do you know she isn't?" Dottie asked archly.

"There must be something in the air. All this talk of brides and weddings puts me in an envious mood. Why should young people be the only ones to share such bliss? How about it, Dottie: Shall we show 'em how it's done?"

"Are you speaking of consummation, or constipation, Neville?"

"I'm quite serious, my darling, even though you aren't."

"My dear old stoat, are you sure you're up to it?"

"I am at the age when I realize time is of the essence; I'm not ready to stare up at a wooden lid and hear the dirt hit the box."

"What a way you have with words, you silver-tongued devil. The answer is yes; how could I possibly resist?"

Alex suddenly realized that her grandmother's money worries were over. Then immediately she felt guilty for the mercenary instinct. Dottie's happiness should have been her first thought. She embraced her grandmother. "You gave him the right answer. Oh, I have an engagement present for you!" She went into her bedroom to get the cashmere shawl. The chamber was filled with too intimate, too recent memories of Nicholas, and she left quickly before they overwhelmed her.

Dottie opened the box from Madame Martine's and lifted out the cream shawl with its black fringe. "Thank you, darling. You know my taste well; anything theatrical delights my *cockerocity*."

"Mine too!" Neville teased.

Alexandra blushed at the bi-play between the lovers and felt decidedly *de trop*. "I really must go, but before I do, can you tell me anything about Nicholas?"

"He's at the Wood Street Compter. Your husband arranged a private room for him, and we are trying to set a date for an immediate inquest. Christopher will fill you in on the details."

"Thank you." Her throat was too tight to say more. She hugged Neville, kissed Dottie, and left. Alexandra's immediate impulse was to rush to Wood Street. *You know they wouldn't let a woman in to see him . . . and if by some miracle you did get to see him, what would you say? That you married his twin?* Her heart plummeted to the same low level as her spirits. Though she felt loathe to go to Curzon Street, she had nowhere else to go. With reluctant steps she walked along Charles Street then turned the fateful corner.

Alex had no key, so she had to knock on the door, dreading the moment when Fenton would open it. She had spent the small hours of Saturday night and Sunday morning here with Nicholas, and Fenton had most definitely not mixed him up with his twin. What in the name of God would the man think of her marrying Kit only three days after changing the sheets on the bed she'd shared with Nick?

When Fenton opened the door his face was inscrutable. "Welcome, Lady Hatton. I took the liberty of taking your trunk upstairs. Would you care for some lunch, my lady?"

"No, nothing, thank you." *Rupert broke the news to him when he brought my trunk!* Alex straightened her back, lifted her chin, and climbed the stairs to the well-appointed drawing room. She sat down and stared off into space. Two hours later, she was still sitting there. Her glance traveled about the chamber. *How on earth will he be able to bear being locked up in the Wood Street Compter?* Then a worse place stole into her mind: *Newgate!*

Its horrors were infamous. *What if he's sentenced to life in prison?* A far worse scenario slipped past her defenses: *What if he is sentenced to be hanged?* A grisly memory of the highwayman they'd seen as children came into her head. *Highwayman!* Nick had done that too! And he'd robbed the Prince Regent! What if it all came out? He was a fearless and reckless rogue who took the law into his own hands to right injustice, but she would never believe he had committed murder. Never.

Alex raised her knees, slipped her arms around them, and hugged them to her chest. Christopher would make sure that Nicholas was set free. She must put her faith in her husband. She suddenly laughed, but it was without mirth. How ridiculous she was to worry over being embarrassed by what Fenton had seen. When her beloved's life was at stake, how little such things mattered.

It was full dark before Nick made his way to Curzon Street. He stabled Renegade, then fed and watered Satin and the two chestnuts. When he praised the stableboy for keeping the place clean, the lad stared at him in amazement; his lordship never praised anyone. Though Nick used his own key, Fenton was in the hall. "Good evening, my lord. Her ladyship is upstairs. Will you require dinner, sir?"

"That would be most appreciated, Fenton."

His steps were measured as he climbed the stairs, wondering what his reception would be. He found Alex sitting in the drawing room. "Why the devil are you sitting here in the dark?" He moved swiftly to the mantle and lit the candles.

"I didn't notice." She blinked at the sudden flare of light.

His eyes swept over her, noting she wore the same sober gray riding dress she had worn this morning when they exchanged their marriage vows. "Fenton will be serving us dinner soon; it will be our wedding supper. Would you like to change?"

"No, I don't think so. What I *would* like is news about Nick."

His heart went out to her. Once again he was deceiving her, but he told himself he only had her welfare at heart. As far as the world was concerned, Alexandra was Lady Hatton, and he would do whatever was necessary to make her believe it too since it was possible he would not win over the jury. "He is being held at Wood Street Compter. He's been moved from a ward to a private room. Neville Staines and Justice Stevenson are arranging for an inquest."

"Neville already told me these things."

"You saw Lord Staines?"

"Yes. Rupert brought my grandmother too. We saw Neville at his . . . er, at Berkeley Square."

Nick knew she had suddenly realized that though she'd told *him* about Dottie's financial difficulties, Kit knew nothing of them. He watched her hug the information to herself. She was secretly glad that her husband had not married an heiress.

"Dottie and Neville have decided to marry."

"That is marvelous news." He gave her a broad smile.

"Nick, I—" Her hand flew to her mouth, horrified at the name that had slipped out. "I am so sorry, Kit; please forgive me!"

"Everyone inadvertently calls us by the other's name occasionally. Why don't you call me Flynn, if you find the name Christopher difficult."

"Lord God, I find more than your name difficult!" She took a deep breath. "I'm sorry. Please try not to be offended. Flynn is a lovely name." *Kathleen Flynn.* Her eyes dropped to her ring. "How is Nick holding up?"

"After France, Wood Street Compter is a cakewalk." He smiled to reassure her. "I took him fresh clothes."

"He will need more than fresh clothes. He will need your support and your help. You must use your title, your wealth, and your influence, as well as your testimony, to gain his release."

Nick was glad that Fenton announced dinner. At the moment he refused to even consider helping his twin. They moved into the small dining room, and he watched her stare at the food with unseeing eyes. "You must eat something, Alex," he urged gently.

She raised her eyes to his, and the pleading look she gave him tugged at his heartstrings. "This morning you asked me to trust you. If you will keep your promise to do all you can for Nicholas, I will keep the vows I made to you."

Neither of them did justice to their wedding supper. When Alex pushed her chair from the table, Nick immediately arose and went to her side. Without looking at him she said, "Will you help me remove my trunk from your chamber? I find that I will need a little time before I can share your room."

Nick's heart soared. If she had gone dutifully to his twin's bed, he would have been devastated.

As she requested, Kit lifted her trunk and carried it across the hall into Nicholas's chamber. Alex watched him set it down at the foot of the bed, then stood stiffly as he kissed her cheek and bade her good night.

The moment she was alone, she was engulfed by memories of the intimacies in which she and Nicholas had indulged with such joyous abandon. She put her hands over her eyes to blot out the images, but this only made them more vivid. His imprint was everywhere, tangible in the room's furnishings—especially the big bed—and intangibly in the very air she breathed. Alex felt overwhelmed by the feelings and emotions the chamber evoked. Gradually, however, she realized that she could not alter the past, and she knew she would not change it if she could. She was now Lady Hatton, Christopher's wife, and the memories of Nicholas would have to last her a lifetime.

As if she were in a trance, she walked to his wardrobe and took out his black velvet robe. Then, slowly, she removed the gray riding dress and the rest of her garments. When she was completely nude, she wrapped herself in Nick's robe, climbed into Nick's bed, and abandoned herself to dream of her only love.

Chapter 34

Nicholas arose early, left the house, and walked the streets of London for five miles, fighting an inner battle over his twin. His initial impulse at Christopher's revelations had been: *Let him rot!* This ignoble sentiment had been replaced by a more detached attitude, to simply let justice take its course and allow the chips to fall where they may.

But, as he walked, Nick realized that he could not remain detached. For one thing, he had pledged his word to Alexandra that he would do all he could to gain his twin's release. The fact that she thought it was Nick was totally irrelevant. If he had any honor at all, his word was his bond. But even setting Alexandra aside, the old habit of coming to his twin's defense died hard. All his life Nick had thought of his twin as the other half of himself, albeit the weaker half. Now he realized that was no longer true. His other half was now Alexandra.

Nick acknowledged that he faced a dilemma. As he went over the alternatives, he had a sudden revelation. It was not his decision to make; it was Christopher's. He would put the facts before him, then Kit would make his own choice.

Later that morning at the Ludgate coffeehouse, he met with Neville Staines and Justice Stevenson, who reported their success in arranging for an inquest into Henry Hatton's death. "I pulled more strings than a harpist, but I gathered a jury. The inquest is set for tomorrow afternoon," Neville added to Stevenson's information, "principally because there are only two witnesses who will testify other than ourselves, you and Jeremy Eaton, who brought the charges against him."

"Eaton is recovered enough to testify?"

"He was lucky—wounded in the shoulder—but I understand the ball missed his heart by only inches," Stevenson declared.

Neville Staines looked at Nick with concern. "Perhaps you should consider retaining counsel in case the jury decides there is sufficient evidence to take it to trial."

"I did that this morning," Nick acknowledged. "Father's solicitor, Tobias Jacobs, recommended someone."

"Good, good. So everything is set for two o'clock at the Old Bailey, in the grand jury room. Shall I inform your brother?"

"I prefer to do that myself. Thank you Stevenson, Neville."

Nick left the coffeehouse and walked the short distance to Wood Street. He didn't yet know what he would say to Kit; he only knew that he must put the fear of God into him. He paid the usual garnish to visit his brother, then paid the turnkey to allow them to be private.

"What the devil did you mean yesterday, when you said *you* were Lord Hatton?" Kit demanded aggressively.

Nick noticed he was dressed in the Weston coat, fitted breeches, and polished Hessians that he had brought him. "You'd better sit down, while we go over your grave situation." He did not tell him yet that the inquest had been set for tomorrow. "Neville Staines and Justice Stevenson have been working tirelessly to arrange the inquest before the authorities ship you to Newgate."

"*Newgate?* I can't go to Newgate; the prison is a cesspool for the dregs of London! I would go mad!"

Fleetingly, Nick wondered if his twin was already mad, but he dismissed the thought. Kit was weak, selfish, and without conscience; loyalty, honor, and integrity had little meaning for him, but he was quite sane. "At the inquest, if the jury decides there is enough evidence to warrant a trial, you will be incarcerated in Newgate, whether it drives you mad or no."

"You must bribe someone, Nick! I cannot go there!"

"Have you given any thought to the fact that if you

are tried for murder, you could be found guilty? The sentence would either be life imprisonment or you would be hanged."

Kit jumped to his feet. "How can you torture me like this? I thought you loved me!"

I do love you, Kit; I just don't like you. "If it goes to trial, I have arranged counsel for you, the best criminal defense money can buy. And there is only one witness against you."

"Too bad Eaton didn't die of his wound!" Kit hissed. "You have to silence him for me, Nick!"

"By killing him? I think not."

"Go and threaten him . . . put the fear of death in him. . . . Tell him that next time we won't miss, unless he withdraws his testimony!" Kit raked his fingers through his hair until it stood on end.

"No. We must convince the jury that it was an accident. We must not let it go to trial. As the coroner, Neville Staines will be asked to testify, as will Justice Stevenson. They, however, can only give testimony after the fact."

"*I* will convince them of my innocence!"

"By lying?" Nick held his gaze until Kit lowered his eyes. "You will not testify. It is *my* testimony, my testimony as *Lord Hatton* that will decide the outcome of the inquest."

Kit sagged to the narrow bed with relief. "Now I understand why you said you were Lord Hatton yesterday."

"I *am* Lord Hatton; today, tomorrow, and henceforth."

Kit stared in outrage at his twin, then his mind slowly began to grasp the alternative that was being offered. "I told you Hatton was like a millstone round my neck; I'll be glad to be free of it!"

"And Alexandra?" Nick asked quietly.

"Her too! She was Father's choice of a bride, never mine!"

"If my testimony sets you free, it would be best that you leave England for some time, *Nicholas*. Freedom brings responsibility. I'll make sure you have money: ten thousand a year for life. The choice is yours."

"I could go to Italy!" Abject fear was replaced by hope.

"The inquest has been arranged for tomorrow afternoon. I will buy you passage on a vessel to Italy by way of Gibraltar. Tonight, I'll go to Hatton and pack your trunks."

"Can you really effect my release?" Kit's voice was intense.

"No guarantees, but I promise you I will do my utmost." He rose to leave. "One thing more; be sure you wear the uniform tomorrow."

As the morning sun streamed through the bedchamber window, Alex pondered what she would wear to the inquest. Since she was unable to speak with him, she wanted to send Nicholas a message of love and hope with her appearance. Finally, she chose a simple skirt and the bright yellow jacket. In such a vivid color, he would see her immediately, and see that she was brimming with hope and confidence in his innocence.

Her thoughts flew back to last night. Her husband hadn't returned home until an extremely late hour. When she heard him on the stairs, she had pretended to be asleep. She avoided him again this morning by waiting until he departed before she emerged from her room. If she hadn't gone to Berkeley Square yesterday, she would not have learned that the inquest was to be held today in the Old Bailey. She was glad she would be sitting with her grandmother in case the verdict was unfavorable. *Unfavorable? What a vapid euphemism. It would be nothing short of devastating. Alex, banish those thoughts; don't even put them in the air!*

She sorted through her hats. Lady Hatton would be expected to wear a bonnet. She put on one decorated with a smart black ostrich plume and looked in the mirror. She snatched it off and threw it across the room. *Convention be damned! I refuse to cover my hair; I shall wear it as a flaming beacon!*

Just after one o'clock when Alexandra entered the grand jury room of the Old Bailey, she was shocked to see the room was filled to capacity by their so-called friends. She clutched Dottie's arm.

"Jackals; I expected as much." Dottie poked the

Duchess of Rutland with her ebony cane. "Make room on the bench, Your Grace." When they were seated, Dottie whispered to Alex, "Not to worry. When Nicholas is exonerated, the *ton* will fawn upon the Hattons."

Alexandra felt many critical eyes examining her. She lifted her chin, then tossed her hair over her shoulder in a defiant gesture.

After what seemed like an eternity to her, a bewigged magistrate entered the room, followed by his court clerk and the men of the jury. Next came Jeremy Eaton, Lord Staines, Justice Stevenson, and Lord Hatton. Alexandra's gaze was riveted on the door. When the prisoner entered wearing the faded uniform, she gave a swift gasp.

"Hear ye, hear ye! All stand!" ordered the clerk. When everyone obeyed he continued, "We are here to determine the cause and circumstances of the death of Lord Henry Hatton, whether it was an accident or whether it was a greater crime." He cleared his throat. "All be seated!"

Nicholas, in the guise of Lord Hatton, listened attentively as Jeremy Eaton was called upon first to give his testimony. Eaton said that in the woods that day, he had been close enough to overhear a violent altercation between the accused and his father. At the height of the argument, a shot rang out, and Henry Hatton was silenced forever. He testified that he believed it was no accident but a deliberate act of murder.

By his testimony, Nick suspected that though Eaton had heard what went on that day, he had not actually seen it happen. Eaton did not confuse the issue by mentioning that it was actually Christopher who had argued with Henry Hatton that day; not Nicholas, and this told Nick that Jeremy feared the twin who had been a captain in the army far more than he feared Lord Hattan.

Eaton answered the questions put to him by the inquest jury, and Nick silently acknowledged that those answers were damning. When he was interrogated about the duel in Green Park, Eaton asserted that it had been forced upon him and that the prisoner's clear intent had been to silence him about Henry Hatton's murder.

Lord Hatton observed the grim faces of the men on the jury and knew he had his work cut out for him.

Colonel Stevenson, Justice of the Peace for Bucks County was called next. He testified that he believed the shooting to be an accident but admitted that he was called to the scene after the fact. "I asked Nicholas Hatton if the Heylin holster pistol found at the scene was his, and he freely acknowledged that it was. I took the word of the Hatton twins that it was a hunting accident as the gospel truth."

Coroner Neville Staines gave similar testimony, then added that in his opinion it was a hunting accident, plain and simple, as he noted on the death certificate. When questioned, however, he admitted that his role was limited to events after the fact.

The spectators began to whisper and shuffle their feet, but when Lord Hatton was called to the box to give his testimony, a complete hush fell over the courtroom.

"What I am about to say is the truth, the whole truth, and nothing but the truth. I have a grave confession to make, gentlemen," Lord Hatton admitted. "It was *I* who shot my father that day of the hunt; not my brother, Nicholas."

Those present gave a collective gasp then fell silent so they would not miss a word of Lord Hatton's testimony.

"Ever since we were children, my twin protected me and shielded me from punishment. I was a fearful boy who shrank from my father's wrath. As my protector, my brother was ever fearless, brave, and loyal. Whenever I did anything wrong, without hesitation he switched places with me and took my punishment. He even did my schoolwork, so that I would receive Father's praise. As you can imagine, I never learned to stand on my own two feet, never learned to face up to life.

"The day of the hunt, my twin lent me his Heylin holster pistols. When I accidentally shot my father, I threw down the gun and panicked. As Nicholas rushed upon the scene, I saw him as my salvation. I reminded him that the gun was his and begged him to say it was he who shot Father. When he hesitated, I threatened to shoot myself, knowing that his love for me would persuade him to take the blame. I acted like a coward. To my undying shame, it was not the last time." Nicholas looked at the jury, then glanced at Alexandra and saw that she, and they, were hanging on to his every word.

"When the will was read, we learned that Father left me everything. He left Nicholas nothing. When my twin was shunned by Society, he joined the army and rose to the rank of captain. No sooner did he leave England than my cousin, Jeremy Eaton, began to blackmail me. Unless I gave him money from my inheritance, he threatened to go to the authorities and lie, telling them that my father's death was not an accident. As was my pattern, I panicked, and because my twin was not there to take my part, I took the easiest path and paid Eaton. When he saw that I was weak and easily threatened, like a bloodsucking leech he began to drain me dry."

Now the eyes of the jury were focused upon Eaton.

"When my twin returned from war, I told him of Eaton's lies and threats to me. When Nicholas encountered him at White's, he accused our cousin of blackmail, and Eaton challenged him to a duel. Then he ran to the authorities with his lies about murder, no doubt hoping to silence Nicholas Hatton permanently.

"Gentlemen, I ask you to look at my twin. Nicholas Hatton has never done anything in his life to dishonor the uniform he is wearing. My brother had nothing to do with our father's death; it was I who accidentally shot him. I am guilty of cowardice, but that is something my twin is incapable of."

The magistrate said, "Thank you, Lord Hatton. You may step down." He had never before heard a Peer of the Realm admit to being a coward; the testimony carried a great deal of weight.

The jury must have thought so too, for after a short deliberation they returned and handed a written statement to the magistrate, which he in turn handed to the clerk to read. The verdict of accidental death came as a surprise to none after the dramatic testimony of Lord Hatton.

A great wave of relief washed over Alexandra, leaving her feeling as limp as wet newspaper. She watched the magistrate confer with Staines, Stevenson, and Nicholas, then they left the room together. Then she saw her husband coming to join her. "Thank you, my lord." Her voice was intense. "Is he free to go?"

"Yes. They are discussing laying charges of blackmail against Eaton." He turned, accepting congratulations, pats on the back, and handshakes from those who had attended the inquest. He introduced Alexandra as Lady Hatton, which informed everyone that they were newly married. Suddenly, the atmosphere became festive, with everyone offering congratulations to the groom and happiness to the bride.

Under the circumstances, Alex realized it was impossible to run to Nick's side. She forced herself to smile for the first time in days. She told herself she had much to smile about: *Nicholas had been exonerated.* She knew that she had her husband to thank for his twin's freedom, and she would be forever grateful.

Lord Hatton kissed his wife's cheek. "I shall see you at home. I won't be late." Then he departed the room through the door that the officials had used.

Alexandra and Dottie took a hackney cab to Berkeley Square. "Come up for a moment, darling. You left something upstairs. The cabby will wait for you."

When they went upstairs, Dottie handed her the box from Madame Martine's that held the lovely new gown. "You may need this tonight." Dottie winked suggestively.

During the short ride from Berkeley to Curzon Street, Alex clutched the box in clenched hands. The very last thing she would wear this evening was the sea-foam green dress she had worn for Nicholas on their last night together. *Our last night . . . our last night . . . it truly was our last night together. How will I ever bear it?*

As she paid the cabby, she glanced up at the sky. Dusk was already falling; night was rushing upon her before she was ready. Alex took her bath quickly; nothing was more conducive to daydreams than lingering in warm water. Wrapped in a towel, she opened the wardrobe door to select a gown. She shuddered involuntarily as she pushed aside Nick's garments and chose the cream silk faille.

Alex dressed, then brushed her hair. Before she set down the brush, she heard her husband speak to Fenton, then she heard his footsteps ascend the stairs. She felt as if her heart was in her mouth, her very dry mouth. Her fingers trembled as she smoothed out the peacock ribbon on the high-waisted dress. *How can I do this? How can I play wife to my beloved's identical twin? He has the same black hair, the same gray eyes, the same cleft in his chin, the same deep voice. Alexandra, you must put one foot in front of the other and take it one step at a time.* She swallowed hard and stepped into the drawing room. Slowly, but without hesitation, she crossed over to her husband. "Kit . . . Flynn . . . I want to thank you from the bottom of my heart. What you did today took a great deal of courage." She raised her fingers to touch his cheek. "You called yourself a coward, but you will never be that in my eyes." *Dear God, Nick's scent is on my gown because it lay against his garments in the wardrobe; it is filling my senses.*

Her husband looked into her eyes, then bent his head to brush his lips across hers. Her fingers left his cheek, slipping up into his dark hair, and suddenly she felt the stitches she had put there! In a heartbeat she knew this was Nicholas; knew that the twin he had saved today was Christopher; knew that the devil kissing her was deceiving her. Outrageously deceiving her!

She felt hurt and betrayed, yet as his scent enveloped her she also felt gloriously happy that somehow, some way, she was married to Nicholas. She couldn't instantly understand what game he was playing, but it was a game two could play!

She pulled away. "Will Nick return to Hatton, do you think?"

"No. He's decided not to bring charges against Eaton because he wants to leave the country and go abroad."

"I think that's a very wise decision." She wanted to show him that Nick's leaving would not break her heart. "Are you dining here with me tonight?"

"Yes." He looked surprised that she had changed the subject.

"Then perhaps we should think of it as our wedding supper." Her words held a subtle invitation.

"Perhaps we should, since our first one was such a disappointment." His words were guarded, his eyes wary.

"My . . . appetite has improved since then."

Alex saw his nostrils flare. Anger? Lust? "Perhaps we could dine in bed?" This time the invitation was anything but subtle.

"You've enjoyed dining in bed before?"

Alex wondered if he was deliberately reminding her of the intimacies they'd shared. She smiled inwardly. "Not that I recall. If I did, it was so unremarkable that I've forgotten it." She watched his eyes darken as she goaded the lion's pride. "Why don't you find out what delicious surprises Fenton has for us, while I light the candles in my chamber and turn down the bed?"

Nick hardened in spite of himself. Alexandra was a born *coquette;* perhaps she couldn't help flirting. He had been so gratified that she had kept him at arm's length since the wedding, because she thought him to be Kit. But now she had thrown him completely off balance. He glanced after her with a puzzled frown and went to find Fenton.

The first thing she did when she entered her bedchamber was change her stockings. She found the white-and-black striped pair she'd worn at Champagne Charlie's, the ones she'd been wearing when she did the private striptease for Nick. She pulled them on, secured them with black garters, then covered them with the demure skirt of her cream faille gown.

When he opened the bedchamber door, Alex was stretching across the bed to turn down the covers. As he glimpsed her ankles, clad in stripes, a full-blown picture jumped into his head of the night she had worn nothing but the provocative black-and-white stockings. His arousal became even more marked. Now, however, he was perversely fighting his attraction.

Alex looked at him, cast down her lashes, and said shyly, "I don't have a maid." Then she raised her lashes and said boldly, "You will have to help me undress."

Nick knew he would be damned if he did, and damned if he didn't. *It's the twin thing. She knows Kit is her husband, but because our looks are identical, she's pretending I'm Nick.* Then he had a far more disturbing thought. *Because we are twins, perhaps she wants to be made love to by both of us!* He approached her with reluctant steps, slowly unfastened the buttons, and stepped back.

With a teasing smile, she pulled the gown from her shoulders, let it fall to the carpet, and stepped out of it with feline grace. Then she lifted her foot to the bed, pulled back her petticoat to expose her legs, and unfastened the garter.

"Striped stockings are not worn by ladies."

She gave a provocative laugh. "Whatever made you think I was a lady?" She shot the garter at him and licked her lips when he deftly caught it. "You forget I've been wooed by Hart Cavendish," she taunted.

Now Nicholas was not only jealous over his twin but livid over the Duke of Devonshire. He stepped forward, took hold of her leg, and stripped the stocking from it. Then he lifted her petticoat off over her head and cast it away with a deliberate gesture.

"You are *impetuous*! What other delightful, wicked secrets will I learn tonight, my dearest lord?"

He crushed her in his arms, and his mouth came down hard and possessive on her soft lips. He forced them apart and thrust inside to the hot wet cave. He didn't release her mouth until she had been thoroughly kissed.

Alex slid her fingers into his black hair, then touched her lips to his ear. "Don't you think it's time I removed your stitches?"

Nick blinked in surprise, then groaned, crushing her in his arms again. "Damn you, Hellion! You enjoyed torturing me."

"When were you going to tell me you were not Lord Hatton?"

He put her at arm's length and held her gaze with pewter gray eyes. "I *am* Lord Hatton. If I were not, then you would not be *Lady Hatton*. Try never to make the mistake of calling me Nicholas even in private. Call me Flynn."

His hot hungry mouth was on hers again before she could reply, then suddenly the talking was done, replaced by far more meaningful and intimate communication.

Two hours later, as she lay in her lover's arms, replete and languid, she murmured against his heart, "I love you, *Flynn Hatton*."

Epilogue

Hatton Hall, July 1815

Lord and Lady Hatton, along with their guests—Lord and Lady Staines, Viscount Longford and his wife, Olivia, their little daughter, Amanda, and his new heir, baby Rupert—were celebrating the victory of Waterloo. They had dined *alfresco* in Hatton's fragrant garden.

"Thank you for a lovely party, Alexandra. We must go; it's time for baby's feeding." Olivia handed the heir to his proud father.

"I'm glad the weather was glorious. We have so much to celebrate," Alex said happily.

"The weather wouldn't dare to do other than cooperate," Dottie declared, "once I agreed to attend. Come, Alexandra, why don't we take these exquisite roses you've gathered to Margaret's grave? I could use a walk after that decadent trifle."

Alex rose and handed her son to his father. She bent to kiss her husband and murmured temptingly, "Flynn, darling, if you amuse your son and keep him from crying for a little while, I'll let you watch me feed him when I return."

Dottie watched the pair exchange an intimate look that told her they were deeply in love after a year of marriage. She hooked her arm through her granddaughter's and, using her ebony cane, still managed to keep her back ramrod straight. When they had walked a safe distance from their men, she said, "Though I pretended otherwise, I always knew you had a crush on the other twin, Nicholas. However, I was wise enough to know that infatuations fade away. Do you suppose he went back to his regiment and fought at Waterloo?"

"No, Nicholas had had enough of war. I feel quite certain my husband's twin didn't fight at Waterloo."

"I saw your husband's eyes on you in that green gown with its pretty love knots. Tell me, darling, now that you've been wed for a year, have a beautiful son, to say nothing of this magnificent home, aren't you glad that I insisted you marry the heir, Lord Hatton?"

Alexandra smiled her secret smile. Mr. Burke was the only one who knew. "I'm more than glad; I am deliriously happy! I thank you with all my heart."

Read on
for a special preview
of Virginia Henley's next
enchanting
historical romance . . .
Coming soon from New American Library

County Roscommon, Ireland—1751

A brilliant beam of sunlight reflecting on the water momentarily blinded him, then in the blink of an eye a radiant vision appeared before him. *Is she real or is she a wood sprite?* he mused. *After all, this is Ireland.*

The girl was slim and delicate, with an ethereal quality about her. As he stared, a sunbeam touched her, forming a glorious halo about her head, and her shining hair, falling in ringlets to below her waist, turned the color of pure-spun gold. She stood amidst the tall grasses of the riverbank while dragonflies and tiny insects with transparent wings flitted about her, rising like motes of dust from the myriad wildflowers. He had the distinct impression that if he moved or spoke, he would break the magic spell and she would vanish into thin air.

John Campbell, unable to help himself, was compelled to quote *A Midsummer Night's Dream.* "Ill met by moonlight, proud Titania."

The queen of fairies turned her head to gaze at him for a moment. "What, jealous Oberon?" She raised a dismissive hand to the dragonflies. "Fairies, skip hence." She lifted a proud chin and glanced away from him with disdain. "I have forsworn his bed and company."

The tall, dark young man took a step toward her and delivered Oberon's line. "Tarry, rash wanton. Am I not thy lord?"

Titania smiled and sank into a curtsy. "Then I must be thy lady."

He closed the distance between them in two strides and, laughing, took her hands and raised her. "What on earth is a beautiful English lady doing unattended in a meadow in the wilds of Ireland?"

He looked compellingly dark and dangerous but her glance traveled over the fishing basket and the rod slung casually across his back. "I live here. I've come to the River Suck for salmon, just as you have, sir. Come, I'll show you a good spot."

He followed her as if mesmerized to a place where the willows hung low on the riverbank to dip their weeping branches into the water, then sat down beside her and cast his line. The enchanting creature was a mystery he could not fathom. Though barefoot and wearing a threadbare smock that shamelessly revealed her ankles, she spoke in a cultured English voice and was obviously well-read.

"You have no trace of Irish dialect in your speech," he said.

Pretending a confidence she did not quite feel, she crossed her legs, cocked her head to one side, and launched into a ditty:

"In Dublin's fair city, where the girls are so pretty,
I first set me eyes on sweet Molly Mallone;
Through streets broad and narrow, she wheeled her wheelbarrow,
Cryin' cockles an' mussels, alive, alive-o!"

Her Irish brogue was rich and authentic; her singing sweet and melodious. Her accent changed from Irish to Scots in a heartbeat as she decided to trust him. "I detect a wee burr in yer own speech, laddie. I'd guess ye've spent time in Scotland."

It was an understatement. He'd spent time in Scotland all right. When the Jacobite rebellion broke out to overthrow the king, his father was appointed to command all the troops and garrisons in the west of Scotland. He'd fought alongside his father and the king's son, the Duke of Cumberland, at Inverary, then at Perth, and finally at the horrific Battle of Culloden where the uprising had been crushed once and for all.

John banished thoughts of war and smiled at her. "My mother is Scottish."

She proceeded to tell him a joke about two Scotsmen concerning what they wore beneath their kilts. The subject matter was quite risque and John was almost overwhelmed by a powerful desire to take the delectable morsel in his arms and devour her whole.

She smiled at him; her golden lashes swept to her cheeks and then lifted and he received the full impact of violet eyes. "I've been trained for the stage." When she immersed herself in a role, acting out a part, she was able to hide her acute shyness. "I'm going to be an actress!" she said importantly.

John Campbell's breath came out in a rush of relief. Here was no lady, St. Patrick be praised, but an *actress*. That made her fair game for seduction. "How old are you?"

"I'm sixteen, almost seventeen—quite old enough," she assured him. "How old are you, sir?"

The corners of his mouth lifted in amusement at the inappropriate question, asked so matter-of-factly. "I'm six and twenty and have all my teeth."

"Do you have a name, sir?" The fine English lady was back.

"My name is John." He did not offer his family name. "As you guessed, I am in Ireland to fish . . . and hunt." He stressed the last word, glancing at her breasts, then his gaze returned to her lips.

"How do you do, John? My name is Beth. These parts are renowned for fine game birds. We have snipe, quail, pheasant, goldcrests, and even partridge, though I've never tasted it."

"Really? It just so happens I have a plump roast partridge and a bottle of wine in my basket. Why don't you share them with me?"

"I'm not the least bit hungry but since it would be impolite to refuse your hospitality, it would be my pleasure to taste the partridge, sir, though not the wine."

"Why not the wine?" he asked, amused.

" 'Tis rumored that it steals the senses. Would you like me to hold your rod, John?"

For a moment her words dizzied him, then he realized that she had stolen his senses—she was innocently offering to hold his fishing rod while he got the food. He handed it to her, then opened the basket and extracted a large linen napkin that held the roasted fowl. He unwrapped it and broke the bird into pieces.

"Take it quickly." She handed the rod back. "I believe you have a salmon on your line at this very moment."

He reeled it in and with a swift motion dipped his net into the water and flipped the fish onto the riverbank. *With any luck, I'll lure another to take my bait.* His dark gray eyes studied the lovely golden female at his side. "Tell me, Beth, how do you intend to catch a salmon without a rod?"

She picked up a leg of partridge with the thigh attached and bit down with relish. "A man needs fancy paraphernalia. A maid must manage without!"

John's dark eyes widened. Had this enchantress made a racy observation regarding their anatomy to provoke his male lust? He watched her select a breast with its wing intact and saw her lick her lips in anticipation. She had denied that she was hungry yet she was making short work of the partridge. When she set down the bones and sucked on her fingers, he felt his cock stir. He moved the napkin closer to her, and when he saw her look at the remaining pieces with longing, suddenly he wished she'd look at him that way.

"You're not hungry, John?"

He shook his head in denial. He was hungry, all right, but not for food. All he wanted at this moment was to watch her eat. With a feminine, feline grace, she quickly bit into the fowl with sharp white teeth, closed her eyes with untold pleasure when she swallowed a morsel, and then licked her fingers to savor the taste. He wondered if she would relish everything in life with such lusty enjoyment, and his imagination took erotic flight.

She devoured the last of the partridge and wiped her hands on the linen. Then she stretched out beside him, prone in the grass, and gazed down into the water's depths. A shadow beneath the surface inched forward. She waited patiently until it edged closer but the moment her hand slid into the water, the salmon darted away. "We've been making too much noise," she whispered, placing a finger against red lips that looked berry-stained.

John stretched out beside her so that their bodies almost touched. *I'll let you hold my rod, sweetheart.* He didn't say it aloud though it was what his body craved. He watched her lovely heart-shaped face as she focused fully on her task. Her skin was like translucent porcelain and while this close he could see the tiny blue veins of her eyelids. As her glance followed the shadow of the fish beneath the water, the tip of her pink tongue slid over her full lower lip, and he was lost.

He hardened instantly and reached for her. His arms swept about her, holding her captive against his hardness, while his lips took possession of her tantalizing mouth. He drank in her loveliness thirstily, knowing he'd never tasted anything as sweet.

Shocked beyond belief, Beth bit down on his lip and sprang to her feet. He stood, too, towering above her, wanting to gentle her to a giving mood. "How dare you try to ravish me, sir?" Her breasts heaved with indignation as she drew back her arm, reached up on her tiptoes, and slapped him full across the face. She turned on her heel and began to run.

"Beth, wait . . ."

Suddenly she stopped, turned around, and strode back to him, violet eyes blazing. She swept him with an accusing glance, then bent and snatched up the fish he'd caught. "My salmon, sir!"

On the journey home Beth's thoughts were filled with the devastatingly handsome devil she'd encountered by the river. He was tall, with a dark, smoldering quality about him that should have warned her he was dangerous, but truth to tell, she hadn't experienced fear until she'd felt the strength of his well-muscled body when he'd held her captive against him. Still, she mused, the fear of him was minuscule when pitted against the fear she felt of returning home without a salmon for dinner.

It would take far more courage than she possessed to face her mother empty-handed.

Bridget Gunning was an extremely attractive woman whose red hair only hinted at her sharp tongue and flaming temper. She was the undisputed authority figure in their household, whom none would dream of disobeying, least of all her husband. Beth's mother never let them forget that she had sacrificed her promising career as an actress on the London stage to marry Jack Gunning and give him two beautiful daughters. She called her husband feckless, which Beth acknowledged was true enough, but she loved her handsome father for his easygoing ways and ready smile.

Jack Gunning's family were well-to-do landowners in St. Ives, Cambridgeshire, but since he was the youngest son and could hope for neither wealth nor title, he had become an adventurer and a gambler. When he wed an actress, his reputation as black sheep of the family had been sealed, and the arrival of two daughters in rapid succession had put an end to Bridget's promising career on the stage. He took them to St. Ives to live off his family's charity, where they were barely tolerated while he haunted London's gaming clubs.

Then by a stroke of fortune, or so it had seemed at the time, Beth's father had won Castlecoote in a card game at White's. The couple instantly packed up their daughters and moved to their castle in Ireland. Castlecoote, it turned out, was no castle at all but a rambling old hall in need of repair. It stood, however, on a lovely piece of rolling farmland in County Roscommon, so they had made the best of their disappointing situation and stayed. Though they were surrounded by prosperous sheep and cattle farms, Jack Gunning was no farmer and eked out a living by tending a few goats and selling the animals' milk and cheese.

The Gunning daughters, Maria and Elizabeth, were exceptionally beautiful girls, and their mother decided to train them for the stage, where they would undoubtedly make their fortune once they were old enough. To this end they were taught to sing and dance and made to practice a scene from a play every night of their lives. Though their mother was a strict taskmaster, Beth knew she was more lenient with Maria, who was older by two years. Because of her exquisite looks, she was their mother's favorite. Beth felt no resentment. It was right and proper that Maria's beauty made her special.

"Elizabeth Gunning, where the devil have you been?" her mother demanded sharply the moment Beth stepped into the kitchen.

Tongue-tied as always in the face of her mother's wrath, she held up the salmon for explanation.

"Is this to be another dumb show, where you practice your mime? Don't think the salmon excuses you from bringing the water from St. Brigid's well. Maria had to wash her face in ordinary well-water today because you forgot."

"Don't fuss, Bridget. Water is water." Jack winked at his daughter as he took the salmon.

"Water is not water, Jack Gunning! Your daughters owe their flawless complexions to the water from Holywell House."

"Beth can run there and fetch a jug, while I fillet the fish."

"Do not call her Beth. Her name is Elizabeth. I picked beautiful names for our daughters, names that will benefit them when they are on the stage."

Beth almost made a grab for the jug but her mother's critical eye stopped her. Instead, she lifted it gracefully from the stone sink and sank into a curtsy. "I shall be pleased to go for the water now, ma'am." She would do anything to please her mother.

"Much better, Elizabeth. Never forget that plainer girls must try harder to please."

"Why didn't you tell her about the letter?" Jack asked, when Elizabeth had left the house.

"And spoil the surprise for Maria? I shall tell them tonight after they've practised their parts."

Elizabeth encountered Maria as her sister came out of Holywell House. The two girls fell into step and they walked toward St. Brigid's well. "I'm sorry, Beth. I told Mother it was your turn to fetch the water today. Will you forgive me?"

"Of course. I met a man today—he was fishing by the river."

"Was he a gentleman?" Maria asked avidly.

"Well, he wasn't Irish, if that's what you mean."

Maria laughed at her sister's droll remark. "I mean was he rich and well-spoken?"

"Yes. English gentry I expect, here for hunting and fishing."

"Ooh-la-la, most likely staying at the royal hunting lodge at Ballyclare. Was he handsome?"

"Handsome in the extreme," Beth said with an involuntary sigh.

"Did he try to kiss you?" Maria asked knowingly.

"How on earth did you guess?"

"Oh, Beth, you're so innocent! How could any man resist you?"

"Well, I resisted *him,* I can tell you!"

"Little goose. You shouldn't have resisted. If he fancied you, perhaps he'd take you to England with him. How else will you get out of this godforsaken country? Tomorrow, I'll come with you and try my own luck."

Beth pulled on the rope and then tipped water from the wooden bucket into her jug. For all her beauty, Maria had no reticence and said whatever thought came into her head, whether it was appropriate or not. "You'd truly let a man kiss you, Maria?"

"I'd let him do anything that pleased his fancy if he'd take me to London, Beth. Only if he was rich, of course."

During the course of the afternoon as John Campbell caught half a dozen salmon, his thoughts were filled with the image of the enchanting wood sprite he'd encountered. She was easily the most beautiful female he'd ever seen but that wasn't the only thing about her that was so arresting. She was direct, without subterfuge, and he found it enchanting. She was also natural and free spirited, speaking her thoughts without coquetry or calculation. And she was completely unaffected, as if she had no notion of her exquisite loveliness.

When he arrived back at the lodge, he saw that his companions who had been hunting had arrived before him. He left his catch with Ballyclare's chef and then joined the other men.

His younger brother, Henry, raised his glass of Irish whiskey in a salute. "You missed out on a damned good hunt, old man. I bagged a red deer."

"How was the fishing?" enquired his friend, William Cavendish.

"Fresh salmon for dinner," John announced with a grin. "I don't think I missed anything." He pictured Beth in his mind. "Enjoyed myself so much I believe I'll try my luck again tomorrow."

New York Times **Bestselling Author**

Mary Jo Putney

"Miss Putney just keeps getting better
and better." —Nora Roberts

VEILS OF SILK 0-451-20455-7
After years of captivity in western Asia, a courageous army major finds hope for the future in a bold woman who dares to accept his marriage proposal, shed her Victorian propriety—and unleash a sensual nature that will set him on fire.

SILK AND SECRETS 0-451-20490-5
Free-spirited Juliet flees the confines of her Victorian existence to live in exotic Persia. But 12 years later, Juliet joins her estranged husband on a mission to rescue Juliet's brother, and the two find themselves renewing the passion they once shared.

SILK AND SHADOWS 0-451-20206-6
Wealthy and seductive Peregrine weaves a web of desire around Lady St. James, who's pledged to wed Peregrine's enemy. Only the burning power of love can pierce Peregrine's chilling silence about his secret past and hidden purpose, and Sara plunges into a whirlpool of uncertainty with a man who has everything a woman could want—and fear.

To Order Call: 1-800-788-6262

S582